FRAC̄ ⎽ ⎺ꓕH

(Ascension Wars Book 3)

(1st Edition)
by Jasper T. Scott

JasperTscott.com
@JasperTscott

Copyright © 2020

Cover Art by Tom Edwards
TomEdwardsDesign.com

CONTENT RATING: R

Swearing: Brief instances of strong language
Sex: Moderate, but not explicit references
Violence: Moderate

Author's Guarantee: If you find anything you consider inappropriate for this rating, please e-mail me at JasperTscott@gmail.com and I will either remove the content or change the rating accordingly.

ACKNOWLEDGMENTS

Finishing this book on time was a monumental task. I couldn't have done it without the fast and timely support of my editor, Aaron Sikes, and my proofreader Dani J. Caile. Thanks also go out, as ever, to Tom Edwards for an amazing cover. I usually commission artwork for my books long before I've finished (or even begun) writing them. This leads to a self-fulfilling prophecy wherein the scene depicted on the cover is one that I strive to bring to life in the book. Read on, and you should recognize it sooner or later.

With this book my deadline was so strict that I sent a draft to my advance readers with only a few days to spare before publishing, but a few intrepid readers still managed to send me feedback on time. Thanks go out to: Davis Shellabarger, Raymond Burt, Karol Ross, Mary Kastle, Lisa Garber, and Gwen Collins. I would also like to thank my wife, Yara, for her support and understanding of all the many hours, lost weekends, and sleepless nights that it takes to do this job.

And finally, many thanks to the Muse.

To those who dare,
And to those who dream.
To everyone who's stronger than they seem.
—Jasper Scott

*"Believe in me / I know you've waited
for so long / Believe in me / Sometimes
the weak become the strong."*
—STAIND, Believe

PREVIOUSLY IN
THE SERIES

Synopsis Of First Encounter

WARNING the following synopsis contains spoilers from book one of this series, *First Encounter (Ascension Wars Book 1)*. If you would prefer to read that book first, you can get it on Amazon: https://www.amazon.com/dp/B07Z6SPM72

The Forerunner ships left Earth to colonize nearby star systems and to search for intelligent life. *Forerunner One* left in 2060 AD under the command of Captain Clayton Cross, bound for the star Trappist-1. After a ninety-year journey to reach it, his ship arrived and made landfall on Trappist-1E. There, the crew discovered a world teeming with life. They encountered the Trappans, an arboreal species of primitive natives with ten legs and hairless brown skin. The initial encounter resulted in a brief conflict, and the ground team was forced to retreat to their shuttle.

Soon after that, they discovered that Dr. Grouse, one of their first contact specialists, was missing. With the shuttle surrounded by Trappans, the crew was forced to venture out. Coming to an understanding with the natives, the crew went looking for Dr. Grouse. They found him via his locator beacon in an underground laboratory. Several of the native Trappans were lying unconscious on metal tables with tubes and wires trailing from their bodies. The same was true for Dr. Grouse, and like the Trappans, he was unconscious.

The crew disconnected Dr. Grouse and fled, but before they could leave, an unknown, avian alien intervened and tried to stop them. There was a brief conflict in which the alien killed the ship's XO, before being killed itself. The remaining crew members fled the laboratory and Captain Cross received word from *Forerunner One* that multiple unidentified contacts had just appeared on an intercept course with *Forerunner One.* They were accelerating at over 10Gs, a speed that the *Forerunner* couldn't hope to match.

Captain Cross and his ground team beat a hasty retreat back to their shuttle. In the airlock, Dr. David Grouse's vitals crashed. His colleague, Dr. Lori Reed was able to resuscitate him with help from the ship's chief medical officer, Dr. Stevens, and Dr. Grouse woke up with a warning: "They know where Earth is."

Back on *Forerunner One,* Captain Cross set an outbound course and readied the ship for a fight. The pursuing alien vessels made no attempt to contact them, but continued closing range at an almost impossible rate.

While retreating, both Dr. Grouse and his colleague, Lori Reed, were placed under quarantine. Lori was cleared, but Dr. Grouse was found to be infected with a mutating alien virus that was systematically altering his DNA. Dr. Grouse was changing before their eyes, turning into something not entirely human. Doctor Stevens gave the order to place him in cryo to halt the progress of the virus.

Just as *Forerunner One* reached the boundary of interstellar space, the alien ships broke off pursuit. To Captain Cross, the message was clear: *leave our territory, or else.*

Right before the crew was set to enter cryo for the journey home, Dr. Lori Reed discovered that she was pregnant. Her birth control implant had failed, and Richard Morgan, the ship's ambassador, was the father. The child was later born during regular crew rotations with features resembling those of the Avari that they had encountered in the underground lab on Trappist-1E. Somehow, Lori's brief contact with Dr. Grouse *had* infected her with the alien virus, but it hadn't infected *her* directly, it had infected her unborn child and turned it into something alien. Lori named her Keera, after the ship's XO who had been killed on Trappist--1E. Richard Morgan refused to acknowledge Keera as his daughter, despite DNA tests revealing that she was in fact related to him.

After just six months, Keera reached a level of development comparable with that of a six-year-old human girl, and she looked more alien than ever. She was talking, walking, and developing vicious claws and teeth. She'd unintentionally injured both of her parents on several occasions, and she was becoming increasingly aggressive. One night she couldn't sleep because she imagined that she'd brutally killed the two officers on the bridge. A little while later, her parents discovered that those two officers really were dead, and they found Keera there, covered in their blood.

The Captain and his section woke up and discovered the carnage. The security logs had been erased, and Keera was the only suspect. The child insisted that she hadn't done it, but no one believed her.

Keera fled into a maintenance tunnel before she could be captured. The crew split up to search for her, and in the process several crewmen were killed, but no one got a good look at their killer. Finally, Keera was captured and placed in cryo, and then everyone went to bed, thinking the crisis past.

In the middle of the night, Captain Cross

awoke to find one of the avian aliens, the Avari, standing over him, and some kind of device on his head. He managed to remove the device, and the alien vanished into thin air, having cloaked itself.

The aliens were on board, and they probably had been this entire time. Maybe Keera really hadn't killed the officers on the bridge. The crew woke up and began hunting for the cloaked alien. Several more crewmen died in the process. The Avari abducted both Lori and Keera, taking them to a cloaked alien shuttle that was docked to one of the *Forerunner's* external airlocks. On board the shuttle, Lori encountered Dr. Grouse, who now looked just like an adult version of Keera. He admitted to killing both of the officers on the bridge and to erasing the security logs. Lori concluded that he must have been brainwashed by the Avari.

Captain Cross and his chief of security, Lieutenant "Delta" Sanders, jumped in a pair of Scimitar starfighters to give chase. During a brief conflict, Delta was killed, and Captain Cross was forced to break off pursuit when the alien shuttle cloaked and disappeared.

Captain Cross returned to the *Forerunner*. He set a course for Proxima Centauri, not Earth, and went back into cryo with his crew for the long journey home.

Upon arrival at Proxima Centauri, almost seventy years later, the *Forerunner* was greeted by Keera, now all grown up, and an Admiral leading an Avari fleet of warships. She told Captain Cross that her people were actually known as the *Kyra,* and she welcomed him to the Kyron Federation. The Kyra had beat them to Earth, having traveled there with FTL drives. They invaded and occupied the planet, annexing it.

Keera demanded permission to come aboard, and Captain Cross met her with his crew at one of the *Forerunner's* airlocks. Keera's mother, Lori Reed, was also there, still alive after all these years thanks to Kyron longevity treatments. Keera saw her father again, but it was an awkward reunion at best.

And there was another surprise waiting for Captain Cross. He was reunited with his long-dead wife, Samara. Prior to her death on Earth, he'd had the contents of her mind saved to digital records. Keera had wanted to repay his kindness and impartiality toward her, so she convinced her people to clone and resurrect his wife from her memories.

This happy reunion blinded Captain Cross to what had really happened during the invasion. After a short journey aboard Keera's ship to reach Earth, he discovered that his home world had been almost entirely destroyed. The devastation was everywhere, cities ruined, and billions had died. Only a few city centers remained, all of them walled off to keep out failed human-Kyra hybrids known as *Dregs.*

During the trip down to what was left of Houston, Captain Cross witnessed one of the Chimeras kill two colonists from the *Forerunner* just because they took too long to get out of their seats.

On this ominous note, Captain Cross vowed to oppose the alien occupation in any way that he could. The invasion might be over, but the rebellion had just begun.

Synopsis Of Occupied Earth (Book 2)

WARNING the following synopsis contains spoilers from the previous book in this series, Occupied Earth (Ascension Wars Book 2). If you would prefer to read that book first, you can get it on Amazon:
https://www.amazon.com/dp/B085RRP16V

One year after his return to Earth, Clayton Cross finds himself living in a walled occupation zone in the center of old Houston. The downtown has been rebuilt as *New Houston,* and he lives in an apartment with his cloned wife, Samara Cross. They discover via a Kyron pregnancy test that they are pregnant and that it is a girl. They are ordered to report to the nearest "Ascension Center" tomorrow morning for her first prenatal check-up.

The avian species known as the *Kyra* that Clayton met on Trappist-1E, and their alien-human hybrids, the Chimeras, take a special interest in human children. Birth control is illegal, so birth rates are high. Schools function as indoctrination centers because the Kyra need soldiers for their war with their mysterious enemy, the Chrona. After years of indoctrination, most children choose to *ascend*, willfully exposing themselves to the hybridizing virus to become Chimeras themselves. These Chimeras are both hardier than Humans and better suited to life in space and other worlds, but because Chimeras cannot breed amongst themselves, Humans are still a necessary part of the supply chain.

But not all conversions are successful. Nearly half of all people who are exposed to the virus lose their minds in the process, turning into violent, infectious beasts known as *Dregs*. These failures are cast out into the *Wastes*, the moldering ruins of Earth's former cities, while their families are told that they were sent to the front lines to fight.

The alien occupation has been on Earth for nearly a hundred years already, but to Clayton, it's all new, and he can't bring himself to accept the status quo. He drives a garbage hauler for the solid waste management department (SWMD) at night, but he's secretly smuggling supplies to a human resistance group known as Phoenix.

Meanwhile, Keera and Lori Reed are aboard the *Sovath*, the flagship of Earth's occupying fleet. Keera Reed has risen to the rank of admiral, and she is overseeing the interrogation of a human prisoner from the resistance. Overseer Damos, the only actual Kyra in the entire solar system, is there conducting the interrogation.

There are rumors that the resistance planted a bomb in one of the Ascension Centers, but the Kyra don't know which one. When the Overseer realizes that the prisoner doesn't even know where the bomb is, he eats the man alive. Lori is there to see it, and this is the final straw for her. She no longer believes that Humans and Kyra can one day find a way to live together, and she solidifies her plans to escape—unlike her daughter, Keera, the first ever human Chimera, she is not an exalted member of the Kyron Federation. She is little better than a prisoner, poked, prodded, and studied to find out why she was able to carry a Chimeran fetus to term. If the Kyra can discover how to make other humans carry Chimeran babies, they won't need to waste time indoctrinating human children. And Chimeran children grow up much faster, so their lead time on new soldiers will be far shorter.

While all of this is happening, Clayton is

out in the Wastes, delivering a load of garbage at the dump. He and his partner run into trouble with Dregs and find another hauler driver stranded on top of his vehicle, shooting down at a horde. Clayton goes to the rescue, but winds up falling off his own truck. His partner doesn't wait around, leaving both him and the other driver at the mercy of the Dregs. The unidentified driver leads Clayton down into an old sewer where they meet a member of the resistance: Sergeant Sutton. It turns out that the driver Clayton rescued was with the Resistance, too. Sutton has a mission for Clayton, and it's much more than a simple supply run. They need his help to smuggle one of their operatives out of the city tomorrow night.

Clayton agrees to the mission. In the morning, after the Dregs have all crawled into their holes to escape the rising sun, Clayton and his new partner flee the sewers and run to the other driver's hauler to call SWMD central for a rescue. Dregs hear them and come scrambling out again, braving the light for a fresh meal. Clayton is tricked into hiding in the back of the hauler while the man he rescued gives his life to operate the switch and shut the hatch. He is sealed inside until Chimeran soldiers arrive to let him out.

Samara Cross has been working all night at her job as a nurse in the Med Center. She learns that Clayton ran into trouble and leaves work early to meet him as Chimeras bring him back to SWMD central. They leave together to go to their prenatal appointment in the Ascension Center, only to discover that it has been shut down due to the bomb scare. Their appointment is rescheduled for the following day.

Clayton and Samara both meet with a resistance operative at a park inside the city. It turns out to be Richard Morgan, the former Union Ambassador from *Forerunner One*—also Keera's father. Clayton receives a signal blocker for the Kyron tracking implant in his hand, and he learns that Samara is also working for the resistance. She has secretly been smuggling vital medications out of the Med Center to help them with their cause.

That night, Clayton conducts his mission for the resistance as planned, but the cowardly partner who left him behind the night before is not sympathetic to the resistance, so Clayton has to drug the man. After slipping a sedative in his coffee, Clayton is shocked to learn that the operative he's smuggling out is none other than Lori Reed, the former first contact specialist aboard his colony ship, *Forerunner One* —Admiral Keera's mother.

Clayton helps her into the back of his hauler and then drives out the city gates. Once they're in the Wastes, Lori comes up to the cab to ride shotgun and keep a lookout for Dregs. Clayton's partner is still fast asleep. Lori reveals the reason the resistance is going to so much trouble to extract her: she's immune. The virus didn't infect her even though it infected her unborn child, Keera. The resistance hopes to use her immunity to formulate a cure to the hybridizing virus.

Soon Clayton is back at the dump where he was the night before. He helps Lori to the rendezvous point—the manhole cover leading to the sewers where he spent the previous night. But just as Lori is climbing down, she is shot and killed by a Chimeran bounty hunter who followed her from the *Sovath*. Clayton escapes, but only barely. He meets Sergeant Sutton in the sewers again, and they flee, taking Lori's dead body with them. Maybe she can still be used to develop a cure.

The next day Samara is told that Clayton is dead. Even the Chimeras believe this, because his tracking implant has been disabled by the signal blocker. Distraught as she is, Samara is forced to attend her appointment at the Ascension Center as planned. The Kyra would interpret her absence as a willful act of rebellion.

Clayton is in the back of a stolen garbage hauler, on the way with Sutton to the resistance base. He and Sutton get out at a midpoint along the way. Clayton sees an explosion at the Ascension Center in New Houston, and remembers that his wife had an appointment there this morning. Furious at the resistance for endangering innocent lives, he strikes out on his own, determined to have nothing more to do with Phoenix.

Sergeant Sutton sends him away with some basic supplies and a weapon, saying he's going to need it. He also advises Clayton to remove the tracking implant in his wrist. The signal blocker won't last forever, and tracking implants are designed to execute people remotely if they get out of line. Once the Chimeras realize he is alive, they'll execute him on the spot.

Clayton leaves Sutton and goes walking back through the Wastes on foot. He plans to make his way to the city and find out if his wife is still alive. Along the way, he encounters an infected woman and her dog, Rosie: a mutt that looks to be part Rottweiler. The woman begs him to take care of her dog. He agrees, and then she kills herself with Clayton's sidearm before she can finish turning into a Dreg.

Clayton continues on with Rosie. Soon after setting out again, he receives a global announcement over his comms. It's from Overseer Damos. After the bomb in the Ascension Center, the Kyra have decided to adopt a new policy: criminals and dissidents will no longer be exiled to the Wastes. They will be executed in the Arenas, which were previously used only for Chimeran "Challenges" (honor duels that determine the pecking order in Kyron culture). And finally, all living exiles in the Wastes now have a bounty on their heads.

With this new edict, Leeto Voth, the bounty hunter that killed Lori, flies out to the Wastes, searching for more exiles to claim bounties on. He discovers the dead woman who was Rosie's former master, shot in the head, but the weapon that shot her is missing. Someone else had to have been there. Leeto tracks the smoke from a nearby fire that Clayton is using to sterilize water and gets on his hoverbike to take care of the exile.

Clayton and the bounty hunter trade shots, but Clayton gets the upper hand thanks to Rosie. Just before Clayton kills the man, Leeto gloats, revealing that he was the one who shot Lori. Clayton steals his hoverbike and weapons and flees with Rosie sitting in the cargo compartment behind him.

The *Sovath* is sent to investigate the bounty hunter's death. Admiral Keera goes down personally with her XO, Commander Treya. The Commander says they need to find whoever did this. The bounty hunter's bike is missing, so whoever did it shouldn't be hard to find. They just have to look for its sensor signature. Keera realizes from the report on her mother's death that this bounty hunter is the one who killed her, and she orders Commander Treya not to pursue the matter. Whoever killed Voth did her a favor.

Clayton flees the Wastes, heading North on his bike to evade detection. He hides in an old school and winds up fighting off the Dregs who are living inside. He locks himself and Rosie in one of the second level classrooms, then sneaks out under the cover of darkness that night to fly back to New Houston and find out if his wife is still alive. He can't use his comms without the signal being traced to him, so he sneaks into a farmer's house to use that man's comms to call his wife. The farmer wakes up and sees him, but they reach a mutual understanding, and the farmer helps Clayton call Samara.

She answers, and Clayton is overwhelmed with relief. But rather than speak and let her know that he also survived, Clayton decides to say nothing. He's an exile now, and it will do her no good to know that he's alive.

He thanks the farmer and leaves. On his way to pick up Rosie, Clayton hears laser shots and a woman screaming. He goes to investigate and finds two Chimeras and a little girl of about four years old. The girl's parents were killed by the Chimeras to claim the bounties on their heads. Clayton kills both soldiers, saving the girl before they can kill her, too. He learns that her name is Nova. He takes her back to see Rosie, and the three of them leave the Wastes together, heading into the *Wilds*.

Keera Reed is so distraught over her

mother's death that she will do anything to bring her back. Kyron medical science has a way; she used it once before to resurrect Clayton's wife. The problem is that the process of cloning and resurrection from digitally stored memories has since become illegal. She sneaks away from the *Sovath,* stealing valuable neutronium fuel to trade for the cost of her mother's cloning and resurrection at an outlaw space station. Commander Treya follows her there, and discovers what she's doing. Now Keera can't go back to her command without being executed for her crimes. She has become an exile.

Ten years later...

Nova is fourteen, and Rosie is still around —somehow she must have also received the Kyron longevity treatments that keep their human breeders alive and fertile. Clayton, Nova, and Rosie have been living in an old log cabin in the middle of the Sam Houston National Forest.

During this time, Clayton has been keeping tabs on his wife and his other daughter, Dora, who is now ten years old. He is in touch with the farmer, Harold Neem, who helped him contact Samara ten years ago, and Harold gives him monthly updates on his wife and daughter. In exchange for that favor, Clayton has been helping Harold stay in contact with the resistance, because his own daughter is one of them.

Clayton makes his regularly scheduled contact with the resistance to get an update for Harold. In the process, Clayton learns that Phoenix is working with Keera and her recently-cloned and resurrected mother, Lori. But that's not all. As an exile, Keera has reached out to the Kyra's enigmatic enemies for help. Clayton learns that the Chrona are actually a form of artificial life—machines that look like the Kyra themselves. They are an offshoot of Kyron society that made themselves immortal by becoming robots. The biological and mechanical versions of the Kyra have been at war with each other ever since.

A Chronan operative known as Specter has helped the resistance to develop a cure to the virus using Lori's clone. The Chrona will use that cure to vaccinate the entire human population of Earth. To this end, they have secretly seeded the water supplies of occupied cities all around the planet. Now all they need to do is break into New Houston and its Ascension Center in order to deactivate everyone's tracking implants. If they don't do that, the Kyra could simply execute everyone out of spite once they learn that the human population is no longer useful to them. While Phoenix is disabling the tracking system, the Chrona have agreed to come to humanity's aid with a fleet. They will defeat the Kyra's occupying fleet and set Earth free.

Clayton realizes that the resistance actually has a chance, and he puts aside old grievances to join the cause with Nova.

They get help sneaking into the city from Harold and his Chimeran girlfriend, Mona. Once inside the city, they meet up with Richard, who helps get them close to the Ascension Center. Phoenix is discovered early and they have to fight their way in. Richard decides it's suicide and flees the battle. Clayton takes over and leads his team instead.

Inside the city, Samara learns that Dora has snuck out. She follows her daughter's tracking signal to the arena and finds her little girl bleeding out from a ceremonial *Sikath*— one of the swords that the Kyra use in their challenges. Dora participated in an illegal challenge with one of her classmates. Samara rushes her to the Med Center in an ambulance.

After a pitched battle, Phoenix makes it inside the Ascension Center only to learn that the city's tracking system has been disconnected from the rest of the tracking network, making it impossible to disable everyone's implants at once. Keera steals a ship and takes Specter up to one of the Kyra's satellites to hack into the tracking network from there.

The Chrona's fleet arrives, and the fighting

begins in earnest. The *Sovath* crashes just outside the city walls and flattens them on one side. Dregs come streaming into New Houston through the gap. They descend on the Med Center where Samara is with Dora. Samara and her colleagues are forced to fight for their lives to fend off the Dregs. Several nurses and doctors die in the process.

Keera and Specter succeed in disabling the tracking network and return to Earth. Chronan troops liberate New Houston. The Kyron fleet has been routed. The battle is over, and the resistance won. Clayton learns that Samara is under attack by Dregs and runs to the rescue with Nova and the rest of the resistance. They arrive too late. Samara and Dora have both been infected by Dregs.

But Lori reveals that they are also immune. Samara is a clone, and her immunity is in her germ cells, so it is passed on to her children. Clayton is reunited with his family, finally, and they are all okay.

The Med Center is secured against Dregs, and everyone takes the time to rest and recover. Four hours later, they wake up to see and hear the Chrona's fleet pulling out. Specter has gone with them. They also learn that the surviving staff of the Med Center are getting sick—even Commander Treya, who was captured during the fighting. But Chimeras like her should be immune to the virus. It doesn't make any sense.

Then they realize what must have happened. The Chrona didn't vaccinate everyone as they claimed. Yet Phoenix knows that the cure *does* work; they tested it. Somehow, the Chrona didn't mass produce and distribute the vaccine in the water supplies. They distributed a new and even more virulent strain of the virus instead. No one is immune to it, not even Chimeras, and this virus turns one hundred percent of its victims into Dregs.

Following the Chrona's betrayal, there is only one thing left to do: flee New Houston and return to the Wastes before the city's inhabitants all turn into infectious, carnivorous monsters. But Phoenix is all out of ammo, and the new virus has a much shorter incubation period, so its victims are already turning...

RUNNING IN THE DARK

CHAPTER 1

The beams of tactical lights bobbed and flashed over bare concrete, parting the darkness inside the stairwell of the New Houston Medical Center. Clayton's knuckles whitened around his hunting knife, and he squeezed his wife, Samara's hand. His EKR-7 rifle dangled uselessly from the shoulder strap. The charge was completely depleted after the assault on the Ascension Center.

That attack had turned out to be for nothing. Their Chrona ally, Specter, had double-crossed all of humanity, infecting them with a new, deadlier strain of the Chimeran virus rather than vaccinating them as the resistance had originally planned.

On Clayton's other side, Samara held the hand of their ten-year-old daughter, Dora, while Clayton's adopted daughter, Nova, walked behind them. Admiral Keera and her mother Lori led them and the rest of the resistance group known as Phoenix down the stairs with Sergeant Sutton bringing up the rear. The only sounds were the echoes of their collective footfalls.

With the medical center and the entire city overrun by Dregs and newly infected people, none of them dared to raise their voices. Dregs had particularly keen hearing. And making matters worse, Clayton wasn't the only one who was out of charge on his rifle.

They continued down the stairwell, passing landing after landing as they descended from the tenth floor. After just a few minutes, Clayton's legs began to ache. His muscles were still sore from all of the activity yesterday.

"How much farther is it?" Dora asked in a loud whisper.

"Shhh!" several people hissed at once.

Both Clayton and Samara gave her a sharp look, to which Dora frowned and looked away.

Step after creeping step, they descended until they reached the bottom of the stairwell. The procession stopped there, and Clayton stood in line behind four others, watching as Admiral Keera leaned around the corner of the open stairwell to check for signs of trouble. After a moment, she turned to look up at them, her matte black cloaking armor making her look like a shadow. She waved for them to follow her, and then crept into the corridor.

As Clayton reached the bottom of the stairs, he saw the dead, half-eaten body of a doctor lying in a dark pool of congealed blood, both human-red and Dreg-black. The Dreg who'd been feasting on him lay face-down beside the doctor. Clayton remembered killing it the day before on his way up to rescue Samara.

She sucked in a shallow breath as they stepped over the doctor's snaking entrails. Clayton looked to her with eyebrows raised. Samara seemed like she was about to say something, but then shook her head. He offered a sympathetic smile, and they carried on in silence. She had worked at this hospital as a nurse, so she probably knew the dead man.

Everyone hurried down the corridor and through a pair of swinging doors to the ER waiting room. The glass doors were shattered and a stack of overturned chairs sat partially blocking the opening. Wedges of broken glass caught jagged reflections from the sweeping tac lights mounted under depleted rifles. Keera and her mother Lori crept over to the doors and peered out to the darkened street beyond.

Samara glanced around with the others, her eyes wide in the darkened waiting area. Seeing no immediate signs of trouble, Clayton released Samara's hand and went to check the entrance with Keera and Lori. They crouched there with the barrel-mounted tac lights on their rifles turned off. Both women had night-vision optics built into their helmets, so they could see more in these conditions than anyone else in the group.

Clayton asked a silent question with an open handed shrug as Keera glanced back. He read tension in her posture. She held up an armored hand, four fingers raised, then jerked a thumb to the street beyond the doors.

Clayton's heart rate spiked. Four Dregs. He glanced back at the resistance fighters and his family. There were eleven of them counting himself and his two kids, but Dora wasn't armed and she was too young to count for much in a fight. And Samara was only armed with a scalpel.

Where they had knives, the Dregs had sharp teeth and claws. All it would take was one scratch or a bite to infect one of them. With the exception of Clayton and Nova, they'd all been inoculated against the original version of the virus, while Samara, Dora, Lori, and Keera were all naturally immune to it. But no one was immune to this new strain that Specter and the Chrona had unleashed. Not even Chimeras like Keera, or clones like Samara and Lori. As far as Clayton knew, there was no way to physically tell which version of the virus a particular Dreg was infected with, so it was going to be Russian Roulette out there.

Keera stepped away from the entrance and gestured for him to follow her. She led him around the reception desk of the ER. Sergeant Sutton followed them.

"So what's the plan?" he asked, his voice

barely audible. He and Keera were the joint leaders of the resistance.

"We need guns and a vehicle," Keera said, matching the volume of his voice. "But we shouldn't all go out."

Clayton nodded, a knot of tension releasing in his chest. He'd already been imagining a bloody fight with the Dregs as they fled the city on foot.

Sutton frowned crookedly, the shiny patch of scar tissue tugging the one corner of his mouth up instead of down. "I'll join you." His dark skin made him blend with the shadows, but it wouldn't matter: Dregs had excellent night vision. Not to mention hearing and smell.

"No. Lori and I will go," Keera said. "We're armored and we can cloak ourselves. The Dregs won't see or smell us."

"Those suits must be running low on charge by now," Sutton said. "How long can you sustain a cloaking shield before they're completely depleted?"

Keera hesitated. "We'll use our charge sparingly."

Sutton didn't look convinced. "When you deplete those suits they're gonna lock up and you'll have to ditch them. What then?"

"I can see in the dark. I'm still the best one to do this."

"And Lori?" Sutton's eyes flicked to her.

"She doesn't have much combat experience."

"I have over a century of experience," Lori replied. "I could out-shoot you with my eyes closed."

"I'd like to see that," Sutton growled.

"Enough," Keera snapped. "This isn't open to discussion. We'll go get a vehicle and then come straight back here to get the rest of you."

Sutton crossed his arms over his chest. "We should all go now before it gets any more crowded out there," Sutton said. "Finding a vehicle won't do us any good if it's being chased by a horde of Dregs. All you'll do is lead them back here. The Chrona infected everyone before they left, so soon there will be thousands of next gen Dregs flooding the streets. Besides, for all we know, you're the most vulnerable of us all. You saw what happened to Treya."

Clayton thought back to the room full of twenty-odd infected survivors from the hospital that they'd left behind on the tenth floor. They'd all been in the process of turning into Dregs, but the first one to turn had been a Chimera like Keera—Admiral Treya of the Kyron fleet, formerly Keera's XO.

Keera shook her head, a human gesture she'd likely learned from her mother. "Treya may have turned faster than the rest, but the outcome will be the same for any of us. No one is immune anymore. And if you're right about thousands of Dregs flooding the streets, then

27

it's even more imperative that we stay hidden. We can't fight against those odds."

"We could if we scavenge weapons along the way."

"Not even then," Keera said. "The population of New Houston was over two hundred thousand humans, let alone Chimeras. Assuming all of them were infected and the virus doesn't kill anyone, then we're looking at just as many Dregs. That means there's twenty thousand of them for every one of us. You like those odds? How long do you think you can run before they overtake us?"

Sutton frowned crookedly once more, but said nothing. Dregs were physically superior to humans—faster and stronger. They would catch up fast and it would be over in a matter of seconds.

"We need a vehicle," Keera repeated. "If possible, we'll get two. We can use one as a diversion while the other comes here to pick you up."

"SWMD Central is just a few blocks from here," Clayton suggested. "You could steal garbage haulers. They're designed to handle the roads outside, and Central will have plenty of guns, too."

"My thoughts exactly," Keera replied.

"Then Lori should give me her armor," Clayton added. "I know the way to SWMD and I also know my way around inside."

Both Keera and Lori regarded him steadily, their expressions hidden by their helmets. "He's right," Sutton said.

Keera looked to her mother. Lori responded by removing her helmet and triggering her suit's release. It splayed open with a flurry of clicking metal joints and Lori stepped out. She looked sweaty and tired. Clayton removed his utility belt and then handed it to Sutton along with his rifle and his knife. Going to the suit, he lined himself up inside, and Lori passed him the helmet. He nodded his thanks and slipped it on. A colorful green heads-up-display (HUD) appeared inside the helmet's glossy faceplate, and the shadows in the medical center retreated with the light amplification settings of the suit's optics. The helmet was designed to read his thoughts, making the control systems highly-intuitive.

He cycled the suit shut with a thought and felt armor plates squeezing around his arms and legs. The suit was a particularly tight fit around his feet due to his bulky boots. Suits like these were best worn with special footwear, but he'd make do.

"Can you hear me?" Keera's voice sounded close, coming to his ears over the in-helmet comms.

"Yes," he replied, making sure to activate the comms first by focusing his attention on the blinking icon at the bottom of his HUD.

He turned to reach for the knife and rifle he'd given to Sutton before putting on the suit of armor, but Keera shook her head.

"We're going to engage our EM cloaks out there. Those weapons will still be visible."

Clayton grimaced, and gave in with a nod.

Sergeant Sutton shouldered the extra rifle and strapped on Clayton's utility belt over his own before sheathing the hunting knife. "You can have them back later."

Clayton focused on the speaker icon to address the others. "The rest of you should hide until we get back," he whispered, his eyes flicking between Sutton and Lori. "We'll let you know via comms when we're close."

Sutton glanced around. "I don't see any cover positions around here."

"Samara will know where to go," Clayton said. "She worked here."

"Good," Keera put in. She nodded to him, and he led the way back to his wife and kids. They stood huddled in the middle of the waiting room surrounded by a circle of resistance fighters armed with knives and empty rifles. Samara was gazing fixedly at the broken glass doors of the ER, as if expecting Dregs to come dashing through at any second.

Clayton touched Samara's arm. She flinched and whirled to face him, her eyes flashing in the dark.

"Lori?" she asked.

"It's me," he soothed.

"Clayton? What are you doing..." She trailed off, her eyes flicking over his armor.

"Keera and I are going to get a couple of haulers from SWMD," Clayton explained. "Is there anywhere close by that you can hide with the others until we get back?"

Samara blinked rapidly as she considered her answer. "The quarantine unit on sub-level one would be the safest. Both the patient rooms and the stairwell access are designed to contain Dregs, so they should keep them out, too. We just need to get the keys from the nurse's station down there so we can lock ourselves in."

"Lead the way," Keera said.

Samara hesitated for a moment, then released Dora's hand and started for the corridor on the opposite side of the reception desk. Dora trailed after her along with everyone else. Samara pushed through another pair of swinging doors, and Clayton caught up to walk beside her in case they ran into trouble. He didn't have his hunting knife or rifle, but now with the augmented protection afforded by his armor, he felt much better about his chances if they ran into Dregs.

But that didn't happen. They reached a gleaming bank of elevators and a door to a stairwell on the wall in front of them. Samara nodded to it, but made no move to open the door. "One level down," she said.

Clayton grabbed the door handle, but Keera caught him by his shoulder and stopped him.

"They can handle it from here," she said quietly.

"We don't know that the sub-levels are clear," Clayton replied.

"We swept them when we were looking for survivors," Keera replied.

"That was hours ago," he objected.

"If there's anything down there, we can handle it," Sutton said, stepping into view with Clayton's knife in his hand. "You two better get going."

Clayton stepped back and turned to Samara, Dora, and Nova. All three of them looked scared, but Nova looked particularly worried.

He pulled Samara into a quick hug. "I'll see you soon. Watch the kids."

"*Kid,*" Nova said, emphasizing the fact that she thought of herself as a grown-up at fifteen. "I can watch myself," Nova said.

"Me too," Dora added, but her small, girlish voice belied that statement.

"What if you don't make it back?" Samara asked.

"We will," Clayton replied. Keera strode by him, walking quickly and silently back the way they'd come.

"Time to go," she whispered over the

comms.

"Stay safe," Clayton said; then he switched from speaker-mode to comms and hurried after Keera.

"Activate your cloak," she said just before they reached the swinging doors to the ER.

He did so with a thought, and watched as his arms and legs shimmered and vanished from his field of view. The HUD highlighted his armor and Keera's with glowing green outlines, but it was still a strange, surreal sensation, as if he'd become a ghost.

"What is your suit's power level?" Keera asked as she pushed one of the swinging doors open with a whisper of protest from the hinges. She held it open as he went through and then hurried back to take the point position as they headed for the exit.

Clayton checked the power icon in the top left corner of his HUD and a stab of fear shot through his system. "Seven percent."

A rush of static crackled through Clayton's helmet. "I'm at nine."

"How long will that last?" he asked.

"With our cloaks engaged, we drain about one percent per minute, and that's if we don't drain the power in other ways."

"Such as?"

"Running. Jumping. Or otherwise using the suits' augmented strength."

Clayton did a quick mental calculation in

his head. It was only four blocks from the hospital to SWMD Central. Less than half a klick. That would only take a couple of minutes if they sprinted the whole way, but they couldn't do that without draining their power levels—not to mention causing a lot of noise and attracting Dregs. "It won't take more than five minutes to walk there," he decided. "We'll still make it."

"Yes," Keera agreed.

But neither of them mentioned what would happen after that. They'd have to ditch their armor soon after they got into the facility, and then they would be utterly defenseless. He could only hope Central had been evacuated during the fighting.

They reached a glittering pool of broken glass just before the doors of the Med Center.

"Careful," Keera warned as she stepped gingerly through the debris, grinding broken glass under her boots. Clayton tried to follow her footsteps, being careful to make as little sound as possible. Then they reached the empty door frames and ducked under jutting chair legs to reach the street. Both he and Keera froze right outside the doors.

Scattered groups of Dregs were picking their way down both sides of the street. Others were down on their knees and haunches, hunching over dead bodies, their heads periodically dipping to feed. Their naked, chalk-white backs shone bright in the combined light of the stars and the light amplification optics in Clayton's helmet.

"I thought you said there were four of them," he said slowly.

"There *were*," Keera replied.

In the span of ten minutes they'd multiplied from four to forty. That didn't bode well.

"We'd better hurry," Keera added. "Lead the way."

Clayton nodded, turning and walking up a slight incline to the right and heading deeper into the city. His suit's power level was down to five percent. He ran the math in his head again: one percent drained per minute. Four hundred meters to cover at walking speed, heading up a hill...

Chances were fifty-fifty that he'd have to deactivate his cloak or ditch his armor before they arrived. And all it took was one look at the roaming, hungry masses of infected monsters to know what would happen next.

CHAPTER 2

"**T**hese are all first generation Dregs," Keera whispered over comms.

"How can you tell?" Clayton asked, eying the ghostly white creatures as they passed each other on the street.

"They're mostly naked. If they'd turned recently, they would still be fully clothed."

"So we *can* tell them apart," Clayton realized.

"For now, but it doesn't matter for you. You weren't inoculated. You're vulnerable to either strain of the virus."

"Right." Clayton glanced at his suit's power levels. Three percent. Roughly three minutes left, and he estimated they were about halfway to the station. He pushed himself to walk a bit faster, hoping the trade-offs between speed and power draw came out in his favor.

By the time their destination appeared on the right side of the street, he was down to one percent and the power icon was flashing red. An audible warning echoed through his helmet: "*Warning, power levels critical. Shutdown imminent. Warning, power levels critical. Shutdown imminent. Warning—*"

"How are you doing for charge?" Keera asked.

Clayton barely heard her over the repetitive alerts from his suit. He silenced those warnings with a thought and headed for the entrance of the facility. "Not good. You might have to carry me in a minute."

"Deactivate your cloak," Keera suggested.

Clayton glanced around quickly, but didn't see any Dregs in the immediate vicinity. He turned off the cloaking shield and the glowing green outlines of his arms and legs turned to shadowy black armor once more. He reached the metal doors that formed the front entrance of the boxy concrete building and hesitated before trying the handle. One of those doors was ajar, a scorched black hole where the door handle and locking mechanism should have been. That saved them from having to break their way in, but it meant that someone else had already beaten them to it. Clayton reached out to open the door, but even as he did so, he felt the growing resistance from his suit.

A new alert sounded: *Power levels depleted. Shutting down.*

And then a series of whirring and clicking noises issued from the suit. It splayed open and a gust of cool air washed over his sweat-soaked black uniform.

Clayton removed the helmet and stepped out of the suit, leaving the frozen armor in front of the entrance like a gargoyle. "At least we made it," he whispered, reaching for the door again.

"Clayton wait!" Keera hissed.

The door burst open with a *bang* and a snarling Dreg leaped out with red, demon eyes flashing and blood-smeared teeth snapping for his throat.

Keera grabbed the creature from behind and gave the head a vicious twist. Something popped, and it went limp in her arms. She dragged it off him and yanked him to his feet.

"Thanks," he breathed.

Keera nodded and led the way through the doors. They hurried through the entrance together, and she snapped on a pair of headlamps that flanked her helmet's visor. Harsh white light played over at least a dozen different corpses in the lobby. Some were Dregs. Others humans. Blood and gore shone dark red and black under Keera's helmet lights. The humans wore gray pants and shirts with neon yellow vests and reflective piping. Hauler drivers.

Clayton spotted their weapons. Gunmetal gray and short-barreled. Standard-issue Kyron Laser Rifles. He ran to get one and checked the charge on the physical display below and behind the weapon's night-vision scope—ten blue segments out of twelve ran in a circle around the number 15. Fifteen shots left. He flicked on the tactical light under the barrel and went around scavenging spare charge packs from other rifles. Almost as an afterthought, he connected his augmented reality contacts (ARCs) to the rifle, and the charge meter appeared in the bottom right of his field of view.

"Which way?" Keera whispered as she recovered a rifle for herself.

Clayton swept the tac light around to get his bearings, then pointed to the far end of the lobby where the elevators to the admin levels were. "This way."

He walked right by the elevators to a security door. It was blasted open just like the front door had been.

"Looks like someone else had the same idea as we did," Clayton muttered.

"Maybe they came in here to hide," Keera suggested.

"Yeah, could be," Clayton agreed. He jammed the barrel of his rifle through the gap between the door and the jamb and connected his ARCs to the scope for a look at what was on the other side. The tac light revealed overturned tables and chairs. Two more dead drivers. One was draped over the legs of a table, her arms and legs dangling. Another one lay face-down on the polished concrete floor with his gun beside him. A dead Dreg was sprawled on the floor between them, its half-naked body riddled with laser burns. No signs of live Dregs, however.

Clayton spied the doors to the men's and women's locker rooms. Beyond that were the hauler bays. He disconnected his ARCs and eased the door open, gesturing for Keera to follow him.

Before they even reached the doors to the locker rooms, he heard the telltale clicking and clattering of Keera's armor as it ejected her before shutting down completely. She emerged, her face ghost-white and flushed with fish scale patterns of black veins underneath. Her red eyes narrowed and cranial stalks rose, twitching from where the helmet had flattened them against her hairless skull. The cone-shaped ears at the tips swiveled to face him. A Chimera's version of ears.

"Let's keep moving," Keera whispered.

Clayton nodded and grabbed the door to the men's locker room. This one wasn't blasted open, and it was locked. Clayton released a noisy sigh between his teeth.

But then, to his surprise, the door popped open. It hadn't been shut properly. As it opened, the sound of running water could be heard. He and Keera shared a worried look, and he placed a finger to his lips before flicking off his tac light and waving for her to follow him in. Someone might have left a shower or a faucet on in the midst of all the chaos, but then why was the door locked?

The room looked empty. Several of the lockers stood open and both SWMD uniforms and regular clothes sat in piles and messy heaps on wooden benches. Clayton led them around the lockers, past the urinals and toilets to the sinks and shower stalls. The sound of running water wasn't steady, but splattering loudly as if someone were scrubbing themselves clean. Whoever it was, they obviously hadn't gotten the memo about the water being infected with a new strain of the Chimeran virus.

Clayton's hands tightened on the grip and handguard of the rifle as they rounded the corner.

A man stood there, hunching over one of the sinks, a black rifle beside him, the tac light on and shining. He was covered from head to toe in glistening black Dreg blood and struggling to clean it off his hands.

"Hey," Clayton said in a gruff whisper. The man spun around, shock flashing in his eyes. His face was cleaner than the rest of him, but still darkly smeared.

"Clayton?" he asked in a familiar voice. Then his eyes darted a few degrees to the left and widened suddenly. "Keera?"

Clayton couldn't believe it. It was Richard

Morgan, Keera's father. He'd abandoned their assault on the Ascension Center at the last minute, saying it was suicide, and left Clayton to lead his fire team.

"You have no idea how glad I am to see you two!" Richard said. "Alive!" he added quickly.

"Shut up," Keera hissed. "What are you doing here?"

"Probably the same thing as you. I was looking for a way to get out of the city, and garbage haulers are one of the only vehicles that can take the roads out there."

"Have you drunk anything since the assault began?" Clayton asked.

Richard frowned. "Of course."

"From your canteen or a tap?" Keera asked.

"Canteen. I was just about to refill it."

"Don't," Clayton said. "Shut off that faucet and dry your hands. The water's infected."

Richard blinked. "What? I thought it was supposed to contain the vaccine!"

"The Chrona betrayed us," Keera explained. "They decided to test a deadlier version of the virus on us instead, and none of us are immune to it. The entire city is busy turning into the next generation of Dregs, and we need to get out of here before that happens."

"That's... how do you know?" Richard looked horrified.

"We saw people turning after we told them to drink the water," Clayton said. "Even a Chimera."

"Shit. No wonder I haven't seen any other survivors." Richard's eyes drifted out of focus, the news seeming to hit him in waves.

"Is that your blood?" He pointed to Richard's glistening black uniform.

Richard didn't reply.

"Morgan. Snap out of it!" Clayton said.

Richard's eyes flicked up, but he still didn't appear to be all there. "Yes?"

"It doesn't matter," Keera said. "He was vaccinated and we haven't seen any next gen Dregs coming out yet. Even if he got bitten, he's not infected."

"That doesn't mean we should take him with us," Clayton replied.

Keera shot him a hard look. "He's still my father, and right now every life is precious."

"Where are the others?" Richard asked. "Did they make it?"

"Some of them did," Clayton replied, unable to keep the accusation from his tone.

"They're at the hospital waiting for us," Keera said.

Richard dried his hands on his pants, grimacing as he dirtied them with black smears of Dreg blood once more.

Clayton eyed the other man, wondering just how contagious the water was. Could casual contact be a problem, or did they have to ingest it to get infected? He resolved to keep an eye on Richard.

"This way." Clayton flicked on his tac light and led Keera and her father back to the lockers. From there, he reached the door to the hauler garage, unlocked it, and opened it a crack to check the other side with his ARCs and his rifle's scope. No Dregs, no bodies, and only *one* hauler. He pulled the door open with a muttered curse.

All of the other haulers must have either been caught out on the streets at the time of the attack or else they'd already been used to evacuate the city. Clayton just stood there, grinding his teeth and trying to come up with a new plan. Keera had suggested they take two haulers so that one of them could act as a diversion to lead Dregs away while they fetched everyone else from the Med Center, but now they would be coming in hot with Dregs chasing them the whole way. How were they supposed to get the others on board with a horde busy swarming them?

"At least they left us with one," Keera pointed out.

CHAPTER 3

Samara sat on the floor with Dora, leaning back against the nurse's station in the center of the quarantine unit. Several of the others stood around watching the shadows with their flashlights and knives. The farmer, Harold Neem and his daughter, Veronica, A.K.A. Pyro, sat with their backs to the door of an isolation ward. Those wards lined both sides of the nurse's station with thick security doors leading to airlocks. Lockers with canary-yellow hazmat suits ran between the rooms. Floor grating instead of solid floors hinted at another security measure: decontamination jets in the ceiling that would spray the entire level with virus and bacteria-killing chemicals in case of a containment breach.

The hospital wasn't meant to deal with infected patients, but sometimes accidents happened when the Ascension Center was already at maximum capacity, so they needed to have a place to keep the infected until they could be transferred. The Kyra had been meticulous about preventing outbreaks. They had to be, because the virus had only two outcomes: Chimera or Dreg, and Chimeras couldn't breed. The human population had to be protected in order to preserve the Kyra's breeding stock.

But all of that was over now that their post-biological brethren, the Chrona, had deliberately infected the entire planet with a new version of the virus. The roaming bands of exiles living in the Wastes and Wilds beyond the cities would soon be the only humans left on Earth.

"They're taking too long," Sergeant Sutton growled as he paced the floor, the beams of tactical lights reflecting off the old burn scars on his face.

"Still nothing?" Lori asked, running hands along her sweaty brown hair to make sure it was still tucked firmly into a bun behind her head.

"You tell me," Sutton replied. Lori shook her head. Samara noticed that both of them were wearing in-ear comms pieces. Everyone else was, too, even that kid—Clayton's other daughter. What was her name again?

Nova, she recalled. Samara studied her. The girl stared back. She was pretty, with blonde hair, hazel eyes, and a soft, feminine face, but there was a hardness around her eyes that suggested she was anything but soft. Dora sometimes had that same look, but she was several years younger.

"What?" Nova demanded, her hands going to her hips.

Samara smiled and shook her head. "Nothing. I was just wondering about you."

"Yeah, likewise," Nova said, still sounding defensive.

"Not in a bad way," Samara added.

Nova nodded and averted her eyes, pretending to busy herself by checking the shadows with her rifle's tactical light for the hundredth time.

Silence thickened the air between them. Some of the others spoke to each other in hushed tones.

"I'm glad Clayton wasn't alone out there," Samara said, trying to keep the conversation going. "And that you weren't, either. Come sit with us. We may as well get to know each other while we're waiting here."

Nova's attention tracked back, and she shrugged before walking over. Dora watched curiously as her stepsister approached and sat down facing them. "What d'ya wanna know?"

"Anything. Everything. How have you survived out there all this time?"

Nova pursed her lips. "We hunt and forage, and Dad goes out to the Wastes to scavenge for stuff that we can trade to the resistance—I mean, Phoenix."

Sergeant Sutton glanced their way at the

mention of his ragtag group of resistance fighters.

"What about fruit and vegetables?"

Another shrug. "Don't really like 'em."

"How have you not gotten sick?" Samara asked.

"Well, there are a few fruit trees and bushes around our cabin. And Dad trades for vitamins."

It was hard to imagine the two of them living on their own like primitive hunter-gatherers for so many years. "Why didn't he just tell me that he was alive?" Instead, he'd let both her and Dora think that he was dead after the Kyra had exiled him from the city.

"I guess you'll have to ask him that," Nova said.

"Oh, I intend to," Samara replied.

A distant clattering sound echoed from the deepest recesses of the sub-level and everyone froze.

"What was that?" someone asked in a quiet voice. It was Harold.

It had sounded like a metal tray being knocked to the floor.

"Shhh," Sutton warned, with a finger to his lips and a hand cupped to his ear, listening for subsequent sounds.

"Maybe a rat?" Harold's daughter, Pyro, suggested. Her curly red hair bounced as she stood up. With that hair and her freckly skin, she looked just like a younger, female version of her father.

Another clatter came, followed by the sound of metal implements scattering, and suddenly everyone was looking to Samara.

"Is there any other access to this level?" Sergeant Sutton asked.

They'd checked the sub-level when they came down, but hadn't found anything to worry about. Samara took a second to consider the question. "No," she decided. "The stairwell and the elevators are the only entrances to the sub levels." She pointed to the gleaming bank of elevators and the locked security door to the stairwell. All the possible entry points were in plain sight.

"The door wasn't locked when we came down here," the Latin woman known as Widow said from where she stood peering into the shadowy depths of the quarantine level. She clutched her knife tightly in one hand, her depleted laser rifle in the other. "Maybe we missed something on our initial sweep."

"Maybe," Sutton agreed. "Widow, Pyro, on me."

"I can go," a man with curly black hair and a bushy beard added, struggling to rise from where he lay slumped against one of the isolation wards. His chest was bandaged from a laser burn he'd suffered.

"No, you can't," said Doc, the Asian member of Phoenix, pushing the man with the beard back down. "You're still recovering."

"You gave me Regenex! I should be good as new by now."

"Listen to the Doc, Preacher," Sutton said.

"What if our ride calls while you're away?" Lori asked as Sutton started past the nurse's station.

He tapped the comms piece in his ear. "Then I'll hear it. If not, you call me."

Samara watched Sutton, Widow, and Pyro leave the group with knives at the ready and tac lights sweeping. The sub-levels were huge —just as big as the other floors of the Med Center. It could take them a while to figure out what was making all that noise. Everyone watched in silence as they faded into the shadows. They reached a pair of automatic doors, spent a moment prying them open, and then passed out of sight.

"What if whatever it is slips by them and comes here?" Nova asked.

Samara shook her head and offered a tight smile. "I'm sure it's nothing. Probably just—"

And then a familiar shriek split the silence and sent hot spikes of adrenaline shooting to Samara's fingertips.

"That's not nothing; that's a Dreg!" Harold said, jumping to his feet and drawing a six-inch combat knife from his belt.

A flurry of high-pitched cries followed,

coming from the direction where Sutton had gone.

"More than one," Doc added, his eyes fixed on the doors through which Sutton and the others had left.

"They must have found a way in," Lori said. "We can't stay down here." She held a finger to the comms piece in her ear. "Scar, come in." she said, using Sutton's call sign. Lori waited a beat, and then tried again. "Scar?"

* * *

Clayton climbed into the driver's seat of the hauler, taking a moment to familiarize himself with the controls. Thankfully, the key was already in the ignition. Someone had left it there in their hurry to get to safety. He glanced around at the switches, buttons, levers and screens. The inside of the haulers hadn't changed much in the decade since he'd last driven one.

"Can you still operate it?" Keera asked, her hairless scalp wrinkling and cranial stalks twitching as she climbed into the co-pilot's seat on the other side.

Richard stood behind her, still covered in black Dreg blood, and peering up at them. "Where am I going to sit?"

Clayton nodded to Keera. "Yes," he said, ignoring Richard's question. He touched the ignition button and the vehicle whirred to life. Thankfully, the vehicles weren't biometric-ally-locked. Control screens tied to external cameras flickered on. He spotted two joysticks to manipulate the robotic loading arms. This version of hauler apparently had one on each side.

Clayton gripped the wheel in both hands and looked to Keera. "Better grab the rifle behind your head." He nodded to the laser rifle mounted on a rack behind her headrest. He had a plasma pistol tucked into a holster in his door and a matching rifle behind him. He took a second to draw the pistol and check the charge. It was down to just below half, with only four shots left. Whoever had brought this hauler in, they'd seen some action out in the Wastes.

"Hello?" Richard prompted, waving his hands to get their attention. "I don't see an extra seat."

"You'll have to ride in the back," Clayton said.

Richard wrinkled his nose dubiously.

"We could use a gunner back there," Keera added, and offered him the rifle she'd taken off the rack.

Richard took a quick step back, his hands upraised. "Are you insane? I'm not going to stand in the back with the hatch open."

Keera hissed loudly between her teeth and shook her head. "Fine. I'll do it."

"Don't," Clayton said.

She jumped down, and Richard shamelessly took the seat she'd left. Clayton glared at him.

"Open the hatch!" Keera said, banging on the side of the truck. Clayton pulled the lever to open the hatch. It began groaning open. He continued glaring at Richard while he waited for Keera to climb up.

"What?" Richard asked, his blonde eyebrows arching up over bright blue eyes. His chiseled jaw and movie-star good looks might have landed him a role as an action hero in a holovid.

Pity the reality is so different, Clayton thought. "She's your daughter," he said.

"She's a *Chimera.* And this is all her fault. Besides, she's a much better shot than I am."

Clayton snorted.

Another bang sounded, this time on the roof of the cab. Clayton checked the external monitors and saw Keera standing in the back of the hauler, her rifle balanced to aim out the garage doors when they reversed. The doors were all shut, which meant that the other haulers had to have left before the facility lost power.

Clayton threw the hauler into reverse and eyed the rearview monitor as he backed toward the exit. The vehicle's backup alarm made a ruckus, beeping loudly.

"Shut that thing up!" Richard snapped.

Clayton killed the alarm after just a few seconds. The hauler had a silent-running mode that drivers used when they left the city walls, but he'd forgotten to engage it. Ten years away from the job had taken a toll. "Relax. We're still inside the garage. Nothing's going to hear us this far out from the street."

Another series of banging sounds reached their ears. One look at the external monitors told him it wasn't Keera. Those sounds were coming from the garage doors. Then came a tooth-grinding screech of sharp claws raking over metal, and more banging.

"Shit." Clayton hit the brakes, his thoughts racing.

"Nice job," Richard muttered. "We should stop and wait here until they go away. At least we're safe in here."

The muffled cries of untold numbers of Dregs reached their ears and the sound of palms banging and claws raking over the metal doors intensified.

"You sure about that?" Clayton asked.

"We could go back to the locker rooms..." Richard suggested, his eyes straying to the doors they'd exited a few minutes ago.

"What's the hold up?" Keera asked, her voice muffled through the roof of the hauler's cab.

"Keep it down!" Richard hissed.

"A little late for that," Clayton added. His

eyes were still on the rearview monitor. He could actually see the garage door behind them shaking as Dregs pounded on it. They had a problem. With the power out, someone needed to operate the manual pulley to open that door, but with Dregs out there it would be suicide.

"We're going to have to ram our way out," Clayton decided. He put the vehicle into drive and angled between pillars to the hauler bay beside theirs.

"What are you doing?" Richard demanded as he came to an abrupt stop and then reversed back the other way, cranking the wheel.

"Turning around. We need to get up some speed, and we'd better be going forwards for that."

"Are you crazy?" Richard asked. "That door is made of reinforced steel."

"And this truck weighs more than twenty tons." Clayton cranked the wheel again, angling the front toward the exit.

"What if we puncture a wheel?"

"Better hope we don't," Clayton replied as the front of the truck swung into line with the door. He threw it into reverse again and backed all the way up to get some distance to accelerate. "Buckle up," he said, hitting the brakes just before they reached the back wall of the garage.

"If this goes wrong, we're all dead," Richard

warned, fumbling with his seatbelt.

Clayton ignored him and lowered his window. The sound of Dregs pounding and scratching to get in grew immediately louder as he did so. Craning his neck out the window he turned to look up at Keera. "Better brace yourself! We're going to hit hard."

She nodded and ducked down below the top of the truck. If she was smart, she'd plant her back against the front wall of the cargo box.

"Here," Clayton reached behind his head for the second rifle and passed it to Richard. "Have it ready. Just in case."

The defiant set of Richard's jaw made it look like he was considering a mutiny, but he accepted the weapon without comment.

Buckling himself in, Clayton nodded once and took a deep breath. "Here goes..." He planted his foot flat. The electric vehicle accelerated with a rising *whir*, moving impressively fast for all its mass. The metal door gleamed under headlights, swelling to fill the entire windshield. A new concern occurred to Clayton just before they hit. One of the reinforcing metal beams running along the width of the doors could easily break free to stab through the windshield and impale either him or Richard.

The impact came with a deafening crash. Followed by the sound of shattering glass as exactly that happened. Clayton reflexively threw up his hands as two twisted metal beams flew through the front windshield, riding a wave of pulverized safety glass.

CHAPTER 4

The hauler bucked up and bounced over the twisted ruins of the door, drawing peals of thunder from tortured metal sheets and crushing Dregs underneath. Clayton grabbed the wheel to steady their course. A cacophony of pitiful screams and popping, snapping bones reached their ears through the broken window as they blasted free of the garage and the twisted remains of the door. Clayton spared a hand from the steering wheel to pat himself down, checking for puncture wounds. Luckily, the metal beams that broke through the windshield had stabbed *between* him and Richard. One look at the other man revealed he was also fine. Pale as a Dreg, though.

"We made it," Clayton said as he gunned the accelerator and steered hard to drive around the facility. Richard just nodded.

Dregs shrieked and growled in the distance behind them. Others scattered under their headlights, their red eyes and sharp, rotting teeth gleaming in the gloom.

Clayton touched the comms piece in his ear. "Lone Wolf to Scar, come in Scar."

Static hissed long and hard.

"What's wrong?" Richard asked as they flew over a speed bump at the entrance of the waste management facility. The street was still crowded with shadowy groups of Dregs hunched and feeding on the dead. At the sound of the hauler's approach they looked up and hissed, and others rose to their feet.

"They're not answering!" Clayton replied, shouting to be heard above the wind roaring in through the broken windshield. The metal beams that had broken the glass shivered and rattled together where they snaked over the abbreviated front end of the vehicle.

"Could be out of range!" Richard suggested.

Clayton shook his head. "We're only four blocks away!" And that was another problem. He glanced at a screen hanging above the left side of his dash. It showed Keera just now standing up and taking aim with her rifle. It also showed a horde of at least fifty Dregs turning to give chase. The hauler was a lot faster than they were, but they'd be stopping soon, and then those Dregs would catch up fast. At most, their pursuit would be lagging behind by a minute. "I'm going to have to circle the block until they reply!" Clayton said.

"Shit," Richard muttered. "Try them again!" The stricken look on his face mirrored

Clayton's own fears. Why the hell weren't they answering?

He tried the comms again, this time calling Lori. "Mother, come in," he said, using her call sign rather than her name.

And again, an empty stretch of static and silence hissed on through his ear piece. Dread filled his chest to the point of bursting, making it hard to breathe. He should have stayed with Sam and the kids. If something had happened to them, he'd never forgive himself.

* * *

The shrieking cries of Dregs grew nearer with every passing second. Samara stood beside the nurses' station with Doc, Lori, Harold, and Nova. She held a rifle with its under-barrel flashlight directed at the doors on the far end of the isolation wards. She clutched a scalpel in her other hand, her knuckles whitening as her grip tightened in anticipation of what was to come. The bare feet of dregs rattled the floor grates like thunder.

"They're coming," Harold whispered.

"Mom..." Dora's trembling voice rose to a terrified pitch.

She'd told Dora to hide under the desk in the nurse's station, but she was just about to get the keys to open one of the isolation wards and lock her in there instead.

"Be quiet!" Lori whispered, then held a hand to one ear in an effort to better hear her comms. "Say again?" she whispered into the device. "Scar? This is Mother, you're breaking up!"

Just then, a flash of movement appeared in the gap between the automatic doors by which Sutton had left. It was him. He slipped soundlessly through the gap like a wraith, followed by Widow and Pyro. The three of them grabbed the doors by whatever handholds they could find and began forcing them shut. It didn't appear to be working. The doors were smooth, with no way to grip them.

"Come on!" Lori said. "We have to help them!" She broke into a run.

"Stay here," Samara said to Dora, just before taking off after Lori. Doc and Harold ran with them, their thundering footfalls competing with those of the approaching Dregs.

The first one arrived in the gap before they did. A naked white arm shot through, long black claws slashing the air, and sharp, rotting teeth bared in a snarl. Spittle flew from the creature's lips, and its cranial stalks writhed furiously above its head. It couldn't get through the doors. They'd managed to force them shut just enough to keep the Dregs out.

Sutton narrowly avoided a sweeping slash of the creature's claws, cursing as he ducked, and Samara saw the doors inching open as he lost his grip. Both Widow and Pyro struggled to regain those inches, but they were narrowly avoiding the Dreg's claws themselves.

Harold reached the doors first. Heedless of the danger, he stabbed his combat knife through the gap—straight into the Dreg's left eye. The creature sunk to its knees, hissing softly. Harold pulled his knife out with a grunt, and a second Dreg crowded into the gap.

"Help us shut the doors!" Sutton cried through gritted teeth. He had both palms pressed to the smooth metal, trying to grip the door with friction. Harold squeezed in to help, while Samara and Lori stood back, keeping out of reach of the Dreg snarling on the other side of the opening. Samara could see at least a dozen more besides that one pressing in behind it.

"Where did they all come from?!" Samara cried.

"We don't know!" Widow said. Her tanned face was beaded with sweat and her dark eyebrows were knitted from the exertion of bracing the doors.

"Did you call us?" Lori asked, looking to Sutton.

"What?" He shook his head. "No! Get that Dreg out of the gap!"

Lori jolted into motion, her knife flashing up and slashing a long dark gash in the Dreg's forearm. The creature hissed and withdrew.

"Now!" Sutton cried.

Everyone pushed as hard as they could

and the doors came together with a thump, muffling the roaring and hissing of the Dregs on the other side. Everyone sagged with relief, but Lori stiffened, her hand flying to her ear again. "Say again! You're breaking up!"

Sutton nodded to her. "That has to be them. We should go now before these bastards pry the doors open again."

"It's radiation shielded..." Samara said slowly.

"What?" Lori asked, her eyes cinching down to slits.

"The quarantine level. It's radiation shielded! It's so that we can bake the whole floor to contain an outbreak."

"Fuuuck me," Sutton drawled. "You coulda mentioned that before we came down here!"

"I forgot!" Samara replied.

"On me, everyone! We don't want to miss our ride!" Sutton sprinted back toward the nurse's station. Samara raced after him with the others.

They reached the stairwell and pushed through. Samara held the door open with Lori, waiting for Nova and Dora to catch up from the nurse's station. "Come on!" she urged, waving to the girls.

A hollow metal banging sound started up, followed by a metallic shrieking noise... Samara's eyes tracked to the sound just in time to see a man in a blood-stained white lab coat stumble out of one of the elevators beside the stairwell. He turned to them with a snarl and wide, feverish eyes, his forehead glistening with sweat.

It was horrible timing. Nova and Dora were running too fast to slow down.

"Look out!" Samara screamed just as Dora passed right within reach of the infected man.

Dora screamed and recoiled from him, but he grabbed her arm in both hands and brought it up to his gaping jaws.

Dora cried out in pain.

"No!" Samara screamed. She lunged toward the doctor, but Nova beat her to it and plunged her knife into the base of the man's skull. He dropped instantly. Dora pulled her arm free and ran sobbing to Samara's side.

"Let me see it," Samara said, reaching for Dora's arm with shaking hands. Her eyes seized on the bite, two horseshoe-shaped marks, dark and glistening with blood. Her heart hammered in her chest, horror swirling like a hurricane.

"No, no, no..." Samara said, shaking her head and crying.

"It hurts..." Dora whimpered in a shivery voice, between sobs and gasps for air.

"It's okay. It'll be okay. We'll fix it," Samara said.

"We have to go!" Lori interrupted. A distant, echoing shriek sounded along with the hammering thuds of Dregs at the far end of the room, still trying to beat their way through the doors. "We'll deal with this later. We have plenty of medical supplies. And your daughter is immune. Just like me and you, remember?"

Samara stared hard into Lori's eyes and slowly shook her head. "He wasn't fully turned yet! He was infected with the new virus. No one is immune to that!"

"Mom, I'm scared," Dora sobbed.

"You don't know that," Lori said.

Nova stood off to one side, watching them as she retrieved her knife from the back of the dead man's skull and wiped it off on the back of the dead doctor's lab coat.

"Listen to me," Lori went on, "We'll figure this out. But right now, we have to go, okay?"

Samara drew herself up with a sharp inhalation and nodded. Maybe there was some way they could fight this. And Lori was right: none of them had yet seen if the Chrona's version of the Chimeran virus would defeat germ line immunity like theirs. Maybe clones and the descendants of clones would turn out to be immune to this new strain of the virus, too.

"Lead the way," Samara said, nodding to Lori. She nodded back and reached for the door to the stairwell, yanking it open once more.

"It's going to be okay, Dora," Samara whispered. She grabbed her daughter's hand on her uninjured side and hurried through, leading her up the stairs. Dora cried and sobbed the whole way—probably as much from the pain as from fear.

But Samara refused to give into despair. She held onto hope. She had to; it was the only thing that kept her from falling apart completely.

CHAPTER 5

Clayton drove past the entrance of the ER with a shrieking scrambling mass of Dregs chasing the hauler. Keera stood in the back firing periodically to deter them. It wasn't working.

"She should save her charge," Richard muttered, watching their pursuit in the side-view mirror. "We can't kill them all."

As if on cue, Keera banged on the roof of the cab. "I'm out! Toss me another pack!"

"What did I say?" Richard muttered. He reached into the side of his door and pulled out a fresh charge pack for the rifle before lowering his window and leaning out. "Hold your fire! Save it for the ones that grab on! We still have to make it through the Wastes after this!"

Clayton hated to admit it, but Richard was right. He watched on the hatch monitor as Keera leaned over the roof and grabbed the spare pack. The old one *clunked* to the bottom of the cargo box, but this time Keera held her fire.

"Try the comms again," Richard suggested.

"Lone Wolf, calling Phoenix. Come in Phoenix!" He was using a channel they all shared, so hopefully *someone* would answer.

Static hissed in his ear for the third time, but this time it cut in and out, and he caught a garbled reply. "Say again, Phoenix, you're breaking up."

Another burst of static, followed by a few more indistinct words. "Damn it!" Clayton hit the steering wheel with the heel of his hand. "There's too much interference."

Richard frowned. "Just keep trying..." He trailed off as they came around a corner. They were just a block away from the walls of New Houston. All of the buildings between them and those walls had been leveled by the Kyron Destroyer that had crashed outside the city. A mountain of ruins over five stories high blocked their view of the hole in the wall where the Dregs had come in. Then they flashed by a side street that gave a clear view to the destroyer. The bulk of it was still intact, but jets of flame shot up from the rear-end where the thrusters and reactor cores lay.

A few sporadic flashes of green laser fire caught Clayton's eyes from around the crash site. Small arms fire. There were survivors down there—Chimeran ones.

"Did you see that?" Clayton asked.

"Yeah..." Richard trailed off, his eyes never

leaving his window. "Looks like we're going to be sharing the Wastes with Chimeras."

Clayton blew out a breath. "I hope they all get infected and die."

"I thought you were above all that petty racial prejudice."

"It's not about race. It's about survival. They're going to wind up competing with us for very limited resources, and they're obviously much better armed than we are."

The streets along the wall were paradoxically less-crowded with Dregs. Perhaps all of the ones outside the walls had already come through.

We should be so lucky, Clayton thought as he turned the corner and drove around the back of the hospital complex.

Clayton's ear piece crackled, and finally the words came through loud and clear. "This is Scar, calling Phoenix Leader. We're at the rendezvous. Where the hell are you?!"

A mixture of relief and concern flooded Clayton as he activated his comms for a reply. "Scar, this is Lone Wolf! We're circling the block with Dregs hot on our six. You won't have more than a minute, so be ready to move!"

"Copy that, Lone Wolf. Ready and waiting. Scar out."

Clayton was about to leave it at that, but then he asked, "No trouble at the center? We had difficulty raising you."

"Some trouble. No casualties. High comms interference due to radiation shielding in the sub-levels."

Clayton released a breath he hadn't realized he was holding. They reached a side street between the hospital complex and a cluster of office buildings beside it, and Clayton turned left. "Coming up on the entrance to the ER now. ETA fifteen seconds."

"Copy," Sutton replied.

He glanced at the rear-view monitor. Dregs were still chasing them, but they'd fallen behind with that lap around the block. Fully half of them had given up on the chase, leaving maybe ten.

A knot of tension between Clayton's shoulders released. Their odds were getting better. He turned left again, and the entrance of the ER swept into view. A scattering of Dregs lurked out front: some feeding, others shuffling along aimlessly. Two of the shufflers were headed straight for the broken doors of the ER.

Clayton leaned out his window to call up to Keera. "We've got two between us and the extraction point!"

"I see them!" Keera called back.

All of the Dregs on the street turned their way at the sound of their shouting and Clayton mentally kicked himself. Keera opened fire on the ones headed for the doors of the hospital.

The first emerald bolt of energy leaped over the roof of the truck to burn a hole through the chest of a Dreg. Its partner spun around and hissed at them. Clayton drew his plasma pistol from the door holster, flicked off the safety, and pulled the trigger. A brilliant white ball of plasma hit the creature full in the gut and lit it on fire. It fell over face-first, and Clayton drove over it for good measure. He grimaced as he both heard and felt the creature's bones crunching under the weight of the vehicle.

A muffled shout heralded the approach of the others from the medical center. Sutton ran out, leading the way. Clayton saw Samara and his kids running close behind.

"Look out!" Keera cried.

A group of five more Dregs, barely twenty feet away, bounded toward them on hands and feet. Richard and Keera both shifted their aim, cutting down two of the five in quick succession. Clayton steadied his pistol in a two-handed grip and cut down a third. It burst into flames as it dropped to the street. The remaining two leaped into the back of the hauler, and he watched on the cargo monitor as they tackled Keera. She cried out as a swipe of claws dug through her cheek. Black Chimeran blood sprayed out and Keera grappled with the first creature as it strained with snapping jaws to rip out her throat.

Richard opened his door and jumped down,

his rifle up and tracking. "I can't get a clear shot!" he cried.

Sutton climbed up on the other side, his knife flashing in the dark. Clayton leaned out his window with the plasma pistol to try for a new angle. He was just in time to see Sutton's blade flash across the Dreg's throat. The furious snarling of Keera's attacker turned to gurgles and it dropped into the back of the hauler like garbage. The second Dreg had been standing on the roof of the cargo box, waiting for its turn. Now its eyes flicked to Sutton, and it snarled.

"Come on!" he cried, his knife dripping black blood onto his hand.

Clayton took aim. And the remaining Dreg leaped off the back of the hauler. Keera brought her rifle to bear, the barrel sweeping into line.

Sutton's knife plunged between the Dreg's ribs. Snapping jaws went for his throat and he threw up his free arm to protect himself. An agonized scream tore from Sutton's lips as sharp teeth closed around his arm.

Clayton and Keera pulled the trigger in the same instant. A ball of superheated plasma hit the Dreg square in the side of its head and Keera's laser blast impaled its back. It fell off the back of the hauler on fire and smoking. "Let's go, let's go!" Sutton cried, waving every-one into the back with his bloody, bitten arm, even as he sheathed his knife and climbed in beside Keera.

Keera's face was a horror of glistening black blood. A set of three parallel gashes ran along one cheek.

"Are you okay?" Clayton called to her.

She met his gaze briefly and nodded. "I'll be fine. Let's go!"

Clayton sat back down and watched on the monitors as Widow and Pyro helped Samara, Nova, and Dora into the back of the truck. Lori came next, followed by Harold, Preacher, and Doc. The Dregs who'd chased them around the block were seconds away now—close enough to see the tattered rags of their clothes flapping in the wind of their approach.

"That's it! Let's go!" Sutton cried, banging on the roof.

"We've got incoming!" Richard screamed.

The sound of a laser rifle discharging drew Clayton's gaze out the other side of the truck to see Richard standing with the rifle to his shoulder, aiming down the sights at the entrance of an apartment building across the street. Another emerald shot lanced into the darkness. Dregs were pouring through the revolving glass doors by the dozen. These were fully-clothed. Next generation and infectious as hell.

"Get in!" Clayton shouted.

Richard snapped off another shot and then lowered his rifle, turned, and leaped back into the co-driver's seat. Clayton stomped on the gas before he'd even shut the door. The shrieking cries of Dregs chased them down the street. He drove down to the ruins along the edge of the walls, to that side street with a clear shot to the Wastes and the crash site of the *Sovath*. Flashing green lasers still lit up the Wastes between them and the crashed destroyer, marking surviving Chimeras in the distance.

"Where the hell are you going?" Richard asked, his eyes wide as he stared at the hostile forces.

"The city's lost power, so the gates are all frozen shut," Clayton said, his words all but stolen by the wind billowing through the broken windshield. "The only way out is this one." Chunks of shattered concrete littered the street between them and the pair of reinforced metal gates that formed the Northern exit. Those doors were twisted and stood halfway open, leaving a gap conveniently large enough to drive a hauler through. The walls and buildings around the gates were damaged and crumbling, but not completely flattened. As they drew near, Clayton saw that the doors were bent *outward*, not in. They must have been rammed by a vehicle on its way out of the city.

Their hauler bumped and rumbled over the debris and out the open gates of the city. Thankfully, the I45 on the other side was considerably clearer.

Clayton touched his comms to activate

them. "Lone Wolf to Scar, is everyone okay back there?"

A rush of static replied, followed by Sutton's voice, sounding strangled with pain. "Doc's busy patchin' us up now with supplies from the Med Center."

Clayton frowned. "That wasn't an answer."

Sutton's voice came back, sounding clipped: "Everyone is fine. Don't worry."

Clayton wondered what the sergeant wasn't saying. His breath hitched in his chest as he thought about the possibility that his wife or one of his daughters had been injured, or worse—infected. But whatever was going on back there, Sutton wasn't willing to go into details. Clayton gave his worries a mental shove and forced himself to focus on the task at hand; even if someone was hurt, there was nothing he could do about it that Doc wasn't already doing. "I'm going to shut the hatch to keep Dregs out," Clayton decided.

"If you do that, we can't cover you," Sutton replied. "Best to keep it open for now."

Clayton glanced in his sideview mirror and saw Widow and Pyro standing up with their heads and shoulders poking out of the hatch, keeping watch. They only had one rifle with any charge left—the SWMD-issue laser rifle—but Pyro was using the night-vision scope on her depleted EKR to act as a spotter and scan for targets. "Your call," Clayton said through a stifled sigh. He'd have felt better with his family locked up safe in the back, but they weren't out of trouble yet, and he and Richard were badly exposed where they sat. They didn't even have a windshield to keep the Dregs out.

"You're heading straight for those Chimeras..." Richard warned.

Emerald lasers stitched the night with fire between them and the flaming ruins of the Kyron Destroyer. The six-hundred-meter-long warship had dug a deep furrow through the ruins and grassy hills beyond the northern end of the city. Dregs were used to hunting exiles in the Wastes by looking for camp fires, so it made sense that they'd be drawn to the crash site.

"Looks like they have bigger problems than hijacking us," Clayton pointed out. "Besides, this highway is the only clear way back to our camp. It's either that, or we go out on foot."

Richard frowned. "We'd never make it through the Wastes on foot."

"No, we wouldn't," Clayton agreed, his eyes on the Chimeras fighting beside the remains of their destroyer. They were about a kilometer away and maybe half that from the highway at its nearest point. But those were just the ones they could see. Hopefully, they'd stick together like any good military unit. If not, then there could be armed Chimeras waiting just up ahead to hijack them.

CHAPTER 6

Samara held Dora tight, wiping her daughter's tears and whispering reassurances in her ear while she sobbed. Dora's arm was a grisly sight. That Dreg had bitten hard and deep, leaving a clear impression of all of its teeth. Doc sprayed her bite wound with Regenex. It fizzed with pink froth. The hauler bumped through a big pothole, jarring them and almost sending her and Dora sprawling. Doc glanced at Keera and Sutton. They'd both sustained injuries of their own. Keera was bleeding from a set of ragged gashes in her left cheek, while Sutton's forearm was soaked in blood from a bite wound just like Dora's. The difference was that neither of them had to worry about their injuries. They'd been vaccinated against the original virus, and the Dregs who'd attacked them were old ones from the Wastes.

"It's okay, Dora. You're going to be fine," Samara lied as Doc grabbed a patch of synthskin from the supplies in his pack and peeled off the packaging. He placed the translucent square over Dora's bite mark. It adhered instantly, sealing the wound, and he grabbed a roll of clean white bandage to add an extra layer of protection while the wound healed.

"There," Doc said, leaning back with a grim smile. "All better. Your mother's right. You'll be fine."

Dora nodded quickly, and she and Samara withdrew to the nearest side of the truck while Doc began working on Sutton's and Keera's injuries.

Samara leaned against the side wall of the hauler with Dora clutched protectively against her chest. Samara let out a strangled breath. It felt like her entire world was collapsing, like her future had just been thrown into a fire and she was watching it burn. They were lying to Dora, but only she, Nova, and Lori knew that.

For her part, Nova watched them quietly, her eyes big and full of fear. Samara sent her a warning look, and the teenage girl looked away. But Lori wasn't being much more discreet. She was sitting on her haunches beside Keera, her eyes on Dora rather than her own daughter as Doc worked to patch up Keera's cheek.

"How are you feeling?" Lori asked Dora.

Samara's eyes flared and she shook her head at the other woman.

"It burns," Dora said.

"Don't worry, that's just the Regenex doing its job," Doc said. "That's how you know it's working. It'll feel numb soon."

Dora nodded, but said nothing.

Either they hadn't found any injectable painkillers in the Med Center, or Doc was saving those meds for more serious injuries. He finished treating and bandaging Keera's cheek and then moved on to Sutton's arm.

The undercarriage of the truck rumbled loudly as it jumped over more potholes and debris. The vehicle rocked from side to side, and Samara banged her head against the metal wall. She saw stars and with that, an image flashed before her eyes, forever burned into her memory: she saw that man in a clean white doctor's coat grabbing Dora's arm and taking a bite. Dora's screams still echoed in her ears.

She was supposed to have germ line immunity because Samara was a clone, and clone's couldn't be infected by the virus. But there was no telling if the Chrona's version would affect her. Chimeras were supposed to be immune to the virus, too, because that was what had turned them into hybrids in the first place, but Samara had seen a Chimera getting sick. And if they weren't immune, then Dora might not be either.

Only time would tell.

* * *

The jagged, windowless walls of century-old ruins flashed by on either side of the highway, along with old, broken down cars and tanks. They drove by the crash site of the *Sovath* without incident. They could hear the weapons fire now. Those Chimeras were pinned down beside their destroyer.

Clayton wove around the old mech that stood blocking the highway, eying the skeleton that dangled from the cockpit. Déjà vu hit him hard. He'd made this run every night for a year, but that had been more than a decade ago. Before Dora was born. Before the failed attempt to smuggle Lori out of the city for the Resistance which had ended in her death and his exile. He'd lost ten years with his wife and daughter because of that night, but he never would have run into Nova if it weren't for that, so he couldn't bring himself to regret those events. And Keera had brought Lori back in a cloned body from a digital copy of her memories, just as she'd done with Samara, so the consequences weren't as dire as they'd seemed back then.

All of that seemed like a lifetime ago now. The ruins flashed by on either side, full of shadows and gleaming eyes. It was slow going from all the potholes.

"I hope you know where you're going," Richard whispered.

"Yeah, me, too," Clayton replied, earning him a sharp look from the other man.

They crested a rise and saw the first strokes of sunrise blushing on the horizon. "Thank God," Clayton breathed. He drove on into the brightening crimson swell of daylight and the night fell away, taking with it the gleaming eyes of Dregs as they retreated deeper into the shadows. Like the Kyra with whom their DNA had been fused, they shunned daylight. The Kyra had evolved to live on the dark side of a world that was tidally locked to its sun, so Chimeras and Dregs alike were light and heat sensitive.

Clayton drove through the designated dump site on the North end of the city, and the smell of rotting garbage filled the open cab, making both him and Richard cough and gag into their sleeves.

"Damn it that's foul! How did you do this for a living?" Richard asked.

"By keeping the windows shut," Clayton replied. "Stay sharp. More Dregs live in the dump than any other part of the Wastes. They feed on the scraps people throw away."

As they cruised slowly through the dump, Clayton's head swam with the stench, but he ignored the sulfurous smell of decay and kept his eyes scanning the shadowy ruins. With daylight rising swiftly, he saw no sign of Dregs. "Looks like they've all gone to bed," Clayton said.

Once they reached open road on the other

side of the dump, the air grew less fetid and the ruins opened up, becoming sparser and more overgrown. Soon they were driving through rolling fields and tall trees waving in the wind. Clayton activated his comms again. "I'm going to need a guide. I don't know the way to Phoenix Base."

"I'll switch positions with Richard," Sutton replied.

Clayton checked his monitors for any signs of trouble before hitting the brakes. The hauler came to a squealing stop, and Richard popped his door open and jumped out.

"Leave the rifle," Clayton told him.

"What?"

"I need whoever's riding shotgun to be armed. They call it shotgun for a reason."

Richard scowled and ducked out of the shoulder strap, placing the weapon butt-first on the floor of the co-driver's side.

Sutton rounded the cab and climbed in, looking bloodied and tired, but otherwise fine. His bitten arm was bandaged, and he held it close to his chest like a wounded bird. Probably hurt like hell, but his face held none of the tension Clayton expected to see from the pain of an injury like that.

"Captain," Sutton said, inclining his head to Clayton as he climbed in.

"I'm not a captain of anything anymore, Sergeant," Clayton replied.

"Once a soldier always a soldier. Besides..." Sutton patted the dash of the garbage hauler and winked. "You've got this old scow. The UNSF Junker."

Clayton smiled wryly. "Where to, Sarge?"

Sutton hesitated, eying the metal beams that had pierced the seat between them when they'd rammed their way out of the garage at SWMD central. "A few inches to the right and I'd be climbing over a corpse," Sutton observed.

"Or talking to one," Clayton added, nodding to the second beam that was lodged a few inches away from his right shoulder.

Sutton looked around with squinting eyes, checking their surroundings. "You can drive on. We haven't reached our turn off yet. I'll let you know."

Clayton hit the accelerator and did as he was told, checking the truck's charge level as he did so—down to sixty-two percent. She had at least another three hundred klicks to go before they'd need to plug her in.

They rode on in silence for the next ten minutes. Sutton spent the whole time playing with the knobs and buttons on the hauler's comms panel, occasionally glancing up to see where they were.

"Who are you trying to reach?"

"No one," he replied, but went on fiddling.

"Then...?" Clayton trailed off, shaking his

head.

"I'd like to know if the Kyra are coming to pick up the survivors from the *Sovath*. They were staying pretty close to the crash site. Makes me think they were waiting for evac. And Specter said the Kyra had a reinforcing fleet on the way."

"That might have been a lie," Clayton said.

"Might have," Sutton agreed. "But if it's not, the Kyra might be on their way here as we speak."

Unease trickled into Clayton's gut. He began to see where Sutton was going with that. If the Kyra came in and did an aerial sweep for survivors, they'd easily pick out a lone hauler driving through the Wastes. One stray shot from a Kyron Lancer Fighter would vaporize them on the spot.

"Even if they are trying to contact their people on the ground, their comms would be encrypted," Clayton said. "We won't hear them."

"Respectfully disagree, Cap. The content *will* be encrypted, but we'll still hear it as noise on our end. That'll give us some warning at least."

"Unless they're using lasercomms," Clayton said. "That's point to point. And besides, even if we do get signal noise from an encrypted source, we have no way of knowing if the sender is in space. Could just as easily be from a ground-based transmitter."

"The Satnet is down," Sutton said. "So are all of the relays in New Houston. At this point, anything with enough range to reach us has to be coming from a ship in orbit."

"You've given this a lot of thought," Clayton replied.

"Got something!" Sutton placed his ear to a crackling speaker while he went on dialing the frequency for clearer reception.

Clayton took his foot off the accelerator and held it poised over the brake pedal, getting ready to stop and pull over somewhere. They would have to hide if the Kyra had ships incoming. "What is it?"

Sutton's face had scrunched up in concentration, his scarred cheek making one side of his face droop. His eyes were squinting shut as he focused on whatever he was hearing. "Doesn't sound encrypted..."

The static cleared and words snapped into focus. "...repeat, this is Lieutenant Commander Tyris of the Kryon Destroyer, *Sovath,* to anyone who is listening. The Kyra have turned their backs on us. We have just five hours before the 42nd fleet arrives to quarantine this planet. If you are able to hear this, know that we are on your side. If you see us, please do not shoot. We do not wish to fight you, but we will defend ourselves if forced to do so.

"Our continued survival now demands

that our two species work together. We have weapons and military training but little else. Many of you will have food and shelter, but none of the means with which to defend yourselves. If we work together, we can thrive despite our current circumstances. Please accept our humble apology for any atrocities that you may have suffered at the hands of the Kyron regime. Know that we were slaves to them just as you were. I repeat, this is Lieutenant Commander Tyris of—"

Sutton killed the comms with a grunt and shook his head.

Clayton sat back in shock and returned his foot to the accelerator. He hadn't seen that coming. Chimeras asking for pity and collaboration.

Sutton arched an eyebrow and smiled grimly. "Well ain't that ironic. Now that they're the ones living under the boot that stomps, they want to work together. Well, fuck 'em! We don't need their help."

Clayton nodded slowly. He couldn't blame Sutton for feeling that way. He had plenty of his own resentment built up. The Chimeras were sell-outs, adults and kids who had volunteered to enlist in the Kyron Guard and fight the Chrona. Until now, they had been the Kyra's boot, hovering over Earth. The Kyra had only had one of their own in the entire solar system—Overseer Damos—and he was likely dead now.

"The Kyra don't know how to fight this strain of the virus," Clayton realized. "They're scared that it could get off Earth."

Sutton nodded. "Fat lot of good it's gonna do them. The Chrona didn't develop a bio-weapon and test it on us just so they could use it on Earth. They'll spread it to other worlds soon enough."

Clayton nodded along with that. "They might win the war."

Sutton snorted. "Yeah. Can't say that gives me the warm and fuzzies, but I don't feel sorry for the Kyra. Good riddance, I say. Couldn't happen to a nicer bunch of aliens."

Clayton frowned. "They're going to wipe out local populations like ours in the process," Clayton added. "And other species of Chimeras."

"Not much we can do about that now. All that's left for us to do is survive and make sure we don't get infected in the process."

"Yeah." It was disheartening to go from collaborating with the Chrona to set Earth free, only to discover that those robotic, post-biological versions of the Kyra were even more ruthless and treacherous than the flesh and blood ones. They'd sentenced millions to infection and eventual death, and Earth was just the beginning.

"You missed it," Sutton said.

"Missed what?" Clayton asked, surfacing from his thoughts like a diver coming up for air.

"The turn." Sutton jerked a thumb over his shoulder. "It's a hundred yards back that way."

Clayton hit the brakes and threw the hauler into reverse, keeping an eye on the rear view monitor as he backed up.

"Hey, buck up, Captain. We're alive."

Clayton glanced at him and shook his head. "A wise person once told me it's not enough just to live. You need something to live *for*."

"Who said that?" Sutton asked.

"My daughter. Nova."

"Well, newsflash, Cap—livin's all we got left."

"Maybe not."

"How so?"

"That Chimeran officer on the comms mentioned a blockade."

"So?"

"So, the Kyra wouldn't be blockading Earth unless there were some way for people to get off the planet. That means they're afraid they've left FTL-capable ships behind."

Sutton snorted. "If Tyris and his crew had a working ship, they wouldn't be on the comms beggin' us for mercy."

"I didn't say *they* have a ship, but somewhere there might be one. New Houston is still largely intact after the battle. If the other occupied cities are in similar condition, I bet we'll find a working Kyron transport in one of them. If we do, Keera could pilot it and get us the hell away from Earth."

Sutton grinned. "Now you're thinking like a captain!"

THE MISSION

CHAPTER 7

Time in the back of the hauler passed excruciatingly slowly. Samara's worries for her daughter circled endlessly inside her head like hungry sharks. Everyone kept to themselves, all preoccupied with their own private terrors. Silence reigned but for the constant rumbling and rattling of the truck as it crossed the broken highway. Samara's butt had grown numb from the lack of padding inside the cargo area.

Dora had fallen asleep on Samara's chest. Patterns of light and shadow fell over them, intermittently flashing through the open hatch of the hauler and the trees flanking the highway. Samara ran a hand lightly over her daughter's head, stroking her dark, sun-warmed hair and working out the tangles. She kept expecting Dora's hair to come away in clumps as she stroked it, but so far she had no symptoms: no hair loss, no sign of fever, her skin hadn't begun to lose its pigment, and her cheeks were still flushed with bright *red* blood, not the black blood of Dregs. It was almost enough for Samara to hope that Dora would be okay, but it had only been about an hour since Dora had been bitten. It was too soon to tell if she was immune or not. And there was another problem: what would happen when everyone else found out?

Samara looked up to see Keera and Lori watching her from where they sat on the opposite side of the hauler. A big white bandage covered Keera's left cheek. Lori still looked grim, and Keera's crimson eyes were hard and unblinking, her expression blank. Did she know? Had Lori told her that Dora might be infected? If she had, Samara had missed that exchange. Would Phoenix cast Dora out of the group when they learned that she could be infected? If so, Samara would have to leave as well, and she suspected that Clayton and Nova would join them.

Samara shook her head and let her worries out in a long, slow breath. Her gaze wandered from Lori and Keera to see Richard sitting alone in the shadows at the back of the hauler. When he'd come back to trade places with Sutton in the cab, Widow had spat on him and called him a coward. Samara had asked about her reaction. Apparently, Richard had abandoned the others during the attack on the Ascension Center, leaving Clayton to lead their team of soldiers into combat. Conveniently,

Richard had survived the chaos and somehow avoided infection with the Chrona's new virus only to catch a ride back with them now. But no one looked happy about it—not even Keera, his own daughter. Their glares had chased him to the farthest recesses of the truck, and he hadn't budged from there since.

Samara looked away from him, and her eyes landed on Nova. She sat cross-legged a few feet to Samara's left, playing with her knife. She spun it on the tip of the blade and stared sightlessly at the stained metal floor of the truck.

"Hey," Samara whispered, thinking that some conversation might help to take her mind off things.

The girl's head turned, her hazel eyes bright in the sunlight flickering through the hatch.

"You mentioned you have a dog?"

Nova's head bobbed once.

"What's she like?"

Nova shrugged and went back to spinning her knife. Something was bothering the girl, but Samara couldn't figure out what it was. Maybe she was just in shock. Or maybe she was afraid that now she had competition for her father, the only family she'd ever known. Samara couldn't blame her for being scared. It would take some time to integrate their two families and make everyone feel like they belonged. Even Clayton would probably feel like an outsider for a while. It had been ten years since they'd been together, and Dora had never even known him as her father. They had a lot of challenges ahead.

"You know, we're not going to take him from you," Samara said.

Nova gave her a sideways look in that wary, skeptical way that teenagers everywhere seemed to have patented. "Who?"

"Your dad. Clayton."

"Oh. I know."

"Good. But you look worried about something," Samara added.

Nova snorted. "Shouldn't I be? The world just ended!"

Samara winced at that reminder. Maybe she hadn't given Nova enough credit. Here she'd thought the girl was worried about disruptions to *her* world, when in reality she was more worried about the larger issues facing all of humanity.

"Maybe it's not over," Samara suggested. "There have to be plenty of other exiles living in the Wastes and the Wilds between the cities. Maybe we can get together and form some type of community."

A snort interrupted that, drawing her attention to the red-haired farmer, Harold. "And then I suppose we'll all gather round a campfire and sing kumbaya!" He rocked his head against the side of the truck. "That's not gonna happen. The people living out here are out here for a reason. Most of them were exiled by the Kyra for actual crimes. Some were petty, some not so petty. Of course, that was before you idiots blew up an Ascension Center." He glanced around at the surviving members of Phoenix. "After that, all the criminals were sent to fight to the death in the arenas instead. A good plan you had there. We've had ten years of no one being exiled, and the existing exiles having their numbers whittled away by Dregs. Any survivors out here will be few in number, and nastier than you care to meet."

"That can't be," Samara said.

"He's right," Pyro added from where she sat beside her father. "The next biggest group that we know of besides our own operates in and around New San Antonio. They call themselves the Reapers. We used to trade with them until we realized where their supplies were coming from—they were stealing them from other exiles, usually killing them in the process. We also believe that they might be eating their victims, so there's that."

Samara gaped at her. "Well..." she trailed off as words failed her and her mouth ran dry. She worked some moisture into it. "That's just one group out of what must be thousands. You can't write off everyone just because of them. And besides, people can change. If we form a community, it will give people a reason to behave in more civilized ways."

Pyro snorted and shook her head. "Yeah, I wouldn't count on that. Living in the Wastes changes people for the worse, not the better. Like it or not, we can only count on each other. I wouldn't trust anyone outside this group—and not even everyone *inside* of it," she glanced at Richard as she said that.

The others muttered snide comments about him and sent dark looks his way. He pretended to be oblivious.

A moment later, the brakes screeched as the hauler slowed to a stop. Samara's back gave a sharp spasm from trying to hold herself erect against that sudden change in momentum. "Why'd we stop?" she asked.

Widow, their gunner and lookout, leaned down from where she stood on the pusher plate in the open hatch. "We're home!" she cried.

* * *

Samara helped Dora climb down from the hauler. Clayton grabbed her arm to help her down, then he appeared to freeze as he noticed the bandage.

"What happened to you?" he thundered.

"I got bit," Dora said with tears welling in her eyes.

"Why am I only learning about this now?" he demanded.

"Because there was nothing you could do," Sutton said as he walked around the front of the hauler to join Clayton. "You needed your mind focused on the task at hand: getting us safely across the Wastes—not worrying about your daughter."

Dora jumped down from the hauler and Samara hurried down next. Her back spasmed sharply, and all at once the feeling came back to her numbed buttocks and thighs, filling her legs with a sparking, biting swarm of pins and needles. She winced and pulled Dora close in a one-armed hug.

Clayton gave a seething look to the sergeant. "You intentionally withheld information from me because you thought I wouldn't be able to handle it? We just spent an hour riding together, and you had the utter gall to hide this from me?!"

"Yes, and I apologize for that, but based on the degree of your reaction now, I made the right call. Your daughter is immune from birth, Captain. Doc treated and dressed the wound. She won't even have a scar from this. And she's not the only one who got bit." He held up his own arm to reveal that it was bandaged just like Dora's. "We'll recover."

Clayton scowled, but gave in with a sigh. "Fine, but you do something like that again, and we're going to have serious problems."

"Duly noted, Captain," Sutton said.

Samara sucked in a breath and held it, wondering at what point she should tell Clayton —and everyone else—that this wasn't just any bite, and that Dora might actually be infected.

But she decided to keep the information to herself for now. The last thing they needed was to be set adrift in the Wastes. At least until Dora began to show symptoms they could avail themselves of the shelter, supplies, and safety afforded by Phoenix.

Nova jumped down beside them, followed by Harold and Pyro, then Lori, Keera, and Richard.

"Welcome to Phoenix Base," Sergeant Sutton said, gesturing expansively with his good arm to a sprawling log mansion in front of them. It had cracked and broken windows, black and green mold growing on the log walls, and thick clumps of pine needles scattered on the roof. It could have been an old ski lodge if they weren't in the middle of Texas.

"*This* is your base?" Dora asked, glancing around at the others for confirmation.

Sergeant Sutton gave a deep, booming laugh.

"That was my reaction, too, Sis," Nova said. "Not exactly high tech, huh?"

"Wait till you see the inside," Sutton said. "It's dirty, the roof leaks, and there are bugs everywhere! Come on, let's get out of the sun." He turned and led the way toward a set of rickety-looking stairs beside an old four-car garage.

The rest of the group fell in behind Sutton, dragging their feet from exhaustion and kicking loose gravel with their boots. Their rifles dangled from the straps, their shoulders rounded, heads down. *This is what defeat looks like,* Samara thought.

Tall trees creaked in a warm breeze, the leaves rustling. Cicadas sang, and a vast, cloudless blue sky soared overhead. Birds chirped and tweeted, flitting from branch to branch.

As far as accommodations went, things could be a lot worse. At least they seemed to be far enough out from Houston that there was no real threat from Dregs.

They reached the front steps and climbed them to the door. Sutton opened it without the need for a key, and Samara saw that the lock was broken. It was an old electronic smart lock, and the socket where the biometric scanner used to be mounted above the door was now occupied by a bird's nest.

The door swung wide and Phoenix tromped inside. The floorboards in the hall were soft and creaky. Planks had been laid over holes that had rotted straight through to the floor below. Glinting cracks of sunlight overhead gave the reason: leaks in the roof.

"How long have you been here?" Samara asked.

"Long enough. Why?" Sutton asked.

"Why haven't you fixed this place up?"

"When you're worried about aerial patrols hunting you, it's better to blend in. A newly-renovated mansion would be a lot more noticeable than a tear-down like this."

"Well, I don't think we have to worry about patrols anymore," Samara said. "We should at least fix the roof."

"Maybe," Sutton replied. "But we don't know that yet. Best to wait a bit."

They reached the end of the hall and emerged in a large great room with a wall of windows and a deck looking out on a lake. A cob-webbed chandelier hung above faded couches and armchairs that were bleeding white and yellow stuffing from the cushions.

"Home sweet home," Sutton declared, while staring at the view.

A loud *woof* split the air, and Nova stood suddenly straighter and tore away from the group, saying, "Rosie! Hey girl! We're back!" She angled for a hallway on one side of the kitchen.

Clayton ran after his daughter with a boyish grin, then slowed briefly and nodded to Samara and Dora. "Come on!" he said.

Dora didn't need to be asked twice. She raced after them with an even bigger grin than Clayton's. Samara brought up the rear at a more reserved pace, walking rather than running. She smiled faintly at her daughter's reaction. Finally, she was seeing Dora act her age. The Kyra's schools had indoctrinated her so thoroughly into their culture of war and violence that she'd run to the arena last night to fight one of her classmates in an illegal challenge. She'd been sliced open with a Kyron Sikath and left to bleed to death in the sand. A ten-year-old participating in an alien deathmatch with ceremonial swords. It was beyond comprehension.

But now she was crawling out of that shadow and finally becoming the girl she always should have been. Samara cracked a smile at that, but it was short lived. Dora might have forgotten that she could be infected with a deadly virus, but Samara couldn't allow herself the luxury of ignorance.

Reaching an open door near the end of the hallway, Samara peeked in. Clayton and Nova sat on the floor, laughing and grunting as a large, wriggling black and brown dog bounded from one lap to another, barking and whimpering and knocking them down to lick them all over their necks and faces.

Dora stood to one side, gaping in awe at the sight of an animal that must have seemed almost mythical to her. She'd only ever heard stories about dogs. Man's best friend. The Kyra didn't let people keep pets in the cities, but when Dora was little she used to have a stuffed animal: a dog. A neighbor had knitted it together for her out of the stuffing from an old pillow and a Chimeran jumpsuit.

It took fully five minutes for the creature to stop jumping around and licking its masters. She stood off to one side panting from the exertion, then her head turned to Samara and Dora. Her tongue popped back into her mouth and her ears perked up. She barked once, then growled. Dora backed up a step.

"Clay..." Samara began. There was a note of warning in her voice. Maybe now was the time to tell him about Dora.

"It's okay," he said, wiping tears from the corners of his eyes. He patted the dog on the back and said, "Friend, Rosie. Friend." He'd misunderstood. He thought she was worried about the dog biting her or Dora.

Rosie stared at them for another second, then looked away and began panting again. She padded over to an empty metal dish and gave it a lick.

"She's thirsty," Dora said.

"I'll get her something to drink," Clayton added, pushing off the floor and grabbing the dish.

He stepped past Samara in the doorway, and she walked through to hold Dora back at a safe distance from the animal. The dog wasn't the main concern here, but Dora didn't need any new bites to worry about.

"Can I pet her?" Dora asked in a small voice.

Nova sat beside the dog, stroking its back. "Sure, you can. She's friendly."

"She just growled at us," Samara pointed out.

"That was before my dad told her you're friends. She's smart. She knows what friend means."

Dora took a hesitant step toward the animal. Samara's whole body tensed up, partly because she was already on edge. Yet she wasn't eager to squash this new, innocent side of her daughter, so she let Dora creep toward the dog. Dora reached Rosie's side and patted her once on the head before withdrawing her hand sharply.

"Don't be scared—" Nova warned. "Friend, Rosie, friend," she said gently beside the dog's ear. "Try it again, but don't jerk your hand away this time. Dogs can sense if you're afraid, and it makes them think that they can't trust you."

Dora patted Rosie again, then stroked her back as Nova was doing.

Rosie arched her back, Dora's hand having discovered an itch that needed scratching. Nova obliged, and the dog sat down and began scratching at it with one of her hind paws. When she was done, Rosie lay down and Dora tried scratching her behind the ear. Rosie seemed content with all of the attention. The tension bled out of Samara's muscles, and she sagged against the door jamb.

Rosie turned her head and gave Dora's hand a lick. She giggled.

"There, see? She's not dangerous," Nova said.

Dora smiled and nodded.

Clayton breezed back into the room with a dish of water and bent to place it in front of the animal. She lapped greedily from the dish without getting up.

A breeze blew against the old sheets that hung over the room's only window, filling them up like a sail and flooding the room with bright pools of sunlight. Samara heard the sound of cicadas buzzing, and that brought back old, distant memories of lazy summers spent fishing with her dad and playing baseball with her friends. She'd been alive before the invasion and she'd died before the invasion—only to be resurrected by the Kyra when her husband returned from Trappist-1. She was a mysterious exception to the Kyra's laws against cloning. Just like Lori.

But Samara's memories were all faded and bittersweet now. She could still picture the world the way it had been, and her heart ached to remember it. Some things would never be the same. Even if the exiles could find a way to work together and rebuild, how many people were left? Samara guessed maybe ten thousand if they were lucky, and all of them would be scattered across the globe. To bring a large group together and unite them in a common purpose would be almost impossible. Not to mention dangerous. There was a reason the exiles were scattered. It made it harder for Dregs and Chimeras to hunt them down.

But if they didn't group up, humanity was done. There weren't enough people left in any one group to ensure the survival of the species.

"Hey." Samara jumped at the sound of the voice. A hand slipped into hers. It was Clayton's. Somehow he'd taken advantage of her inattention and sidled up beside her. "It's going to be okay," he whispered, nuzzling her ear. "I have a plan."

She looked to him, her eyes searching his. Had he been thinking along the same lines as her?

"We're going to find a ship and go colonize some distant corner of the galaxy where there are no Kyra and no Dregs."

Samara felt a mixture of confusion and hope begin swirling through her. Was that even possible? Getting away from it all? It seemed like too much to wish for, especially now. And how would Dora fit into that plan? They could be taking a Dreg with them if she was infected. Samara shivered at the thought and pushed it from her mind. "You know where we can find a ship?" she asked, her voice a ragged whisper.

"Not yet, but we'll find one. If..."

Samara raised her eyebrows. "If?"

"If we can convince the others to send out a team to look. Keera and Sutton are holding an emergency meeting in the living room to discuss it and take a vote."

"Now?" Samara asked, her voice pitching up sharply. "Shouldn't we rest and recover first?"

Clayton shook his head. "On the way out of New Houston we received a message from a group of Chimeras that survived the *Sovath*. They were asking us to put aside our differences and work together."

"And they have a ship?" Samara asked, dubious at the thought of working with Chimeras. Keera notwithstanding, they couldn't be trusted.

"No, if they had one, they would have used it already, but they told us that the Kyra are coming here with a fleet to blockade Earth. At the time of the transmission, that fleet was just five hours away. Now it's less than four. We have a small window of opportunity to find a ship and use it to escape, and the clock is ticking."

Samara's gaze tracked over to Dora and Nova, both girls watching them with big eyes. Even Rosie observed them intently, her jowls drooping with a solemn frown.

"Do we get to vote?" Nova asked.

"Let's go find out," Clayton replied. "Come

on."

CHAPTER 8

Clayton walked into the great room, leading his family toward the couches and chairs where the group of ragtag resistance fighters that made up Phoenix had gathered. Most of them sat or slumped on the furniture and floor, their eyes half-lidded, looking exhausted. Clayton could sympathize. He could fall asleep standing up, but this wouldn't be the first time that he'd had to forego sleep. There wasn't any time for it anyway.

Clayton went to the nearest couch, where Harold and his daughter, Pyro, sat. The old farmer looked like he'd been crying, and Pyro had her arm wrapped around his shoulders, making the big man look somehow small and frail. Clayton stopped beside Harold, who glanced up at him and Samara with red eyes before looking away. Nova and Dora each took a seat on the floor. Rosie had followed them. She plopped down in front of the girls, and they took turns scratching her behind the ears.

"All right, now that y'all are here, we've got

something important to discuss," Sutton said, his southern accent breaking through.

Clayton followed his voice to see him and Keera standing at the head of the group near the hall that led to the garage and front door. They were the joint leaders of Phoenix, though Clayton still wasn't entirely sure who was actually in charge. He'd seen Keera take the lead in the attack on the Ascension Center, but Sutton had been with Phoenix a lot longer, and he was *human*.

Sutton went on, "We have less than four hours before the Kyra arrive to blockade Earth with their 42nd Fleet. That gives us just one chance to find a ship and escape."

"How do you know that they're four hours away?" Widow asked. The Latina woman sat in an armchair facing Sutton and Keera, looking both angry and tired. She had her arms crossed over her chest, and her rifle sat on the floor beside her feet, leaning against her legs.

Sutton took a deep breath and explained about the transmission they'd received from the surviving crew of the *Sovath*.

"That could be a trick designed to lure us out," Pyro said from where she sat beside Harold. She leaned forward, elbows on her knees. Her curly red hair turned a vibrant copper with the sunlight streaming in from upper-level windows of the living room. "How do we know it's true? The 42nd fleet could already be in orbit."

Keera spoke next, her deep, husky voice filling the echoing room: "Specter discovered the same thing when he hacked into the Satnet. At the time, he said the Kyra were twenty light-years away. That was about six hours ago, and Kyron destroyers travel at approximately two light-years per hour."

Widow scowled. "So, according to Chimeras and the robot-Kyra who single-handedly made humans an endangered species on this planet, we have a small window of opportunity. It sounds like we're better off keeping our heads down and getting a good night's sleep."

"I agree," Pyro said.

"We'll get to a vote in a minute," Keera said, holding up her hands for patience.

"What is she even doing up there?" Widow added. "She's a Chimera! A former admiral of the occupying fleet! And *she's* the one who convinced us all to go along with Specter's plan in the first place! How do we know she wasn't a part of it?"

"If that were true, wouldn't I have escaped with him and the rest of the Chrona?" Keera asked.

"Maybe you were going to, but then he betrayed you, too," Widow said.

Harold and Pyro leveled suspicious looks on Keera.

"Are you all crazy?" Lori asked, jumping up from the couch opposite theirs. "She's just as vulnerable to this virus as the rest of us! You saw what happened to that Chimera in the Med Center. Barely four hours after exposure to the new virus and she was already three-quarters of the way to becoming a Dreg."

Doc stood up beside Lori. "She's right. If anything, Chimeras are more vulnerable than we are. That officer turned before any of the surviving doctors and nurses did."

"And what would Keera possibly have to gain by going along with the Chrona's plot?" Lori asked.

"An in with the Chrona?" Widow suggested. "She was already wanted by the Kyra for cloning and resurrecting you illegally, so maybe this was her only option: get a foot in the door with their enemies." Widow's eyes slid back to Keera and narrowed to slits. "Now she's here among us as a spy."

"A spy?" Keera demanded, her red eyes flaring wide with indignation. "Earth is no longer of any tactical significance to the Chrona or the Kyra, except that it's teeming with a deadly infection that the Kyra need to keep from escaping. Why would the Chrona need a spy on the ground? They've already done everything they needed to do."

"What was the point of infecting Earth?" Pyro asked. "They should have slipped the virus into some heavily-populated world or a space station with constant comings and goings."

"We don't know that they didn't," Doc pointed out. "Earth might have been one of several places that the Chrona targeted simultaneously."

Widow muttered something under her breath and looked away, as if she couldn't stand to even look at Keera anymore.

"Hey!" Sutton clapped his hands for attention. "Y'all shut your pieholes and listen up. We're not here to discuss Keera's loyalties or speculate about the how's and why's of what's happened. It is what it fucking is. All we need to figure out is whether or not we're going to make a run for it while we still can."

Clayton cleared his throat. "Do we have any idea where we might find a ship?"

"As a matter of fact, we do," Sutton replied. "New San Antonio."

"Not New Houston?" Harold asked, sounding disappointed.

"No," Keera replied. "I've already been to the landing pad at the top of the Ascension Center. The only ship there was the fighter I stole with Specter."

Harold looked like he wanted to say something more, but Pyro looked at him and shook her head. Clayton made a mental note to ask them about it later.

"How do we know New San Antonio will have a ship?" Samara asked from beside Clayton.

"We don't know," Sutton said. "But there is a strong chance that it will. New Dallas probably will, too."

"It's around two hundred miles to New San Antonio from here," Harold said. "Same for New Dallas. You said we only have four hours. How are we going to get to either of those cities in time?"

"We have eight hoverbikes in the garage," Sutton replied. "I propose we send out four. They'll fly in over the heads of any Dregs infesting the city, straight up to the landing pad at the top of New San Antonio's Ascension Center. Going at a hundred miles per hour, straight as the crow flies, we'll be there in under two hours."

"We should send two teams of two," Clayton said. "One to New San Antonio, another to New Dallas. We're only going to get one shot at this. If one team fails, the other might not."

"That's not a bad idea, but we only have one pilot," Sutton said, nodding to Keera. "If her team doesn't find a ship, but the other team does, then who's going to fly it?"

"I can," Lori said.

All eyes turned to her.

"I know enough of their language to understand the controls, and Keera can give me a crash course in the rest."

Clayton and Sutton both regarded her dubiously, but Keera said, "Kyron controls are intuitive and our ships are easy to fly. It's not ideal, but I can prepare her."

"In ten minutes?" Sutton pressed. "Because that's all we can afford to waste before you leave."

Keera hesitated, her cranial stalks twitching. "Yes."

"Good. Then it's settled. Two teams of two. All that's left is a vote. All in favor of this plan raise your hand."

"Wait," Widow said. "If we do find a ship, where are we going to go?"

"Anywhere that the Kyra and Chrona aren't," Clayton said. "We'll start a colony."

Widow didn't look happy with that. "With twelve people?" Her gaze passed swiftly over the group. "I count four women, two girls, five men, and one sterile Chimera. So our plan for the continued survival of the human race is to pair up and get all of the women pregnant as many times as possible before we eventually die in labor? Doesn't sound any better than the occupation. We'll have gone from breeding soldiers for their war to breeding kids for the survival of the species, a petty distinction if you ask me."

"Let's not get ahead of ourselves," Doc said. "No one is going to be forced to have children or pair up, but ideally that will happen naturally over time."

Widow snorted and shook her head. "No offense, but I'm not attracted to any of you. And the Captain is already spoken for. Unless we are aiming for polygamy to repopulate the species..." She smiled sweetly at Samara. "Wanna be sister wives?"

Samara tensed up.

"Put a fucking cork in it, Widow!" Sutton snapped. "We can discuss your prospective love lives when we're all safely away from here. Right now, we need to vote and get a move on. All in favor, raise your hands." Sutton stuck his hand up.

Clayton went next. Doc and Lori followed, and Preacher half-raised his hand, wincing as the movement disturbed the bandages around his laser burn from their attack on the Ascension Center last night. Pyro raised her hand. Samara didn't. Clayton sent her a questioning look. She shook her head and slowly raised her hand as well. The kids kept their hands in their laps, but their vote probably didn't count anyway. Only Harold, Widow, and Keera didn't raise their hands.

"That settles it," Sutton declared. "By majority vote, we proceed with the mission."

Everyone dropped their hands.

"You don't think we should go?" Widow asked Keera, her voice dripping with suspicion. "Maybe I should change my vote."

"It's a good plan," Keera said. "But only if it works. To me the risks outweigh the chance of success. New San Antonio is Reaper territory. And as for New Dallas, we don't know anything about it. For all we know, it's even more dangerous. Add to that the possibility of running into surviving Chimeras in both cities, and all the Dregs we're going to encounter..." She trailed off hissing softly between sharp teeth. "I'm afraid that one or both of our teams will wind up dead or captured, and that we will have nothing to show for it."

"We have to try," Clayton whispered.

"And we need you," Sutton added. "You and your mother both. You're the pilots. Without you we wouldn't know what to do with a ship even if we found it."

Keera inclined her head to that. "I didn't say that I wouldn't go, just that I don't think we should."

"Noted," Sutton said. His eyes left her to regard the group. "We need two other volunteers."

"I'll go," Doc said.

Sutton shook his head. "You're too valuable. You're the only doctor we have."

"Well, I'm expendable," Preacher croaked, struggling to rise from where he sat on the couch.

"And wounded," Sutton said. "We need

able-bodied operatives, not a liability."

Clayton stuck up his hand again. "This was my plan. I'll go."

Samara seized his arm in a taloned grip. "Clay, don't. There's something you need to know..."

He regarded her with eyebrows raised, but Sutton interrupted before she could go on.

"That's four," Sutton said as he thrust up his own hand. "The rest of you will stay to hold down the fort around here. Doc, you'll be in charge while I'm gone."

"Yes, sir," he replied.

Widow snorted. "How convenient. The Chimera and her mother are leaving. I guess I won't be able to say I told you so when that albino science experiment tells the Chrona where to find us and we all get slaughtered in our sleep. Screw it, I'm going, too. I'll join the team with Lori. That way if Keera betrays us, I can slit her mother's throat."

"I'd like to see you try," Lori said.

Keera flashed a predatory smile. "Touch her and I'll make you watch as I rip out your heart and eat it."

"Enough!" Sutton roared. "We have less than four hours and we're fighting like a bunch of children! Widow, you're staying here, end of discussion. You don't like it, feel free to strike out on your own, is that understood, soldier?"

Several seconds of tense silence stretched

between them. "Yes, sir," Widow said quietly.

"I didn't hear you! What was that?" Sutton cupped a hand to his ear.

"I said, I'll stay, sir!"

"Good call. Captain, Admiral, Lori, it's time to kit up. We leave in ten. The rest of you, go get some sleep and stay close to base, understood?"

A few *yes sirs* echoed back. Others nodded and slowly rose from their seats. As the group broke up, Lori walked over to Doc and pulled him aside. She whispered something in his ear and the man's eyes flew wide. Clayton watched as he turned around and stared directly at Nova and Dora. When he noticed Clayton looking, he looked away quickly and nodded along with something else that Lori said.

The conversation only lasted a few seconds, but Clayton knew it concerned his family. He left Samara's side, running to catch up to Lori. She was hurrying down the hall to the basement where Sutton and Keera had gone.

"What was that about?" he demanded as they both reached the door to the stairs.

"What was *what* about?" Lori asked.

"You and Doc. I saw him look at my daughters."

Lori appeared to hesitate, then shook her head and cracked a tight smile. "I was just telling him to look out for your kids. We don't need them wandering off because they get bored waiting for us to return." Lori smiled reassuringly, then started down the stairs.

Clayton stared at her back as she went, quietly wondering if that was the whole truth.

"Clay." Samara came striding over from the living room. He saw that her eyes were brimming with tears. "Why do *you* have to go?" she asked as she stopped in front of him.

"Because it was my idea, and someone has to."

"But what if something happens to you? Let Widow go!" Samara said, jerking a thumb to the armchair where she still sat. "She *wants* to go! And they must call her *Widow* for a reason. She's probably already lost everyone, but we just got you back. You still have a family, and we need you."

"This is our only chance, Sam. When the Kyra get here, they could do a lot more than just blockade the planet. They could sterilize it in an attempt to wipe out the infection. Even if we live through that—do you want to be here for a nuclear winter? Because I don't."

Samara bit her lower lip. "Still. Someone else can go. What's the difference?"

"You said it: I have a family. That means I have more to lose. That's why *I'll* succeed and how I know that I'll be back."

"Don't do this," Samara insisted, slowly shaking her head. "Please..."

"I have to," Clayton replied. He pulled her

in for a hug, and then kissed her lightly on the lips. "I love you."

He pulled away, and Samara looked like she wanted to say something else. Before she could, both Dora and Nova came running over. Nova gave him a hug. "Let me go with you," Nova whispered against his chest.

Clayton looked his daughter in the eye. She wasn't crying like Samara, but he could see the threat of tears lurking there.

"It's not up to me," he said.

"Please," Nova pleaded.

"I need you here to look after your sister. And Rosie. It's important. Can you do that for me?"

Nova sucked in a shuddery breath and nodded.

"Thank you." He dropped a kiss on the top of her head and then hurried down the stairs after Sutton and the others. If this plan was going to work, then they needed to move fast.

CHAPTER 9

One hour earlier...

"**T**hey didn't reply, LC. I have a clear shot on the wheels. Should I take them out?" Lieutenant Akora asked.

Tyris watched the lumbering garbage hauler drive by. "After telling them we won't shoot? That might send the wrong message. Besides, their vehicle is of no use to us if we disable it."

"We could still learn where they're going and then take their base for ourselves."

Tyris regarded his second-in-command steadily. She had taken her helmet off due to an injury that made it uncomfortable to wear. Akora was attractive, despite the dark swollen lump above her right eye, with softer, more appealing facial features than he possessed. When they reached a more secure location, he would try his luck again. Perhaps this time she wouldn't reject his advances. But even if she did, there were other ways to get what he wanted.

"We need to get away from the city soon," Akora added, bringing his mind back to the situation at hand. She glanced over her shoulder to indicate the flaming hulk of the *Sovath.* That destroyer had been V'tan Company's posting until just a few hours ago when it had been shot down by the Chrona. Now they were stranded down here with a virulent new strain of the Chimeran virus and the Kyra were on their way with a reinforcing fleet to quarantine the entire planet—hopefully, not to sterilize it.

Tyris's cranial stalks twitched at the distant reports of laser rifles discharging around the *Sovath.* His surviving crew mates were busy holding off shrieking hordes of Dregs besieging them from both the city and the Wastes around it. "We will have to move out on foot," he concluded.

"And go where, sir?" Akora asked. "Our rations were all in the aft section, and it's gushing flames. We need food and shelter."

"We could hunt for food," Tyris suggested.

"And build our own camp?" Akora's tone was disapproving. "We should just take theirs." She pointed to the vanishing speck of the garbage hauler. "This is all their fault, anyway."

They'd been eavesdropping on that group's comms before they'd even left the city. Their use of known resistance call signs and comms encryptions had given them away. *They* were the ones who had attacked the Ascension Center. They'd been seen working with the Chrona, and the Chrona had somehow infected the water supply of every occupied city on the planet. They'd turned millions into Dregs, most of them humans. *They'd rather commit genocide on their own species than let the Kyra continue to enlighten their children. Ignorant* Dakkas.

Tyris's gaze tracked back to the highway, to the receding black speck of the garbage hauler and the pink glow of dawn now swelling above the horizon.

"Did you hear me, sir?"

"Go with Corporal Rathos on the hover-bikes," he replied. "Follow the resistance to their camp and report back here once you have a location for their base. We'll barricade our-selves into the forward section of the *Sovath* until then."

"Aye, sir." Akora dropped her rifle from her shoulder and saluted smartly before darting back through the ruins. Tyris watched her go.

They didn't have enough hoverbikes for everyone to follow the resistance now. Be-sides, it wouldn't be wise to attack before they'd scouted the enemy's defenses. For all they knew, the resistance could have hun-dreds of fighters waiting at their base. Tyris had barely sixty-two Chimeras under his command, and most of them were wounded. Patience would win the day, not a hasty charge into unknown territory.

A snarl echoed from a nearby mountain of ruins, and a Dreg leaped out from behind it to surprise Akora. She must have heard it coming, because her body was already twisting to evade the creature's claws and teeth. She tore out its throat with a deft slash of her own claws, saving the charge on her rifle.

Tyris smiled as the creature fell in a twitching, gurgling heap. Being stranded on Earth and exiled from the Kyron Federation was *not* what he'd had in mind when he'd signed up to become a Chimera nine years ago. Nevertheless, this crisis would pass just as soon as the Kyra figured out how to fight the Chrona's plague. Until then, all they had to do was survive, and the resistance fighters in that garbage hauler were going to help them. They'd already been living in the Wastes for years, so they must have perfected a way to do so.

A cold smile curved Tyris's lips. A flashing yellow arrow appeared at the bottom of the HUD in his helmet, indicating that something was creeping up behind him. A quick look at the sensor display in the top right of his field of view showed two yellow blips approaching fast, fifteen meters away. He waited. Ten meters. Four—

He heard the snarling snorts of the Dregs as he spun to face them. Fully-armored as he was, there was little they could do to harm him. He caught the first one by the throat and let it scratch impotently at his armor. Teeth gnashing, spittle flying, and red eyes wild with hunger and insanity. He sidestepped the second Dreg and squeezed the first one's throat, crushing its windpipe with the augmented strength of his suit. The Dreg fell thrashing at his feet, clawing for air.

The second came circling back, keeping a wary distance and hissing. Dagger-sharp claws flexed restlessly at the ends of its fingers. Tyris waited a few seconds for it to grow impatient and charge him, but the creature bided its time, still waiting for an opening to attack. *Not as dumb as you seem,* he thought.

His right arm dropped to the holster on his hip and flashed back up, now holding a Stinger pistol. He shot an invisible, silenced laser bolt between the Dreg's eyes, and it dropped like a rock to the rubble-strewn ditch beside the highway. Tyris holstered the smoking weapon and scowled. That Dreg had been wearing clean clothes, which meant it was from the city. One of the former citizens of New Houston. Based on the size and shape of its frame, he guessed that this was a teenager. A girl. Her cranial stalks hadn't even emerged yet, so she was still in the process of turning.

Tyris dropped to his haunches beside the dead creature, careful not to touch it. This was one of the new generation of Dregs, contagious even to him and his crew. Her mouth was slowly opening and closing, bloodshot green eyes roving in her head. She was still alive even with a hole in her brain. Tyris stepped back and drew his pistol again. A shot to the heart ended her struggle and the light left her rabid gaze.

Rather than pity or remorse, he felt nothing but raw, simmering anger. This girl was just a few years away from graduation and her own ascension ceremony. She probably would have become a Chimera and joined the Federation, but the resistance had stolen that chance from her and millions of others. Tyris glanced back to the highway where the hauler had gone. The sky was now drenched in a bloody sunrise, as if the ground were so saturated with blood that the clouds were soaking it up.

The resistance would pay for what they'd done. He'd make sure of it.

CHAPTER 10

Clayton accelerated down the long, tree-lined driveway of the log mansion that was Phoenix Base. The wind roared past external audio pickups in his helmet as he watched his wife and kids waving to him in one of the bike's side view displays. It was hard leaving them so soon after they'd been reunited, but this was their best shot at survival. Not just for his family, but for the survival of the species, too. Kyron ships could cover two light years per hour. Even if they only found a small hyper-capable transport, they would be able to explore several star systems before they ran out of fuel, air, and other vital supplies. At this point, humanity had a better chance at starting over somewhere new than trying to rebuild a civilization on Earth with Kyron ships in orbit, waiting to invade again.

Clayton's family disappeared from view around a bend in the driveway. Another minute later, Clayton and the others reached the end of the driveway; Sergeant Sutton accelerated down a rubble-strewn residential street lined with old, rotting homes peeking through curtains of old-growth trees and waist-high grass.

They wound through the neighborhood until they passed beneath a big archway that said *Welcome to Eastshore Estates* across the top. The road beyond was the one they'd driven in on with the hauler, cracked and crumbling, pocked with deep holes and sprouting trees and grass from wide fissures in the asphalt. Even a dirt road would have been better. Fortunately, the hoverbikes wouldn't be slowed down by debris and rough terrain.

Clayton, Keera, and Lori pulled to a stop alongside Sutton, and he removed a discolored black helmet, stolen ages ago from a Chimeran soldier. He wasn't wearing the accompanying suit of armor, however. Clayton removed his own helmet, taking the opportunity to scratch his scalp through long, sweat-matted hair. It was still early morning, and already hot as hell.

"This is where we part ways," Sutton said. He looked to Clayton, then Keera. "We won't be able to stay in comms contact with each other for long, so if you run into trouble out there, you won't be able to call for help."

"There won't be any time for rescues, anyway," Clayton replied.

"All the more reason to watch each other's

backs," Sutton replied.

"Be safe, Keera," Lori added, her voice coming simultaneously to them over the comms and as a muffled muttering that escaped her own helmet. She was going with Sutton to New Dallas while Clayton and Keera went to New San Antonio. Keera had spent ten minutes giving her mother a crash course in how to fly a Kyron ship. Clayton and Sutton had listened with half an ear while gathering equipment to pack into the backs of their bikes.

"Likewise," Keera replied to her mother over the comms. Her helmet turned a few degrees to face Sutton, and she added, "I'm trusting you with her safety, Sergeant."

He nodded, but said nothing to that. "Look, an Admiral outranks a Captain, but as far as I'm concerned, Clayton is in charge. Is that going to be a problem for you, Keera?"

She held his gaze for a beat, her red eyes unblinking behind her helmet. They looked darker than usual behind the tinted visor. "Not a problem," she said.

"Good," Sutton replied. "Fly safe and stay the hell away from Reapers and Dregs. Hooah!"

"Hooah," Clayton replied.

Sutton put his helmet back on, then twisted the throttle and tore down the right side of the street, heading north. Lori hesitated for a beat.

"Go," Keera prompted. "We'll see you back

here in a few hours. Hopefully with a ship."

Lori smiled tightly and nodded before sending her bike whirring after Sutton.

Clayton watched them for a moment. Cicadas buzzed like circular saws in the rising heat of the day. It was still early morning. By midday the Kyron fleet was due to arrive. He checked the time on his augmented reality contacts: *8:35*. They only had three and a half hours left.

"Ready, Captain?" Keera asked.

"Let's go." He slipped on his helmet and then gripped the control bars tightly and flattened himself to the seat behind the windshield. Twisting the throttle a few degrees, he went whirring down the left side of the street, heading south toward New Houston. With the Satnet down, they had to navigate by landmarks, not GPS, but that was nothing new to him. He used to do that all the time while scavenging in the Wastes. Sparing a hand from the control bars, he worked the nav and sensor display in the center of the dash. He kept half an eye out for any saplings breaking through the road that could knock him off the back of the bike, but so far the street was clear.

Zooming out on a satellite map, Clayton searched for a path to New San Antonio. The imagery was too old to show the recent devastation from the battle between the Kyron and Chronan fleets, but the old I-10 ran straight between New Houston and New San Antonio. No need for detours, just a straight shot between the two cities, and the highway would be easy enough to see from the air.

Keera's voice came hissing through the comms in Clayton's right ear. "You know where you're going?" she asked.

"I do now." Clayton pulled up to an altitude of twenty meters to avoid any obstacles, and then gripped the control bars tight as he twisted the throttle around to fifty percent. The bike surged forward, threatening to tear out of his grip and send him tumbling off the back. The sheer thrill of it was simultaneously terrifying and exhilarating. Airspeed hit two hundred and five kilometers per hour in about five seconds, and he backed off the throttle to keep it steady.

At this rate, we might even arrive early, he thought.

***

"I should be going with him," Nova said, watching as the hoverbikes disappeared around a bend in the driveway.

"Do you think he'll come back?" Dora asked in a small voice.

"Of course he will!" Samara said. "They won't be gone long. We'll get some rest, and then he'll be back and we'll all leave together."

"We're supposed to leave Earth in four hours or less, right?" Nova asked.

"Right..." Samara answered slowly.

"Well, what if the sergeant finds a ship, but Dad and Keera don't? It takes two hours to fly there, and two hours to fly back. We have less than four, so that means they won't make it back here before we have to go."

"The bikes can go faster than that," Samara said. "If they're running low on time, they'll just increase their speed on the way back."

"I guess," Nova muttered.

"Why don't we take Rosie for a walk?" Samara suggested. At the mention of the word, Rosie barked and spun around in a circle, chasing her tail.

Nova smiled at the dog's reaction. "I'll go get her leash," she said, and ran for the house.

"Me, too!" Dora added.

Rosie ran barking after them, thinking it was a game.

* * *

Samara watched as the girls ran back to the house with Rosie yipping and barking at their heels. There were still no signs of Dora succumbing to the virus. Clayton had left, and for some reason, she hadn't found a way to tell him about Dora. But why hadn't she? He might have stayed if she'd told him.

Yet she already knew why she hadn't said anything. She knew if she'd told Clayton the truth, he would have stayed, but he also wouldn't have kept the information to himself. He would have told the others just to make sure that they didn't get too close to Dora. And maybe they would have reacted by putting her in some kind of quarantine—or worse, she'd be exiled. And how long would she and Dora last out there on their own?

No, Samara couldn't yet trust Clayton to treat Dora like his other daughter. He hadn't raised her like he had with Nova. He would favor the welfare of the group over Dora's. And besides, all of Samara's worries might be for nothing. So far, Dora was symptom free. For all they knew, she would turn out to be immune.

"You're lucky," a gruff voice said.

Samara flinched at the sound, having thought that everyone had gone back inside. She turned to see Harold and Pyro watching her.

"Lucky?" Samara asked. She and Harold went way back. He'd been a regular at the hospital, always coming in with bite marks on his neck and shoulders from his Chimeran girl-friend. He used to ask a lot about Dora, but it turned out that was for a reason: he'd been act-ing as Clayton's conduit of information, a way for him to check up on her and Dora.

"You escaped with your daughter," Harold explained. "I was separated from Veronica for a long time," he nodded sideways to indicate Pyro. "And now, I've lost Haley. And my wife, too." The corners of his mouth drooped and his eyes grew watery.

Pyro wrapped an arm around his shoulders and pulled him close. "You don't know that they're gone."

"I do. I watched as we drove past my farm. Everything was destroyed. During the fighting I told Mona to take Haley and head for the entrance of the sewers where we snuck in, but even if she made it, that section of the wall was flattened. And I lost comms contact with them just after the *Sovath* came down."

Samara winced. "I'm sorry, Harry. But the sewers run below the walls. There's still a chance—"

"That they're buried under a mountain of debris? Or that they made it out only to get eaten by Dregs?" Harold shook his head. "If I thought there was any chance that they'd made it, I'd be on a hoverbike right now, headed for the city."

Pryo rubbed her father's back, looking almost as distraught as he did. "Just keep your kids safe, and be careful on that walk. We haven't established a perimeter since we got back."

"I'll go with them," Pyro suggested, and patted her sidearm—a bulky plasma pistol that hung low on her hip.

Harold glanced at her, then nodded and took in a shaky breath. "Good idea. I'm going to rest. You girls be safe..." He put on a fading smile. "And have fun, too."

Samara smiled back and watched as he shuffled toward the house. She was exhausted, too, but the kids still seemed to be full of energy. Hopefully a few laps around the property would wear them out so they could all follow Harold and get some sleep.

Nova and Dora burst through the front door of the house with Rosie in the lead at the end of her rope leash. Both girls laughed as Rosie bounded down the steps, dragging Nova along. The three of them flashed by Samara and Pyro in a matter of seconds, with Nova barely managing to keep up with Rosie. "Give her to me!" Dora said. "I wanna walk her, too!"

"Don't get too far ahead!" Samara called after them, but her words fell on deaf ears.

"We'd better catch up," Pyro said. "Come on!" She sprinted after the girls, and Samara pushed through her exhaustion to run after them.

They flashed down the driveway past walls of trees full of rustling leaves and flickering sunlight. They had to weave around potholes and thick clumps of grass growing through the pavement. "Rosie! Slow down!" Nova cried.

Samara's legs and lungs started burning, and she began to regret suggesting that they take the dog out for a walk. Rosie had obviously confused walk for run.

"Take her off the leash!" Samara called after

them.

Pyro was catching up with them, but Samara was done. She gave up and stumbled to a stop, gasping for air and leaning heavily on her knees. She dropped to her haunches and hung her head between her knees to get the blood flowing back to her brain.

Rosie barked, but this wasn't like her excited barks from before: it was a single deep-throated *woof!* And then the air went achingly still and even the cicadas stopped buzzing. Samara glanced up from the ground to see the dog and the girls all stopped and staring through the trees. Samara followed their gazes over a field of tall brown grass to a neighboring house—a hunching two-story cottage with a fallen tree leaning on top of it and half of the roof caved in.

The inside of the structure was cloaked in shadows. Anything could be hiding in there: a family of Dregs, a roving band of exiles, or just squirrels and termites. Samara pushed off her knees and ran down the driveway to reach the others.

As soon as she arrived, Rosie barked again, and this time she pulled toward the neighboring house.

"Easy, girl," Nova said, stroking the dog's back to calm her down.

"What do you think she saw?" Dora asked.

"It's probably nothing to worry about,"

Pyro said.

But Rosie barked again, as if to contradict her.

Samara looked to the other woman. "And what if it *isn't* nothing?"

A muffled crash dragged their eyes back to the house in question, and Pyro drew her plasma pistol. "Take the girls back," she said. "I'll go check it out."

Samara nodded. "Come on. Walk's over."

"What? Why?" Dora complained. "I can handle Dregs!"

"With what?" Nova countered, looking skeptical. She patted the knife on her belt. "You don't even have a weapon."

"Then give me yours."

"We're not going in there," Samara replied, taking hold of Rosie's leash and yanking her up the driveway. Rosie gave in with a sigh and trotted along beside her, but Dora screwed up her face in a pout.

"But, Mom..."

"But nothing."

"Come on, sis," Nova added, wrapping an arm around Dora's shoulders. "We'll walk Rosie later, okay?"

Dora sighed dramatically. "Okaaay, fine."

Samara smiled at their exchange. Hopefully Rosie's next walk would be on an entirely different planet. But that raised a swirling storm of questions that Samara hadn't even begun to ask due to all of the more pressing concerns about Dora.

There were good reasons why the Kyra didn't allow native species to leave their worlds. For one, Chimeras were engineered for interstellar travel. They were immune to most pathogens and plenty of toxins, too. They were also stronger and hardier than humans, so they could endure greater amounts of radiation and larger variations in atmospheric pressure and surface gravity. How would a group of un-altered humans handle those environmental threats? They would need pressure suits and oxygen tanks for most planets. And even the ones with breathable atmospheres could still turn out to be deadly in a dozen other ways.

Clayton's plan to get away sounded good until they started to think about the logistics of relocating to another world with nothing but basic survival gear and a small transport to shield them from the elements. What if they found a planet where everything was perfect, only to discover that the water or the soil were poisonous?

Samara felt the beginnings of a sharp, stab-bing headache building behind her eyes. She hoped Clayton had thought that far ahead. He'd already been on a mission to another world, so hopefully he had a plan.

CHAPTER 11

Back inside the house, Doc, Preacher, and Harold were gathered around the kitchen island, eating chunks of meat and blackened ears of corn. Catching the scent of food, Rosie pulled toward the island even as Doc waved them over.

"You three want some?" he asked while gnawing on a glistening white rib big enough that it might have belonged to a cow. His eyes lingered on Dora while he waited for a reply.

"Yes, please," she said.

"Me, too," Nova added.

Samara's stomach growled and her mouth began to water. She noticed there were only two ears of corn, but six pieces of meat. "Serve them first," she suggested.

Doc put down his food and peeled open the ears of corn before snapping them in half with his bare hands. "There's enough to go around," he said, then served a piece of meat and corn onto three chipped and discolored plates. He slid the plates over one at a time.

"Thanks," Nova said, and Samara echoed her sentiments. Dora said nothing, but Samara was too tired to nag her about her manners.

She grabbed her chunk of meat and started eating. It had a strong, gamy flavor, and it was dry, tough, and too salty for her tastes.

The girls pulled out rusty bar stools and hopped up to eat their food. Rosie sat down beside Samara and looked up at her with sad brown eyes and drooping jowls. The dog licked her lips once, her gaze never leaving the meat. Samara smiled and tore off a piece.

It never touched the ground. Rosie snapped it out of the air and swallowed it whole, then licked her lips again, waiting for another morsel to fall from Heaven.

Doc was watching Dora again. "How are you feeling?"

Samara felt a tickle of dread course through her with that question. Did he *know?*

"Tired," Dora said around a mouthful of corn.

"The bite still hurts?"

She shook her head. "Not anymore."

"Good," Doc said, then turned and opened a rusty old fridge behind him. Samara watched him curiously as he withdrew a big pitcher of water and poured a glass for each of them. If he knew about Dora, would he be so nonchalant about his inquiries? *No,* Samara decided. He was just showing concern over an ordinary injury.

"Yuck," Dora said, her lips curling around a mouthful of the meat. "What *is* this?" she asked, holding it up like a dirty sock.

"Venison," Doc replied. His teeth and lips shone with grease as he smiled. "You'll get used to it."

"Not if we find a ship and leave," Nova said.

"God willing," Preacher added.

Harold looked up from his plate while chewing endlessly on his own venison. He had a faraway look in his eyes, but they quickly swam into focus, and the crow's feet around them tightened with concern. He swallowed visibly, then asked, "Where is Veronica? Wasn't she walking with you?"

Samara took a sip of water to wash down the meat. "We heard a crash from the neighbor's house. She told us to go back while she went to check it out."

"And you *let* her go?" Harold's expression darkened. He reached down and snatched up a rifle by the strap. Slinging it over his shoulder, he turned and ran for the door.

"We didn't want to worry anyone," Samara called after him. "It's probably nothing!"

The door slammed behind Harold.

Doc looked worried, the Asian man's typically smooth, youthful features now tense with concern.

Preacher scratched absently at his curly

black beard. "Could be Dregs," he said. "They'll have gone indoors to hide from the light."

"This far out?" Doc countered.

"Well..." Samara trailed off. She hadn't thought about that. She'd actually been thinking that the sound was just a wild animal, but what if it was another group of exiles, planning to ambush them and steal their supplies? Her gaze tracked back to the hallway by which Harold had left. Maybe he was right. Maybe they shouldn't have let Pyro go.

Doc held a hand to his comms piece. "Pyro, it's Doc. Come in."

Samara stopped chewing and watched him for a breathless moment, then he visibly relaxed. "Good to hear. Your dad's on the way to back you up... I know you can. He was worried. Keep us posted. Doc out." He nodded to Samara. "It's okay. She's fine. The house is empty."

"Any sign of what caused the noise?" she asked.

Doc shrugged as he covered the remaining food with an old cookie sheet and put the pitcher of water back in the fridge. "Could have been anything. A tree fell on the place a few weeks back. Maybe something shifted under the weight. Finish up and go get some rest. Take the food to your room if you want. It won't be long before the recon teams return, and then we'll be on the move again."

Hopefully, Samara added quietly to herself.

She nodded and picked up her plate and glass from the bar counter. "Come on, girls. Let's go."

The girls took their food and glasses of water and jumped off the bar stools. They followed Samara down the hall to the room where they'd found Rosie, and the dog padded along beside them, her long nails clacking on the old wooden floors. Samara opened the door with her elbow and pushed it shut after the girls came in behind her. She eyed the locking mechanism built into the metal handle for a second before setting her glass of water down and twisting the metal knob to lock the door. Samara tested the handle to be sure. The lock worked. Good.

Turning away, she saw the billowing bedsheets covering the broken window. The door wasn't the only way in. Walking to the opening, she peered out and saw that it was at least fifteen feet to the ground. She let out a sigh of relief. The house was built on a slope, facing the lake, and the basement was a walkout. They'd be relatively safe at this height, even with a broken window. It was still possible for someone to climb in while they slept, but not very likely. And besides, Dregs were the main threat, and they wouldn't be out walking around in the middle of broad daylight.

Samara sat down heavily on one of the two bare mattresses in the room and went back to eating her food, this time focusing on the corn rather than the tough, gamy meat. "Finish up your food and let's get some rest," she told the girls.

"I'm done," Dora said as she pushed her plate toward Rosie. The dog grabbed her hunk of venison and ran to the farthest corner of the room with her prize. She lay down, holding the meat between her paws and began gnawing on it with her back teeth as if it were a bone. Samara smiled wryly at that. *You know meat is tough when even a dog can't wolf it down.*

Dora came over to Samara's mattress and lay down beside her. The girl's eyes sank steadily shut, succumbing to sleep in a matter of seconds. Samara watched her as she finished her corn and then gave the rest of the meat to Rosie. She lay down behind Dora, wrapping an arm around her, and hoping to God that when they woke up Dora wouldn't be symptomatic.

Nova watched them steadily while slowly chewing on her meat. Her corn was already picked clean. She had to be used to food like this.

Samara lay there, her body numb with exhaustion, her mind tortured with fear. She listened to Dora's steady breathing, and to the birds chirping and cicadas buzzing outside the window. The breeze filled the sheet-curtains, and bright waves of sunlight washed over them. Dust motes sparkled, drifting lazily in the air. The growing heat and the sounds of the birds and bugs carried Samara to the edge of sleep. She wondered briefly where Clayton was now, and if he was okay. Then her eyes slid shut, and a blanket of darkness fell over her, smothering all of her worries with merciful oblivion.

She woke up what felt like only a few seconds later as Rosie let out a muffled bark. The dog raised her head and looked intently at the door, cocking her head one way, then the other, listening.

"What is it, girl?" Samara whispered.

Rosie hesitated, then lay her head back down with a heavy sigh. She worked her tongue around in her mouth a few times, probably trying to dislodge bits of meat stuck between her teeth.

Samara waited a few more seconds, listening to the saw-like buzzing of the cicadas. A gust of wind went by the window, sucking the curtain out this time instead of pushing it in. Outside, the trees creaked and rustled.

Nothing but the wind, Samara decided. She took a moment to check on Dora, feeling her forehead for a fever, but she was cool to the touch. No other signs of the virus, either. With that reassurance, Samara let herself drift off to sleep once more, and this time nothing woke her.

* * *

Clayton flew ahead, leading the way

through the Wastes around New Houston. They'd had to slow to a crawl near the city and drop down low to avoid the possibility of Chimeran snipers watching them from the wreckage of the *Sovath*. He took a wide berth around the jagged, smoking remains of the Kyron destroyer to be safe. The ship had cracked in half when it crashed outside the city last night. It had dug out a massive crater, sending century-old rubble from the Wastes airborne to flatten the walls on the North end of the city.

They'd seen dozens of survivors fighting around the crash site when they'd left the city in the early hours of the morning, but there was no sign of them now. Clayton checked the bike's sensors once more.

"Not a blip," he said over the comms.

"They could be cloaked," Keera replied.

Clayton frowned, troubled by that possibility. He'd been surprised by cloaked Chimeras before. That was how Lori had died and he'd wound up exiled to the Wastes.

"Maybe the Dregs got them all," he suggested. "Or they might have left already. No sense waiting around here for hordes from the city to swarm them."

"Maybe," Keera replied. "But it's day now. The Dregs will have scurried away to hide from the sun. Do you see any hordes?"

"Guess not," Clayton replied.

"Their ship is a secure position with supplies and valuable equipment. They'll have to leave it eventually, but if I were in command, I wouldn't go anywhere until I'd found somewhere to go."

"So you think they're still there?" Clayton asked as he pulled up to fly over the twisted remains of an old traffic light.

"Maybe," Keera replied.

They flew on in silence through a maze of debris-strewn streets and old buildings. Glinting eyes watched them from the shadows of gaping windows and jagged holes in the crumbling facades of old stores and houses.

After about half an hour, they rounded the North end of the city. The spires of the tallest buildings glinted in the sun, some pristine, others ragged with scars from the recent battle. A murky haze of smoke hung low over the city from fires that had burned through the night.

Clayton watched the crash site of the *Sovath* vanishing in his side and rear view displays. He waited a few seconds more before daring to fly above the rooftops of ruined buildings around them. He twisted the throttle up, and the wind became a muffled roar in his ears even through his helmet.

Within minutes they reached the I-10 on the west end of the city. A broad avenue of cracked and broken asphalt stretched as far as the horizon. Overgrown ruins lay on either side of the highway, while old derelict cars, trucks, mechs, and tanks lined the outer lanes and shoulder, leaving a narrow gap of just two lanes free down the center. The debris and vehicles had been pushed aside decades ago to make a path for garbage haulers and armored troop transports to leave the city.

Then they reached the exits to the designated dump site. Stinking mounds of trash rose like so many ant hills, choking the air with rotten fumes. And soon after that, the highway was no longer clear, but completely choked with rusted vehicles. Chimeras used to travel between occupied cities by air, not the ground, so they didn't bother to clear the roads and highways beyond a certain point.

Fortunately, hoverbikes were aerial vehicles, so they didn't need a clear path to get around.

Clayton took a breath to steady his nerves and rolled his shoulders to work out some of the tension building from hunching on the back of the bike. He kept an eye on the sensors to watch for signs of Reapers or other Exiles who might try to shoot them down and steal their gear, but no blips appeared. And at this speed and altitude, even if someone did see them, they'd be hard to hit.

As the immediate threats faded to the back of his mind, more distant ones came to the fore. What if neither his team nor Sutton's found a hyper-capable ship?

Or better yet, what if they did? Where would they go? He had a few ideas. The first thing they would do is follow up on the missions of the other three Forerunners. His ship, Forerunner One, had been one of four interstellar exploration and colony missions sent out before the Kyra had invaded. Clayton and his crew had gone to Trappist-1 and encountered the Kyra as well as the native, ten-legged Trappans. Their encounter with the Kyra had forced them to flee back to Earth, but no one had ever heard back from the other three missions.

Furthermore, what had happened to his ship? They'd arrived at the UNE outpost at Proxima Centauri to find Admiral Keera waiting for them. She'd transferred all of them to the *Sovath* for transport back to Earth. So what had happened to *Forerunner One?* Had they just left it there, drifting around an abandoned UNE outpost? If they could find his old ship and sneak aboard, they would find all the supplies they needed to deal with interstellar exploration. But finding a ship was just the first in a long series of other challenges.

Clayton pushed those concerns from his mind. *One obstacle at a time.* He checked the time in the top right corner of his ARCs: *10:09 AM.* They'd been traveling for over an hour and a half already, but they'd had to slow down to go around New Houston, so he estimated they were only halfway to their destination. *Less than two hours left before the Kyra arrive,* he thought.

The comms in Clayton's ear crackled with Keera's voice just as something began flashing at the leading edge of his bike's sensor display. "Unknown contact. Three blips at twelve o'clock, one klick out. Somewhere around that overpass up ahead."

"I see them. Could be trouble. Cut your throttle."

"Copy."

Clayton backed all the way off the throttle and hovered at a safe distance and an altitude of about twenty meters.

A crumbling bridge arced high above the old interstate at eye level with them. The overpass was too far away to see people standing on or beneath it, but the bike's scanners showed them clearly: a pair of yellow, human signatures standing in the middle of the highway, not moving and about forty feet apart. And there was a purple Chimeran signature about ten feet away from the leftmost human, also not moving. Despite Commander Tyris's appeal for peaceful cooperation, humans and Chimeras traveling together was unlikely unless one species had captured the other. Since the Chimera was only close to one of the two humans, Clayton suspected they'd captured a

Chimera rather than the other way around. *Exiles.*

"Could be Reapers," Keera suggested.

"Either way they're not friendly. It's some kind of road block. We'd better go around." The distance between the two humans was tactical, designed to flank incoming targets. *Targets like us,* he thought. "Stay close," Clayton said just as he twisted his throttle up gently and began veering off to the right.

In that exact moment, a bright green laser flashed by his left shoulder, so close that it warmed his skin even through his jumpsuit. "Taking fire!" he cried, and pushed the control bars down to dive for the relative safety and cover of the ruins below. A flurry of laser bolts chased him down, and Keera screamed.

CHAPTER 12

"**K**eera!" Clayton shouted over the comms. He hit the street level, pulled up hard, and applied the air brakes under his right foot. He coasted to a stop in front of a sprawling, two story building, the bulk of which blocked him from line of sight with the overpass. Keera came crashing down beside him, her bike gushing black smoke. She slammed into the wall and flew over the control bars. Her helmet cracked against solid concrete, and she hit the ground with a thud.

"Shit!" Clayton jumped off the back of his bike and ran to see if she was okay. He found Keera struggling to rise, and pulled her up by the arm to eye level with him.

She seemed dazed, her crimson eyes blinking slowly behind a cracked visor, her expression slack with shock.

"Are you okay?" he asked, holding her at arm's length to check her over. There was a dark, smoking patch on her right thigh. A laser burn. No wonder he'd heard her scream. Her helmet's visor was starred with a spider's web of cracks. She reached up with shaking hands and pulled it off. Clayton did the same.

"Sit down," he said, while guiding her over to the wall and helping her sit with her back to it.

"My equipment," Keera said, swallowing visibly and pointing to the cargo compartment on the back of her bike. The machine was still gushing thick black smoke, but now he glimpsed a bright orange flicker of flames. If that fire reached the IEDs and charge packs in the cargo area, they'd be killed in the blast.

"Shit," Clayton said again. He ran to her bike, opened the cargo compartment and began pulling out all of Keera's gear. In particular, the two rifles and the ten spare charge packs. He threw everything out as quickly as he could, then reached past Keera's canteen, poncho, and tent to a pair of IEDs the size of soup cans. He pulled them out gently and ran to set them down beside his own bike.

When he was done, he noticed that Keera's vehicle had stopped gushing smoke and the flames had guttered out. Maybe they could still salvage it. At least there was no rush to remove the rest of her gear.

Breathing hard, he looked around to take stock of where they were. It looked like they'd landed beside an old covered parking garage. He remembered seeing the rest of the sprawling complex from the air and guessed that it might have been a shopping center before the invasion. The roof of the garage would have contained landing pads for air cars, while the lower two floors provided covered parking for ground vehicles.

The wall they'd crashed into was open at waist-height between the columns—except where it had collapsed. Clayton drew his pistol and crept carefully over to the nearest gap in the wall, peering into the shadows.

Shafts of sunlight illuminated the interior of the structure, pouring down through at least half a dozen places where the roof and second floor of the garage had collapsed. The interior was relatively well-lit and full of dusty old vehicles. He decided it was too bright to make it a good nest for Dregs.

Holstering his plasma pistol, Clayton hurried back to Keera's side. Her eyes were shut, her cheeks and scalp shining with sweat and cranial stalks drooping. Her lips were slick with black blood that leaked in a trickle from one corner of her mouth. That made him worry about internal injuries.

"Where does it hurt?" he asked.

"Everywhere," Keera mumbled, then she cracked a bloody smile and slowly shook her head. "I'll be okay. Just focus on the laser burn."

Clayton blew out a shaky breath and ran back to his bike. He had to hurry. Those two on the overpass might be a kilometer away, but they hadn't been shooting for target practice. They were obviously scavengers, and that meant they'd be following up with a second attack soon. On the bright side, they were most likely on foot so it would take them a while to get here. Clayton tore open the cargo compartment in the back of his bike, quickly rifled through the contents, and then pulled out a medkit. He ran to Keera's side, opened the kit, and withdrew a pair of scissors to cut her jumpsuit away from the burn on her thigh. The material had fused with her skin, melting into it and making his job that much harder.

"Hurry," Keera urged through gritted teeth.

"I'm trying!"

He finished cutting, but when he tried to peel away the fabric, her skin peeled off with it. Keera screamed as he exposed a large patch of raw flesh to the air. A dark, thumb-sized hole cut through the center of the injury where the laser beam had hit. At least lasers cauterized veins and arteries on the way through, so he didn't have to worry about Keera bleeding out. He cut away the fabric and skin and quickly sprayed the raw wound with Regenex. The healing fluid fizzled and bubbled as it came into contact with the injury. Keera breathed raggedly from the pain. He applied a large transparent patch of synthskin, then began to wrap the area with a bandage.

"Don't forget the exit wound," Keera said. "The bolt went straight through and hit my bike." She rolled onto her side, and Clayton hurried to repeat the process on the back of Keera's thigh. The damage wasn't as bad at the exit wound, with none of the fusing between her skin and clothing, so he just sprayed it with Regenex and wrapped the leg in a bandage. When he was done, he noticed the silver cannisters of a couple of stim shots and painkillers. Pulling out one of the latter, he pressed it to the side of Keera's wounded leg and depressed the button on the back of the cylinder. It injected a potent painkiller with a soft *hiss.*

"Should have done that first," Keera muttered through a sigh.

Clayton grimaced. His thinking was scattered by the looming threat of those scavengers coming to finish them off. "Can you stand?" he asked.

"Only one way find out," she replied, and began pushing off the grassy, rubble-covered ground.

He helped her up, and she stood leaning heavily against the wall. She was clearly trying to keep weight off her injured leg.

"We need to arm ourselves," Clayton added, supporting her on one side and helping her to limp over to her bike. They reached one of the two rifles that he'd tossed out earlier, lying about five feet from the bike. It was the EKR-7, an automatic rifle like the ones they'd used during the assault on the Ascension Center. Besides having a greater number of shots per charge pack than the average laser rifle, EKRs were mainly characterized by the addition of a *stealth* setting that fired invisible, silenced laser bolts. That would come in handy when they had to deal with Dregs. Clayton let go of Keera and bent to retrieve the weapon.

And that was when he heard it—a loud crunch of gravel grinding under a boot. He snatched up the rifle and spun toward the sound, flicking off the safety with his thumb.

"Drop it," a deep voice said. All Clayton could see was the barrel of a laser rifle peeking over the top of a jagged chunk of concrete.

He shifted his aim half a foot to the left, taking a guess at where the person holding the rifle was. Hopefully that rubble wasn't too thick to shoot through.

"I wouldn't do that if I were you," a second man said. Clayton's eyes darted to the source, and he saw another rifle barrel peeking at him from around the rear bumper of an old air car. Both men were aiming at them from the safety of cover, leaving nothing but their weapons sticking out. That meant they were either using augmented reality contacts or helmets stolen from Chimeran soldiers to connect to the scopes of their rifles. Either way, it meant that these exiles were unusually well-equipped. They had to belong to a larger group like Phoenix. *Reapers,* he thought. From what little he'd heard about them so far, they were bad news. He'd been planning to take precautions to avoid them as they drew near to the city, but he hadn't expected to run into them this far from New San Antonio.

"Listen, we don't need to fight each other," Clayton said. "You can take whatever you want, just leave us the bikes. We need them to get to where we're going," Clayton said. He made no move to drop or lower his weapon.

The first man chuckled darkly. "First off, the bikes are the most valuable thing you got, so no can do, sir. Second, I have a counter proposal for you: you tell us what you're doing traveling with that red-eyed demon, and maybe we'll let you live."

Clayton swallowed thickly. "She's on our side. A defector."

More laughter rippled back, this time from both men. "Well, now I've heard everything!" the first man said. "Shit, she's on our side, Terry! What a relief. Say, you two wouldn't be more than just travel companions, would ya?"

Clayton caught the man's meaning and shook his head. "No."

"Hmmm. Question is, should I believe ya? What do you think, Terry?"

"Just read 'em their rights, Zack."

"All right, all right. You have the right to remain silent. Anything you say or scream can be held against you. You have the right to a quick death if you cooperate. Do you understand your rights as I have read them to you?"

Ice spread swiftly through Clayton's veins. He was outgunned and outmatched, and these two were obviously complete psychopaths. They had no intention of letting either him or Keera live. "You're Reapers," he said slowly.

Another laugh answered from both men. "Well, shit. Looks like we're famous, Terry!" Zack said.

"Fame and fortune," Terry replied.

"Wicked vices, but someone's got to have 'em," Zack added. "You didn't answer the question, sir. Did you understand your rights or do I need to illustrate by putting a hole between that demon's antennae?"

CHAPTER 13

Samara awoke bathed in sweat, her head thick and groggy with sleep. She heard a muffled cry followed by a *thud,* and then Rosie barked once, sharply. The dog got up and began sniffing at the door.

"Mom?" Dora asked, sounding confused.

"Shhh." Samara gave her a sharp look and placed a finger to her lips. Even as she did so, a burst of relief coursed through her. Dora still looked fine. Maybe she was immune to both strains of the virus, after all.

Nova jumped up from her mattress, awake and alert in an instant. She stepped lightly to the door, drawing the hunting knife from her belt along the way. Samara cast about for some other kind of weapon, but there was nothing she could use.

Nova placed her ear to the door, listening. Rosie sniffed and snorted loudly at the bottom of it. Samara jumped up and joined the dog and the teenage girl by the door. She placed her ear to it opposite Nova and listened...

The sound of the cicadas and birds and the wind sighing through the trees outside filled her other ear, but nothing from inside the house. No sounds followed that *thump* and muffled cry. Samara thought about possible causes. Dregs wouldn't be so stealthy. They'd hear them stomping through the house, hissing and shrieking—or at least feeding on their victims. But that was another giveaway. Dregs wouldn't have overwhelmed the armed guard outside or the occupants of the house without a fight. They'd have heard guns firing, people running around and shouting warnings to each other. This was something else. Something much more dangerous than Dregs.

Chimeras. It had to be. They were likely commandos wearing cloaking armor with weapons set to *stealth* mode.

Nova peeled away from the door and looked to the open window. Samara followed her gaze. She read the girl's thoughts without either of them having to speak. They had to get out now while they still could and that window was their only chance.

Dora watched them quietly, now sitting up on the bare mattress, her green eyes big and blinking. Samara and Nova crept to the window and carefully removed the rocks that pinned down the sheet. Peering out, Samara noted the fifteen-foot drop to the ground, and this time found herself wishing that the window were on the ground floor. Even if they dangled by their hands from the window sill it would still be a nine-foot drop, and the ground was sloping at the bottom. They'd land unevenly, with all of their weight on one foot. It was an almost sure-fire way to break or twist an ankle.

Samara looked to Dora. The girl was light enough that Samara might be able to lower her down and reduce the height of the drop.

Nova had other ideas. She was struggling to pull down the sheet from where it was tied crudely around the old, sagging curtain rod above the window. Samara helped her and the sheet fell in a puddle at their feet. Nova quickly rolled and twisted it into a crude rope. She handed one end to Samara and took the other for herself. She pointed to her chest, then to the ground below. She expected Samara to hold the sheet while she climbed down. Samara nodded quickly and wrapped the sheet around her wrist for a better grip. She braced both feet and leaned back, watching as Nova climbed over the window sill. Samara braced herself, hoping she'd be strong enough to hold the girl's weight.

A moment later that was tested as an almost unbearable weight tugged her toward the open window. Samara's arms snapped straight, and she leaned back with all of her weight to avoid being dragged out the window. Nova wasn't much smaller than she was, but probably fifty pounds lighter. It worked. She felt steady tugs on the sheet rope as Nova climbed down...

And then a sudden, unexpected release that sent her tumbling over. Samara fell on her rear with a sharp pain and a teeth-clacking jolt.

That was followed by a steady clomping of heavy footsteps as someone ran down the hall outside the door. Rosie began barking and snarling incessantly at the door. Samara jumped up and waved Dora over. The girl hesitated for a brief instant, then catapulted off the mattress. Samara pulled the sheet up and gave her daughter the other end. She nodded reassuringly. Again, Dora hesitated. She stared out the window, sizing up the distance to the ground.

Then the door handle jiggled as someone tried to get in.

"Go now!" Samara whispered sharply. "Hold tight." She showed Dora how to wrap the sheet around her wrists.

Rosie snarled and scratched at the bottom of the door while Dora climbed over the sill, holding the sheet. This time Samara took up the slack and began lowering Dora down. She wouldn't have the strength to climb or rappel down like Nova had. Samara lowered Dora steadily.

The door thumped and shook as someone

on the other side rammed their shoulder or boot into it. Samara's eyes darted to the door and saw Rosie now backing away, still barking and snarling. Samara reached the end of the improvised rope. Her back and arms were screaming for her to let go, and she couldn't feel her hands where the sheet was wrapped around them. She fought through it, bracing her shoulder against the wall and peering over the window sill to make eye-contact with Dora. She was dangling about five feet from the ground. *Jump!* she mouthed.

Thump! The door shook with another impact.

Dora winced and shook her head. Her grip on the sheet slipping. She was going to fall. Samara did the only thing she could, and let the sheet slide slowly through her grip, running hotly through her hands and buying Dora an extra foot.

The daughter gave a stifled cry as she fell. Samara watched as she hit, dropped, and rolled twice before coming to a stop beside a bush. Nova crawled out, crouching in the tall grass and pulled her up. The two of them spoke briefly, exchanging words that Samara couldn't hear. Both girls looked up. Nova gestured for her to join them, and Samara contemplated the drop. She could risk it. Maybe she would get away with a light sprain. Or maybe she would wind up so badly injured that she would only slow them down and make it all for nothing.

Samara shook her head and waved them away. Dora hesitated, but Nova looked away and grabbed her by the arm, leading her away. The two girls crouched low in the tall grass, using the side of the house for cover. They were headed for a line of bulrushes and trees growing along the shore of the lake.

Thump! This time the door jamb splintered and it burst open. Samara spun away from the window and saw—

Nothing. The door groaned, swinging slowly open with residual momentum, askew on its hinges.

Rosie growled softly.

And then a bright flash of light leaped out of thin air and hit the dog in the head. She dropped with a *thud*, her legs kicking spasmodically and nails skittering on the wooden floor. Horrified, Samara spun back to the window, irrationally planning to leap out and risk the fall.

But a second burst of light drove a hot spike between her shoulder blades before she could take a single step. Her whole body went limp and she crumpled to the floor in front of the window, vaguely aware of her muscles spasming and limbs jerking involuntarily. Her eyed blurred with tears and her mind blanked just as the air above her shimmered and a dark shadow appeared standing over her. It was the last thing she registered before losing consciousness.

CHAPTER 14

"**D**rop the gun. This is your last warning," Zack said.

Clayton laid the rifle down slowly. "Listen to me," he said as he straightened up. "You need us alive."

"I don't think he got the part about whatever he says being used against him," Terry said.

"No, he did not," Zack replied as he stepped out from behind the chunk of concrete he'd been using for cover. At the same moment, Terry emerged from behind the skeleton of the old ground car. Both men wore old, sweat-stained and faded t-shirts and jeans. Clayton sized them up in the span of a few seconds —Zack was tall and fit with tanned skin. He looked to be about thirty, with a quarter-inch of dark stubble and the same on his head.

The other man, Terry, was shorter than Clayton at about five foot eight, with light blue eyes, a bushy blond beard, and matching hair pulled back into a ponytail. Terry looked meaner and more dangerous than his partner, despite being the smaller of the two. Spiky black tattoos ran around both of his bulging biceps as well as a stylized skull on one shoulder. Terry had the dead-eyed stare of a trained killer, unblinking, no emotion. He also held his rifle higher and closer than Zack and his movements were more fluid. Terry was just waiting for an excuse to shoot them. He stopped beside Clayton's bike and began checking it over, keeping half an eye on them while he fiddled with the controls.

"It's in good condition," Terry said, not noticing the pair of IEDs on the ground on the other side of the bike.

"Good," Zack purred.

Clayton contemplated drawing his pistol or diving for the rifle he'd set down. If he could hit one of the explosives next to the bike, he'd probably blow the guy up. And then Zack would gun him down. If he went over to join Terry by the bike, however, then Clayton might have a chance to get them both.

"Don't," Zack warned. His aim shifted a few degrees to the right, and Clayton saw that one of Keera's hands had dropped to the sidearm holstered on her hip.

"Enough pussy-footin'. Let's just shoot 'em," Terry said.

"Not yet." Zack jerked his chin to Clayton. "You were saying we need y'all alive. Now why is that, sir?"

Clayton wondered at Zack's polite language. He thought back to the Chimeran blip they'd seen on their sensors from the air. If these two had chosen to capture rather than kill a Chimera, then maybe they weren't the cold-blooded killers they seemed to be.

"We were on our way to New San Antonio to steal a Kyron transport," Clayton said. "We're getting off this planet before things get any worse."

"Oh yeah?" Zack appeared to contemplate that. "Sounds like a good plan. And I suppose bright-eyes over there is gonna fly it."

Clayton nodded. "You can come with us, but we need to move fast."

"Why the hurry?" Zack asked.

"Because the Kyra are coming with a fleet to blockade Earth." Clayton glanced at the time on his ARCs. It was 10:32 now. "We have an hour and a half left before they arrive." Hopefully by now Sutton and Lori had reached New Dallas. Maybe they would succeed even if Clayton and Keera failed.

"How do you know that?" Zack's eyes flicked to Keera and back. "The demon told you?"

"Yes."

Zack made a *tsking* sound. "Haven't you learned? You can't trust them! Look, the demons abandoned the planet and turned everyone into mother-lovin' Dregs before they left! What does that tell you? It tells me that they're not coming back."

Clayton hesitated. The Reapers didn't know that the Chrona were the ones who had released the new virus. Did they even know about the battle in orbit? Maybe most of the fighting had centered around New Houston. Clayton picked his words carefully. He couldn't reveal the Chrona's part in things without implicating himself in their plot. "Maybe the Kyra won't come back down to the surface, but they can't afford to let anyone leave, either. The planet is teeming with a virus that's just as deadly to them as it is to us."

"You know that for a fact?" Zack asked. "Have you seen any Kyra get sick?"

"No, but there weren't any Kyra on Earth."

"Exactly!" Zack nodded, agreeing with himself. "Those devils wrote us off and the demon-Chimeras along with us. Probably the new virus only infects the *human* Chimeras. Maybe a bunch of them rebelled or something and this is their punishment. Whatever the case, they're not comin' back. They don't need to tie up resources blockading a dead planet."

Clayton decided not to argue further. "Let's say you're right. We're still better off leaving Earth than staying."

"Let's say you find a ship, and that demon of yours *can* fly us out of here," Zack said. "Where do we go from here?"

"I have a few ideas," Clayton replied. "I was a Captain with the United Nations Space Force before the invasion."

Zachary blinked. "A captain? No, shit."

"He's lying," Terry said. "There's no way he's that old."

But Zack looked more curious than skeptical. "Hard to tell these days... what with the Kyra messing with our biological clocks. Hell, I'm supposed to be fifty-two, and I sure don't look or feel it. And McKayla is ninety-seven but she doesn't look a day over twenty. Let's say I believe you," Zack went on. "Why New San Antonio? You know if there's a ship you can steal out there?" His gaze shifted to Keera once more.

"Yes," she answered.

Zachary gave a slow smile and shook his head. "Well, I hate to dump on your plans, but your demon buddies set off a bomb there last night. There's nothing but a smoking crater where the city used to be."

Clayton blinked in shock. "What?"

Zack's smile widened. "We went to see if New Houston was still around. Just came from there, in fact. We were on our way back when you two came along."

"Now you're lying," Clayton said. "You were waiting for us on that overpass. We stopped at the edge of sensor range, but you opened fire almost immediately. We would have been nothing but dots to the naked eye at that distance, which means you had your weapons out and your scopes trained on the horizon."

Zachary's brow furrowed. "We just stopped to stretch our legs and relieve ourselves. Considering how many Chimeras we saw fleeing the city on bikes when we arrived this morning, we'd have been remiss to let our guard down. Fact is, we thought you were both Chimeras. Seeing that one of you is a human was a real surprise."

"We can still find a ship," Clayton insisted, getting back on topic.

"Where? In New Houston?" Zack shook his head. "You'd be there right now if the demons had left behind a ship you could use."

"There are plenty of other cities we can search," Clayton replied.

"But you just said we're short on time before the devils return and blockade the planet. You can't have it both ways. I think you're stalling. I think you'd say anything to keep me from putting a hole in your head."

Clayton frowned, trying to decide whether to press his argument further. His gaze flicked to the rifle at his feet. Terry was still standing by Clayton's bike and the IEDs.

"We're with Phoenix," Keera said quietly.

"You're with *who?*" Zack thundered. He

raised his rifle to his shoulder, aiming at her. Maybe mentioning them hadn't been a good idea.

She went on anyway, "If your group joins forces with ours, we could take back Houston from the Dregs. There's a lot of supplies there. Enough to keep us all going for years."

Zack appeared to hesitate.

"I've heard enough from this abomination," Terry said. "Shoot her or I will."

Zack dropped his rifle. "Actually, the demon's right. Working together's not a bad idea."

"Dammit, Zachary! Have you lost your mind? The others will never go along with that."

"Oh, I didn't mean *that*," Zack replied. "We can work with Phoenix. Even you." He nodded to Clayton. "But you've got to prove that you can be trusted first. Turn around and draw your pistol. No sudden moves, mind you. Shoot the demon between the eyes and then we can all break bread together like civilized folk."

A cold weight settled in the pit of Clayton's stomach. He couldn't shoot Keera. There had to be another way out of this.

"Go on. About face," Zack insisted. "Let's do some target practice. Take a life to save a life. Namely yours."

With his heart slamming in his chest, Clayton slowly turned to face Keera.

"Now draw your weapon, nice and slow," Zack instructed.

Clayton reached for the weapon with a cold and clammy hand. His palm touched the cool metal of the grip, but he didn't draw the pistol.

"He can't do it!" Terry crowed. "These damned perverts *must be* screwing each other."

"A real live succubus," Zachary added in a dark whisper. "I'm gonna count to five. If you haven't pulled the trigger by the time I reach zero, then I will."

"Go ahead," Keera whispered. "They're going to shoot me anyway."

Clayton gave his head a slight shake, his mind racing for an alternative. *Any* alternative.

And then Zack began to count: "One... two..."

CHAPTER 15

An idea popped into Clayton's head. Possibly suicide, but it was the only way they were both walking out of this alive. He mouthed to Keera: *Play dead.*

"Three..." Zack intoned.

Keera's eyes widened fractionally, the only sign that she might have understood.

"Four..."

Clayton's arm snapped up; his plasma pistol cleared the holster and came into line with Keera's head. He shut one eye and hoped to God his aim was good enough.

"Five!" Zack declared.

Clayton pulled the trigger. A bright flash of super-heated plasma leaped out, and Keera dropped to the ground.

Terry laughed darkly and Zack whistled. "Now, that wasn't so hard, was it?" Clayton steeled himself for action. His heart was beating so hard he thought it might stop. Footsteps approached, crunching through the pebbly, debris-strewn ground. Clayton lowered his gun just as Zack appeared on his left, entering the furthest limit of his peripheral vision. The man's rifle was aimed at him. Clayton averted his eyes, pretending to be in shock. He was actually trying to hide the glow of active displays on his ARCs. He'd just connected the sights of the pistol to a display over his right eye. His weapon dangled loosely from his right hand, the barrel aiming at the ground. He was only going to get one shot at this.

"Set the gun down. Slowly," Zachary said.

Clayton released the grip of the weapon, allowing it to dangle by his forefinger and the trigger guard as he bent down. Gravity and the weight of the weapon sent the sights and barrel swinging backward. Clayton glimpsed his bike and the IEDs beside it as the weapon dangled from his finger. He manipulated the weapon subtly between his forefinger and thumb, bringing the sights into line with the nearest of the two IEDs. He was about twenty feet away from the target, and an upturned chunk of concrete stood waist-high between him and the other IED. He hoped it would be enough to shield him from the blast.

Clayton held his breath and froze halfway through a squat. Then he pulled the trigger.

There came a blinding flash and a deafening *boom* just before a superheated gust of wind knocked Clayton flat on his face. He lay there for a second, stunned, with sharp pebbles digging into his cheek. He tasted blood. Muffled reports of laser fire sounded through the ringing in his ears.

Clayton pushed off the ground to see Keera sitting up and shooting bolt after dazzling green bolt at Zack, who was limping and stumbling away as fast as he could. Keera's shots were missing wildly, as if she were shooting blind—and she likely was. Her eyes were even more sensitive than his, and he was still seeing spots. Clayton felt around for his pistol, but it had been knocked clear out of his hand by the blast. Zack disappeared around the corner of the parking garage. Keera tried to push off the ground, but fell back down with a grimace as her injured leg gave out.

Clayton succeeded in stumbling to his feet and glanced back to where Terry had been. Clayton's bike was gone, and so was the man who'd been standing behind it. Both IEDs had blown, along with all of the explosive material in the back of the bike. There was nothing but a few flaming bits of debris left. The upturned chunk of concrete between him and the back of the bike was scorched black, having taken the brunt of the blast.

Turning away from the scene of destruction, Clayton ran over to Keera. That was when the first wave of pain hit, staggering him. His back felt like it was on fire. He reached around to check, and his hand came away bloody.

Keera was still staring after Zack, at the far corner of the garage, as if expecting him to return or start shooting at them from that position of cover. Clayton helped her to her feet.

"Come on!" he shouted through the ringing in his ears. "We need to find cover!"

She nodded, and they stumbled away together. Clayton spotted the rifle he'd been trying to get to when the Reapers ambushed them, now covered in a fine layer of concrete dust. He made long, clumsy strides to snatch the weapon off the ground, hoping it still worked.

They ran behind the twisted remains of an ancient air car and crouched behind it. Clayton studied Keera, checking for signs of injuries. His shot had scalded the top of her head, leaving a bright red patch of skin where the ball of plasma had made a near miss, but otherwise she seemed to be doing better than he was. She'd been lying flat when the shock wave had hit, so she likely didn't have any shrapnel wounds.

"I need you to check my back," he said just as another blinding wave of pain hit and sucked the air out of his lungs. At least his hearing was starting to return.

Keera nodded, and he turned around.

"Well?" he prompted when he didn't immediately hear back.

"You're bleeding from at least ten different places, but none of them look urgent. Still, I can't see how deep the wounds go without removing your jumpsuit. You'll probably need surgery to remove the debris."

Clayton let out a ragged breath and turned to face her once more. "That will have to wait." He connected his ARCs to the rifle's scope and popped the weapon out of cover, using it like a periscope to check for signs of Zack. "Any sign of him?" Keera asked.

"I don't—"

The rising *whirr* of a hoverbike's engine interrupted him, but the sound quickly faded into the distance.

"He's leaving," Clayton said.

"We can't let him escape," Keera replied.

He looked to her with a frown. "Why not?"

"Because the Reapers know where Phoenix base is!"

"What? Why would they know that?"

"Phoenix used to trade with them," Keera said. "There were always plenty of closer targets for Reapers to hit around New San Antonio. But now that their city is gone..."

"They'll be coming to ours," Clayton concluded.

"If they weren't looking to raid us before, they will be now. We killed one of theirs."

"Right. I'll go check on your bike," Clayton said. He ran out of cover, ignoring the hot waves of pain radiating from his injuries. Neither he nor Keera was in any condition to go chasing after Zack, but it didn't seem like they had a choice.

Keera's hoverbike was resting on the ground rather than hovering—not a good sign. He slung the rifle over his shoulder, wincing as he did so, and then hopped on the bike to see if it was operable. He flicked the ignition switch and got nothing but a sullen *click.* A series of error codes flashed on the nav display:

Power cells offline.

Gravity generators offline.

Stability control offline.

Air brakes inoperable.

Automatic elevation control malfunctioning.

Clayton glanced over his shoulder to see Keera limping out of cover. "It's not going anywhere," he called to her.

Keera hissed with displeasure.

Clayton fought a wave of nausea and dizziness. He felt hot and cold all over; his hands grew clammy and began to shake. It was probably just the adrenaline wearing off, but their current situation didn't help.

"Now what?" Keera asked as she stopped beside him.

Clayton gave her a blank look. Both of them were injured, and they were at least a hundred and fifty kilometers from Phoenix base. Their bikes had been taken out, so now they would have to go back on foot through the Dreg-infested Wastes, and Keera could barely walk.

Even if Sutton and Lori found a ship in Dallas, they'd never make it back in time to catch a ride off-world. Would Sutton wait? He hoped not. They'd end up stranded on Earth when the Kyron fleet arrived, and if Keera was right, Reapers would be coming for them soon.

"Captain?" Keera prompted. "We need a plan."

Clayton's mind spun with possibilities. As he scanned their surroundings, he realized the truth. He didn't have a plan.

CHAPTER 16

Nova heard the piercing reports of a weapon going off from the house—one shot. Two. Dora gave a strangled cry and pulled back the way they'd come. Nova yanked harder on her arm.

"We can't help her!" she whispered sharply to her younger sister, even as she warred with herself not to turn around. There'd been two shots. That meant one had been for Rosie.

They reached the edge of the lake and crashed through a wall of bulrushes. Both girls crouched low behind the cover of the reeds, breathing hard. Nova released Dora's arm and drew her hunting knife in a white-knuckled grip, imagining what she would do to the intruders when she got the chance. She peeked through the curtain of reeds, checking for signs of pursuit.

But there was nothing. Nova's breathing and heart rate slowed.

"She's dead!" Dora sobbed. She was whispering far too loudly for Nova's comfort. The sound of frogs croaking and cicadas buzzing was probably loud enough to drown them out, but they couldn't afford to make assumptions.

"Shhh! We don't know that."

"They shot her!"

Nova grabbed Dora's arm and squeezed it hard. "Shut *up*," she said through gritted teeth. Fresh tears sprang to Dora's eyes, and she shook her head. But at least this time she kept quiet.

Nova released her sister's arm. "Listen to me. We won't do either of them any good getting ourselves killed. That weapon might have been set to stun."

Dora suddenly stopped sobbing. Her eyes flared wide, and she nodded eagerly. She wiped both cheeks on her sleeves. "I didn't think of that."

Nova thought back, trying to remember the tone and pitch of the weapon. Stun bolts were softer than lasers and plasma bolts when they went off. They discharged with a muted *crackling* sound, like a miniature bolt of lightning or electricity. Nova couldn't be sure, but she thought that was what she'd heard. Rosie and Samara could still be alive, and clinging to hope was better than giving into despair, so on she clung.

"What do we do now?" Dora asked.

"Whoever attacked us likely doesn't know that we escaped. That gives us a chance."

"A chance for what?" Dora asked.

Nova glanced at the other girl. She was sitting in a puddle and didn't even realize it. "To strike back."

Dora appeared to consider it, but then she shook her head. "Our dad will be back soon. We should wait for him."

Our dad. Nova felt a strange flash of annoyance at the other girl for that choice of words. Dora hadn't even realized that she had a Father until last night. Nova had never had to share him before, and this was his *real* daughter...

She gave those thoughts a mental shove and shook her head to clear it. "If we wait for him, he'll run straight into a trap," Nova replied. "We need to make our move before that." Her mind raced, trying to come up with a plan. She looked back to the house, peering through the reeds. They needed guns. The armory was in the basement, but the way back to the house was completely exposed. Nothing but grass and a few trees. There was no way to reach the basement without being seen. She could risk it and hope no one was watching...

"So what are we going to do?" Dora prompted.

Nova glanced back at her and noticed the shimmering surface of the lake behind them. That gave her an idea. Her eyes scanned along the shore of the lake until she spotted a dense line of trees that ran all the way from the water's edge to the other side of the house.

"Can you swim?" Nova asked.

Dora shook her head. "No."

"Well, then I guess I'll be on my own."

"I want to help," Dora insisted.

"You can't."

"I can fight. I fought a challenge in the arena. I almost won, too, but the other girl cheated. One of her friends distracted me."

Nova blinked in shock with that revelation and slowly shook her head. "A challenge?" Clayton had told her that it was common for Kyra and Chimeras to challenge each other to duels to settle petty disagreements or to steal coveted positions from each other. "That's with swords, right?"

Dora nodded solemnly. "*Sikaths.* It's very dangerous. I almost died."

"Have you ever fired a gun?"

Dora hesitated. "Only the cadets get to train with guns."

"So that's a no. You can help by staying out of the way. If I don't come back in an hour, you hide and wait for my dad to come back, okay?"

"He's my dad, too."

"Yeah, yeah I know." But Nova didn't feel the truth of it. Dora and Clayton might be related, but Dora wasn't his daughter the way *she* was his daughter. "Stay out of sight," Nova added, pushing those thoughts from her mind as she sheathed her knife and crept to the water's edge.

She began wading in. Despite the growing

heat of another summer's day, the water was still cold from last night. She shivered as it slid up her legs. Soon she was in up to her neck, and then doing the breast stroke along the shore, being careful to keep her body below the water and not to break the surface with even the slightest splash.

* * *

Samara awoke sitting in one of the armchairs in the great room. She found herself slumped against one side of the chair, eyes staring at the floor. She tried to sit up straight, but hot cords tightened around her wrists and ankles, sparking with loud *pops* and sharp jolts of pain that raced up her arms and legs. Samara bit back a cry and lay gasping for air in the wake of those shocks.

"Careful," a woman said. Samara placed the voice as Widow's a second later. She was the one who'd been standing watch outside. Maybe she'd been taken out first.

Being more careful this time, Samara raised only her head and turned to see the other woman sitting in the armchair across from hers. Widow's ankles and wrists were bound with jointed metal ropes. Samara noticed that hers were, too. Stun cords. Kyron tech.

The others were all there as well. Harold and Pyro were still out cold on one of the two couches with Harold snoring away softly. Doc,

Preacher, and Richard were awake and sitting up on the couch opposite theirs. Doc's usually straight black hair was sticking up at odd angles, making Samara think that he'd received more than his fair share of shocks from the stun cords when he'd woken up. His gaze met hers, but he said nothing.

Everyone was there except for Rosie and the girls. Samara cast about quickly, looking for Dora and Nova, but there was no sign of them. One corner of her mouth tugged up in a smile. They'd escaped.

But what could two kids do to help them? Hopefully they'd have the sense to stay away. "Who did this?" Samara asked, not seeing any sign of whoever had attacked them.

Widow's face scrunched up with disgust. "Chimeras. Two of them, both cloaked. They hit us before Pyro and Harold came back and after you and—" She stopped herself before she could mention the girls. "—after you went to your room," she finished. "They split up and took out Preacher and Doc at the same time as me. Richard tried to run for it, but they caught him." Widow flicked a nasty grin at him.

"I was going to come back," Richard said. "I couldn't fight back against an enemy I couldn't even see."

"Sure, because that's what stopped you," Widow said.

Richard looked like he wanted to say something else, but he clamped his jaw shut with a visible effort.

Widow's gaze swept back to Samara. "They got you next. Pyro and Harold were last."

"Why didn't I hear them shooting?" Samara wondered.

"Stun bolts are much softer than live lasers," Preacher said. "And we were downstairs, so the sound would have been muffled from the distance."

Widow nodded along with that explanation. Samara realized that she and the girls had been asleep at the time. She'd awoken to the sound of a *thud* which in retrospect had probably been the sound of someone collapsing to the floor.

A muffled scratching sound caught Samara's ear, coming from one of the bedrooms. *Rosie.* It had to be. Samara let out a stale sigh and looked back to Widow. "So they were waiting until we split up to attack."

Preacher nodded. "They had to even the odds somehow."

"Even the odds?" Widow echoed. "With that cloaking armor they could have taken us all out in a straight fight."

"So why didn't they?" Samara asked. "Why did they stun us? And where did they go?" Samara glanced around, checking the living area once more.

Doc caught her eye and quietly said, "I'm

189

not so sure they did." He flicked his eyes around to indicate their surroundings.

He made a good point. How better to gather useful intel about their group? Have them wake up together and start talking freely amongst themselves. Make them think they were alone. No wonder Doc had been so quiet.

A heavy silence fell as everyone took the hint. There was no sense giving their captors any more information than necessary. Clayton and the others would be back soon. Hopefully they would realize what had happened when they saw that no one was standing guard outside. Assuming more Chimeras didn't arrive before then, there was a good chance that they could turn this around.

Harold awoke with a loud snort and sat up. His bonds sparked and crackled, shocking him into submission. Pryo received the same shocks, since she was leaning on him. She came to with a yelp, recoiling from her father. They both took turns asking the same questions that Samara had. Who had attacked them? Why? Where were they?

"So much for claiming to want to work together," Harold muttered.

"You're alive aren't you?" a deep voice said, slithering to their ears from the shadows. The voice was vaguely feminine, but definitely not human.

Samara's gaze snapped to the source, but

there was nobody there. A floorboard creaked. Then another. Footsteps approached, stepping lightly but audible in the pregnant silence of the house. Rosie barked once, sharply, the sounds having reached her ears, too.

And then the air shimmered, and a Chimera in matte black armor appeared, standing between Samara's chair and the couch where Harold sat. The helmet turned fractionally to look at her.

"Where are the two girls who were with you outside?"

Samara's stomach tightened with fear. "What girls?" she asked.

"I saw you. Walking the dog. Tell me where they are."

Samara lifted her chin and gave a defiant smile. "They're long gone."

A sharp hiss escaped the helmet. "It would be best if you cooperated. We have sensors in our armor. If they get anywhere close to this house, we'll see them coming. I would hate to have to accidentally kill one of them." The helmet turned away. "Who's in charge of your group?"

No one answered.

A long-barreled sidearm cleared the holster on the Chimera's hip. She aimed it at Harold's head. "I don't need all of you alive. Cooperation might ensure your survival."

"I'm in charge," Doc said.

The Chimera looked to him. "When will the others be back?"

"What others?" Doc asked, feigning ignorance.

"The ones who left on hoverbikes."

Doc said nothing to that. *They've been watching us all morning,* Samara realized. This was bad. Even after Clayton and the others returned, the Chimeras would be here waiting for them. But maybe they would come back with a ship. The sensors on a starship were more advanced, and they might detect something through the cloaking shields.

It was a slim hope, but better than nothing.

"What do you want?" Doc asked.

"What do I want? That's a good question. Let's start with answers. Why did you help the Chrona? Was it worth it? You defeated the occupation by sentencing everyone on the planet to death."

"What are you talking about?" Widow blustered. "We didn't—"

The Chimera's weapon snapped into line with her head. "Don't. We saw you leaving the city, and we were listening to your comms. We know what you did."

"We thought it was a vaccine, not a new virus," Doc said. "The Chrona betrayed us, too."

The Chimera laughed. "Well, now you know what they're really like. They don't care about biological life. We're all the same to them."

"My turn," Doc said. "What are you going to do with us?"

"That's not for me to decide. Commander Tyris will determine your fate."

"When does he get here?" Samara asked.

The Chimera's helmet turned to look at her and they stared at one another for a handful of seconds. "Soon."

With that, her armor shimmered, and she vanished into thin air once more.

CHAPTER 17

A plan. Clayton's mind spun around endlessly searching for one. "We need to take inventory. See what supplies we have left." He walked over to Keera's hoverbike and began pulling items out of the cargo compartment and gathering them on the ground beside it.

Keera stood to one side, leaning hard on her good leg while Clayton consolidated their equipment. A canteen, full. A bed roll, a tent. One medkit. A poncho. Two laser rifles. A Stinger pistol. A dozen spare charge packs, eight for the rifles. Two each for the sidearms. Clayton's own sidearm, a plasma pistol, down to half charge with just five shots left. Two meal bars, both plainly packaged, and obviously smuggled out of the city from a Kyron dispensary. A knife. A spear made from another knife with a sturdy metal pipe for a handle. A Kyron solar lantern.

"It's not much," Keera said. "We lost your equipment with the bike."

Clayton shrugged. "I've survived in the

Wastes with less." That much was true.

Keera suddenly tensed up. Her head turned one way, then the other, both of her cranial stalks swiveling independently as she did so.

"What is it?" Clayton whispered.

"There's a Chimera nearby."

Clayton grabbed one of the rifles and slid the safety off. Staying low, he kept the damaged hoverbike at his back and quickly scanned their surroundings. Rusting cars, clumps of grass, and chunks of concrete covered the ground all the way out to the highway. There were plenty of places for someone to hide. "Where?" he whispered.

Rather than answer him, Keera drew her sidearm and crept over to the hoverbike. She swiped away the error messages and checked the sensor display. A single purple dot indicated the Chimera's position. It was in the same direction that Zack the Reaper had escaped, around the far corner of the parking garage. Was this the one the Reapers had captured? If so, how did it get here? Maybe Clayton had read the situation wrong. It was possible that they hadn't captured a Chimera at all. Maybe it had been watching the Reapers on the overpass without them even knowing that it was there.

Clayton stepped around the back of the bike, taking the lead. He held the rifle at the ready and flicked the fire-mode selector pin to *stun.* If they could capture that Chimera, they might be able to learn something useful from it.

He reached the far corner of the parking garage and stopped there. Connecting his ARCs to the scope, he poked the rifle around the corner to check for signs of their quarry.

Nothing. But there was one obvious cover position in view. An old container truck, the container-part of which had rusted straight through in several places. The Chimera could be hiding in the back, or behind the truck. If they stepped out of cover, they'd be easy targets.

Keera brushed by him, limping as she went.

"Wait!" Clayton whispered sharply. He reached for her arm to pull her back, but she was already out of reach.

"She's tied up," Keera said, not even bothering to whisper.

"What? How do you know that?"

Clayton waited a few seconds, not daring to follow until he saw that no one was firing on Keera. Maybe she was right, but that still didn't explain how she knew that the other Chimera wasn't a threat.

He darted out of cover, moving fast and low to catch up. "Hey. Are you going to explain yourself?"

Keera just looked at him. She appeared to hesitate. "Not now."

They rounded the back of the container truck to see a hoverbike parked and hovering there. Clayton's spirits soared with that discovery. The vehicle had been modified with a flatbed in the back. And the Chimera they were tracking was chained up in the farthest corner of it. A bright red piece of cloth had been tied around her mouth as a gag, and her head was swollen and discolored with bruises. Her brow and bottom lip were split, her nose crooked and bloodied.

"She's been beaten," Keera said, her voice thick with disgust. She limped to the back of the vehicle with the other woman's eyes watching her the whole way.

"Why'd the Reaper leave her here?" Clayton wondered aloud. They'd obviously wanted this Chimera alive for a reason, but after going to all the trouble of taking her as a hostage, Zack had fled and left her behind.

"This bike would have been too slow," Keera suggested.

Clayton noticed how the vehicle was sagging to one side, unbalanced with the flatbed and the Chimera's weight. A long, straight metal pole with counter-weights had been affixed to the front to keep it from flipping over.

Keera reached the other woman and removed her gag.

"Thank you," she said in a croaking voice.

"What is your name?" Keera asked.

"Ava," she said.

"I'm Keera, and this is Clayton." She jerked a thumb to him.

Clayton glanced about nervously. "We need to leave. That Reaper could be on his way back with reinforcements by now."

Keera caught his eye with a nod. "I agree. Maybe you should go get our supplies."

Clayton hesitated, watching Ava for a second, but she was chained up so she didn't pose a threat to them. He took off at a run and came back a few minutes later with both rifles, the stinger pistol, and an armful of their survival gear. He dumped it all in the back of the flatbed in the opposite corner from the captive Chimera.

Keera was busy talking to the other woman in low tones, but he couldn't hear any of what passed between them. He ran back for the rest of their gear and then returned and dropped it beside the first load. None of it was secured, so it would shift around as the bike flew. Clayton looked for a way to tie it down and noticed that the bike's original cargo compartment was covered by the flat bed. Upon closer examination, he saw that there was a hatch in the floor.

Grabbing a folding metal handle, he tugged, and the floor came away to reveal the bike's cargo area chock full of the Reaper's gear.

Clayton pulled it all out as fast as he could: a sleeping bag, a coil of rope, a jacket, a lunch kit, a bottle of water, a few rusty knives, a Kyron solar lantern, and a pack that likely contained personal effects. He also found spare charge packs, but left them where they were.

Clayton worked fast to pack all of the weapons into the compartment. The spear that had been clipped to the side of Keera's bike wouldn't fit, so he used the rope to tie it to the pole and counter-weight at the front of the bike.

By the time he was done, the clock on his ARCs read: 10:56 AM. *One hour to go before the Kyra's fleet arrives.* Getting off Earth before that happened was looking more and more unlikely, but it was still possible that Sutton had managed to find a ship in New Dallas. They had to make it back to Phoenix Base before midday, or else there was a chance that Clayton's family would leave without him.

"Ready to go?" he asked Keera, interrupting the ongoing conversation between her and the other Chimera. *What have they been talking about?* Clayton wondered.

Keera came over and pulled him aside. "She says she knows where we can find a ship."

Clayton's eyebrows shot up. "How do you know she's telling the truth?"

Keera appeared to hesitate. She glanced back at Ava, then leaned in and whispered, "Because I can read her thoughts."

"You can do what?"

"Shhh. I'd like to keep that to myself if you don't mind."

"How?" Clayton whispered.

"It's a long story."

Clayton pulled her even farther from Ava so they could be more certain that she wasn't listening. "Give me the short version."

Keera explained that telepathy was an ability some Kyra were born with. It supposedly meant that they were descendants of a royal line and it all but guaranteed their rise to power. As far as Keera knew, no Chimeras were telepaths except for her. It was how she'd risen to the rank of Admiral.

"It could be something to do with how you were conceived," he said. "You're also the only Chimera to ever be born to a Human. Maybe your conception was engineered rather than accidental as we thought." Her mother, Lori, had discovered she was pregnant on the trip back from Trappist-1. That was after being exposed to the Chimeran virus, but maybe it wasn't that simple. They'd also had at least two Kyra stowaways on board the *Forerunner*. Those aliens had conducted experiments on him during his sleep. He'd put those visitations down to night terrors, but in reality they'd been scanning his mind while he slept, learning about the human race. It was possible that Keera was the result of another experiment that they'd been conducting on board.

"It's possible," Keera agreed.

"So where's the ship?"

"The Reapers have it," Keera said.

"You're joking."

"I wish I were. They were planning to get Ava to fly it. That's why they captured her instead of killing her."

"Then why did the surviving Reaper leave Ava behind?"

Keera shook her head. "Like I said, he probably thought we'd catch up with him if he took the slower vehicle. He wasn't willing to risk his life to get the pilot back."

"Maybe," Clayton agreed. "But that means we have something they need. They'll definitely be coming for us now."

"They also have something we need," Keera added. "That means we can't go back yet."

Clayton frowned. "Even if this is all true, we don't have time. The Kyra will be here with their fleet in less than an hour."

"We could fly a ship back to Phoenix base in a matter of minutes. That gives us at least half an hour to steal it. Besides, the Kyra won't be able to get in position immediately. Once they drop out of FTL it will take several more hours to set up their blockade. We still have time. And this ship has a cloaking shield."

Clayton scratched at his beard. "I thought

Kyron sensors can see through cloaking shields."

Keera shook her head. "Nothing can see through cloaking shields unless you know where to look with active sensors. For passive sensors to work, a cloaked ship needs to be under active thrust. So as soon as we reach escape velocity, we cut the engines and engage the cloak, and we'll vanish. This is our best shot to escape. We have to take it."

"Does she know where the Reapers are?"

"No."

Clayton blew out a breath and shook his head. "What if Sergeant Sutton finds a ship in Dallas?"

"The odds of that are slim to none."

"And what do you think are the odds that we'll be able to find the Reapers' base and steal a ship out from under their noses?" Clayton countered.

"It's your call, Captain. What do you want to do?"

He took a minute to consider the question. "Where do we look first?"

It was Keera's turn to think. Her brow furrowed, and her cranial stalks twitched. Her eyes widened. "I think I might know."

Clayton nodded. "Go on."

"If they have a ship and they're looking for a pilot, then they can't be far from New San Antonio. The Kyron Guard wouldn't have landed a ship in the middle of nowhere, so that transport the Reapers found is probably sitting in the city's garrison, or even landed on top of the Ascension Center. The Reapers wouldn't want to let something that valuable out of their sight."

Clayton frowned. "They said Chimeras detonated a bomb in the city."

"Something must have survived. Remember Kyra ships have reinforced hulls. The transport might have even been shielded at the time. It could have survived the blast."

"True. All right, we'd better get going."

"What about Ava?" Keera asked, her gaze sweeping to the flatbed on the back of the Reaper hoverbike.

Clayton shrugged. "We take her with us. Abandoning her out here without any weapons would be as good as killing her ourselves." Clayton glanced at the time on his ARCs once more. *11:08 AM.* "Let's go," he prompted, and they both headed for the bike, their footsteps crunching in the patchy, debris-strewn grass. He winced as the movement provoked a fresh wave of pain from the shrapnel wounds in his back.

"You need to do something about those injuries," Keera said.

"We don't have time," Clayton replied.

"There's no time for you to faint in the middle of the next fight either."

Clayton stifled a sigh. "Okay. Make it fast."

Keera nodded and went to get their medical supplies from the back of the flatbed. She came over with Regenex and painkillers. "Strip to the waist and lie down," she said, nodding to a clump of grass in front of him.

Clayton unzipped the top half of his jumpsuit and gingerly pulled his arms out of the sleeves. He lay down on his stomach, and Keera set to work, picking a few of the larger bits of shrapnel out by hand, and digging for the others with a set of tweezers he hadn't seen her carrying.

"Damn it, Keera!"

"Don't be such a *sikun*."

"A what?"

"Nevermind."

He heard her spraying his wounds with Regenex, then heard them fizzing and felt them growing numb as the nanites did their job. Then came the muted sting of a painkiller being injected.

"Couldn't you have given me the painkiller *before* you started digging shrapnel out?"

"It's not fast acting, but it will keep you from succumbing to the pain later on. All done," she declared. "It's the best I can do in a hurry."

Clayton eased off the ground and zipped his jumpsuit back up without so much as a wince. He was already feeling a lot better.

Striding over to the hoverbike, he climbed on behind the control bars and Keera jumped in the flatbed with Ava. She shuffled over to examine the chains that bound the other Chimera.

Clayton watched them over his shoulder with a frown. "Are you sure releasing her is a good idea?"

Keera grabbed the Stinger pistol and fired it into the chains. They broke and fell to the flatbed with a clatter.

"We're going to need all the help we can get," Keera explained, and handed the Stinger pistol to the other woman. Ava reached hesitantly for it with a furrowed brow. "We can trust her," Keera added.

Clayton understood. She was relying on her telepathy to warn them if Ava tried anything. He nodded, then looked away. "Brace yourselves," he warned, and then twisted the throttle and jetted up and away from the ruined shopping center. The wind flooded through his long, sweaty hair, reminding him that he'd forgotten to retrieve his helmet before taking off. He hunkered down behind the windshield of the bike to shield his eyes from the wind. At least it would be cooler this way. A brief thrill of exhilaration ran through him.

A grim smile twitched at the corners of his mouth as he remembered countless trips like this one, scouring the Wastes for food and survival gear that he could use to keep Rosie and Nova alive.

Clayton peered up at the pale blue sky, a thin haze of smoke from the war that had raged through the night now clouding and dimming the sun. He imagined the vast immensity of space beyond, and the perilous voyage that still awaited them even if they succeeded in escaping Earth. Finding the Reaper's stolen transport and commandeering it for themselves was just the beginning. Flying that ship to a safe and habitable world would be far more difficult.

One problem at a time, Clayton chided himself. At least now he had a plan.

CHAPTER 18

Nova waded out of the water under cover of the trees growing along the shore. She headed for the sliding glass doors in the walk-out basement below the first floor. The windows had been boarded up in places where they were broken, but a few still remained intact, giving a view to the shadowy interior of the basement. Nova crouched behind the thick trunk of a cedar tree and peeked around the side, taking a moment to catch her breath from the long, cold swim around the house.

She was dripping wet, her clothes heavy with water, her skin itching where they clung. Once her breathing slowed, Nova took a moment to listen for signs of trouble—but she only heard birds chirping from the trees, frogs croaking in the rushes along the water, and cicadas buzzing in the midday sun.

Steeling herself, Nova gauged the distance to the basement doors. Maybe fifteen feet. She could cover that in a couple seconds. Glancing up, she shaded her eyes against the sun and scanned the length of the wraparound deck on the first floor. The railings were clear. Assuming the basement itself was empty, this was her chance. Nova grabbed the hilt of the hunting knife on her belt and drew it in a white-knuckled grip.

Time to move.

She burst out of cover, staying low and making long strides rather than running in order to keep her footfalls quiet. She reached one of the boarded-up windows and peeked around it to a sliding glass door. The view through the dirty glass was hazy at best. Nova curved her hands into binoculars against the glass, shading her eyes from the glare of ambient light.

She saw the dim outlines of benches lined with spare charge packs and various types of weapons. No sign of anyone down there. No guards, no prisoners. It was almost too good to be true. Was this a trap? Or maybe they thought they'd already captured everyone, so they weren't guarding against a counter attack.

Nova ducked back behind the wooden boards covering the broken window where she stood. She worried her lower lip and glanced around, her eyes darting for signs of Chimeras watching her. But as far as she could tell, no one was sheltered in the long grass or hiding behind the trees. And if they were, what were they waiting for? Now was as good a time as any to pick her off with a rifle.

Her heart slamming in her chest, Nova gritted her teeth, and sucked in a deep breath. She had to risk it.

She dashed around to the sliding glass door and tugged at it. The door ground open noisily on a dirty rail. A pure shot of adrenaline jolted through her system and she flew through the opening, heading for the nearest table full of guns. She reached the counter top, sheathed her knife, and grabbed an automatic laser rifle. Her fingers seized around cold metal. It was an older model, but it would do.

She flicked the selector switch from safety-on to kill, and checked the hazy red number that glowed to life just below the holographic sights. It read 14/30. Less than half a full charge pack. Also good enough. If she couldn't take out these Chimeras with fourteen shots, she almost certainly wouldn't live long enough to fire a fifteenth.

Whirling away from the bench, she scanned the basement one last time, found it empty, and then started for the stairs.

She put her foot to the first step, and froze. Had she just felt something brush her back?

Then it came again, jabbing sharply this time. A weapon barrel.

"Where's the other girl?" a deep female voice asked.

Nova swayed on her feet as all the blood drained from her head to her legs, her body automatically preparing to make a run for it. She swallowed hard and forced herself not to give into the temptation to do just that, or to spin around and make a play for the Chimera's weapon. "What girl?"

"Your sister. There's no need to play dumb with me. I saw you outside with your mother, walking that mutt."

"Her name is Rosie and she'd better be alive," Nova said through gritted teeth.

"Relax, I only stunned her. Now answer the question." Another sharp jab landed between Nova's shoulder blades and drew a wince and a gasp from her lips. "Set your weapon down. Now."

Nova did as she was told, despair sweeping through her as she did so. She should have waited and done more surveillance. Her gut instinct had been right. This had been a trap. Of course Chimeras wouldn't leave the armory in the basement unguarded.

* * *

The wind was a deafening roar in Clayton's ears as he flew along the old I-10, heading west to New San Antonio. The highway was a river of broken asphalt undulating gently beneath them and littered with smashed cars, trucks, and cargo haulers. He kept to an altitude of about twenty feet to avoid all the debris, pulling up to crest the occasional overpass. His bike's sensors showed no signs of Zack the Reaper. Clayton couldn't hope to spot him with his naked eye. But he took that for a good thing—it meant they weren't visible to Zack, either. They were almost certainly going to be outnumbered at the Reaper's base, so they needed to stay hidden until the last possible moment.

Just a few moments later, a jagged line of skyscrapers came marching over the horizon, followed by the city's perimeter wall. He gaped at the sight. Zack and Terry had said that Chimeras blew up the city in the early hours of the morning, but nothing could be further from the truth. Everything looked perfectly normal. At least, from a distance it did, but he knew the city would be teeming with Dregs from the Chrona's virus.

A muffled exclamation came from the back of the hoverbike at the edge of Clayton's hearing. Probably Keera or Ava remarking on the same thing he'd just noticed.

As they drew near to the city walls, the city's Ascension Center appeared, nestled between two taller skyscrapers. It was the same as the one in New Houston: a giant windowless black dome rising to fifteen stories with four pillars soaring up to support a flat landing pad at the top. He couldn't see what, if anything, was landed up there without ascending to an altitude that would make them a conspicuous target for any Reapers watching the horizon. Instead, he dropped even lower to skim over the fields of wheat and corn and grazing cattle that encircled the city. As he passed over a cattle ranch, he noticed the glowing red lines of a razorbeam fence designed to keep Dregs out, followed by a more conventional fence to keep the cattle from slicing themselves to pieces on the laser fence.

They reached the wall and Clayton slowed right down, trying to decide how to proceed. The gates of New San Antonio were shut. For all he knew, the city had escaped infection with the Chrona's virus. But there weren't any guards on the wall, and no one shot at them as they approached. A quick look at his bike's sensors revealed the same thing: no life signs. But if the residents of the city had all turned to Dregs, then they were just hiding inside to avoid the sun. He wouldn't want to be around at dusk to see what happened when they all came crawling out.

"What are you waiting for?" Keera asked quietly.

With the wind no longer roaring in his ears, he heard her clearly. Glancing over his shoulder, he met her crimson gaze. "Just making sure we're not flying into an active occupation zone."

Keera shook her head. "The Reapers are the

only ones who will be out in the open right now."

Clayton nodded. "Hang on." He pulled up and twisted the throttle to fly over the walls. A street lined with ten and twenty-story apartment buildings appeared on the other side. It was deserted. Somehow he'd expected to find it covered in debris and dead bodies from the fighting the night before. Yet, there were no signs of any kind of battle. As he'd suspected, the fighting had centered on New Houston. Here the devastation would be limited to whatever mess the former inhabitants had made as they lost their minds and turned into vicious blood-thirsty monsters.

Clayton flew slowly down the street, keeping an eye on the sensors. The only sign that anything was amiss was the fact that it was the middle of the day and the city was eerily quiet. No pedestrians, no automated Rydes cruising the streets, and no Chimeran bikes or troop transports. It was a perfect ghost town.

"The Reapers lucked out," Clayton said. "Not a single sign of resistance anywhere." Clayton kept his eyes on the landing platform at the top of the city's Ascension Center. It was to the right, about two blocks away. "Hold on tight. I'm going to fly up to the roof of one of these buildings," Clayton said.

He checked the bike's side view display to see both Keera and Ava holding tight to the sides of the flatbed. Clayton pulled up, and turned down the alley between two buildings on his left to spiral up and around so he wouldn't have to climb too steeply—it would also help to shield them from view of the Ascension Center, which was the most likely place that Reapers might have found a Kyron transport.

Apartment windows and glass doors flashed by as he went; some of the windows were broken, the jagged shards glinting in the sun. Others were left open with curtains billowing ominously in the wind. No sign of Dregs, but they would be hiding deeper in the building to avoid the light of day—hunkering together in hallways, bathrooms, and closets.

The bike crested the roof of the building, and Clayton flew to the stairwell and set down behind it. He jumped off the bike and stretched out his aching legs and back. Keera and Ava stood up and climbed over the tailgate while Clayton walked around and opened the storage compartment at the back of the bike. He pulled out his rifle and went to the edge of the roof that faced the Ascension Center. Up here they were at about the same height as the landing platform, but Clayton couldn't see any ships landed there.

Propping his rifle on the low wall running around the edge of the roof, Clayton bent to peer through the scope and played with the roller switch to set the zoom level. It took a moment to find the landing pad, but as before, he could see that it was empty.

"Anything?" Keera asked from beside him.

Clayton pulled away from the scope with a sigh. "No."

He heard footsteps approaching and turned to see Ava. He watched her with a frown. She held the Stinger pistol in a loose grip, relaxed at her side as she approached. But her eyes were wary and never left his. Her cranial stalks twitched furiously, and there was a bright sheen of sweat on her chalk-white face. She was afraid. It took him a moment to realize that she was afraid of *him*. It was strange to think of a Chimeran soldier being scared. He'd always thought of them as cold, unfeeling, and stolid—as if the process of turning had somehow stripped them of all emotion. Maybe he was just as guilty of racial prejudice as anyone else.

Clayton deliberately softened his expression and nodded to Ava. She gave a tight smile and looked away, glancing around the rooftop.

"We should check the Garrison," Keera said. "They have a landing field for transports to pick up and drop off soldiers, but it's on the ground. We'll have to approach it carefully to avoid being seen."

Clayton nodded. His ARCs read 11:52 AM. They had just a few minutes before the Kyron fleet was set to arrive. He started back toward the bike.

"Wait!" Ava hissed. "Look!"

Clayton turned around, squinting against the glare of the sun to see Ava pointing to the landing pad at the top of the Ascension Center. Something strange had appeared up there. A dark gray rectangle *floating* in the air. It was the open door of a cloaked ship, the interior visible despite the active cloaking shield on the exterior hull. Flickers of movement appeared within the opening, and a pair of tiny human shapes jumped down and fanned out along the roof. A moment later, the familiar black wedge of a hoverbike streaked up and landed there. The pilot jumped off. A glint of sunlight reflecting off a rifle's scope was their only warning.

"Get down!" Keera warned.

They flattened themselves to the roof just as a bright green laser bolt flashed between them, dazzling their eyes. Clayton lay with his cheek pressed to the hot concrete roof, his nostrils itching with the sharp tang of ozone from ionized air.

"They spotted us," Ava said.

"No shit," Clayton replied.

CHAPTER 19

"**T**urn around. Slowly," the female Chimera standing behind Nova said.

Again, Nova did as she was told—and came face to face with a soldier in matte black armor holding a long-barreled sidearm. A Stinger pistol. The Chimera's features were perfectly hidden by the helmet. Nova almost would have preferred the nightmarish visage of an alien hybrid to this faceless mask.

"Where is your sister," the woman asked again.

"I don't have a sister. I'm an orphan."

That quip earned her a blow to the gut from the butt of the woman's rifle. Nova doubled over in pain, gasping soundlessly for air. She tried to stumble in the Chimera's direction, using her incapacity as a guise to make a grab for the soldier's weapon.

But the Chimera backed up quickly and flipped the weapon around again. Pity. Nova winced as her diaphragm recovered enough to let in a painful whisper of air.

"Last chance to talk," the soldier warned.

Nova straightened and lifted her chin with a defiant grin.

And then she saw it. Dora creeping up behind the Chimera with a heavy rock in her hands. Nova froze, trying not to let her reaction show. But the soldier was already twisting toward Dora, her weapon sweeping out of line...

Nova didn't waste her chance. She whirled away, ducked, and swept up her rifle in the span of a heartbeat. The soldier realized her mistake and brought her weapon back into line—

Just as Nova pulled the trigger.

A bright flash of emerald light snapped out and hit the woman in her right shoulder. The weapon dropped from her hands with a noisy clatter, and a muffled cry escaped her helmet as she staggered back a step. Then Dora arrived with the rock. She slammed it into the back of the woman's helmet, staggering the soldier the other way. Nova fired again, this time hitting the woman in her side, just below the ribs. She went down with a heavy *clack* of refractive armor hitting the bare concrete floor of the basement. Dora screamed, heaving her rock in the air above the woman's head. The Chimera held up the hand on her uninjured side, feebly trying to block the assault.

"Wait!" Nova cried.

Dora froze, confusion flashing across her face. She took a few steps back and dropped the rock, her eyes wide with horror at what she'd been about to do.

Nova hefted her rifle at the woman. "Take off your helmet."

The Chimera's hands came up slowly, and she twisted it off, revealing the bald, bony features of the enemy. Her cranial stalks were drooping, and her face was contorted in agony.

"What did you do with my mom," Dora asked in a shaky voice.

The Chimera glanced at her, then back. "They're all upstairs."

"And the rest of your team?" Nova asked.

The woman shook her head and spoke in a low, rasping voice choked with pain. "Just one. I sent him back... to report to our Commander."

Nova's eyes narrowed swiftly. She wondered whether she could trust anything this woman said.

"We didn't hurt anyone. I'm still alive. Let me treat my wounds, and I'll leave you alone."

"And then you'll come back with reinforcements," Nova said. "I don't think so. Dora, get a gun. Watch her. I'm going to see if there are any others upstairs."

Dora nodded quickly and ran to the nearest bench full of weapons.

"If there were others, don't you think they

would have heard your rifle going off?" the Chimera asked. "I'm alone. But I won't be for long. Reinforcements will be coming whether you let me go or not."

"What's your point?" Nova demanded.

"My point is, you need to keep me alive, and I'm going to die if you don't let me treat my wounds."

Nova narrowed her eyes on the Chimeran woman. Dora came back from the bench with a plasma pistol. She stopped in front of the enemy and held the weapon in shaking hands. Nova strode over to her, and kicked the Chimera's pistol out of reach along the way. Switching her rifle to a one-handed grip, she kept the Chimera covered and took Dora's pistol with her other hand.

"The safety's on," Nova said through a snort.

"Oh," Dora said.

"Keep your finger outside the trigger guard. Like this." She turned the pistol side-on so Dora could see. Her sister nodded, and Nova handed the gun back.

"How long before your reinforcements arrive?" Nova asked.

The Chimera coughed up a clot of black blood and let out a rattling breath. "Not long."

Again, Nova wasn't sure she could trust anything the Chimera said, but it would be wise to hurry all the same. "Keep her covered, and don't get any closer, do you understand?" Dora nodded quickly, but her eyes were wide and glassy with shock. Nova hesitated. Leaving Dora alone down here was a bad idea. "You know what, I have a better idea." She flicked her rifle to stun and aimed it at the Chimera's head.

"Wait!" the woman said, throwing up her good hand to shield her face.

Nova pulled the trigger, and the stun bolt hit straight between her eyes. The Chimera fell over backward, her whole body skipping and bucking with involuntary spasms as bright blue electrical impulses arced and flickered over her.

"That's for stunning my dog," Nova said.

* * *

Clayton was hunkered down with Keera and Ava behind the low wall that ran around the roof. Another laser zipped by, above their heads, hitting the rim of the wall with a loud *crack* as super-heated concrete exploded and sent pulverized shards flying out in all directions. Bits and pieces rained down all around them. Clayton cursed through the ringing in his ears and connected his ARCs to the scope of his rifle before popping the weapon out of cover and maneuvering it to get a look at the roof of the Ascension Center.

He zoomed out, then in on two men lying prone along the edge of the landing platform.

He was about to line up a shot on one of them when he noticed that the hoverbike they'd seen fly up there a moment ago was now nowhere to be seen.

"What do you see?" Keera whispered.

"The bike is missing," Clayton said.

Keera's brow furrowed in confusion.

"They're coming after us," he explained. "At least one. Maybe two." His gaze snapped to the stairwell and their modified hoverbike landed beside it. "We have to go. They'll be here any second."

"Wait," Keera said.

He arched an eyebrow at her.

"If we get on the bike, they'll just follow us and shoot us down," Keera said. "And we still need to steal that ship."

"So what do you suggest?"

"We lure them into the building and take them out."

Clayton's gaped at her. "There must be hundreds of Dregs in there!"

Keera nodded. "If we're lucky they'll kill the Reapers for us."

Clayton heard the approaching *whirr* of a hoverbike's engine. They were out of time.

"Fine. Stay down! Those snipers are still watching us from the landing pad."

Keera nodded and the three of them scurried out of cover, crouching low and running for the stairwell. A laser bolt zipped by, hot and close—followed by another.

And then Clayton reached the shelter of the stairwell. He stood behind the door with Keera and Ava, neither of whom appeared to be hurt. So far so good. He faced the rusty metal door that barred the stairs and pushed the barrel of his rifle against the seam between the door and the jam. Clayton pulled the trigger, and something *popped.* He grabbed the door handle and gave it a sharp tug. The door burst open, revealing a darkened stairwell winding down. The whirring roar of the Reaper's hoverbike was almost upon them.

"Let's go!" Clayton whispered, ushering the others down ahead of him.

He shot a rueful look at the hoverbike with all of their other gear in the cargo compartment. They'd be sorry they left it behind if the Reapers simply came, stole the bike back, and then left.

A flicker of movement caught Clayton's eye, and then another hoverbike came sailing over the top of the stairwell. He snapped off a quick shot with his rifle—missed, and then pulled the door shut with a resounding *bang.* With no lock to hold it, it bounced back open, leaving a gap of a few inches.

"Let's go!" Clayton whispered to the others, and the three of them began jogging down the stairs. The whirring sound of the Reaper's bike rose and fell as it circled the rooftop. Clayton stopped on the nearest landing with one ear cocked and listening. Then the sounds died to an idling whisper, and he heard voices: two men shouting to each other on the roof. Next came footsteps, approaching fast.

"Go, go, go," Clayton said.

Keera's plan was working. He belatedly realized *why* as he flew down the stairs, holding to the banister and jumping halfway down to the next landing. The Reapers were here because they needed a pilot—either Ava or Keera would do.

Which means I'm expendable, Clayton realized.

The door at the top of the landing banged open, and a familiar voice shouted down to them:

"Stop yer runnin'! We can all fly outta here together, just like you said. We don't need to fight!" It was Zack again.

And at the sound of his indiscreet shouting came another type of shout: the shrieking roars of Dregs waking up. Hundreds of them.

"Keep going!" Clayton cried as he jumped past Keera and Ava to the next landing.

CHAPTER 20

Footsteps thundered down the stairwell after them. "Hey, wait up! We just wanna talk!" Zack called.

But Clayton kept running. It felt like the echoing shrieks and roars came from everywhere. Dregs were waking up all throughout the building.

A flash of light tore down from above, and the concrete wall beside Clayton exploded with superheated fragments.

"We have to get out of the stairs!" Clayton shouted.

A door banged open somewhere above them, and the shrieking roars of the Dregs grew suddenly louder.

Clayton stopped briefly and leaned toward the railings to peer in the direction of those sounds.

"Shit!" Zack cried.

Another laser bolt flashed out. A Dreg's screams died abruptly, and it toppled over the railing, falling twenty floors straight down. Its head *clanged* on metal railings a few times.

Emerald fire flashed out steadily from above.

"Leave 'em! We gotta go!" someone else said.

"Fuck!" Zack cried.

And then the sounds of laser fire receded, along with the collective shrieking of Dregs.

Clayton exchanged a wide-eyed look with Keera and placed a finger to his lips. The sound of boots beating on concrete stairs rose ever higher and farther from hearing—then they heard the metal door at the top of the stairwell bang open once more, and the sounds of the horde and periodic laser fire of the retreating Reapers faded into near silence.

"They drew them off," Clayton whispered. He took a couple of slow, careful steps back up to the previous landing.

"What are you doing?" Keera hissed.

He didn't reply. Better not to risk making any more noise. From the landing above he glimpsed the door the Dregs had opened, two flights up on the next level. He could shut that door, but then the Dregs who were on the roof might keep on heading down the stairs rather than go back to whatever holes they'd crawled out of.

Clayton hurried back down to Keera and Ava. Both watched him, waiting for him to explain himself. But now wasn't the time for that. He waved to them over his shoulder and kept on down the stairs. Keera nodded, understanding the need for quiet. Once Zack and his partner took off, the Dregs would give up. Their thirst for blood would be enough to overcome their aversion to sunlight, but only for a few seconds. After that, they'd head back down the stairs and return to bed.

Clayton thought about all the equipment they'd left behind on their stolen bike. His throat began to ache for water. Even their canteens were on the bike. He swallowed painfully, his tongue scraping the roof of his mouth like sandpaper. The water in the city would all be contaminated. It might be a while before he could get a drink.

A few seconds later, the distant sounds of Dregs hissing and muttering to each other came echoing down the stairs. They were coming back inside.

Clayton picked up the pace, hurrying down two more flights. The stairwell was growing progressively darker—apparently the power was out in New San Antonio just like it was in New Houston. One of the only signs that there'd been any fighting at all here last night. None of them dared to turn on the tac lights attached to their rifles. Not with those Dregs still filing down the stairs above them. The slightest flash of light would catch their sensitive eyes, and then it would be game over.

The air was thick and hot inside the close confines of the stairs. Their footfalls were almost perfectly silent, but their breathing had grown swiftly louder in volume and pitch as they exerted themselves. Clayton could only hope that the Dregs were making enough noise to drown out any sounds they were making. His feet touched another landing—

And a sharp hiss filled the air. Clayton froze and whipped his rifle up. A flash of green eyes appeared beneath his sights, lying close along the floor in the corner beside the door on this level. It took a moment for his brain to catch up.

A cat. Either a stray or an illegal pet.

Clayton's heart hammered in his chest, his lungs filled to bursting with a stale breath that he had yet to release.

The cat hissed again, then gave a loud meow and padded toward them. He watched it walk between his legs, rubbing its side and back on him, its tail erect and flicking the air. Another loud *meow!* It was probably hungry.

He shot a quick look back up the way they'd come. No sign of Dregs coming down to investigate the noise.

"Get rid of it," Ava breathed.

Clayton turned to her with narrowed eyes. "How? Shoot it?"

"Snap its neck," Ava suggested.

Another *meow!* came from the animal, as if

in protest, as it rubbed itself on his other leg.

Clayton's guts churned with a revulsion at the Chimera's suggestion. He had to remind himself that Chimeras had all started out as indoctrinated human children who'd never been allowed to have pets. They'd been taught that cats and dogs were vermin. Several generations of humans, brutalized by Kyra teachings.

"Let's just keep going," Clayton muttered. "She'll leave us alone eventually."

"Wait—" Keera said suddenly.

He turned to see her staring back the way they'd come. As he watched, she leaned over the railing and peered up through the center of the stairwell. It was too dark for him to see anything but the faintest outlines of stairs and railings rising above them. But Keera's eyes and ears were both much more sensitive than his.

She looked away suddenly, her crimson eyes big and gleaming in the dark. "They're coming," she breathed.

"I don't see..."

"Run!" she hissed. Not waiting for him to react, she flew down the next flight of stairs, colliding with the wall in her hurry to escape. Ava ran after her, and that was when Clayton heard them: a horde of Dregs, now snarling and hissing and slapping the stairs with countless footfalls. In the next instant, his eyes registered a flicker of movement—just one floor up.

The Dregs hadn't lost their trail, they'd been quietly and cleverly stalking their prey.

Clayton jolted into motion, flying down after Keera and Ava. The cat hissed and streaked down beside him, quickly outrunning all three of them. And that put him at the top of the Dregs' menu.

Tossing a glance over his shoulder, Clayton caught a glimpse of the nearest Dreg: eyes gleaming and teeth shining in the gloom. It was only one flight away.

"We have to get out of the stairwell!" Clayton called down to Keera before she reached the next level. She didn't reply, but tore open the door and held it for him and Ava.

The cat bounded through first, then Ava. Clayton leaped off the bottom stair and let his momentum carry him through. Keera went next, and pulled the door shut behind them.

Before she could even release the handle, it twisted in her grip and the door began to open. Keera threw her weight against the door, holding it shut. Dregs shrieked and clawed at the other side, bouncing the door open and closed in its frame. Clayton jammed his rifle into the gap between the door and jam and fired a shot into the horde. The shrieks grew momentarily louder, and the door slammed shut as Dregs scattered from the laser blast. The reprieve lasted only for a moment, and then they were back.

"We can't stay here!" Clayton whispered sharply.

"If I let go, they'll tear us apart!"

A new sound reached Clayton's ears. A door clicking open in the hall where they now found themselves. Someone coming out of their apartment. Clayton whirled around to see a group of three Dregs standing there in a pale wedge of light spilling from the open door. One adult and two children, all of them fully clothed, almost civilized-looking. A low hiss sounded from the adult, and then both children dropped to their hands and feet.

A blinding laser bolt shot out and hit the first kid before it could take a single step. Ava appeared, standing beside him with her pistol in a two-handed grip. Clayton took aim and fired at the second kid. Both of them dropped to the carpeted hallway in a muted *thump*. The adult Dreg screamed and sprinted toward them. A third shot from Ava dropped the creature and sent it sprawling. And then more doors began clicking open, one after another. "Keera now! We have to go!" Clayton cried.

She released the door and it burst open, Dregs falling on each other in the hallway, kicking and clawing to be the first to sink their teeth into fresh meat.

Clayton and Ava ran for the open door with Keera right on their heels. A scurrying wall of pale shadows and gleaming eyes appeared. The nearest ones were all neighbors of the family Clayton and Ava had just gunned down. Not daring to slow down, Clayton sprayed the corridor with pulsing green fire until his weapon clicked dry and a sharp hiss of steam escaped from the coolant vents. A wave of Dregs fell under that onslaught, and others cringed away, buying them precious seconds to reach the open door. And then they were through, and Keera pulled the door shut behind them. This time, she flicked the deadbolt into place with a manual lever, and planted her back against the door for good measure. The Dregs arrived and began thumping and scratching on the other side, but the door appeared to be holding.

Clayton planted his hands on his knees and bowed his head as a wave of dizziness swept over him. Ava sank to the floor. All three of them gasped loudly for air in the short hallway leading to a messy living room and kitchen. The windows looking out were all set to their most opaque setting and barely letting in any sunlight. The family living here would have developed a strong aversion to the light before they finished changing. Clayton cringed with the memory of shooting that kid. He had to remind himself that they weren't human anymore. Barely even self-aware.

"Now what?" Ava asked. She jerked her chin to where Keera still stood, bracing the door. It shuddered violently behind her with periodic impacts, as if the Dregs were trying to batter it down by throwing themselves against it.

Clayton straightened with a grimace and cast about the apartment, checking for signs of any more Dregs hiding within.

"This door won't hold them forever," Keera warned.

"It's the only exit," Clayton said.

A loud *meow* issued from the floor, and he spotted the cat, now seeing it fully in the pale light pouring through the living room windows. It had blue-gray fur and bright yellow eyes.

Clayton smiled ruefully as it rubbed up against his legs first one way, then the other, meowing piteously for food. *We're not going to eat, we're going to be eaten,* he thought grimly. He looked up from the animal, and checked over the furniture in the room, trying to decide how best to arrange it into barriers that would help block the door and create a kind of *pillbox* from which they could fire safely on any Dregs that broke through.

"What about the balcony?" Ava asked.

"What balcony?" Clayton replied.

Rather than explain, she hurried to the picture windows on the far side of the living room, and pulled one of them open, revealing that it was actually a sliding glass door. Blinding sunlight poured in as the polarized glass slid away. A narrow balcony appeared on the other side.

"We could climb down from one balcony to the next," Ava suggested.

"With what rope?" Clayton countered.

"Sheets?" she suggested.

"That'll get us down one floor. What about the next? And there'll be Dregs in each and every apartment we climb down to, so we can't keep repeating the same strategy. Worse yet, it wouldn't take much for them to break through those sliding glass doors to reach us."

"Do you have a better idea?" Ava demanded, squinting at him as her sensitive eyes adjusted to the light now gushing into the apartment.

Clayton glanced back to Keera. Even she was wincing against the glare, and she was wearing auto-polarizing contacts to protect her eyes. But the Dregs had no such protection. "We need to break all the windows," Clayton said. "Let's flood this place with light."

CHAPTER 21

Samara heard the muffled sounds of raised voices coming from the basement. She picked out Nova's voice. And that Chimeran soldier's. A sharp stab of dread went through her chest, and her eyes burned with hot, angry tears that never fell. She strained her ears to listen, but didn't hear Dora. Maybe she was still safe.

"They should have stayed away," Widow said with a rueful shake of her head.

Others frowned and grimaced or averted their eyes. Things were going from bad to worse. This was Phoenix, a militant resistance cell that had fought for years against the Chimeras and the Kyra. Now they'd become prisoners of the very Chimeras they'd fought, and it was hard not to imagine what horrors awaited them.

What had possessed Dora and Nova to run headlong into danger? How could they possibly have thought they could get the upper hand on professional soldiers?

The muffled reports of a weapon firing shot

through Samara's consciousness like lightning bolts. She heard a *thud* and more muffled voices. It sounded like Nova talking. And... Dora! The third voice was Chimeran.

"I don't believe it..." Widow muttered.

A third shot rang out, and Samara flinched.

"It's okay," Doc said quietly. "That was a stun bolt."

Footsteps came thumping on the stairs, rising steadily. More than one set. Confusion creased Samara's brow. She twisted around to look at the door to the stairs, receiving a mild shock from her stun cords in the process.

The door to the basement creaked open, and both Nova and Dora came running out.

Relief crashed over Samara like a wave, and for more reasons than one: Dora still looked healthy; there were no signs of her turning, and by now she should have been showing symptoms of some kind. Tears that Samara had been holding back burst free like a flood from a dam breaking. Nova and Dora ran into the middle of the living room, both of them holding weapons, their eyes tracking warily through the room.

"I don't believe there's anyone else here," Doc said. "There were only two. The other one left to report back."

"Better cut us free fast before that changes," Widow put in, jerking her chin to indicate the front door behind Samara. "Reinforcements could be here any minute."

Nova nodded quickly and let her rifle dangle from the shoulder strap. She drew a wicked-looking hunting knife and hurried over to Doc. Sergeant Sutton had left the Asian doctor in charge. Samara was surprised that Nova had remembered that. She struggled with the knife to cut the stun cords binding Doc's wrists. Electric shocks sparked and popped, drawing a grimace from his lips. Nova flinched as she received her own shock. "Damn it!"

"Don't touch me," Doc said. "The handle of the knife is insulated. Just cut as fast as you can."

Nova nodded and stepped back in to work on the stun cords again. It took a few seconds, all the while with Doc gritting his teeth and trying not to scream.

"You're going to knock him out!" Richard said.

"I can take it!" Doc replied.

His bonds snapped with a final *pop!* And fell sparking to the floor. He grabbed the knife from Nova and then deftly sliced the cords that bound his ankles, receiving only a mild shock this time. That done, he went to Widow next.

Samara caught Dora's eye while she waited for her turn. "Maybe you girls should go let Rosie out." The dog's whining and scratching at the bedroom door was still going on in the background.

Nova straightened suddenly, as if only now remembering her beloved pet. She took off at a run. Dora tore after her a second later.

"Wait!" Doc called out. "Where's the Chimera?"

"Stunned in the basement!" Nova shouted back.

Widow jumped up as soon as she was free and ran for the stairs to the basement.

Doc continued around the room, freeing people in order of priority—Pyro, Harold, and Preacher. He deliberately skipped over Richard.

"Hey, what about me?" Richard complained.

Doc gave no comment, but Samara understood why. He hadn't prioritized her, either. He was first freeing the people who would be more useful in a fight, and Richard had proved time and again that he was a coward who would run at the first sign of trouble.

"Now what?" Harold asked as he ran hands through his short red hair and scratched furiously at his nose and scraggly beard, taking advantage of the fact that he finally had his hands free to scratch all of the maddening itches that must have been accumulating.

"We arm ourselves and get out before the rest of them get here," Doc said as he finally set to work on Richard's restraints.

The sound of claws skittering on rough wooden floors drew everyone's attention to a sleek black blur tearing down the hallway past the kitchen. Rosie launched herself into the air and bounded over the couch where Doc had been sitting with Preacher. She was a bundle of nervous energy, barking and wiggling her way around the room, wagging her entire hind-quarters with her tail and fixing them with a giant grin and wild brown eyes. She'd been cooped up for far too long. Even the stun bolt she'd received couldn't dull that much pent-up energy. Samara smiled at the display.

Doc hurried over to Samara as everyone ran for the armory in the basement. "Ready?" he asked her.

Samara nodded, and he sliced the stun cords around her wrists with a single stroke. A sharp jolt went through her, but it only lasted for a split second before the flexible cords fell sparking to the floor. Samara noticed then that they weren't actually solid metal, only coated with a thin metallic mesh. The underlying material was filled with some kind of clear liquid gel that oozed out from the ragged ends of the freshly-cut bonds.

Doc cut the cords around her ankles next, and Samara stood up, rolling her shoulders to work out the tension from sitting perfectly still for so long. Nova and Dora came and gathered around her. Nova bent to pat Rosie on the head and scratch her behind the ears, while Dora wrapped an arm around her waist in a hug that felt both affectionate and needy at the same time.

Doc watched her for a moment, his eyes hard. Then he appeared to notice her bandage, and he grabbed her arm, holding it out. "You're bleeding."

"I am?" Dora asked, blinking in shock at the horseshoe-shaped marks that had soaked through her bandage—a clearly defined bite, marked in blood.

"That should be impossible," Doc said. "By now the Regenex and Synthskin should have done their job and you should be good as new."

Samara chewed her lip, fretting over what that might mean, and also over the possibility that Doc might learn about Dora.

His gaze found Samara's. "I think it might be time that we told the others what we're dealing with, don't you?" He released Dora's arm and straightened to regard Samara steadily.

Samara felt like a hot stake had just gone through her heart. "You know."

Doc nodded. "Lori told me before she left. She asked me to keep an eye on Dora."

Dora looked confused, but Nova was clearly nervous, her eyes darting back and forth between them and the stairs where the others had gone.

"What does he know?" Dora asked, revealing that she had conveniently blocked out the significance of her injury and the type of Dreg that had inflicted it.

"We can't tell them," Samara pleaded. "Please. She's not showing symptoms. She can't be contagious."

"No? And how do I know that? She could be asymptomatic and still be contagious."

"Please. I'll make sure she's careful not to share drinks or anything. Just give me more time. If she's not showing symptoms yet, it might be because she's immune. The others will overreact if they find out. Especially Widow."

Doc gave an unhappy frown. "Fine, but the instant she starts to feel bad, I expect you to tell me, or I will make sure that both of you are exiled from this group. Do you understand me?"

Samara nodded quickly. "I promise I'll let you know the minute anything changes."

"Good. In that case, follow me," Doc said, and he turned and headed for the stairs. "We need to hurry."

Rosie barked once, loudly, as if to voice her agreement, then pranced eagerly after him.

"What was he talking about?" Dora asked, looking up at Samara.

She shook her head and smiled. "It's nothing to worry about."

"I'm infected, aren't I," Dora said, revealing that she wasn't as oblivious as she'd seemed.

"No, but you should be, and we don't know why you aren't. That's a good thing."

"It is?" Dora asked.

"Yes, because it gives us hope. The first vaccine was developed with Lori's help, because she was immune to the original virus. Maybe we can develop a new vaccine one day with your help."

Dora smiled. "I'd like that."

"Me, too," Samara said. "Now come on. We'd better go arm ourselves in case those Chimeras come back."

As Samara hurried after Doc with both girls, she noticed the deadly plasma pistol dangling from Dora's hand. She reached for it carefully and said, "Let me take that."

Dora shot her a look of wounded pride, but let her take the weapon. "I need a gun," she said by way of protest.

"You've never handled one before," Samara argued as she carefully engaged the safety on the weapon.

"I just did! Besides, neither have you," Dora replied.

She made a good point.

They arrived at the door to the basement stairs and ran down together. Upon reaching the basement landing, Samara saw the Chimeran woman lying on the floor, her helmet off and cast to one side. Two crusty patches on her armor indicated where she'd taken laser bolts to the torso. Samara looked away with a grimace to see that everyone was already busy arming themselves, clicking charge packs into rifles, holstering knives and sidearms. Clipping on utility belts.

Samara joined Doc at the nearest table. He glanced briefly at her before handing over a belt and holster for the plasma pistol she'd taken from Dora. He grabbed a rifle for himself and stuffed his pockets with spare charge packs. Dora eyed the weapons eagerly, but kept her hands to herself. Harold and Preacher went over to the Chimera and stared at her.

"What do we do with her?" Harold asked, looking to Doc.

"Get her up. We might need a hostage to negotiate with if we run into trouble on our way out of here."

Both men nodded and bent to the task. Samara looked away. Doc came over carrying a short-handled spear with a sturdy-looking blade tied to the end of a metal pipe. He handed it to Dora. "Here, take this."

She accepted it with a smile.

Samara walked down the line of tables, passing over weapons and looking for other types of equipment. She grabbed a Kyron solar lantern and a canteen, clipping both to her belt. She grabbed an extra canteen for Dora and passed it to her daughter. Nova grabbed one for herself. Finally, Samara found heavy packs stuffed with basic survival equipment at the end of the line of tables. She hefted one of those off the table, and abruptly sagged under its weight. Grunting, she looped the straps over her shoulders and winced as they dug in.

"All right everyone! Let's move out!" Doc said as he fitted a comms piece to his ear. Rather than head back up the stairs, he led the way out the sliding glass door in the basement. Samara passed through the opening behind Nova and Rosie with Dora close behind.

They stepped out into a sun-soaked field of grass and wildflowers and walked through the shadows of giant cedar and oak trees growing up alongside the house. Climbing a short hill, they rounded the old log mansion and came to the front entrance and garage. The hauler they'd left New Houston with last night was still sitting in the driveway. Doc and Widow led the way past the sagging front steps and around the front of the hauler to the garage. Behind them Preacher and Harold carried the Chimeran prisoner, stumbling and grunting as they struggled under her weight. Somehow they'd found the time to tie her ankles and wrists with thin black ropes.

Everyone else had their rifles up and sweeping for the slightest signs of trouble. Doc reached the open side of an old four-car garage and turned to stand guard at the entrance. "Two to a bike," he said as he waved the others through.

"What about the prisoner?" Harold asked as he and Preacher set her down with a noisy clatter of armor on the crumbling driveway. Both men were breathing hard, their brows beaded with sweat from the exertion.

Doc appeared to hesitate.

"We only have four bikes left," Widow pointed out, poking her head out from the garage. "There's nine of us, not counting the prisoner or the dog, and the bikes only have room for two."

"We could fit the two kids on the back of one," Doc replied.

"Or we could leave Richard," Widow replied, speaking through a thin smile.

Doc frowned. "We need to leave a lookout behind to tell Sutton and Clayton where we went when they return."

"Still doesn't solve the problem," Widow said. "Unless you're planning to strand them here on foot."

"Sutton's and Clayton's recon teams have one man to a bike. When they get here they can pick up the lookout."

"And the prisoner?" Harold prompted.

A rising *whirr* came rushing in at the edge of hearing. Everyone spun toward the sound just in time to see a pair of hoverbikes racing down the driveway, ablur with the speed of their approach.

"Too late!" Richard cried, his rifle snapping up to take aim on the incoming bikes.

CHAPTER 22

"**L**ower your weapon, you idiot!" Doc snapped.

Both hoverbikes whooshed to a stop in front of them, and familiar faces snapped into focus. Sergeant Sutton and Lori Reed jumped off the backs of their bikes.

"Doc, report!" Sutton cried, striding swiftly over to them. His gaze took in the Chimeran prisoner and the group's state of readiness in an instant, and he jerked his chin to Doc. "I see you ran into some trouble."

"We did. There's more of them on the way. They're the ones from the *Sovath*. We were just about to leave."

Sutton arched an eyebrow at that. "I see. Where's Captain Cross?" He looked around, deferring the question to the rest of the group.

"He's not back yet," Samara said quietly.

"We can't wait for them," Doc added.

"No, we can't," Sutton agreed. "All right, listen up everyone. We didn't find a ship, but we did find something else. And it's going to come in real handy now."

Doc cocked his head curiously, waiting for Sutton to elaborate.

"We're headed for greener pastures. Harold, Pyro, and Preacher, you're flying three of our six bikes."

"I can fly one, too," Nova put in.

Sutton looked her up and down, and the girl squared her shoulders. "You've flown a hoverbike before?"

"Yes, sir," Nova said.

"Well, then. In that case, you and your mother take one of the bikes. Lori and myself will fly two more. The last one will stay with Widow so she can catch up to us later." He looked to her.

"Catch up?" Widow asked.

"I need you to wait for the captain and the admiral to return. But keep your head down. Last thing we need is you getting picked up by Chimeras when they get here."

Widow nodded back. "I'll be a ghost, sir."

"Better be. Doc, Richard, Preacher—you'll be taking the hauler we rolled in on from the city last night."

"I thought you wanted me on a bike?" Preacher asked.

"Change of plans. I need someone reliable riding shotgun with Doc." He glanced quickly at Richard as he said that. "You'll take as many supplies as we can pack over the next five minutes, and the prisoner along with 'em. The bikes will fly out ahead and you'll rendezvous with us up north. The rally point is a straight shot along the I45 to New Dallas, about two-thirds of the way there. You'll come to a bridge over an old dried up river delta on the shore of a big lake. The highway isn't exactly clear the whole way out there, but the hauler should be able to bulldoze a path. If you get stuck, don't worry, we'll circle back to pick you up. Any questions?"

Doc raised a hand. "Just one. Where are we going?"

Sutton flashed a tight smile. "Our new home. A place called The Enclave. They've got walls to keep out the Dregs, and food enough to feed an army. Now let's move!" Sutton clapped his hands. "Double time! We push out in five."

Doc walked over to Sutton, shaking his head. "We should leave the hauler and just take the bikes. Forget the prisoner. We can't afford to be slowed down."

Sutton grabbed Doc's shoulder in a firm grip. "We might need her for negotiations. Besides, we can't pack all of our gear into the bikes, and it would be a damn shame to let it fall into Chimeran hands when they get here."

"How do you know they're not already here?" Samara asked as she walked over to them. "They could surprise us before we have a chance to get away."

"We got a good look at things from the air as we flew in," Sutton said. "No sign of Chimeras yet."

Lori joined their circle, nodding along with what the sergeant said. "We have time. Maybe not much, but a few minutes won't make a difference."

"Let's hope not," Doc added.

"Faster we pack, faster we can go," Sutton replied. "Let's get this hauler loaded up!"

* * *

The door still thundered with impacts as Dregs tried to claw and batter their way in. Clayton crouched behind a wall of sofas, beds, and overturned cabinets. They'd managed to pile the furniture from the apartment into a wall almost two meters high, leaving gaps to shoot out of. In addition to that, they'd broken all of the windows, letting in a warm breeze and more light than any Dreg would be able to stand for more than a few seconds.

It was the best they could do to fortify themselves, but so far the door was holding. Clayton flexed sweaty hands on his rifle, staring hard at the door, watching it shiver with each impact, and waiting to see some sign that Dregs were breaking through. Instead, he heard and saw the frequency of the impacts decrease, and then disappear altogether. Shuffling footsteps thudded off, and they heard doors slamming shut as the Dregs returned to their respective apartments—almost as if some remnant of their humanity remained.

Keera pulled back from the top of the couch she was aiming over, relaxing her guard. "Seems like they've given up," she said.

Clayton waited a few more seconds, blinking sweat from his eyes. But the attacks didn't return. He and Ava pulled away from the fortifications next. The three of them sat staring out the broken windows of the balcony, listening to the wind whistling through. They were about thirty floors up, so the gusts were loud and strong. Their feline friend sat on the back of a padded armchair, along the left side of their makeshift pillbox, her tail swishing and eyes fixed on the door. She'd given up begging for food, but that wouldn't last long.

"How are we going to get down?" Ava asked.

Clayton shrugged. "We wait a few more minutes and make a run for the stairs."

"It's already past midday," Keera pointed out.

Clayton grimaced, noticing the time in the corner of his ARCs. 12:25 PM. By now the Kyra had to have arrived with their reinforcing fleet. They'd be maneuvering into position to blockade the planet, and after that, escaping Earth in any kind of ship would be extremely dangerous.

"So that's it?" Ava asked. "We just give up

and leave?"

"No," Clayton replied. "There's no way we'll make it back on foot."

"We could find bikes at the city Garrison," Keera pointed out. "We don't have to steal them from Reapers."

Clayton looked to her. Her pale features and hairless scalp were slick with sweat from the stuffy heat inside the apartment, and the exertion of moving all the furniture around. "You're assuming the Reapers won't have found and commandeered those vehicles already."

Keera sighed. "We could steal a hauler from the city's waste management department."

"We could," Clayton agreed. "But the Reapers might see us leaving, and they'd catch up to us in seconds on their bikes."

"You're still thinking we should steal that ship," Keera said.

"I don't think we have a choice. Besides, even if we can't use it to escape Earth, a cloaked troop transport would be a hell of an asset, don't you think? Better we have it than Reapers."

"It's landed at the top of the Ascension Center," Keera said. "Looks like they're using the interior as a kind of shelter up there, so most of the Reapers will be inside the ship waiting for us. Making matters worse, the only way up there is the stairs or the elevators in the four support columns. Those will all be guarded."

"Okay, so we need a distraction to draw the Reapers out, and a way to sneak up to the landing platform."

"If we find hoverbikes, we could fly up there," Ava said.

Clayton looked to her. "*If* we find them, yes, but that's still not going to even the odds. We'll be outnumbered, and likely get picked off by those snipers before we even reach the landing platform."

"You have another idea?" Keera asked.

"I might. Who uses cloaking transports?" Clayton asked.

"Chimeran Commandos and Elites."

"And Elites wear aerial cloaking armor."

"Exosuits," Keera clarified.

Clayton nodded. "If we find a few suits of that armor, we'll be able to fly up to the landing platform and stay invisible at the same time. We could walk right past the Reapers and they'd never know it."

"That would give us a tactical edge," Keera replied. "But we don't know what happened to the soldiers that came in on that transport. They could be anywhere. For all we know they're still alive and they fled the city."

"Without their ship?" Clayton countered.

"He's right," Ava said. "They are either dead or turned to Dregs."

Clayton nodded. "And in the latter case, they would have removed their armor before they turned. If you're feeling deathly ill and vomiting every five minutes, you don't want to wind up wearing the contents of your stomach."

"So how do we find a bunch of empty exosuits?" Ava asked.

Clayton looked to Keera. "I was actually hoping you might have an idea. Shouldn't they have tracking IDs or some type of comms beacon for friend-foe identification?"

"Not if they're actively cloaked," Keera replied.

"But they won't be. Why would they keep the cloaking shields active after they took off their armor?"

"Good point," Keera replied. "Okay..." She ran a hand with long black claws along her sweaty brow and flung away several droplets of sweat. She swallowed visibly and nodded. "The city Garrison's operations center will have a tracking system for all friendly units. It should be able to pinpoint the locations of any idle exosuits—but that's assuming they're still powered on. If they're not, we won't detect anything at all."

"What if there isn't any power at the Garrison?" Clayton asked.

"They have backup power cores," Keera said.

"And the exosuits? How long do their power cores last?" Clayton asked. "Could one of them still be running if it had been left on all night?"

"Idle mode barely uses any power. Cloaking shields and active energy shields drain the most, so it's definitely possible that we could find something."

Clayton pushed off the floor, and winced as one of his calf muscles seized up in a cramp. He pointed his foot and massaged the stiff knot of muscle. Dehydration was setting in. He rapped the canteen on his belt with his knuckles and heard the hollow report of an empty container. "We should gather our strength first. This place must have something to eat and drink." He turned toward the kitchen, his eyes sizing up a gleaming black refrigerator.

"Not worth it. The water is infected, remember?" Keera said.

"The water is. Not the food. And we might just get lucky in the beverage department." He reached the fridge and pulled the door open. A weak gust of cool air spilled out, but the light didn't come on inside. He scanned the contents, eyes passing over containers of leftover food until he found a pair of reusable bottles of vitamin water. It was a common beverage in occupied cities, designed to enhance human fertility and keep the Kyra's breeding stock healthy. He grabbed one of the bottles off the shelf and quickly twisted off the cap, chugging down the contents. The flavor was vaguely acidic, like lemon water without sugar, but in that moment he could have sworn that nothing had ever tasted so sweet.

Belatedly remembering he wasn't the only one who was thirsty, he saved the last third of the bottle and turned to Keera and Ava. "Heads up," he said, and tossed the full bottle to Keera. She twisted it open and gulped as he had. He walked over to Ava with the remainder of the one he'd drunk from and held it out to her. She regarded him skeptically.

"How do I know you're not infected?" she asked.

"If I were, you'd know it by now."

"Not if you got infected *here,*" Ava said.

Clayton frowned. "We were careful about what we touched. Besides, the virus is transmitted through fluids, not the air or surfaces."

"This is a new strain," Ava added. "We don't know how catchy it is yet."

"You're in here with us. We're all in contact with the same elements."

Ava still didn't reach for the bottle.

Clayton shrugged and half raised the bottle to his lips. "Last chance."

Ava looked away and Clayton finished off the contents of the bottle. When it was empty, he tossed it aside and nodded to Keera. She was just finishing hers. "Ready to go?"

She dropped the bottle and rose to her feet. Clayton took that for her answer and headed around the wall of furniture for the door. He spared a glance at the cat. It meowed as he approached and stopped him in his tracks. They couldn't take her with them. They had no way to carry her and aim their weapons at the same time.

Thinking about the poor animal's fate, trapped in this building and surrounded by carnivorous beasts, he turned and went back to the fridge. Removing several likely looking containers, he checked the contents and laid out the ones with meat inside.

"Psst!" he called to the cat. She looked his way, tail swishing, and he lifted one of the containers for her to see. She got up lazily and stretched, as if she were doing *him* a favor, and then hopped down from the armchair and padded over slowly, meowing softly as she went.

Upon reaching the kitchen counter, the animal jumped up and her head dipped into the first container.

Ava walked over, looking weak and unsteady on her feet. "Is there anything else to drink in there?"

Clayton turned back to the fridge with a frown and made a more thorough examination. There was a jug of water, but that wasn't worth the risk. There was also a pitcher of what looked like orange juice. The Kyra didn't waste time cultivating more than the basic necessities, so it wouldn't be actual fruit juice. More vitamin water, prepared from powder. He pulled it out. "It might not be safe. Unless they prepared it before the Chrona infected the city reservoir."

Keera shook her head. "With how fast the symptoms started in Houston, I'd guess they had the virus on a timed release. If they prepared it last night, it's infected, but if they prepared it before that, it should be fine."

Ava hesitated, her eyes darting between them. She looked at the pitcher, and licked her lips with a black tongue. "No. Let's go. We'll stop at a dispensary."

"Good call," Clayton said, and set the pitcher down on the counter beside the food he'd laid out for the cat. He headed for the door again, this time making it all the way around their fortifications. When he reached the door, he saw the state of it and let out a low whistle. The door was made of metal, but the frame was made of wood, and the beams around the lock were splintering. A few more good blows and it would have burst open.

"We got lucky," he whispered, glancing back at the others. Keera nodded, but neither woman said anything. They needed to be as quiet as possible from here on out. Clayton kept his rifle in a one-handed grip as he reached for the deadbolt with his off hand. He turned the lock, and the door popped open without even needing to turn the handle. The hinges squealed in protest and sunlight flooded the darkened hall. He eyed the widening gap, his heart beating hard in anticipation. If the corridor wasn't clear...

The door opened all the way, and he stepped out, checking both ways. Not a Dreg in sight. He signaled to the others over his shoulder, and soon they were padding softly down the hall to the stairs.

They reached the open stairwell and Clayton covered Keera and Ava from the door, watching their backs as they went in. Once they were through, he considered closing the stairwell door behind them, but the thought of that cat in the apartment gave him pause. If they left the doors open for her, at least she'd have a chance to escape.

Leaving the stairwell open, Clayton turned and hastened down into utter darkness with the others. He had to hold to the railing to keep from tripping, and even so he nearly tumbled down more than a few times. Their footsteps cascaded with muted echoes that may as well have been cannonades. The entire building was teeming with Dregs. All it would take was for one to wake up and hear them...

They raced down flight after flight of stairs until Clayton's legs were shaking and his lungs burning for air. Keera was leading the way now, her eyes more suited to the darkness than his. A dense, festering stench rose from the depths below, and Clayton heard Keera and Ava suddenly halt their progress. Clayton ran straight into one of them before he could stop himself. He heard Ava grunt in protest.

"What is it?" Clayton whispered, struggling to see through the gloom.

The stale heat inside the stairwell didn't help with that smell. Clayton brought his sleeve up in an attempt to shield his nose.

"It smells like rotting meat," Keera whispered, leaning over the railing to peer down to the lower levels.

"Maybe garbage?" Clayton suggested.

"No." He heard Keera sniffing the air with long, deep inhalations. "I smell blood. And it's still fresh."

"We need to get out of here," Ava added.

A loud snort rose to their ears, followed by a sharp, muttering hiss.

Keera looked to Clayton. The only thing he could see was her eyes—a faint gleam in the dark. No one said anything this time. They dared not even to breathe. Footsteps sounded below, rising slowly, just a few flights down. Another hiss rattled out of the darkness, followed by a snort. At least one Dreg. It had caught their scent. Clayton lifted his rifle to his shoulder and felt around with his forefinger for the selector switch above the trigger guard.

He set the weapon to *Stealth* mode for a silent kill and then stepped past Keera and Ava. Peering down the weapon's adaptive night-vision scope, he aimed through the fuzzy green darkness, waiting for the Dreg to reveal itself at the bottom of the nearest flight of stairs.

A quiet *pinging* of aging springs caught his ear and he glanced away to see the door beside him slowly sweeping open to the muted light of the hall. A flash of crimson eyes and a low growl were his only warning before something leaped through the door. He pulled the trigger and an invisible laser cut the beast down at his feet.

But it didn't die. It shrieked and screamed and thrashed, gouging out deep furrows in the cement landing with its claws.

The one sneaking up from below gave an answering cry. And then those calls were echoed dozens of times over throughout the building, coming from several different floors at once.

"Run! We're almost there!" Keera cried. She flew down past him with her rifle up and tracking. The Dreg below came bounding into view and she shot it between the eyes. It fell with a *thud* and Clayton leaped over the fallen body as he jumped from the third stair to the next landing.

Ava and Keera led the way. Footsteps and shrieking roars sounded from above, approaching fast and breathing hard.

They hit the final landing and Keera tore open the door. Light poured in from the ground-level lobby, and Clayton saw the source of the rotten smell. A pair of humans lay at the bottom of the stairs, half-eaten, with jutting bones glistening white where they'd been picked clean by Dregs. The Dreg who'd fallen from higher up had landed on top of them, practically exploding from the force of the impact.

Clayton skidded through a congealing pool of blood and flew out of the darkened stairwell. He slammed the door behind him as he followed Keera and Ava to the shining river of light that was the street beyond the apartment. They burst through the glass doors and emerged into the midday sun, gasping for air and stumbling around on the pavement. Clayton glanced back and saw the stairwell door thrown open as the Dregs reached it. He glimpsed a clambering mass of bone-white arms and legs: pale, dirty faces, red eyes and flashing white teeth. They shrieked and recoiled from the flood of light that entered the stairwell before scurrying away from the open doorway.

Clayton sucked in a ragged breath and straightened. "We'd better not still be here when dusk falls."

"Second that," Keera said, squinting and

holding a hand to her brow to shield her eyes from the glare.

"Which way to the Garrison?" Ava asked.

Keera took a moment to get her bearings, then pointed up the street in the direction of the Ascension Center. They couldn't see the landing platform from here, but one of the support columns and the edge of the dome was visible, peeking out from behind a building at the end of the street two blocks up.

"It'll be close to the Ascension Center, but we need to watch our approach to avoid being seen by Reapers." Keera led them under the eaves of a nearby Kyron dispensary. Ava cupped her hands around her eyes and peered through the window. "Looks empty," she said. "I'll be right back." Ava went to the sliding glass doors and pried them open.

Clayton was about to follow her as she slipped through the gap, but Keera stopped him with a slight shake of her head. "We'll wait for you out here," she said.

Clayton stood under the eaves with Keera, waiting for Ava to pass out of earshot. After a few seconds, he decided to risk it. "Still think we can trust her?"

Keera glanced at him. "For now."

"That sounds like a *no* to me."

"She's from the *Sovath*. Everyone in her unit died, except for her. She doesn't seem to know that some of the crew survived. If she finds out... she might try to join them."

"You got all that from her thoughts?"

Keera nodded slowly. "That, and she thinks you smell bad."

Clayton's eyebrows shot up, and a wry smile touched his lips. "Yeah, well she's not exactly a bouquet of roses herself."

Keera looked away, up to the far end of the street. Bathing was the least of their worries right now, though their stench probably didn't help to hide them from Dregs. If all went according to plan, they'd be back at Phoenix base in a couple of hours. Clayton imagined going for a swim in that lake behind the house, Rosie barking as she ran splashing in, and Nova swimming laps along the shore. He wondered if Dora even knew how to swim. When would she have had a chance to learn? He doubted the Chimeras taught kids how to swim, and there weren't exactly any rec centers in the cities. Hopefully soon he'd have a chance to teach her.

Ava slipped back out carrying an armful of flavored vitamin waters. "Here," she said, passing the bottles around. "Fill your canteens."

Clayton nodded, accepting two bottles from her. "Thank you."

Ava nodded back, her red eyes boring into his without so much as a hint of a smile. As he poured the first bottle into his canteen, Clayton thought over what Keera had said about Ava, that she was from the *Sovath*. Phoenix was directly responsible for the Chrona's attack. The Chrona had brought down the destroyer that this woman had called home. How many of her friends had been killed in the fighting last night? If Ava learned what they'd done and who they were—members of a resistance cell —she would probably shoot them both.

Keera tossed two empty bottles aside and replaced the cap on her canteen. Clayton did the same and nodded to her. "You know the way better than I do."

"Right," Keera replied, then turned and started up the street, being careful to stay as close to the adjacent buildings as possible. Clayton trailed behind, bringing up the rear so he could keep an eye on Ava. Of all the ways to die out here, getting shot in the back by a supposed ally would have to be one of the stupidest.

CHAPTER 23

"**A**re you sure you know how to fly this thing?" Samara asked as she climbed on the hoverbike behind Nova.

"My dad taught me," Nova replied, her voice muffled by the helmet she wore. The armory didn't have enough helmets left for everyone, so only the hoverbike pilots wore them.

Samara nodded and wrapped her arms around Nova's skinny waist. She still couldn't believe that this girl was now her stepdaughter.

Glancing to her left, she saw Dora on the back of Lori's bike. "You hold on tight, okay?"

Dora flashed a mischievous grin and wrapped her arms around Lori's waist as she'd seen her mother do. Riding on the back of one of these bikes must seem like a thrill ride to her.

Samara peeked around Nova to the back of the hauler. Rosie was riding in there along with the prisoner and Richard. Between him and the dog, they were supposed to keep that Chimera from trying anything stupid when she woke up. Her hands and ankles were bound, and she was still badly injured despite Doc's hasty attempts to dress and clean her laser burns. But even bound and injured, that Chimera could still be a threat. For one thing, they'd dumped all of their weapons and other gear from the house in the back along with her, so someone had to make sure she didn't get her hands on a weapon. Samara wasn't sure that Richard was the best choice for that job, but at least they could count on Rosie.

A comms unit crackled to life in Samara's ear and Sutton's booming baritone came through with surprising depth and volume: "All units on me, loose wedge formation with a five meter spread as long as we're in the open. Stay sharp. We could still run into Chimeras on the way out."

Sutton's bike began gliding forward, swiftly picking up speed. The hauler kicked into drive and spat out a wave of gravel and dust from its rear wheels, accelerating faster than Samara would have thought possible for such a heavy vehicle. She imagined Rosie sliding around in the back, claws skittering.

Lori, Harold, and Pyro jetted by the hauler with a sharply rising and falling *whirr* of their bike's engines. Dust and pebbles settled in their wake, and all of the vehicles vanished around a bend in the tree-lined driveway.

Nova made no move to follow.

"Is everything okay?" Samara asked.

"Just reminding myself where the brakes are. Are you ready, Sam?"

"You forgot where the brakes are?!" Samara cried.

Rather than reply, Nova hit the throttle and rocketed after the others at top speed. Samara felt her hands slipping from the girl's waist, her inertia threatening to yank her off the back of the bike. "Slow down!" she shouted to be heard above the wind now roaring in her ears.

But she doubted Nova heard anything through her helmet.

"I'm going to fall off!" Samara shouted into the wind.

At that, Nova did slow down, but it wasn't because Samara had asked her to. The hauler had appeared at the end of the driveway up ahead, making a wide turn onto the street, and Nova had to slow down to make the corner.

They banked hard, leaning into the turn at forty-five degrees. Samara watched the broken pavement blurring by within just a few feet of her nose and squeezed her thighs as hard as she could to stay rooted on the back of the bike. Up ahead, the other four hoverbikes were nothing but receding specks at the end of the street. Nova accelerated again, jetting after them.

She pulled alongside Lori's bike, and then backed off the throttle to keep them even. Dora spared a hand from Lori's waist to wave. She had a huge grin on her face. "This is so *spectral!*"

Samara fixed her daughter with a dark look. "Hold on with both hands!"

Lori's helmet turned a few degrees, and she reached around and grabbed Dora's hand, planting it firmly around her waist again.

Thank you! Samara mouthed, but Lori's eyes were on the road. They hit another bend and banked hard, leaning the other way this time. Samara struggled to hold on and keep her lunch of venison and corn down.

A few seconds later they'd reached the end of the rural streets and the highway appeared in front of them. They jetted onto it, zipping over old broken-down cars and past a solitary tank with the boxy barrel of a rail gun mounted on its turret. They flew down the crumbling highway, blurring past an endless stream of ruin.

Samara's comms crackled with Sutton's voice once more. "I'm going to get some altitude and see if I can get eyes on the enemy. Everyone else stay down."

A stream of clicking sounds came back over the comms along with a solitary, "Copy that," from Doc.

The sergeant's bike angled up sharply, clawing into the clear blue sky and receding from view until it was no bigger than a gnat.

Moments later Sutton's voice came over the comms and his bike swooped back down. "We're clear out to about twenty klicks. Past that, it looks like we have an army marching this way on foot."

"You think they might have spotted you?" Doc answered.

"Doubt it. I was only up for a few seconds. Popped up and down like a periscope."

"Well, they have at least one other hover-bike besides the one they came in on, so we need to be careful."

They hadn't found the vehicle that the Chimeran prisoner had used to get to their base, but it was a reasonable assumption that she hadn't come on foot.

"From here on, we stay off the comms unless it's strictly necessary," Sutton said. "Can't be sure they're secure."

More clicks sounded through the comms piece in Samara's ear. She glanced over her shoulder, squinting against the wind whipping around the bike, and saw the hauler vanishing into the distance behind them. It stuck to the center of the road, weaving around obstacles. Just then she saw it slow down to push through a wall of rusty cars with no clear path between. The shrieking roar of metal on metal on pavement was like thunder even from this distance.

At least the Chimeras were far enough away that they wouldn't hear anything, even with their sensitive ears. Samara's gaze lingered, and her thoughts turned to Clayton. He still hadn't returned, which meant they must have run into trouble out there. She could only hope that he was on his way back by now and that he would beat the Chimeras to Phoenix base.

She turned back around and swallowed past a growing knot in her throat. She refused to think the worst. Last time she'd done that, she'd spent a decade mourning and wallowing in grief over a dead husband who had actually been alive. Clayton still had a lot to answer for. He could have at least found a way to let her know he was alive. Especially since he'd been in contact with Harold all that time.

Samara pushed those thoughts away. She set her mind on their destination instead. Sutton hadn't explained anything about this *Enclave* other than that it was supposedly safe and had plenty of food for everyone. She just hoped it would live up to those expectations. Who were the people that lived there, and why were they so willing to let a group of strangers in? Especially armed militants like Phoenix. Samara had a bad feeling about where they were going. She resolved to ask Sutton more about the Enclave as soon as they reached the rendezvous.

CHAPTER 24

The Garrison was a cement-walled compound two blocks down from the Ascension Center. Clayton stood in the shadows of an opposing alley with Keera and Ava. No sign of Reapers or Dregs in the street, but a scattering of dead bodies, soldiers and civilians alike, spoke of a struggle last night. None of the dead Chimeras looked to be wearing the characteristically dull black cloaking armor or exosuits that they were looking for.

"What's our move?" Clayton asked. He'd let Keera take the lead at this point, because she would know her way around the Garrison better than he.

Keera peered down the scope of her laser rifle and aimed it at the top of the Ascension Center.

"We'll have to move quickly to avoid drawing fire from the Reapers up there," Keera said as she lowered her rifle.

"Can you see them?" Ava asked.

"No, but that doesn't mean they won't see

us."

Clayton scanned the painted black walls of the city Garrison, looking for a way in. The gates were shut, and the walls had to be at least twenty feet high. Too smooth to climb. "Any ideas about how we get in?" he asked.

"Over there." Keera pointed to a plain black metal door that served as a pedestrian entrance beside one of the guard towers that flanked the main gates. "We can shoot through the lock like we did with the top of the stairwell in that apartment building. Ready?" Keera asked.

They both nodded.

Keera darted out of cover, crouching and running at the same time. Clayton and Ava both ran behind her, keeping their footsteps as quiet as they could. Wounds stabbed and ached in his back as he went, reminding him of his injuries. Feeling the hair on the back of his neck prickle, his gaze snapped up to the landing platform at the top of the Ascension Center. He saw the dark, square edges of it, but no sign of Reapers aiming down. They reached the door beside the gate tower and Keera's rifle snapped up. She fired soundlessly into the locking mechanism, her weapon set to stealth mode. She tugged hard on the door and it popped free with a groan of rusty hinges, revealing a narrow cement corridor that cut though the base of the wall to the other side.

Keera led them through to a parking and landing area. The landing pads were empty, but several large, six-wheeled black troop transports sat in front of the main building, their sides sloping at sharp angles, laser turrets mounted on top. In here, there weren't any dead bodies like they'd seen out on the street.

Clayton peered up at the Garrison building: a big black edifice with no windows that rose fully eight stories. It hid them from view of the Ascension Center, so they didn't need to worry about Reapers picking them off.

The roof of the Garrison likely also had landing pads, but Clayton didn't see any ships sitting up there. Then again, he'd barely *seen* the one at the top of the Ascension Center, either.

Keera cut across the parking lot, heading for the main building.

"Wait," Clayton said, whispering sharply.

Keera turned.

Rather than explain, he turned and jogged the other way, heading for the four big circles of landing lights that he'd assumed were for aerial transports. Stepping gingerly into the first circle, he slowed down and began feeling around with one palm raised. In his other, he held his rifle, ready for the first sign of trouble.

"What are you doing?" Ava asked, sounding exasperated.

"Reapers found a cloaked transport, but

maybe it's not the only one," Clayton explained. He wasn't really expecting to find anything. But if they did, it would eliminate the almost impossible task of stealing that ship from the Reapers.

He stumbled his way through the first landing pad like a mime trying to find his way out of an invisible box. The next two were the same.

By the time he reached the final landing pad, he'd all but given up hope. He was just going through the motions, ruling out even the remotest chance.

And then his foot *clanged* into something, and he went sprawling to his hands and knees. Keera and Ava ran over to see what he'd found just as he jumped back up, his jaw slack with anticipation. Feeling around carefully with both palms, he encountered the smooth, cold surface of a cloaked vehicle. Keera and Ava joined him in feeling around, but they wound up swiping empty air. Their faces collectively fell as they realized what it was, but Clayton recovered with a tight smile.

"It's not a ship," he said.

"It's an exosuit," Keera added.

"I guess we won't have to go inside the Garrison looking for them, after all," Clayton added.

"But why is it just standing here, sealed up and actively cloaking?" Ava asked. "It should be powered down, or at least be standing open after the pilot abandoned it."

"Not if the pilot was afraid that someone might steal his armor after he got out," Keera said. She joined Clayton beside the invisible suit, feeling around for some type of activation switch or touch panel that only she knew to look for. He stepped back and watched, keeping a wary guard with his rifle.

Keera touched something, and a sudden *whirr* of clicking metal joints sounded. The invisible armor shimmered and peeled open, revealing a darkly padded interior.

"There's only one suit," Ava pointed out. "Who's going to use it?"

"There might be more than one," Keera replied. She ducked out of her rifle's strap and passed it to Clayton as she stepped into the armor. A moment later, the suit folded up around her, and she vanished into thin air. Ava glanced at Clayton, her brow tense with suspicion.

"Don't worry. She's not going anywhere without me," Clayton said as he looped the strap of Keera's weapon over his head and slung it across his back.

"You seem pretty sure about that," Ava replied.

The air shimmered once more, and the suit re-appeared standing there like a statue carved from obsidian. The statue came to life as Keera took a few plodding steps. She tested integrated weapons in the arms—laser barrels folding out of gauntlets, and racks of anti-personnel rockets rose out of her shoulders.

"The core is down to five percent power. It won't last more than ten minutes with the cloak engaged—less if I'm moving around and shooting while I'm cloaked."

"What about flight time?" Ava asked, nodding to the roof of the Garrison to indicate the Ascension Center beyond that. "You'll have to fly up to the landing pad."

"Five minutes," Keera replied. "But it won't take more than thirty seconds to reach the landing pad."

"From here it'll take more than that," Ava countered.

"I can walk to the base of the building first."

"We're wasting time and power talking about this," Clayton said. "Keera, can you do this on your own?"

"She doesn't have to. Check the sensors," Ava suggested. "If there are any other exosuits powered on around here, you should be able to detect them."

"I already checked. Not a blip," Keera replied.

"There could be more suits inside the Garrison. In the armory," Ava suggested. "Power down to save the charge and we can all take a look."

"There could be hundreds of Dregs in there," Keera pointed out, shaking her head. "It's too risky."

"So is sending one soldier to attack a numerically superior force," Ava replied.

"I will be invisible. That's all the advantage I need."

Clayton raised both hands for silence. "Enough." The two Chimeran women looked at him, Keera's expression inscrutable behind her helmet. "Go," he said. "We'll wait here for you. You can land the transport here and pick us up when you're done."

"With Reapers chasing her on their bikes?" Ava asked.

"I'll keep the cloak engaged. They won't know where I went. But you two had better stay out of sight."

Clayton nodded.

"See you soon," Keera added.

Not bothering to cloak herself again, she took off at a jog, her boots clanging on the pavement as she ran for the tunnel entrance they'd passed through a moment ago. She vanished inside the narrow corridor, her footfalls receding into silence.

The door in the wall gave a rusty shriek, and Ava let out a noisy breath. "When she leaves us here, you're going to wish you hadn't been so naive."

"What makes you so sure that she'll leave

us behind?" Clayton asked.

"Because she's a traitor and a coward."

Clayton's eyebrows shot up. He knew about Keera's past, but he was surprised that Ava did. Keera used to be the admiral of Earth's occupying fleet; she'd gone AWOL to resurrect her mother, Lori, through an illegal cloning and memory transfer process. But that had been more than ten years ago.

"You knew her."

Ava nodded. "I did."

"Then you should know that she's not the kind of commander who leaves her soldiers behind."

Ava cracked a grim smile at that. "Tell that to the fifty thousand soldiers she left behind on Talos Four."

Clayton frowned. "What are you talking about?"

"Before she became an admiral, Keera Reed was a *Protomark* in the Guard. She led several successful campaigns against the Chrona. Until we were sent to take back Talos Four. After a week of heavy losses, our fleet pulled out. We were being hounded by a superior force, cut off with no chance for retreat and no hope for extraction. Then we took back an old Kyra hangar and found an assault shuttle with a cloaking shield. She told us we weren't going to use it, that we'd fight to the death if we had to. But that night she and three of her lieutenants stole the transport and left us behind. Soon after that, our entire division was slaughtered."

Clayton gaped at her. "If that's true, then how did you escape?"

Ava's smile grew thin and brittle. "I didn't." She reached up and pulled down the zipper of her uniform, revealing her bare torso underneath. He blinked in shock at the sight of her naked breasts, but Ava didn't appear bothered by it. His eyes tracked down to a puckered mass of scar tissue over her left side.

"I went down with everyone else and woke up some time later, covered in blood and piss, buried under a pile of fifty men. A few hours later, Keera came back with a destroyer she'd stolen from a nearby shipyard. She had the dumb luck and timing to arrive just after the Chronan fleet jumped out. Uncontested, she flew over the battlefield, and decimated the Chronan army. Then she landed and picked up the handful of survivors who'd made it through the night. And for that, she was awarded a promotion, transferred to fleet command and promoted to Captain."

Clayton took a moment to consolidate his thoughts. He was only getting one side of the story, and it sounded like Keera hadn't really run from the battle. She'd snuck off to get reinforcements. There had probably been a good reason that she hadn't told her army where she'd gone and why.

But rather than say all of that, he inclined his head to the enraged woman standing half-naked in front of him. Her red eyes blazed and cranial stalks twitched in agitation. She'd obviously lost people she'd cared about in that battle. "I get it, but maybe you should give her a chance to explain."

"She *had* that chance years ago," Ava replied, zipping her uniform back up.

"Well, trust me. I've known her since she was a child. She's not going to leave us here," Clayton added.

"No, she's not," Ava replied, turning away from him and stalking toward the Garrison. "Because this time, I'm not going to give her the chance."

Clayton hurried after her. "Where are you going?" he asked, whispering as they approached the reinforced metal doors. He'd just noticed that one of them was ajar.

"I'm going to look for another exosuit," Ava said.

"Keera could be back here any minute," Clayton pointed out. "We shouldn't risk it." He grabbed Ava's arm to pull her back as they came within reach of the doors, but she jerked free of his grasp and rounded on him with a snarl. "I don't take orders from Dakkas."

Turning away, she held her stinger pistol at the ready and grabbed the handle of the open door, pulling it slowly open.

A gulf of shadows appeared on the other side. The perfect haven for Dregs. Despite what Keera had said about there being reserve power cores at the Garrison, the lights were out.

"You can stay here if you want," Ava suggested as she stepped inside, her pistol now clutched in a two-handed grip.

Clayton watched her disappear inside, and glanced back over his shoulder to the landing pads in the courtyard. Keera would be landing there in just a few minutes. He warred briefly with himself over staying out here and leaving Ava to her fate. But she didn't stand a chance on her own. Especially with nothing but that Stinger pistol. Even if the charge pack were full, she'd only get ten shots with it, and she'd already fired the weapon several times.

Eying the wall of shadows beyond the door, Clayton connected his ARCs to the night-vision optics of his rifle's scope, and maximized that view so that it was the only thing he could see. Bringing his rifle up and holding it steady, he forged ahead, using the rifle's scope to see what his naked eyes couldn't.

Ava appeared in his view, her body heat revealing her as a shining white silhouette.

"You are much braver than the average Dakka," Ava whispered as he pulled alongside her.

"Maybe because I'm not a Dakka," Clayton replied. The word roughly translated to *sewer rat* in Kyro—as common of a pejorative for humans as demon, chalkhead, and devil were for the Chimeras.

"Maybe so," Ava agreed. "The armory should be that way. Sub-level three."

She pointed to a gleaming bank of elevators and an open stairwell beside them at the far end of the receiving area where they currently found themselves.

"How do you know?" Clayton asked. "Aren't you from Houston?"

"I'm from the *Sovath*," she replied. "But all of the garrisons have the same floor plan."

"What about the op center?" Clayton whispered. "We could use it to see if there are more exosuits around here, like we were originally planning."

"Only if they're powered on. The armory will be faster," Ava replied, starting in the direction that she'd indicated.

There was no sign of Dregs yet, but as they approached the open stairwell, Clayton heard distant echoes from the sub levels: the sound of naked feet slapping polished concrete floors. He wondered at that—if these Dregs had been Chimeras as recently as yesterday, then shouldn't they still be wearing their boots? Maybe as they'd lost their minds, they'd devolved to the point that shoes felt strange and unnatural to them.

Clayton's heart rate spiked as he followed Ava into yet another darkened stairwell. He swept his rifle around quickly to check both the flight above and the flight below for signs of danger, but the immediate area was clear.

In the apartment building he'd been able to get by with his eyes, but here it was impossible to see without the night-vision and light amplification optics in his rifle's scope. Unfortunately, it had an extremely limited field of view, which would make it easy for Dregs to sneak up on him.

Clayton swept the rifle around constantly as they hurried down the stairs. The sounds of Dregs' bare feet shuffling and of muttering hisses rose steadily to their ears. Neither he nor Ava dared to speak, but Clayton was beginning to wish he'd stayed outside.

CHAPTER 25

"**M**om, I'm *thirsty...*" Dora whined.

"Me, too," Nova said. The cicadas buzzed ceaselessly around them, grating on Samara's nerves. More distantly, frogs croaked in the pebbly, grass-lined trough that used to be a river delta. Maybe it still was, but only when it rained.

"They'll be back soon," Samara reassured the girls. She noticed that the bloodstains on Dora's bandage were darker and redder than before. She was tempted to unwrap the bandage and see what was going on, but without Doc here and medical supplies to redress the wound, that could be a bad idea. It was probably just from all of the recent activity and excitement pushing up Dora's blood pressure and making her wound bleed.

Regardless, Samara was no longer worried about a possible infection. Dora was still symptom free and it had been more than half a day since she'd been bitten. Everyone in the Med Center last night had been showing symptoms after just a few hours, so Dora had to be immune.

"Maybe I should go after them," Nova said. "It's been a while..." She twisted around to look at their hoverbike. They'd parked it between a pair of ash trees and covered it with leaves and grass—just in case they ran into trouble with other exiles. Samara wasn't sure if the Enclave was the only group out here, but she didn't want to make any assumptions that could get them into trouble.

"You're not going anywhere," Samara said.

"You can't make me stay."

"Maybe not. But you're better with a gun than I am, and if you leave, something could happen to us while you're gone."

Nova gave up with a sigh and began restlessly plucking up blades of grass around her legs.

They sat in the shade of a thicket of scraggly trees beside an old road that ran parallel to the highway. The highway bridge that was supposed to be their rendezvous was just in front of them, on the other side of the road. Samara peered through the concrete pillars of the bridge to a sparkling slice of the lake that Sergeant Sutton had mentioned. Her mouth ached with the thought of all that fresh water lying right in front of them. They hadn't brought much in the way of provisions, and most of what they had brought was in the back of the hauler. Sutton had claimed that they'd be able to drink and eat to their hearts' content in the Enclave. They'd taken him at his word, but now Samara realized that the wait for that proverbial land of plenty could be much longer than she'd first assumed.

As soon as they'd arrived at the rendezvous, Sutton had sent Pyro and Harold back to check on the others who were bringing up the rear in the hauler. Meanwhile, he and Lori had left for the Enclave to formally accept the invitation to join the community. Samara wasn't sure she understood the politics involved, but for some reason Sutton was hesitant about showing up on their doorstep unannounced, and to Samara, that spoke volumes about the situation. Maybe the Enclave wouldn't be as welcoming as the sergeant had led them all to believe.

"Why do you think my dad didn't come back?" Nova asked suddenly.

The girl's hazel eyes found Samara and burned a hole straight through to her core. Nova was such a tough, capable young woman that it was easy to forget she was still just a kid. Samara held her gaze for a long, silent moment, trying to decide between a candid answer and a comforting lie.

"I think he ran into some trouble," she said, deciding to go with the truth.

Nova nodded slowly, and her eyes dipped

to the ground again. She went back to plucking up the grass. "Do you think he's alive?" she asked quietly.

That was harder to answer. "I do," Samara said, but doubts swirled into the silence that followed.

"Why?" Nova managed.

"Well..." She took a moment to consider her reasons. "I guess as far as I knew, he was supposed to be dead ten years ago. That turned out to be a lie, so I'm not ready to fall for the same thing twice."

"Yeah. I get it. But that's not really a reason for me to hold onto hope, is it?" Nova said.

Samara smiled at the girl's answer. "Sure it is. It means your dad is harder to kill than you think."

"If he's gone, I won't have anyone anymore. Just Rosie."

"And us!" Dora put in brightly, somehow missing the tone of the conversation and the fact that Clayton was *her* father, too.

Nova looked up with a bitter smile. "Yeah, but we're not blood. I'm not *really* your sister."

"Sure you are," Dora went on, undaunted. "You are my dad's other daughter. So that makes you my sister."

Samara's smile widened. "She's got you there, Nova."

"I guess she does."

"She's right, you know."

Nova met Samara's gaze again, but waited for her to go on.

"I'd like to be able to call you my daughter, too. If you'll let me."

Nova shrugged, then hesitated. A faint smile tugged at the corner of her mouth. "Does that mean I have to call you *Mom,* and go to bed when you tell me to?"

"You can call me whatever you like, and we can talk about bedtime."

"Fair deal," Nova replied.

Samara nodded in agreement. She got the feeling that Nova still hadn't really dropped her defenses yet. But maybe that would just take time.

The sharp *crack* of a stick breaking caught Samara's ear and interrupted her thoughts. A sparking flood of adrenaline shot through her, and she fumbled for the plasma pistol holstered to her hip. Nova was already up and crouching behind the nearest tree, her rifle aimed in the direction of the sound they'd heard. Heavy, thumping footsteps came thundering toward them, followed by more breaking sticks. Someone was running their way from the direction of the trees. Nova flicked off the safety on her rifle; then planted her cheek to the butt of the weapon and peered down the scope.

Those footfalls were rising swiftly in volume, getting closer with every passing second.

Dora's eyes were wide, her lips parted, the lower one trembling. "What is it?" she whispered.

"Quiet," Samara answered, even though she was sure the sound of her heart thudding in her chest was far louder than Dora's whispers. She crept over to the nearest tree and used it for cover while aiming her pistol around it, mimicking Nova's posture as best she could.

As she crouched there, listening and watching, sweat prickled her back and scalp. The crashing footfalls sounded like they belonged to a human to her—maybe more than one—but that could also mean Dregs or even Chimeras. *It can't be Dregs, can it?* she wondered. It was the middle of the day. But the forest grew thicker and darker the farther it got from the road. Wild Dregs could definitely stand to live in a place as gloomy as that.

Remembering her encounters with those monsters last night, Samara's hands began to shake. She'd seen two of her colleagues die, and she'd been badly injured herself. If it weren't for the supplies on hand at the hospital, she might not have survived.

Thud, thud, thud, crack! Those footsteps were almost upon them.

Samara flicked off the safety on her pistol, and then her finger ducked into the trigger guard. This wouldn't be like last night. She had a gun this time, not just a scalpel. She wasn't defenseless.

A wall of leafy green branches in front of them shivered with the rushing approach of whatever was coming. A guttural snorting sound erupted—a sound that could only belong to beast, not a man.

Dregs, Samara thought, and her entire body grew cold. Time seemed to slow to a crawl. She caught flickers of movement between the branches and took shaky aim. Then the trees and shadows were thrown aside like curtains, and *it* stepped out into the light.

Samara screamed and pulled the trigger before she'd even fully registered the shape and form of her target.

A human man sank to his knees, clutching a fiery hole in his chest.

And then the real monster crashed through the trees behind him: a wild boar. It squealed and snorted, goring him from behind with its tusks. Nova opened fire, and her shot felled the animal with a burst of a light and a sharp report. And then a deathly silence fell, and Samara had a moment of calm to fully grasp the horror of what she'd done.

"No..." she whispered, her eyes fixed on the motionless body lying face-down in the dried leaves and grass. The cicadas resumed their buzzing. Wind shuffled through the trees, sending patterns of sunlight and shadow fluttering across the dead man's back. Bloody puncture wounds glistened where the wild bore's tusks had torn him open. And the exit wound from Samara's shot was clearly visible, a charred black hole the size of her open palm from the bolt of plasma that had incinerated his heart.

"Is he dead?" Nova breathed as she straightened from cover.

But Samara didn't have to wonder. No one could have lived through that. Dora stood up and stared at the dead man for half a second, and then she let out a piercing scream.

CHAPTER 26

Clayton walked into Ava's back as she stopped suddenly at the reinforced door on one of the landings. She tried the control panel, but it was dark and unresponsive, and the door was locked.

"So much for backup power," Clayton muttered.

"Someone shut it down," Ava whispered.

The door to sub-level one had been standing open, but levels two and three were both locked. The Chimeras at the Garrison had obviously taken pains to restrict access to sensitive areas after they'd started turning. They'd probably realized that people would try to break in here and steal the guns.

A distant shriek sounded, echoing down the stairwell.

"Let's just shoot the lock," Clayton said.

"We can't," Ava replied. "The door *slides* open. The locking mechanism is inside the wall. She knocked on solid concrete with a fist.

Clayton blew out a breath. "Then this mission is over. We're leaving."

"Go ahead," Ava replied as she worked her claws into seams in the door and gave it a tug. The heavy slab of metal didn't budge.

Another shriek. Closer now.

"If you stay down here, you're as good as dead," Clayton gritted out quietly.

"I will be if you keep drawing them to us with your rotten stench!" Ava replied through a hiss. She tried to force the door again, throwing her weight against it this time. But it was futile. The door was locked, and the lock was electronically activated via the control panel.

Ava turned away and started down the next flight of stairs.

"Where are you going?" he asked.

"To turn the power back on," she said.

Clayton hesitated, warring with himself over following Ava or leaving her to her fate and going back up to meet with Keera.

Another suspicious sound echoed from the levels above—a loud snorting. Dregs sniffing them out. Ava was right about one thing. The smell of his sweaty, unwashed body was going to draw the Dregs to them like flies. Their olfactory glands were tens of millions of times more sensitive than a regular human's—more akin to a dog's.

Recalling that factoid gave Clayton the kick in the pants he needed. He turned and hurried back up the stairs, holding his rifle like a flashlight ahead of him. The shadowy green overlay of the night-vision scope was enough to see by, but it made it easy to trip. He had to feel for the stairs with his feet rather than see them.

As he neared sub level one, he slowed down and swept his rifle toward the open door, pressing himself to the railing as he slipped by to give himself as much time as possible to react.

He stepped into view of the open door—

Saw a mass of shaded white thermal signatures in the sea of green and black. A sharp hiss and collective roar of shrieking voices told him that they'd seen him too.

An electric jolt of fear shot through him. He flicked the fire mode to full-auto and sprayed the corridor with laser fire. Agonized screams erupted, followed by skittering claws as the survivors trampled the dying to reach him. Clayton kept raking his rifle back and forth, the weapon intermittently blinding his scope with strobing flashes of light. Then it clicked dry and a scalding wave of steam gushed from the coolant vents.

A trio of surviving Dregs scrambled over a pile of at least fifteen dead and dying. His weapon was useless. He still had Keera's strapped to his back, but he didn't have time to reach for it. Instead, he turned and ran up the stairs as fast as he could, using the railing to pull himself up two and three steps at a time. He heard claws and bare feet slapping and scraping on the concrete steps behind him. Ragged, panting breaths chugged along behind him, seeming only inches away. His feet touched the top landing and he skidded with his momentum, grabbing the door handle and pirouetting around to slam it shut in the Dregs' faces.

The door thumped with heavy impacts, and a pair of pale, dirty faces appeared, pressing against the square of bullet-proof glass at the top of the door. They shrieked and hissed, gnashing their teeth at him as if to bite him through the glass. Clayton held the door handle with both hands, bracing it. There wasn't any locking mechanism that he could see. His mind raced, and he cast about desperately for some way to barricade the door. Nothing in reach. All he could use was his rifle, and that wouldn't work. He needed a chair.

Then came the inevitable. The Dregs stopped trying to claw their way through, and found the door handle. He felt an impossibly strong grip, twisting and wrenching the handle, inching it open despite him holding it with both hands and all of his strength. Clayton felt his head growing hot, tendons and veins popped out all over his face, neck, and arms. His lungs seized up as his entire core turned to stone to support the effort his upper body was making.

But he couldn't hold it. They were coming through, and he still couldn't spare a hand to reach for the fresh rifle strapped to his back.

He had just one chance for survival. He glanced at the swath of sunlight pouring in through the door they'd left open from the parking lot outside. If he could beat the Dregs there, they wouldn't chase him out into the light of day.

At least, he hoped not. Only one way to find out. Clayton took in a deep breath, his lungs straining against rigid walls of muscle...

And then he pushed off the door and ran for his life, riding a wave of sheer adrenaline.

He heard the stairwell burst open a split second later. A scrabbling shrieking horde of Dregs boiled after him, their footsteps a stampede, thundering in his ears alongside his racing heart.

* * *

Keera stood at the base of the Ascension Center, gazing up at the landing pad on top of the massive, windowless black dome that was the facility itself. Until the Chrona released their plague, this had been a training center for human cadets before they made the decision to become Chimeras. Now the interior of the facility had to be teeming with failed conversions—a new generation of Dregs. The old virus had a forty-two percent failure rate, but the new one looked to be right near a hundred. They had yet to encounter someone who had caught it and not turned into a mindless Dreg.

Checking the power bar in the top right of her helmet's display, Keera saw that the exosuit was down to three percent power. Once she engaged the cloaking shield, it wouldn't last more than five minutes. And that wasn't even factoring in that she still had to use the suit's grav thrusters to fly forty-five stories straight up to the landing pad above the dome.

She was running out of time.

Keera activated the suit's cloaking shield with a thought. Her armor shimmered, then vanished. The power bar immediately began flashing in warning. She engaged the grav boosters at full thrust, and her stomach plunged into her feet as the suit rocketed into the air. The blood left her head in a rush, and a dizzying swirl of black spots danced across her vision.

The bottom of the landing pad grew swiftly larger and closer, and she backed off the thrust in preparation for a landing. Keera passed the top of the dome, then angled her body and the thrusters in her arms and feet to fly up alongside one of the support columns to the landing pad itself. She cleared the top of the landing pad and backed gradually off the thrust to make a controlled landing. Her feet touched down with a soft *thunk* that was hopefully muffled by the wind whipping across the landing pad.

Clear blue sky and a scattering of clouds wrapped around her and overhead. No sign of Reapers anywhere—no... wait. There were two of them standing in the middle of the landing pad, and four hoverbikes parked at the far end. The cloaked transport must have been at their backs; the door was now shut, and the landing ramp had been raised, so it was completely invisible. Whoever was inside, they'd clearly discovered how to operate at least those basic functions.

Keera quietly started toward the two guards, raising both her arms to take aim with the suit's integrated gauntlet lasers. She set both weapons to stealth mode, and locked on to her targets.

She fired both lasers at the same time. Invisible beams leaped out soundlessly, and both men crumpled to the landing pad with quarter-inch black holes burned through their heads.

The power bar in the top right of Keera's HUD began flashing more insistently. The weapons were independently powered, but her estimates of the power drain from flying up here must have been off, because now she was down to just one percent power. An audible warning broke the silence inside her helmet:

"Warning, power levels critical. Shutdown imminent."

Keera silenced the alert and quickly used the suit's active sensors to probe the area where the transport had to be. A shaded green overlay revealed the ship. It had a hexagonal body and sharply-angled sides. The vessel was aerodynamic, if not actually capable of generating lift. She stepped up to the door and the control panel beside it. She tapped the button at the bottom of the panel, and the door to the transport slid open, revealing three Reapers sitting on the other side of the door. They jumped to their feet, instantly alert, and another three crowded into the entrance, peeking around the sides with rifles and sidearms.

"Hey what gives?" one said.

"Shit!" another cried as he noticed the two dead guards crumpled on the ground.

Keera marked targets and fired just as fast as she could move her arms. Five Reapers fell, some struggling, others dead before they even hit the deck. And then two bright green laser bolts snapped back at her, aimed blindly. The first one hit her shoulder, barely warming Keera's skin through the armor, but the second hit a joint in her leg and she felt a sharp spike of pain shoot through her knee. Her leg gave out, but the suit held her up.

Then the HUD went dark, and the air shimmered, revealing her where she stood. Three more lasers slammed into her armor, and again barely made it through to scald her skin.

"Hey, it's not moving!" someone said.

Keera had frozen solid, a prisoner inside her own armor. She couldn't even twitch. The suit had reserved its final gasp of juice to let her out, but she couldn't step out of her armor until she was sure the Reapers wouldn't simply gun her down the moment she appeared.

"The armor seized up!" one of the surviving Reapers crowed. Keera counted four of them by their weapons peeking around the edges of the door. They were firing without looking, no doubt using augmented reality contacts to connect to the scopes of their weapons.

"Come on out!" one of the Reapers shouted. That voice was familiar.

"Either you peel out of that suit, or we'll keep shooting until you boil like a lobster," another said.

"*Ka'ra!*" Keera cursed in Kyro. This fight was over. She'd lost. But she could still bargain for her life. "You need me alive!" she shouted at the top of her lungs, hoping they'd be able to hear through the suit. Without power to the external speakers, she couldn't be sure that they would.

"We'll be the judge of that!" the first one added. "Come on out and let's talk."

Keera triggered her suit open. A flurry of

whirring and clicking sounded, and the suit splayed open, letting in a burst of fresh air that cooled her sweat-soaked body.

"Well, looky who it is, y'all!" the one with the familiar voice said.

"Hands up!" another added. Four weapons were still aimed around the sides of the door at her.

Keera slowly raised her hands and limped out of the exosuit, her injured knee barely strong enough to support her weight. The man with the familiar voice stepped into view with a big grin. Tall and fit with tanned skin and a quarter inch of dark stubble and hair. It was Zachary, the surviving Reaper of the two they'd met on their way over from Houston. Keera fixed him with a glare. "I need to speak with your leader. I've come to negotiate." That wasn't true, but maybe he'd buy it.

Zachary jerked his chin to the dead guards outside the transport, then turned to regard the five Reapers that she'd shot after opening the door. Only one of them was still alive, but he was lying clutching his side and gasping for air. It sounded to Keera like he had a collapsed lung. He wouldn't last much longer without treatment.

Zachary fixed her with a cold look. "So you thought killing half of us would strengthen your position for negotiations?" He crossed thick arms over his chest and slowly shook his head. "I'm not the fool you take me for, chalk-head. You were trying to steal our ship."

Keera scowled. "Fine. But I failed. And you need me to pilot it, so I think we can come to terms, don't you?"

"Do I need you?" he countered. He strode to the edge of the open doorway, jumped down, and stopped with his nose just a few inches from her face. He was at least a foot taller than her, and this move was clearly designed to intimidate, but she wasn't going to give the man the satisfaction of a reaction. She briefly fantasized about ripping his throat out with her claws.

His lips parted in a thin smile, as if he'd read her thoughts. Not for the first time, she wished her telepathy worked on humans.

"Where's your human concubine?" Zack asked.

"He's not my—"

"Answer the fucking question."

Keera shook her head. "He's dead."

"And the other Chimera?"

"She's dead, too."

Zack's smile widened. "You're lying."

"Get me your leader," Keera tried again. "I'm not going to waste time negotiating with you."

"Sure thing, darling."

Zack began turning away, as if to do as she'd asked. And then he turned back with a wink and another smile. "The name's Zachary Lee Taylor, but you can just call me *master* for short." Chuckles and muted laughter issued from the interior of the transport.

Keera was shocked to note that no one had made a move to help the wounded man. Either they didn't know how to treat his injuries, or they didn't care to try. If that was how they treated their own, she didn't want to know how they might treat her. Keera's eyes cinched down to slits, but she said nothing to Zachary's introduction.

"All right, let's negotiate. What are you offering, chalkhead?" Zack asked.

"I can show you how to fly this ship," she said, ignoring the insult. "But I need something in return."

"And that is?"

"A hoverbike, and your guarantee that you'll let me go after I show you how to fly the transport."

"That's all? After killing seven of my men, you give us a flying lesson and somehow it's all squared away?"

"Six. That one's still alive," she said, pointing to the wounded man. "And it's the best deal you're going to get. Without my help, this ship isn't going anywhere, and I don't see any other Chimeras around here offering to help you fly out of here."

"No, I suppose you're right about that. But

why should one of us go through flight school when we've already got a pilot?"

"I'm not going to fly for you if I'm a prisoner. Either I teach you and I'm free to leave, or you keep me around as a useless hostage. Your choice."

Zachary chuckled darkly, his shoulders heaving. "So defiant. For a woman in your position, I'd think you'd be a little more... agreeable. Makes me think we need to take you down a notch or two. What d'ya think boys? Should we teach this bitch a lesson?"

"Be my pleasure," another Reaper said, stepping out of cover and into view. He cracked his knuckles and grinned, revealing three missing teeth. He was short and out of shape. Long, thinning brown hair hung on either side of his pudgy, florid face. Three more followed the first: one was big and brawny with blonde hair, equal parts muscle and fat. The next was a short, skeletal man with straight dark hair and cold blue eyes, and the last one, to her surprise, was a woman: thin and pretty with wide hips, long dark hair and piercing blue eyes. She had a weapon like the men around her, so she wasn't a hostage.

"The only question is, how do we break a hardened soldier..." Zachary tapped his chin and lifted his eyes to the sky, as if searching for inspiration.

"Pin her down," the woman suggested. "Let

the boys have her. Might stop 'em from staring at *my* ass all day."

More laughter followed that comment.

Keera's hands clenched into fists, her claws pricking sharply through the skin of her palms.

Zachary regarded the woman standing behind him. "That it might, my love, that it just might. All right, you heard McKayla! Let's get it over with."

The three men inside the transport jumped down beside their leader one after another, and fanned out, surrounding Keera as they advanced.

She began backing away slowly, limping and favoring her wounded knee. She hissed sharply at the overweight man with the stringy brown hair. He eagerly outpaced the other two with a nasty, gap-toothed grin.

"Here kitty, kitty, kitty," he said.

"Touch me and I'll rip your throat out."

"Rip his throat out, and we'll gut you like a fish," Zachary replied as he trailed behind the other three.

Keera shot a quick glance behind her, to the edge of the rooftop. Entrances to the stairwells and elevators stood in the four corners of the landing pad. She could make a run for the nearest one and hope they didn't decide to simply shoot her. Keera sucked in a deep breath to steady her racing heart. *Run.* It was her only option—that, or let them have her, but she'd sooner jump and make a dent in the pavement below.

So she ran, taking long, loping strides with her good leg and all but dragging her wounded one. Booted feet thundered after her, the Reapers catching up fast. The stairwell was too far. But the edge of the roof was just 15 feet away. She angled toward it. She felt a light tug on her shoulder as one of the Reapers caught up to her, but she ducked out of the man's grasp and ran faster, pushing through the sharp stabs of pain radiating up and down her leg.

"She's gonna jump!" McKayla cried.

"Stun the bitch!" Zachary added.

The first crackling stun bolt zipped past Keera's ear. She flinched away from it, her entire body shaking with rage, indignation, and horror. She couldn't let them—

But the next shot hit her dead-center between her shoulder blades. All of her muscles seized up in a full-body cramp and she fell face-first to the pavement, mere feet from reaching the edge. A dark haze descended over her. The muffled sounds of footsteps and laughter carried to her ears, fading fast into the shuttered silence of a dream-like sleep.

At least I won't be awake... she thought.

CHAPTER 27

Clayton ran so fast that it felt like his legs didn't even belong to him, but it wasn't fast enough. Those Dregs were right behind him, panting hard in ragged, grunting snorts. He reached the entrance of the Garrison and slammed into the heavy metal door, pushing it wide open and letting in a flood of light. The Dregs breathing down his neck shrieked in pain as the light hit them.

Clayton twisted around to look as he ran into the sunlit courtyard. A few Dregs stumbled out with him, their momentum carrying them. They stood screaming and clawing at their eyes, as if to fight back against the light. The others piled up in the entryway, hissing and scrambling over each other in their hurry to retreat. All of them wore Chimeran uniforms. They were barefoot, as he'd heard, and some of them had their uniforms zipped open to reveal chalk-white torsos. The Dregs vanished from the entrance, and the ones who'd mistakenly barreled after him into the courtyard now scrambled back inside.

Clayton stopped running and collapsed on the dusty pavement, gasping for air and seeing spots. He dropped his head as low as he could to get the blood flowing back to it, and blinked furiously as stinging drops of sweat dripped into his eyes.

As soon as his vision cleared, he pushed off the ground and walked woodenly over to a pair of armored troop transports. He sat in the shady gap between them to stay out of sight while he waited for Keera to arrive—just in case Reapers made a fly over and spotted him.

Silence rang loud in his ears alongside his thudding heartbeat, now steadily slowing with each shuddering breath he took. He stared at the empty landing pads, trying to figure out how much time had passed since Keera had left. It had to have been at least ten minutes already. Maybe fifteen. Either Keera had succeeded, or her suit had run out of power and the attack had failed.

A frown creased Clayton's brow as he considered what he would do in that case. Ava was still in the Garrison looking for more suits of cloaking armor. If she found them and made it out past the Dregs, maybe they could stage a rescue. Until then, all he could do was wait. He leaned back against the nearest of the two troop transports and let out a frustrated breath.

* * *

Keera woke up with a suddenly racing heart and blinked her eyes open to see the sun beaming down on her, burning her sensitive skin. Zachary was crouching over her with a needle in his hand. Her arm stung where he'd just injected her with whatever had been in that syringe.

The leader of the Reapers smiled. "Good, you're awake."

Remembering what had been about to happen before she was stunned, a sick weight settled in Keera's stomach, but she was still fully clothed. Maybe they hadn't done anything to her.

"How are you feeling?" Zachary asked.

She tried to lunge for his throat, but her hands and legs were bound, and her muscles were still weak and sore from the effects of the stun blast. She fell back down with a grunt.

"Easy," Zack said, chuckling softly.

Keera worked some moisture into her mouth. "If your men so much as laid a finger on me, they're going to wish they—"

"Relax," Zack replied, shaking his head. "I didn't think it would be fair if you couldn't fight back. Besides, I'm kinda hopin' you and I might yet be able to see eye to eye."

"I told you my terms," Keera said.

"Your terms!" Zachary reeled back on his haunches with a booming laugh and slapped his knee. "That's a good one, chalkhead!" Abruptly, he stood up and gestured to someone she couldn't see. "Get her on her feet. Let's find out where the others went."

The brawny blonde man and the chubby Reaper with stringy brown hair stepped into view and bent down on either side of her, each of them taking her under one arm and hoisting her up. Since her ankles were bound, they dragged her with her feet trailing behind. Her injured knee erupted with blinding stabs of pain. They obviously hadn't wasted any time or resources to treat the injury.

"Where are you taking me?" Keera asked even though she could clearly see that they were dragging her to the open door of the shuttle. The landing ramp was down now, and Zachary's mate stood in the opening with a rifle across her chest, waiting. The skeletal Reaper with black hair was nowhere to be seen, but Keera decided he was probably waiting inside the transport. That, or he was on one of the hoverbikes, looking for Clayton and Ava. Keera winced at the thought of them. She hoped that they wouldn't try to rescue her. At this point, the best thing they could do was get back to Phoenix base and return with reinforcements. They'd missed their escape window, anyway. By now the Kyron fleet had to have arrived and set up their blockade.

The Reapers dragged her up the ramp and

into the transport. Gone were the bodies of the ones that Keera had killed; the survivors had probably thrown them off the roof like garbage. McKayla stepped aside in the entrance of the ship, glaring at Keera as they came face to face. This was the woman who'd suggested that the Reapers rape her as a form of punishment. That told her everything she needed to know about this group.

"Where are the others?" McKayla asked.

"Go to hell," Keera said, and then she spat in the woman's face.

McKayla's lips twisted in revulsion and she recoiled a few steps. "You bitch!" She wiped her face on her sleeve and her rifle snapped up, aimed straight at Keera's chest.

Zachary stepped between them and pushed McKayla's rifle aside. "Enough."

"You may as well kill me," Keera said. "I won't help you."

"Maybe you won't, but the other demon will, and you're going to tell us where she went," Zachary said. Before Keera could wish him luck getting that information out of her, he looked away and nodded to someone she couldn't see. "Seth, put the helmet on her."

Keera struggled to see who he was talking to. The transport was relatively small inside, the bulk of it devoted to the troop bay where they stood. She caught a glimpse of a flicker of movement behind Zachary and McKayla. They parted to reveal the missing Reaper. The skeletal man with dark hair and blue eyes. He came striding down the aisle between bench seats. In his hands he held a pair of gleaming black helmets, connected to each other by a thick bundle of wires. Keera recognized the technology immediately. It was a Kyron brain scanner.

A cold trickle of dread snaked through her. With that device, her every thought would be laid bare for these perverted psychopaths to browse through at will. In some ways it was an even more grievous violation than what they'd been planning before they'd stunned her. And it was certain to lead to Clayton's and Ava's capture, if not their deaths.

CHAPTER 28

Samara crouched over the dead man, staring sightlessly at his contorted face. He looked so young, but then, almost everyone did nowadays, thanks to Kyra longevity treatments. Samara scanned his features, committing them to memory. A shadow of light stubble on his square jaw. Short sandy blonde hair. Handsome. Did he have kids? A wife? He was dressed relatively well—in a checkered green button-up shirt and jeans, and he wasn't dirty like most of the exiles she'd met.

Samara's guts heaved again and she turned away, preparing for another wave of guilt to come gushing out. But there was nothing left in her stomach. She turned back to the dead man. Fresh tears stung her eyes.

"It was an accident," Nova said quietly. A hand found Samara's shoulder and lightly squeezed. "You can't blame yourself."

"Why not?" Samara asked. "I pulled the trigger."

"But you didn't know. It could have been

a Dreg. Or even a Chimera! It was an accident. That's all." Samara felt Nova trying to pull her away, but she resisted, her eyes fixed on the corpse lying in a bed of grass and fallen leaves.

"Come on... Mom," Nova said awkwardly. Samara looked to her, shocked to hear the girl address her that way. She blinked once, and Nova offered a grim smile and jerked her head to the road where Dora was pacing back and forth and muttering to herself. "Your daughter needs you. You can't afford to fall apart. Look at her..."

Nova was right. Samara pushed off the ground and sucked in a shaky breath. She and Nova went over to Dora.

"Hey, sis!" Nova called. Dora's mutterings ceased and she stopped pacing to watch as they approached.

Samara came to a stop in front of her, saw the blank look of shock on Dora's face, and realized just how badly all of this was affecting her. She wasn't nearly as desensitized as Samara had thought. She pulled Dora into a hug and kissed the top of her head. "Hey," she said. "I'm fine. You hear me?"

Dora nodded against her chest. "Is that man going to be okay?"

Samara frowned and pulled back to an arm's length to regard Dora with a grim look. Her daughter's green eyes were big and glassy. "He's dead, honey." Hearing herself say the words made it doubly real, and a heavy weight settled around Samara's shoulders, rounding them and pushing her down. She knew she would carry that weight for the rest of her life. This wasn't some Dreg she'd killed. Not even an armed assailant. It was an innocent man.

Dora blinked once. "Oh."

"Let's sit for a minute," Samara said as her legs began to shake. She all but collapsed on the side of the road. Dora crawled into her lap, and Nova sat down beside them and leaned her head against Samara's other shoulder. She barely registered it. Her entire body felt numb. The three of them sat there, seemingly oblivious to the mid afternoon sun blazing down on them.

"It wasn't your fault," Nova said again. "I could just as easily have made the same mistake."

"Except you didn't. You held your fire."

"I have more experience with weapons than you do."

Samara nodded slowly and sucked in a ragged breath. And that was just it. She had no business holding a gun. She never wanted to touch one again for as long as she lived.

Samara swallowed past her sandpaper tongue, her throat parched and scalded by the acid in her vomit. Time dragged by in an infinity of silence and regret. Eventually, the sun dipped behind the trees, drawing a curtain of shadows over them.

Some while later, a whirring roar pricked through the suffocating haze in Samara's head. She sat listening to it for several seconds before she realized what it was. Hoverbikes. Her head jerked up and around to watch as they approached. Three of them. She picked out Sergeant Sutton's camo fatigues moments before his bike glided to a stop in front of them. Lori's bike arrived next, followed by a third—a big man wearing a leather jacket and jeans. He didn't have a helmet on, and his hair was tied in a ponytail behind his head. Dark eyes settled on them, crows' feet pinching in silent scrutiny. Samara decided that he must be from the Enclave. Sutton pulled off his helmet and regarded them steadily without getting off his bike.

"The others aren't back yet?" he asked.

Samara slowly shook her head.

"You look like hell."

Nova nodded. "Well, there was an inc—"

Samara grabbed Nova's arm and squeezed as hard as she could. The girl shot her a bemused look.

"It was a long, hot wait," Samara finished for her. "And we're badly dehydrated."

Sutton nodded along with that. He reached down to his belt, unclipped the canteen, and threw it at her. "Here."

Samara fumbled the metal bottle and

dropped it in the gravel beside the road. She picked it up, unscrewed the cap, and lifted it halfway to her lips before remembering that the girls had to be just as thirsty as she was. She passed it to Dora first, showing an unspoken preference. If Nova noticed, she didn't say anything. Dora drank greedily for several long seconds, rivulets leaking down her chin.

"Okay, that's enough," Samara said. She pulled the canteen away and passed it to Nova next.

"Thanks," she said, and raised it to her lips, but she only took one sip before passing it on to Samara. "You have the rest. You need it more than me."

Samara was too tired to argue. She drank until the canteen was almost dry, and then passed it back. Nova drained it, and the three of them stood up together. Samara noticed that Sutton, Lori, and the stranger had all climbed off their bikes and were standing to one side, arguing in low tones.

Samara walked over to them. "What's the problem?" she asked.

The stranger fixed her with a dark look. "The problem is they want to wait around for your friends, and we don't know that they weren't intercepted by Chimeras. It's bad enough that your friends could tell them about us, but at least they don't know where we are. If Chimeras catch us here, they could use us to lead them to the Enclave. We need to leave *now,* before that can happen."

"We should at least leave a scout behind," Lori said.

"I agree. I'll stay here," Sutton said. "I know how to stay hidden. No one will see me."

The stranger looked between them with a scowl. "Out of the question. And it's not your call to make. That was the deal, remember? You want to join us, that means you follow *our* rules, and my orders are clear."

"What's your name?" Samara asked.

"Logan Hall, ma'am."

"I'm Samara Cross. It's nice to meet you." He inclined his head to her, and she went on, "Mr. Hall, what about this: what if you let *me* stay here. I don't know where the Enclave is, so I can't lead anyone there even if I *am* captured. That means there's no danger to you or your people."

Logan hesitated, and everyone looked to him, waiting for his answer.

"We can't just leave them," Samara added. This wouldn't make up for the man she'd killed, but maybe over time small acts of courage and selflessness like this would be enough to somehow make things right.

"I guess that would be fine," Logan said, giving in with a sigh.

"Good," Sutton declared. Looking to Samara, he said, "We'll be back for you."

Samara nodded. Nova handed him his empty canteen. He took it without looking, his eyes narrowing on Samara. "Where's your gun?"

A jolt of dread shot through her, and her hands began to twitch. Sweat prickled her scalp as her mind raced for a suitable answer.

"It's right here," Nova said, producing the weapon with a smile. "She gave it to me because I'm better with guns."

Samara blinked in shock to see the girl holding up her plasma pistol. She must have missed when Nova had retrieved it.

"Fair enough," Sutton said. "But you better give it back now. Sam's gonna need something to defend herself."

Nova held the weapon out to her with a hesitant smile. Samara experienced a visceral reaction. She recoiled from the weapon, stumbling away with her eyes wide and staring.

"What's the matter with her?" Logan asked. "You'd think the girl had just handed her a snake!"

Samara was saved from having to reply as for the second time a whirring roar of hoverbikes came racing toward them. Everyone spun away from her, their weapons flying from their holsters.

Two hoverbikes burst over the tops of the trees and circled back.

Logan took aim, sighting through his

scope.

"Wait!" Sutton said. "That's them!"

The bikes were heavily-laden with two riders each. As they rocketed down for a landing, Samara identified familiar faces. Pyro and Harold were behind the controls—a telltale mane of curly red hair leaking out of Pyro's helmet. Richard and Doc were riding on the backs of those bikes, but there was no sign of the Chimeran prisoner or preacher.

"Where's Rosie!" Nova cried as the bikes slowed to a spot in front of them.

"Doc, report!" Sutton said.

Doc jumped off the back of his bike and hurried over. Samara noticed that his clothes were covered in blood.

"They ambushed us! We managed to escape, but they took the hauler, and Preacher got hit."

"How bad?" Sutton asked, his eyes tightening as they flicked up and down, taking in Doc's blood-stained clothes.

Doc just shook his head.

"And Rosie?" Nova asked.

Doc winced. "I don't know. I don't think they hurt her, but..." He looked to Richard for an answer.

"I didn't stick around long enough to find out," he said.

Doc looked back to them with a helpless shrug. "Sorry, Nova."

"We have to go back and get her!" Nova cried, tears streaming freely down her cheeks.

"Too dangerous," Sutton replied.

Samara wrapped an arm around the girl's shoulders and held her as she cried. "It's okay," she whispered. "I'm sure she's fine. We'll find a way to get her. I promise."

Nova said nothing, but her sobs quieted somewhat.

"Were you followed?" Logan shouted to them.

"No!" Doc yelled back.

"You could have missed something," Logan replied, gliding over on his bike.

"The Chimeras stayed with the hauler," Doc went on. "We kept checking our sensors for signs of pursuit, but they were clear the whole way." He gestured to the center console below the control bars of Logan's bike. "Do you see anything?"

The man in the leather jacket leaned back and crossed his arms over his chest. "Doesn't mean they're not there. They could be powered down and watching us from a distance."

"Then why haven't they taken a shot at us yet?"

"Because they're waiting for us to lead the way to the Enclave!" Logan thundered.

"You're paranoid," Doc muttered.

"You would be, too, if you saw where I live."

"Well standing around here arguing about it isn't doing any good," Sutton said. "You're the boss, so you tell me—do we stay here and wait for Chimeras to catch up, or do we bug out now while the gettin's good?"

Logan pursed his lips, considering the question. After a few seconds, he gave in with a sigh and grabbed the control bars of his bike. "We'll have to risk it. Everyone mount up!"

Doc ran back over to hop on behind Pyro, while Samara started after Sutton with the girls.

"You can ride with me, ma'am," Logan said, stopping her in her tracks.

"Okay," she replied, hesitating briefly. Nova caught her gaze, the girl's eyes red and gleaming with unshed tears.

Nova followed Sutton to his bike, and Dora climbed on behind Lori.

"Hang on tight," Logan said. She circled his waist with her arms, and he gunned the throttle, pulling up and banking around, high above the trees where they'd left that dead man's body. Samara had stopped Nova from telling the others about the incident for a good reason. That man was too clean and well-dressed to have been camping out in the Wilds on his own. He must have come from a community of exiles. A community like the Enclave. And something told Samara that they wouldn't be very welcome anymore if Logan realized what she'd done—accident or not. Maybe she would confess, but first she had to be sure that none of the others would be made to pay for her mistake.

The bike flew low over scattered forests and plains, heading West toward the sinking sun. Tree tops rustled in the wind of their passage. Samara tried to calm her racing heart. With all this wild, untamed countryside, what were the chances that body would be found?

Samara let out a shaky breath and pushed her guilt down. But a new concern promptly took its place.

What had happened to Widow? Was she still back at Phoenix base, waiting for Clayton and Keera? Or maybe they'd met up already and they were on their way to the rendezvous right now. But if that was the case, they were going to arrive only to discover no one there waiting for them.

Why hadn't Sutton said something? She could have stayed behind to wait as she'd suggested. Then again, it wouldn't have made much difference. Samara didn't know the way to the Enclave, so she couldn't lead anyone there. Maybe Widow would be smart enough to wait at the rendezvous until Sutton had a chance to come back for her.

That had to be it. Given the way Logan had reacted to the suggestion that they leave people behind, it made sense that Sutton hadn't mentioned the rest of their people.

Samara had to believe that Widow, Clayton, and Keera would catch up to them eventually. If Clayton was actually dead this time, she wasn't sure if she'd be able to hold it together anymore. Everyone had their breaking point, and hers was fast approaching.

Come on Widow, she thought. *Bring my husband back to me...* And as she thought that, Samara wondered about the woman's call sign. The irony of it hit her: she was counting on a Widow to keep her from becoming one.

CHAPTER 29

Commander Tyris watched the lumbering garbage hauler come down the driveway to the old log home. That crumbling mansion had served as a base for the resistance cell that called itself Phoenix. As the hauler ground to a halt, the doors flew open and three Chimeras jumped out. Another four emerged from the cargo box at the back. Along with Lieutenant Akora. They helped her out, all but carrying her down from the back of the hauler. Tyris went to greet her and get a sitrep, but she appeared to be in significant pain from two separate laser burns. "Get her to a medic," Tyris ordered to the pair of corporals carrying her between them.

"Yes, sir!" one of them replied.

Akora's eyes met his, and she looked like she was about to say something, but he stopped her with an upraised palm. "Save your strength." She gave in with a nod, and the men helping her along carried her off. Tyris turned his attention to the Sergeant whose team had rescued her. "Sergant Harmon, report."

The man stopped in front of him and saluted smartly. "Commander," he said. "We recaptured the hauler and forced the exiles farther north. We shot one, but the other two got away when their reinforcements came on hoverbikes." A resounding *woof* interrupted, coming from within the hauler.

"You didn't think to track them?" Tyris demanded, while staring with narrowed eyes at the back of the truck. Another woof echoed from within. "What in *Dogoth's* name was that?"

"It is a dog, sir."

"A... *dog.*" Tyris felt his nose wrinkling with disgust. "Why didn't you just kill it?"

"We were about to, but the exiles made an attempt to rescue the creature and lost one of their own in the process. Based on that, we assumed it might serve as bait later on."

"Curious," Tyris said. "For terrorists, they are unusually sentimental, aren't they?"

"Yes, sir."

The high-pitched report of a laser rifle sounded somewhere in the distance, and Tyris whirled toward the sound. "What was that?"

Sergeant Harmon slipped on his helmet and stepped in front of him, his rifle up and tracking. "Get behind me, sir."

Another shot echoed out, followed by a flurry of return fire. Tyris's in-ear comms crackled with the voice of one of his men.

"This is Corporal Galon in sector two twelve. Target neutralized. One human female."

"Sergeant Harmon here. Is she dead?"

"No, sir. We stunned her."

"Good," Tyris nodded to himself. "She's worth more to us alive."

Harmon nodded his agreement. "Any casualties, Corporal?"

"None dead, but we have two injured. We're treating their injuries now."

"Corporal, this is Commander Tyris, take a fire team and scout the area. Make sure there aren't more of them out there."

When the corporal's voice returned he sounded winded, as if he were running. "Already on it, sir."

Tyris looked to Sergeant Harmon.

"You think Phoenix is still here?" Harmon asked as he glanced around slowly, his gaze probing the walls of trees growing along the driveway. Tyris joined him, but saw nothing besides the dozens of white canvas tents being erected in the grassy fields around the house. There were fifty-eight of them in all, too many for everyone to fit inside the house. "Maybe that hauler they sent out was a decoy," Sergeant Harmon suggested.

"Maybe," Tyris replied, his cranial stalks twitching in agitation. "Or maybe they left one of their operatives behind to gather intel on us. Either way, I intend to find out." Tyris turned and headed down the driveway. Sergeant Harmon kept pace beside him.

"You're going to interrogate her?" Sergeant Harmon asked as they climbed the front steps together and passed inside the building.

"Of course," Tyris replied. He stopped and turned to the sergeant in the entrance of the house. "Go secure the captive and have one of the medics wake her with a stim shot. I'll be there in just a moment."

"Yes, sir," Harmon replied, before turning and running back outside.

Tyris continued on. Dead ahead, the living room and kitchen at the end of the entry hall were buzzing with activity. Officers bustled about carrying heavy packs and deploying equipment. Tyris saw them laying out solar sheets on the deck to charge weapons and power cores. Mobile auto-turrets were going up on tripods in the windows. Soon this place would be a veritable fortress. If those terrorists were planning an attack, they'd be repelled easily.

Tyris ducked through an open doorway just before reaching the living room and hurried down a flight of stairs to the basement. More soldiers were down there, busy laying out equipment on a line of tables along the far wall. Spotting the device he was looking for,

Tyris angled for a pair of gleaming black helmets connected by bundles of wires.

A mind scan of the captive would reveal where the others had gone.

* * *

Clayton sat in a shady aisle between two armored troop transports, watching ever-lengthening shadows march across the Garrison courtyard. The clock on his ARCs now read 2:17 PM. In just a few more hours night would fall, and then all hell would break loose in the city. He had to do something before then. Keera should have been back twenty minutes ago. And there was still no sign of Ava. The fact that Keera hadn't returned could only mean one thing: she'd failed and been captured by Reapers. Even if she was still alive, there was no way to effect a rescue without a suit of cloaking armor. The only viable option was to take one of the troop transports and escape, but even that was a dim prospect. The Reapers would see him and give chase on their hoverbikes. And without someone to man the gun turret while he drove away, he'd be defenseless. Pity there weren't any hoverbikes parked down here. The Reapers must have taken them all.

A rusty groan interrupted Clayton's thoughts. He turned toward the sound and found himself staring at the side of the nearest transport. The sound had come from the entrance of the Garrison. *Ava,* he thought. It had to be. He stood up and went to look—

But there was no sign of anyone. One of the doors to the Garrison stood wide open, but that didn't mean anything. The Dregs had left it open when they'd chased him outside. Clayton stood frowning into the shadows of the entrance. Maybe the wind had moved the door? Either that, or...

A cold voice slithered to his ears: "Not so brave, after all, Dakka."

Clayton spun toward the sound of Ava's voice just in time to see the air shimmering as she disengaged her cloaking shield. It wasn't an exosuit like the one Keera had used, but it was good enough. "You found it," Clayton said.

"No thanks to you," Ava replied.

"The Dregs could smell me. I didn't want to draw them to you. Was that the only suit of armor you found?"

"No, there's several more. At least a dozen, but it's too heavy to carry out, and you've already proven you can't make it down there to get it for yourself."

Clayton grimaced.

"Where's Keera?" Ava asked, her helmet turning back and forth as she scanned the courtyard.

"She must have been captured."

"Or she abandoned us just like I said she would."

A new sound pricked Clayton's ears, the rising *whirr* of approaching hoverbikes. His gaze snapped up to the sky just in time to see a pair of them streak out over the top of the Garrison.

"We've got company!" Clayton cried, grabbing Keera's rifle in both hands and tracking the bikes as they flew by. They banked sharply, circling around.

"Ka'ra!" Ava cried. "You're on your own!" The air shimmered, and she vanished into thin air once more.

"Now who's the coward!" Clayton cursed under his breath as he darted between the troop transports to stay out of sight. Those bikes were roaring back in. He heard the pitch of the engines reach a peak and then die away completely. For a moment, he dared to hope that they'd left, but then he heard hushed voices and footsteps approaching. Clayton eyed the gap underneath the nearest transport, then thought better of it. They must have detected him with sensors on their flyover. They knew exactly where he was hiding.

"Come out with your hands up!" someone called to him in a booming voice.

Clayton hesitated.

"We know you're there!" another said.

A flicker of movement appeared between the two troop transports, and Clayton ran around behind them. He planted his back to one, and aimed his rifle around the edge, using his ARCs to connect to the scope and aim without exposing himself to enemy fire. Neither of the two Reapers were visible, but he caught sight of one of the hoverbikes. If he could somehow reach that vehicle...

"You have three seconds before I toss a plasma grenade under those trucks and call it a day."

A sharp jolt of adrenaline sparked through Clayton's extremities. Was that a bluff? If they had grenades, his cover would be blown wide open. Literally. Not even an armored transport would survive that.

"What the—"

A muffled thud sounded—

"Hey! Where—"

Followed by another, and then a heavy silence.

"Clayton, let's go!" Ava shouted to him.

He burst out of cover, running for the nearest hoverbike. He saw two Reapers crumpled on the ground with thin curls of smoke rising from their backs. The air shimmered and Ava appeared running for the other bike.

"We have to get Keera!" Clayton said as he swung his rifle around to his back and jumped behind the controls of one of the hoverbikes. The vehicle was still powered on, idling silently and hovering a few feet above the ground.

"Are you crazy?" Ava said. "I'm not going

after her. We don't know how many more of them are up there, and there's no cover on the roof."

"You can cloak!"

"And I'm not risking my life for that traitor. Good luck!"

With that, Ava gunned the throttle and pulled up hard, her bike's engine whirring loudly as it streaked away. A bright emerald laser flashed after her, missing by several dozen feet. Clayton hesitated briefly before deciding that a solo rescue was suicide. Scowling to himself, he vowed to come back for Keera as soon as he could.

He twisted the throttle up to the max and pulled up hard to climb over the Garrison walls. That sudden burst of acceleration threatened to rip him off the bike, but he held on with everything he had and focused on evasive maneuvers, twisting the control bars, left, right, up and down to avoid enemy fire.

A flurry of laser bolts flashed by on either side. He flew down the street, juking furiously and then braked and banked hard at the nearest cross street to put a wall of skyscrapers between him and the Reapers' line of fire. Laser bolts stopped flashing past, and Clayton spared a quick look at the sensor display in the center of his dash. Ava's bike was a bright purple blip already halfway to the edge of the bike's sensor range. Reaching the end of the street, Clayton turned right down the next one, following Ava east.

The city walls soared at the end of the street, and he saw Ava's bike, a mere speck at this distance, flit up and over the top before ducking down again on the other side. He twisted the throttle higher to catch up and gritted his teeth against that fresh burst of acceleration.

Whatever he could say about Ava, she'd just saved his life, and they would stand a much better chance crossing the Wastes together. Besides, Phoenix could use all the able-bodied soldiers it could get. Maybe she would agree to join them.

Clayton checked the bike's sensor display again. Besides his bike and Ava's there were no other blips on the screen.

He glanced back over his shoulder and scanned the jagged spires of New San Antonio for moving specks that would indicate hoverbikes giving chase. Nothing he could see. His gaze lingered, watching the towers of that city shrinking steadily into the distance. The top of the Ascension Center peeked over those buildings—a big flat platform with four pillars. There was no sign of the troop transport or any Reapers up there, but they were too far away to see anyone, and the transport would still be cloaked—unless Keera had stolen it.

But Clayton extinguished that trickle of

doubt just as soon as it entered his mind. How would the Reapers have known where to look for him and Ava if they hadn't forced it out of Keera? And with that thought, a sick weight settled in Clayton's gut. How had the Reapers extracted that information? By torturing her? Despite Ava's suspicions to the contrary, he doubted Keera would have given them up easily. How much would it have taken to break a hardened Chimeran soldier like her? She'd been an admiral no less, and Chimeras were bred and trained to be ruthless warriors, inured to hardship and pain. For the Reapers to have broken her that fast, they must have beaten her within an inch of her life.

That realization spurred another: by the time Phoenix could return to rescue Keera, there might not be anything left of her for them to rescue.

THE ENCLAVE

CHAPTER 30

Samara clung tight to Logan's waist as they climbed high over the walls around New Dallas and flew down a canyon of high rises. Walls of glass and concrete raced by in a blur. The wind was a deafening roar in Samara's ears and flung her hair out straight behind her head like a flag. Now and then a crosswind would gust down an alley or a side street between buildings and slap her in the face with her hair. The streets were empty, but here and there vehicles stood frozen—automated Rydes and troop transports. There were no signs of the battle that had raged over New Houston—no crashed starfighters, no fields of dead bodies or ruined buildings. But that only made the lack of activity in the city even more strange. Everyone here must have already turned into Dregs, and that meant the streets were empty because they were all inside sleeping.

Samara shivered at the thought of what this city would look like when the Dregs woke up and came out to scavenge for food. And that thought triggered another, even more terrifying one: what would happen if the Enclave found out that Dora had been bitten? Just because she hadn't turned into a Dreg yet, didn't mean that they would let her in. They'd worry that she could be contagious, and they'd exile her to the Wastes. Samara grimaced. She couldn't let that happen. If they saw the bandage on her arm, she'd tell them that Dora had cut herself on a piece of broken glass. Or better yet, she'd make sure that no one saw the bandage. Maybe by now the bite was almost healed. Samara pushed those thoughts from her mind with a shaky sigh. Everything was going to be okay.

Logan banked left down the first major street they came to and flew on, leading the group due west—straight into the sun. New Dallas's walls snapped into focus, dead ahead, about half a mile away, and beyond that... nothing but a vast, rolling field of ruins.

Samara frowned as she realized that those ruins were their destination. They flew straight over the walls to a massive field of debris beyond. Ancient skyscrapers had been reduced to mountains of rubble. Here and there a skeletal frame remained with beams and crumbling walls rising to barely ten or fifteen stories where before there had been fifty or even a hundred. Highways and overpasses had collapsed in massive chunks of concrete, each the size of a small house. Ancient traffic jams choked what was left of those streets, but the cars were swept into high berms along the shoulders, like driftwood pushed up on a beach by a wave. In this case, *shock* waves. Not all cities had been this badly devastated, but the Kyra had made examples of the ones where they had encountered more resistance by dropping antimatter bombs on them.

Samara grimaced at the sight of those cars. Each of them was like a coffin, home to one or more bodies—incinerated before they could escape the twin cities. No doubt the only ones who'd actually escaped the invasion were the wealthy with their air cars, but they would have escaped only to become breeding stock for the Kyra.

Samara glanced around as they flew over the devastation. The Kyra had focused their reconstruction efforts on Dallas, and left the Fort Worth side as a monument to the sheer destructive power of their weapons. Perhaps to them the two cities were counted as one and only merited one occupation zone.

Samara began to wonder where Logan was leading them. Was the Enclave hidden in some forgotten section of these ruins? Maybe an underground tunnel, or a building that had somehow survived the invasion despite appearances to the contrary. Her mind began to spin with possibilities, but none of the ones she came up with fulfilled Sutton's promise that they'd be able to eat and drink to their hearts' content in the Enclave.

Logan steered away from the sun, heading north, and that was when she saw it: surrounded by ruins, a massive glass pyramid soared into the sky. Rotating sails sprouted from the top on long poles, catching wind and sun at the same time to generate electricity. Within the sloping glass sides of the structure, Samara saw nothing but the lush greens of growing things. Horizontal beams sprouted from the pyramid's sides, like branches with landing pads of varying sizes for leaves.

"*That's* the Enclave?" Samara exclaimed, unable to contain her amazement. This wasn't some re-purposed derelict from a bygone era of human civilization. It was some type of megastructure. But that called into question its purpose. The Kyra must have built it, but why? And for what? And was it overrun with Dregs like everywhere else? "Is it safe?" Samara shouted.

Logan didn't reply. Maybe he hadn't heard her through his helmet. Samara watched as the facility grew larger and closer with their approach. It was easily ten times the size of the typical Ascension Center. The greenery growing within resolved into orderly fields of crops and neatly-curated gardens, all perfectly contained within a giant greenhouse. People walked among the crops, tending to them—they looked no bigger than ants, giving a new sense of scale to the structure.

They came to within just a few hundred meters of the building, and now it was all Samara could see. Logan gradually slowed and looped down toward one of the smaller landing pads. A high concrete wall ran around the otherwise vulnerable glass pyramid. More farms lay between those walls and the pyramid itself, with different types of crops divided by tall rows of trees. People walked along the shady, winding streets between the fields. To Samara's surprise she even saw a few dogs down there, walking at the end of their leashes.

Logan landed them on a circular platform suspended about five floors above the fields and trees below. More bikes swooped down and glided to a stop beside them.

Samara didn't waste time with more questions. She leaped off the back of the bike and ran on wobbly legs to the edge of the landing pad. She was soon joined there by Dora. Pyro, Doc, Harold, and Richard weren't far behind.

"What *is* this place?" Nova marveled. "It's amazing!"

Dora nodded along with that and took a step toward the edge of the landing pad to look down. Samara had the presence of mind to pull her back. "Careful. There's no railing."

"I *was* being careful," Dora replied, but she didn't try to duck out of Samara's grip.

The sound of children laughing and screaming far below mingled with dogs barking and fountains bubbling—sounds of joy and bliss that Samara could only remember hearing from before the invasion.

"It's some kind of self-contained community," Harold said. "A veritable utopia."

"I don't believe it..." Pyro added. "How have we not heard about this place?"

"The Kyra built this?" Doc asked, his voice pitching up with disbelief.

"Who else?" Richard said.

Samara glanced back to see the massive solar sails slowly spinning atop their masts in the winds gusting over the glass pyramid in the center of the complex.

Sutton, Lori, and Logan strode over, just now joining them at the edge of the landing platform.

"What do you think?" Logan asked. Nova stayed with the bikes, leaning against the side of one of them. She was looking around curiously, but eschewing from social contact— probably drawn inward by grief and worry over her father, and now Rosie, too.

Logan spread his hands in an expansive gesture, catching Samara's eye once more. "Not bad, huh?"

Samara fixed him with a look of unbridled

shock. He wore a smug, knowing smile on his face, as though he could have guessed that they would react this way. It took Samara a moment to process all of the conflicting feelings raging through her, but the one that came out on top was outrage. "You've been living here, like this, all this time?" she demanded. What made them so special that the Kyra had treated them so well? Were they some type of collaborators?

"I realize this must be a shock for you," Logan said.

"Where are the Chimeras?" Harold asked.

"There aren't any. We govern ourselves."

"You govern... how many of you are there?" Pyro asked.

"Four thousand seven hundred and sixty-two," Logan replied. "We have capacity for five thousand, but the Kyra recently took a group of cadets to the front line, and we have yet to replenish our numbers. We have a large number of pregnant mothers, however, so we anticipate reaching full capacity again in about eight to nine months."

"What is this place?" Doc asked.

"It's a city. You might call it New Fort Worth, but we call it the Enclave. It was an experiment conducted by the Kyra when they began rebuilding city centers as occupation zones. A high-ranking engineer in the Kyron Guard believed that we would produce a larger quantity and higher quality of recruits if we could see and appreciate the advantages of membership in the Kyron Federation for ourselves. He also believed that Chimeras who were a product of such a rich environment would fight harder to defend the federation than Chimeras who had been born and raised in hardship."

"Did it work?" Samara asked.

"No," Logan replied through a tight smile. "Our cadets consistently underperformed in battle simulations. But they demonstrated more aptitude for cerebral roles such as supply line management, battle strategy, research and development, and the medical corps. So the Enclave was allowed to persist, and we became one of a very small number of occupied cities producing Chimeran officers."

"It's like ROTC," Sutton said.

"Similar I suppose," Logan replied.

"Well, it's incredible," Pyro said.

"No one here got infected with the Chrona's new virus?" Samara asked.

Logan shook his head. "Our water supply is highly recycled, and as such there are sensors to detect contaminants. We detected the nano virus during its dormant phase, over a month ago, when it was first inserted into our reservoirs."

"A *month* ago?" Samara echoed.

Sutton nodded. "The Chrona needed time

to seed the water supplies of all fifty-seven occupied cities. It was a bit of a logistical nightmare, but we left it to them, and apparently they pulled it off without a hitch. In hindsight, I wish they'd run into more obstacles."

"Did you know what the virus was when you found it?" Samara asked Logan. She was wondering if they'd realized what was going to happen, but had kept quiet about it because it would result in their independence.

"Yes and no," Logan replied. "We had some idea about what it would do and how virulent it might be, but we assumed that it was a Kyra experiment on the Enclave to boost our output of Chimeras or cull our numbers. We quietly neutralized the virus and remained vigilant, while making plans to escape if the need arose, but there were no subsequent attempts to infect our water supply."

A new thought occurred to Samara and she looked to Sergeant Sutton once more. "If the Chrona infected cities a month ago, why aren't we sick?" Samara asked. "I was living in New Houston until last night. So was Dora. We were drinking the water right up until then."

"The water wasn't infectious until last night," Sutton replied with a shrug. "The virus was designed to be remotely activated, and we had to time it to simultaneously vaccinate the entire planet, or else the Kyra might have realized what was happening and found a way to stop us. Little did we know, the Chrona were planning simultaneous *infection*."

"The dormant molecules are not dangerous," Logan added.

Samara looked back to the farms below and let out a long, slow breath. It was hard to imagine that a place like this could exist. An oasis in the middle of all the chaos. Somehow that made it feel even more fragile, like a rose growing in a desert.

"What about the Kyra's reinforcing fleet?" Doc asked.

Samara looked to Logan and waited for his reply.

"We've been keeping an eye on the skies since the battle last night. When Sutton mentioned the Kyra's reinforcements, I was also concerned, but so far there's been no sign of any fleet."

Samara frowned. Was it possible that Keera had been mistaken? Maybe Specter *had* lied to her about the Kyra's reinforcements. But no, that Chimeran commander who'd been broadcasting from the Wastes outside New Houston had mentioned a reinforcing fleet as well.

"Maybe they're running late," Samara said.

"Or they were intercepted by the Chrona," Logan replied. "We'll remain vigilant. But for now, perhaps you would like to get settled? You all look like you could use a warm shower and a hot meal."

"Hooah!" Sutton cried.

Doc echoed that sentiment with a grin. Dora said nothing, holding her wounded arm close to her chest. Samara noticed that and gave her shoulder a squeeze, hoping she'd get the hint—*just act normal and everything will be okay,* she thought.

Doc glanced their way and his grin faded dramatically as he noticed the way Dora was holding her arm.

"Come on then, let's go." Logan turned and started toward the far end of the landing pad, oblivious to the exchange that had just taken place. Lori was watching them too, her eyes tense with worry.

Samara's mouth watered at the prospect of a warm meal, and a hot shower sounded like a forbidden luxury, but she couldn't focus properly on any of that. Suddenly, she was terrified. Dora was starting to act suspicious, and if she wasn't careful she would give herself away. As they crossed the landing pad, Samara waved for Nova to join them. The girl came over, and they all walked together to a pedestrian bridge with metal railings that spanned the gulf between the landing platform and the shining glass pyramid.

The steady *whoosh, whoosh, whooshing* of the gleaming solar sails spinning on their masts grew louder as they approached, setting Samara's nerves on edge.

Dora looked up at her with a worried expression. "Mom, what if they—"

"Quiet," Samara warned sharply. Dora's eyes widened in terror. "It'll be okay," Samara added to put her daughter at ease. But she was keeping another secret, too. Horror and guilt twisted her stomach up in an even tighter knot. She was a murderer. She didn't deserve to live in a place like this. Even if they didn't find out about Dora, they might still exile *her* for killing an innocent man.

Or maybe they'd understand. Maybe Nova was right. After all, it *had* been an accident. And they'd flown a long way to reach the Enclave. Odds were it was just some random Exile from the Wastes. For all she knew, he'd been expelled from New Dallas because *he* was a murderer. Samara tried to comfort herself with that thought, but she knew she was just rationalizing her guilt.

As they reached the end of the pedestrian bridge, the walkway broadened to a semi-circular terrace in front of the sloping glass side of the pyramid. A big panel of glass slid aside, and a pair of armed guards in faceless black armor came out and stood blocking the way. A stab of dread shot through Samara, and everyone froze, their weapons snapping up in an instant. Everyone except for Sutton and Lori. The two guards responded by drawing their sidearms.

"Stand down!" Sergeant Sutton said.

"What the hell is this?" Pyro demanded, aiming her rifle at Logan rather than the armored guards.

Logan walked to the front of the group and turned to face them. "Relax. They're our men, not Chimeras." He nodded to the two guards and said, "Lower your weapons and take off your helmets." The guards hesitated briefly, then twisted off their helmets with a soft hiss of escaping air. Human faces emerged. A black man who could have been Sergeant Sutton's son, and a woman with razor short blonde hair and bright green eyes.

"There are a few formalities that we need to go through before you can go inside," Logan explained. "First, all of you must hand over your weapons. Only our *arbiters* are allowed to carry weapons inside the Enclave."

Samara looked to Sutton for his reaction, but he seemed to have already known about this. He led by example, flipping his pistol around and handing it butt first to Logan. Samara was surprised to see him yield so easily, but then again, he'd probably already been given the grand tour. He and Lori had gone ahead to check out the Enclave, so they surely knew about the rules.

"What's the other formality?" Doc asked as Pyro and Harold followed Sutton's lead, passing their rifles to Logan one after another. Lori did the same, followed by Richard, but Nova didn't step forward with her weapon.

Logan passed the weapons back to the guards, and they set them down against the side of the Enclave.

"The other matter is that you must submit yourselves to a blood test, but that rule goes for anyone who goes out, so it applies to me as well. We have to be certain that none of you are infected."

Samara glanced sharply at Dora, and her daughter gave her a stricken look. Would that test reveal that Dora had been bitten? The virus could be in her blood in some kind of a dormant state.

"Do you accept these terms?" Logan asked, his gaze passing over each of them in turn.

Nods and muttered affirmations answered.

Logan's eyes settled on Nova and narrowed fractionally. "Your weapon, please, young lady."

She shook her head but said nothing.

"You can't come in if you don't give it to me."

"Go on, Nova," Samara urged. "You don't want to be stuck out here alone."

She bit her lower lip. "What if I want to leave?"

Logan frowned and a curious smile lifted the corners of his mouth. "And why would you want to do that?" He gestured to indicate their surroundings. "You want to leave even after you've seen how we live here?"

"Those Chimeras have my dog, Rosie."

Logan nodded and crossed over to Nova. His expression was sympathetic, but his eyes were hard. He stopped in front of her and regarded her steadily. "I promise you, we will go after them, and we will bring your dog back with us after we've eliminated the threat."

Nova's eyes pinched to suspicious slits.

Logan went on, "You won't stand a chance against them on your own."

"I know how to fight."

"I'll bet you do, but those Chimeras are professional soldiers, and they'll outnumber you. It doesn't matter how many of the demons you've killed or how great a marksman you are —no one is that good. You'll need support."

Nova glanced back at the hoverbikes on the landing pad behind them, as if she were considering making a run for one of them.

Logan looked to Samara for support, and she laid a hand on the girl's shoulder. "It's okay, Nova. No one is giving up on her."

Nova's head snapped around, her eyes flashing. "And what about my dad? And Widow?"

Samara shook her head. "For all we know, Widow is there with Clayton right now, and the two of them are busy plotting to rescue Rosie."

Nova held her gaze for a long, silent moment, then heaved out a frustrated sigh. "Okay.

Fine." She handed over the rifle.

"Thank you." Logan took the weapon and went to set it down with the others. Then he stood in front of the guards and waited while one of them removed a handheld scanner from his belt and aimed it at Logan's forehead. The device beeped, and the guard nodded. "Temperature normal."

The other one produced a smooth black cylinder that could have been a grenade. Logan pressed his thumb to the top of it, and the device began pulsing with waves of blue light. Then it flashed green and a pleasant chime sounded.

Logan turned to them with a smile. "That's it. Who's next?"

Samara shrank back a step, not wanting to volunteer herself or Dora. She'd been attacked by a Dreg last night. Maybe she was also harboring the virus. That test might flag them as infected even though they weren't contagious.

"I'll go," Dora said, her hand shooting up before Samara could stop her.

Her sleeve fell down, revealing the bandage on her arm. The bite had never fully healed, despite the Regenex and Synthskin Doc had used on it. A clearly defined horseshoe-shaped bite mark had soaked through her bandage, marked in blood. The guards saw her injury and recognized it instantly.

"The girl's been bitten!" the male guard

cried as he drew his sidearm and aimed it at Dora.

CHAPTER 31

Clayton saw the trouble a long way off, even before the cluster of blips appeared on his sensors. Flying in just above the tallest trees, he could see that Phoenix base was teeming with Chimeras. They had white canvas tents set up all around the house, and several bonfires burning bright against the encroaching swell of dusk. They were probably cooking meat from whatever animals they'd been able to hunt since they'd arrived. Based on the organized state of their camp, they had to have been there for several hours already. Clayton's thoughts jumped to his family and a thick knot formed in his throat. Would the Chimeras take prisoners, or just kill everyone and be done with it?

Clayton didn't have radio contact with Ava, so he gestured to his eyes and then pointed to the camp below. But she was already slowing down and losing altitude. Clayton did the same, and they both came to a stop, hovering a few feet above the winding residential street that led to Phoenix Base. They flew slowly along it until they found cover behind an ancient moving truck. The rusting, slumping skeleton of the vehicle hid them from sight of any perimeter guards who might glance their way from the direction of the camp.

A warm breeze blew through the trees, but it felt hot compared with the hundred-mile-per hour winds that had been whipping around their bikes a moment ago. Ava removed the helmet of her cloaking armor and balanced it in her lap. "Those are Chimeras," she said, jerking her chin in the direction of the camp.

"Yeah, I noticed that..." Clayton added. He hesitated, wondering if he should say *where* they must have come from. Those were almost certainly the ones from the *Sovath*—Ava's old crew. Based on that, it seemed obvious to him where her loyalties would lie. He thought about Keera's rifle slung behind his back, and wondered how quickly he could reach for it.

"Based on the size of their camp, there have to be at least fifty of them," Ava said. "Did you see any of your people?"

He shook his head. "It's too dark. Did you?" Her sight was much sharper than his—the difference between an eagle and a human. In fact, much of Chimeran DNA was from the Kyra themselves—a winged bird-of-prey species used to hunting in the perpetual darkness of their tidally locked home world.

"I saw something. Maybe. A dog and one person on her knees sitting beside one of the fires, surrounded by about twelve Chimeras."

Clayton's heart sank and he felt the blood drain from his face. "Just one? Are you sure? How old?"

Ava nodded. "An adult."

Clayton let out a long slow breath. The dog was clearly Rosie. But why would the Chimeras keep a dog alive and not the people? They had even less time for pets than they did for humans. Maybe the rest of the prisoners were inside the house. If not...

He pushed that thought from his mind. Until he knew for sure, he refused to give in to despair. But one thing was for sure, he couldn't leave his people at the mercy of their Chimeran captors, and if he was going to set them free, he could really use Ava's help. That cloaking armor of hers would make all the difference between success and failure. The problem was, his people and *her* people were on opposite sides. He rested a hand on his thigh, as close as he could get to actually reaching for the rifle behind his back.

But Ava tracked his movement with a hiss and bared her teeth at him. "Relax. I am not on their side."

"You're not?"

"The *Sovath* is gone. That unit down there belongs to Commander Tyris, and he is a chauvinistic pig with at least three counts of rape that *I* know about. I'd sooner challenge him to the death than submit to his leadership."

That news took Clayton by surprise. "What about the soldiers under his command?"

"They aren't much better. I'm not with them for a reason. It's not because I didn't know that they survived."

"I see. In that case, will you help me rescue my people?"

Ava nodded once. "Yes, but first we need to see who actually needs rescuing. I'll conduct recon of the area, and we'll make a plan."

Clayton nodded. "Better do it on foot. They'll see your bike coming a mile away."

Ava jumped off her bike and put her helmet back on. She walked the bike into an overgrown field beside the street—what used to be the front lawn of someone's house. Now the house was a decaying ruin and the yard was full of weeds and waist-high grass. Ava powered down the bike and it sank into the grass, disappearing from sight. Clayton walked his bike over and did the same just as Ava vanished in a shimmering swirl.

"I'll be back soon," she said in a gravelly whisper.

* * *

"She's immune!" Samara cried.

"What?" Logan hesitated, his eyes narrowing sharply. He strode over from the doors, closing the gap between them and the entrance of the Enclave. Logan shook his head, and his pony tail whipped back and forth across his shoulders. "Maybe you'd better explain."

"We're all immune," Sergeant Sutton added. "We created a vaccine and inoculated ourselves." He rolled up his sleeve and revealed his own bandage, but unlike Dora's, it wasn't bloody. He'd healed just fine. "A few of us were bitten early this morning when we were fleeing New Houston," Sutton explained.

"Is that so..." Logan mused, thoughtfully rubbing the stubble on his chin. "How do you expect me to believe that your tiny group managed to create a vaccine? We have a lot more resources here, and we've been trying to do that ourselves for years."

"But you never had access to someone who was immune," Sutton replied.

"No one is immune," Logan said.

"Clones are," Lori said. "I'm a clone. So is Samara. And she passed her immunity on to her daughter. Why do you think the Kyra made cloning illegal?"

"They made it illegal for their own people, too," Logan said.

Lori shrugged. "Regardless. It's true. You can test us and you'll see."

"So you all have antibodies to the virus?" Logan asked.

"No. It's germ line immunity," Lori explained. "It's a result of genetically engineering our germ cells to make us mature to adulthood faster—among other things. The vaccine is actually a retrovirus based on those genetic differences. It alters the hosts DNA to align it with that of a clone with germ line immunity."

"We'll have to test you all to verify that," Logan explained. "We can't take the risk that one of you is actually contagious. Even if you are immune, you could still be carriers and infect us."

"That's fine," Sutton replied. "You can do whatever tests you need to. We'll cooperate."

"Good. Stay here. I'll bring a medical team up."

"You're not going to let us in?" Samara called out to him.

"I'm afraid that would be unwise until we know more."

"If we were infected, we'd be showing symptoms by now," Samara added.

"The incubation period is twelve to twenty-four hours," Logan said.

"Not for the new strain," Samara argued. "It has a much shorter incubation period."

Logan cocked his head suddenly to one side. "And how would you know that?"

Lori and Doc exchanged a quick look. She shook her head and he frowned.

Logan didn't miss it. "What was that?"

Samara's chest ached with a sudden pressure; she held her breath, waiting for one of them to say something about Dora's condition. She'd already said too much. She shouldn't have reminded anyone about the differences between the new virus and the old one.

Lori cleared her throat and said, "We saw the effects of the new strain first hand, before we left Houston. People were succumbing to it much faster."

"I see. We also saw that in San Antonio, so we can say with some certainty that none of you are infected with the new virus. But we still don't know if you've caught the old one, and I only have your word for it that you're all immune. We need to verify that before we let you in."

"Isn't that the point of your tests?" Samara asked, nodding to the guard who'd tested Logan's temperature and his blood.

"The tests are not perfect," Logan explained. "They'll only reveal an active infection. It will take more thorough testing to verify that you won't later sicken from a recent infection. Like that bite." He pointed to Dora's bloody bandage. "Rest assured, if none of you are contagious, this will turn out to be nothing but a formality. I'll be back soon. Try to be patient until then." Logan strode back to the guards and the open door of the Enclave. He stepped through the door, and one of the guards waved it shut behind him.

Samara pulled Dora close and took a few deep breaths to calm herself.

"I'm thirsty," Dora sniffed.

"I know, honey. So am I," Samara said, rubbing her daughter's back to reassure her. "This will all be over soon."

Doc came striding over. "Let me take a look at that bite," he said, and kneeled in front of them. "It might be infected."

"How?" Samara whispered. "I saw you treat her with Regenex and Synthskin." She'd been a nurse in New Houston. She knew how quickly those treatments should have healed Dora's injury. And the Regenex would have made it impossible for an infection to set in.

Doc looked up at her with a frown and gave his head a slight shake as he unwrapped Dora's arm. "I don't know. Maybe we took the wrong meds from the center. They might have been expired."

"Except Sutton's arm is fine," Lori pointed out as she walked over with the others. Everyone gathered around to watch as Doc finished unwrapping Dora's bandage.

Samara's breath caught in her throat when she saw the bite: a crusty, oozing wound that was red and inflamed. It was definitely infected.

Dora whimpered at the sight of her own arm and turned her face into Samara's chest.

"That looks bad," Nova said.

Doc just nodded as he unslung his pack and zipped it open. He pulled out a medkit and removed a syringe and several vials of nanobiotics.

"Shit," Lori breathed.

Samara gave her a sharp look.

"That must hurt," Nova added.

"A little," Dora admitted.

Sutton nodded to them. "Should we treat her before Logan returns? They might have better meds."

Doc hesitated before injecting Dora with the nanobiotics.

"We don't even know if that will work," Lori added in a quiet voice. "Maybe it's time we told everyone the truth."

Sutton looked up sharply from Dora, his eyes turning to beady specks in the gathering darkness. "The truth?" he whispered back, his eyes flicking between Lori and Samara. "About what?"

"Don't," Samara said.

"Dora was bitten by one of the new Dregs," Lori revealed.

Sutton rocked back on his heels. "How am I only finding out about this now?" Somehow he managed to keep his voice down even though his eyes were flashing with fire. "We left her in our camp. For all we know she's passed it to all of us."

"Not without any symptoms," Lori said. "The virus is transmitted through fluids, not casual contact."

"So maybe she shared a glass with someone. You took a big fucking risk keeping this to yourself."

The guards at the entrance of the Enclave shifted noisily from one foot to another, Samara glanced their way, but there was no sign that they'd overheard. She looked back to Sutton with a scowl. "Dora should be showing symptoms by now, so she has to be immune."

"Do you *know* that?" Sutton demanded. "Maybe she's just resistant, not immune. That bite should have healed by now. There's a reason it hasn't."

Dora started crying, and Samara rubbed her back. "Would you contain yourself?" she snapped at the sergeant. "What's done is done."

Sutton snorted and spun away, muttering under his breath. He walked to the edge of the semi-circular terrace where they all stood and leaned on the railing, overlooking the crops below. Now they were illuminated by a silvery glow from streetlights. Looking away from him, Samara noticed that the pyramid structure in the center of the Enclave was a shining beacon of light, casting a pale glow over them. But nothing could light the darkness encroaching on her heart.

Doc sat back on his haunches with a sigh

and put the syringe full of nanobiotics back in his medkit. "I guess we should wait for Logan to see this before we administer treatment. We'll have to level with him, too."

"Absolutely," Lori replied, nodding slowly.

"But Samara's right about one thing," Doc said. "She could be immune. The wound looks bad, but she's not showing any symptoms."

"That would be a stroke of luck," Harold said.

"How so?" Pyro asked her father.

Doc answered, "Because we made a vaccine to the first strain by analyzing someone who was immune. Maybe we can do it again."

"Would be a hell of a thing," Harold said. "The Kyra and Chimeras get ousted and we find a way to immunize ourselves. The planet would be ours again."

"If we can create a vaccine, so can the Kyra," Lori pointed out.

Harold grunted. "Yeah, I guess that's true. Maybe these people will have more answers after they conduct their tests."

A new concern crept into Samara's thoughts. If Dora was immune and the Enclave decided to use her to develop a vaccine, she would become some kind of lab rat. Samara glanced back along the walkway to the landing pad where they'd left their bikes. The path and landing pad were illuminated now by glowing white strips of light, marking them clearly against the blank black canvas of the night. Beyond that, the Enclave's walls were also lit up with floodlights. It reminded her of the walls around any other occupied city, and she realized that the Enclave might not be very different. At least, not for her and Dora. She wondered if she should make a run for it now —before it was too late. Would those guards open fire? Or would they let her go?

But as Samara glanced back, she noticed that Lori, Pyro, and Harold all had their hands resting on the butts of their sidearms. They would just stun her and Dora if they tried to leave. They weren't about to let their only hope for a new vaccine escape.

For better or worse, she and Dora were trapped here.

CHAPTER 32

Clayton crouched behind a window in the porch of the rotting house where he and Ava had hidden their hoverbikes. He had his rifle propped on the sill, and was peering through the weapon's combination night-vision and infrared scope to scan for signs of Chimeran scouts. So far, he hadn't seen any heat signatures that corresponded to Chimeras, or even Dregs.

Clayton eased back from the rifle, rolling his shoulders to work out the kinks from sitting that way for so long. He would have connected his ARCs directly to the scope and avoided the need to lean over the rifle, but this wasn't an advanced weapon adapted for use with ARCs. It was a stripped down model that the Solid Waste Management Department used to arm garbage hauler drivers and co-drivers.

Impatience festered inside Clayton, rearing its ugly head and bursting free with a stifled sigh. Ava had been gone for at least half an hour. How long did she need to conduct recon?

He needed to know where his family was and whether or not they were okay. Not that he supposed a few extra minutes would make a difference one way or the other, but the longer Ava took the more he began to worry that she'd been spotted and captured herself. *That, or she lied about her opinion of Commander Tyris, and she didn't go to conduct recon at all.* Maybe she'd left to get reinforcements to deal with him.

Clayton jammed his eye socket to the rifle's scope once more, sweeping the barrel around to check the trees and the other side of the street for signs of enemy heat signatures creeping up on him. Movement caught his eye, and his finger tensed on the trigger.

It was just the grass swaying in the overgrown yard as the night breeze played through it.

Unless it was swaying because cloaked Chimeras were creeping toward his position. Clayton felt the hairs on the back of his neck rising. He leaned back from the scope again and glanced around the darkened interior of the old home. The roof had collapsed, blocking the stairs in a twisted tangle of rotting wood and moldy shingles. There was nowhere to hide, and even if he did find a place, Ava knew he was waiting here.

Clayton cursed under his breath. He had to go. Jumping to his feet, he grabbed the rifle in a two-handed grip and started for the door.

He was halfway there when a floorboard creaked loudly—but the sound had come from farther away, out on the front porch. He stepped to the side and flattened himself against the wall beside the door.

Blinking stinging drops of sweat from his eyes, he aimed the rifle sideways at the open doorway and stuck out his foot, hoping to hook a foot as whoever it was came through. He couldn't rely on his sight to find them, but even a cloaked soldier could still trip over his outstretched leg.

It worked. He felt a foot hit his, and then came a loud crash on the ground just inside the entrance. He snapped his rifle up to his shoulder and his finger ducked into the trigger guard.

"It's me!" Ava hissed, and the air shimmered around her as she de-cloaked in front of him. She held up one hand in surrender.

Clayton hesitated rather than lower his weapon or reach down to help her up. "Are you alone?" he whispered.

"Of course I'm..." She trailed off, and her helmet bobbed as she began nodding with comprehension. "You thought I might betray you."

Clayton leaned around the door frame to check for signs of more Chimeras approaching. But the front lawn and the street beyond were empty. At least, as far as he could tell in the pale silver light of the stars and crescent moon.

Clayton ducked back into cover.

Ava bounced to her feet with a grunt. "I was telling you the truth. I'd sooner kill Tyris than follow him. Anyway, I scouted the house and the camp as best I could, but I didn't see any signs of additional captives."

"Are you sure?"

"I was pretty thorough, but we'll know more after we free the one they captured."

"Any ideas about that?" Clayton asked.

"One idea. I found their armory and stole these." Ava patted a cloakable EKR rifle dangling from a jointed metal strap, then she reached for a pair of black cylinders on her belt. "Plasma grenades," she explained. "I'll toss them into the middle of their camp, and then lead them on a foot chase through the neighboring fields. You can use the distraction to sneak in and free the captive. They might leave a few guards, but you can stun them silently with this." Ava drew the Stinger pistol from the holster on her hip and handed it to him. "This weapon is designed for covert ops so the stun setting is quieter."

Clayton shouldered his rifle and accepted the pistol with a nod. "Stun bolts might be quiet, but it can fire lasers both silently and invisibly."

"Not all of Tyris's men are as degenerate as

he is. If you want my help, you'll stick to stun."

Clayton nodded. "Fine. Is there a path we can take to approach the camp without being spotted?"

"No. The perimeter guards will see you coming. You should wait here until I've drawn them off."

"All right," Clayton agreed.

"I'll lead the Chimeras away, then cloak myself and circle back around to meet you here. We'll use the bikes to make our escape."

Clayton nodded. "And if you don't make it?"

"I'll make it. Just be sure that you do, too, because I won't stick around and wait. I'll just assume you were captured and bug out."

"Fair enough."

The air shimmered as Ava cloaked herself once more. Her EKR-7 commando rifle vanished with her, and he heard footsteps creaking as she left the house and hurried across the front porch. Clayton went back to his window sill and to using the scope of his rifle to keep a lookout.

His heart beat hard and fast inside his chest as he peered through the scope. His breathing was short and shallow. Anger and a bloody thirst for vengeance rose up like a black tide inside him. He tried not to think about what he would do if he learned that the woman the Chimeras had taken captive was actually the only survivor.

CHAPTER 33

"**T**here are no signs of a systemic infection," Aria Dartmouth, the Enclave's chief virologist declared.

Samara's spirits soared with that news. "So she's fine?"

Aria hesitated. She and her two unnamed colleagues were wearing clean white hazmat suits. Rather than answer, the doctor turned and waved Dora out of the portable Kyron body scanner. Three hovering rings of black spheres encircled her at varying heights.

Dora stepped carefully over the lowermost ring and ducked under the middle one, but the hovering spheres parted to let her out as soon as she drew near.

"I didn't say she's fine," Dr. Dartmouth clarified as Dora ran back to Samara's side.

Samara wrapped an arm around her daughter's shoulders. "What do you mean?"

"The wound is not healing for a reason. Her body's immune system seems to have contained the virus to the site of infection, but the bite is teeming with the virus and it is actively contagious. All it would take is for Dora's wound to bleed or ooze on something that later comes into contact with your eyes, ears, nose, or mouth and you would become infected yourself. The fact that the wound has been covered is likely the only reason that none of the rest of you are infected."

"So we cover it up again!" Samara said. "We'll be careful."

"I'm afraid I can't condone that. It's too much of a risk. And what happens when she bathes? Our residual waters are treated and then recycled. The treatment process might not completely eliminate active particles of the virus. The only way I can admit her to our facilities is if you'll agree to quarantine her in one of our isolation wards."

"I won't agree to that," Samara said. She looked to the others. "You don't have to subject yourselves to anything. We'll leave, and you can stay, but I'm not going to let these people turn my daughter into a science experiment."

"I promise you we will do everything in our power to help her," Dr. Dartmouth said. "And it will only be necessary to isolate her until her wound heals and the virus is eliminated by her immune system.

"No!" Samara said again.

Logan looked on from the entrance of the

Enclave, his eyes shadowed by a prominent brow. He looked angry.

But no one was more angry than Samara. Dora looked up at her with big, terrified eyes, and something inside of her broke just that much more.

Sergeant Sutton came over and held up both his hands in a placating gesture. "Listen to me, Sam. If you leave, how long do you think you'll last in the Wastes on your own? A week? A month? Maybe two if you're very lucky." He slowly shook his head. "And leaving won't help Dora. She could still sicken and turn while she's in your care. Or she could infect you, and then you'll turn and eat your own daughter alive. Is that what you want?"

Some of the fight left Samara, but she wasn't ready to give in just yet. "I don't trust them," she said, glancing at Dr. Dartmouth as she said it.

Sutton followed her gaze to the virologist, then back. "I don't believe she intends to harm your daughter."

"Of course not!" Aria said.

"Let them help her," Sutton urged. He grabbed one of Samara's hands and sandwiched it between both of his. "Please. This is important. The fact that her body is fighting this infection at all is a miracle, let alone the fact that she seems to have fought the virus to a standstill. We need to learn more about what makes her resistant. Do you have any idea how many lives she could save if she is able to help us develop a cure?"

"Not that many," Samara said. "There can't be that many of us left after what the Chrona did."

"Wrong," Sutton replied. "She will save an entire species and all of its future generations. We could be talking about *trillions* of people, Samara."

"And what if she can't help us develop a cure?"

"Then we will have lost nothing by trying," Lori put in.

"They're right," Dr. Dartmouth said. "Humanity needs this. Now is not the time to be thinking selfishly."

Samara looked at Dora, and with that, so did everyone else. "What do *you* want?" she asked. "They're going to put you in a room, by yourself, and you won't be allowed to leave. I won't be able to stay there with you, and the only people allowed in will be doctors."

Dora's face screwed up in terror. "You won't be able to see me?"

"We can arrange supervised visits," Dr. Dartmouth said. "Your mother would need to wear a protective suit like mine, but she can still see you."

Dora hesitated.

"What the hell are we even talking about?"

Logan shouted from where he stood at the entrance of the Enclave. "Who said the girl even has a choice?"

Aria Dartmouth rounded on him. "I say."

Logan looked like he wanted to say something else, but he held his tongue.

The doctor looked back to Dora. "Well, honey? What do you think? Do you want to help us save lives? We can't do it without you."

Dora gave the woman an uncertain look, then nodded once, quickly. "Okay," she said in a shaky voice. "I'll do it."

Dr. Dartmouth smiled broadly inside her hazmat suit. "Said like a true hero." She turned to regard her two colleagues. "Get a suit for the girl. We need to be sure the virus doesn't infect anyone while we're escorting her to isolation."

Both men nodded and started for the entrance where Logan stood. Some of their gear was standing there, including what looked like a garden sprayer. They began spraying each other with the pump-operated device—disinfecting their suits before they entered the facility.

Samara looked away and her guts clenched up with unease as she watched Dr. Dartmouth bandaging Dora's bite without even trying to administer a treatment. She didn't want the bite to heal. Not until she could study it and discover what Dora's body was doing to keep the virus in check. She wouldn't care if the wound spread or if Dora's arm later had to be amputated because they'd waited too long to treat a simple infection.

Their goal was to study her, not cure her. And that fact encapsulated all of Samara's fears and reservations about submitting Dora to their care. They wouldn't care if she died, just so long as they got their vaccine.

CHAPTER 34

Clayton saw the flash of light from the explosions a split second before he heard them: a rolling thunderclap, followed closely by another. He leaned back from his scope, blinking spots from his eyes as twin fireballs leaped high above the scraggly shadows of the trees.

Jumping to his feet, Clayton ran out of the aging house and dashed through the overgrown lawn. He passed the hoverbikes they'd hidden there, and stopped to catch his breath at the edge of the street. He waited behind an old cedar tree for cover. Peeking around the bole of it with his rifle, he checked for signs of heat signatures coming from the direction of Phoenix base. He caught a glimpse of solid white silhouettes running toward the explosions, and heard their voices raised and shouting to one another in alarm.

Clayton waited a minute for them to pass completely out of sight, then dashed across the street and hid behind another tree. Now he was on the same side as Phoenix base, but still a few hundred meters from the actual building. Scanning once more for targets, Clayton found none in the immediate area. He moved quickly down the street, keeping an eye on his surroundings through the rifle's scope. Still nothing. It looked like Ava's distraction was working.

Clayton switched to a one-handed grip on his rifle and drew the Stinger pistol Ava had given him. It was already set to stun. When he came within a hundred feet of the driveway to Phoenix base, he saw what perimeter guards remained. Leaving his rifle to dangle by the strap, Clayton went down on one knee and balanced his aim on his other arm. He fired. Once. Twice. And dropped both guards where they stood.

Breaking into a sprint, Clayton ran right by the fallen Chimeras and ducked behind the line of trees that followed the curve of the driveway. He stopped again behind the cover of a tree and scanned his surroundings with the rifle's scope. He detected a few more heat signatures at the end of the driveway, some sixty meters away. No sign of them detecting *him* yet; the trees would help shield him for now. He tried to orient himself, racking his brain to recall exactly where they'd seen the prisoner from the air. She was in an open area between the tents, next to a camp fire. Clayton followed the tree line down the driveway, crouching low and keeping both of his weapons at the ready. He aimed for the slash of white canvas tents shining bright like a beacon with the light of the moon and stars. The muffled shouts of Chimeras guided him in—then a loud bark, followed by growls and snarls. Rosie was in trouble.

Clayton sped up. He saw the tents just up ahead, some fifteen feet away. He needed to cross open terrain to get there. Peeking out from behind another cedar tree, he scanned his surroundings with the rifle's night-vision scope. A pair of Chimeras stood guard at the entrance of the log mansion that had been Phoenix's headquarters. They weren't looking his way, but if they did, he wouldn't be hard to spot as he ran across the field to the tents. Not that he had much choice.

A sharp whimper erupted from the direction he'd heard Rosie barking, followed by a woman shouting a curse. Clayton gritted his teeth and forced himself to be patient. Someone else emerged from within the building and the two guards standing on the front steps turned to regard that person. Clayton saw that as his chance and dashed out of cover. He reached the back of the nearest tent in a blink, and crouched there in the tall grass, panting hard, with his pulse thundering in his ears. He didn't hear any shouts of alarm, or other signs that he might have been spotted.

Another sharp whimper sounded, and this time Clayton heard a Chimera's deep, throaty laughter, followed by another shout of protest from the woman, and then a pained scream.

Clayton hurried to the corner of the tent and peeked around it with his rifle. He had a clear line of sight to the bonfire where the prisoners were being kept. Two Chimeras were teasing Rosie, circling her. As he watched, one of them darted in and delivered a sharp kick to her hindquarters. Rosie yelped and snarled. Rounding on her attacker, she ran after him. He darted just out of reach and her chain pulled taut, yanking her back violently by her neck. She whimpered again and coughed, having choked herself with the leash.

"Stop it!" the woman chained on the other side of Rosie said.

"I think the human wants more attention," the second Chimera said.

And the first started circling toward her, his black lips parted in a grin, red eyes gleaming with leaping tongues of flame from the bonfire.

Clayton clamped down on a dark surge of fury and quietly slid the fire-mode selector on his pistol from *stun* to *stealth*—one of the *kill* settings. Ava had insisted that he spare lives, but these two clearly weren't worth sparing.

Rosie strained to reach the Chimera as he approached the female prisoner. She was snarling and barking, straining at the end of her leash, but both the human prisoner and the dog were chained up too far from each other for one to help the other. Clayton crept quietly down the side of the tent. The next one over shielded him from view, and both the darkness and the tall grass helped. He didn't trust any of that to be enough against a Chimera's sharp night vision, but these two were focused on their victims, lulled into a false sense of security by the fact that they were in the heart of their camp and supposedly within a secure perimeter.

The Chimera advancing on the human prisoner stopped.

"What are you waiting for?" the human woman spat. She stood with fists balled, ready to fight.

The Chimera grinned and spread both his hands. Sharp black claws gleamed at the tips of his fingers, as if they were already wet with blood. The Chimera hissed and Clayton saw him rear back as if to lunge.

He pulled the trigger, and an invisible laser shot out and hit the hybrid right between the eyes. The grin vanished and a look of confusion flickered over the Chimera's face. His legs gave out, and he fell with a muffled *thump.*

"Kevan? What's wro—"

Clayton fired again and his companion crumpled to the trampled grass beside him.

Wasting no time, he ran into the open. The human woman turned, her eyes widening at the sight of him. One cheek was sliced open in ragged furrows from a Chimera's claws. That entire half of her face was covered in blood, but he still recognized her easily. Clayton's heart sank. It was Widow. Part of him had been hoping it would be Samara. At least then he'd know if she was alive.

"You're late," Widow accused quietly as he reached for the chains that bound her wrists together.

"This is going to hurt," he whispered, noticing that there was no way to shoot her chains off without them scalding her wrists as the laser superheated the metal.

Rosie barked once at the sound of his voice, and he grimaced at the noise, hoping she wouldn't begin barking more steadily.

"Do it," Widow insisted.

He fired another silent laser into her chains. They glowed molten orange and Widow gritted her teeth and stumbled back a step, staggered by the pain as they sizzled against her wrists. She strained her arms briefly against the chains and they snapped and fell in a pile at her feet.

Clayton ducked out of the rifle strap and passed it to her before moving to free Rosie. She began jumping up and spinning around, barking and wagging her tail. "Shhh!" he hissed at her. "Quiet."

Rosie calmed somewhat, seeming to have sensed the danger they were in. He grabbed her chain and shot a bolt directly into it. Again the metal links glowed brightly, and he gave the chain a sharp tug to snap it. Keeping hold of the end still attached to Rosie, he looped it around his wrist and grabbed a handful of it. He didn't trust her not to run out after the nearest Chimera and sacrifice herself.

Turning away from the fire, he nodded to Widow. She'd already fallen back to the shadows between the tents and was busy watching their backs with the rifle. She waved him through, and then he took the lead. "Follow me," he whispered. He led her around the tents, keeping Rosie on a short leash.

Rather than head back the way he'd come, he judged the distance to the street. It was about forty feet to the cover of the trees growing there. Fifteen to the ones hedging the driveway, but that area was in direct line of sight of the Chimeras guarding the front doors of the house.

Assuming no others were watching from the direction of the camp as they ran, it would be safer to run straight across the property.

"Well?" Widow prompted from where she crouched in the tall grass beside him.

"Don't hold back," he said, and then he burst out of cover and ran across the property as fast as he could. He heard Widow running right behind him. Rosie kept up easily, even leading the way and tugging at the end of her leash.

A bright emerald beam of light split the air right beside them and crashed into the street with an explosion of superheated asphalt. Clayton reflexively angled away from the direction of fire and ran faster still. His nostrils flared and itched with the smell of ozone. Another laser flashed by him, this time hitting the ground in front of his feet. It burst into flames and he ran straight through before the heat could so much as singe a hair on his head. Widow cursed and returned fire.

And then they were running through the cover of the trees along the road. "Keep running!" Clayton urged.

He turned up the street, the way he'd come earlier, and angled across it to the cover of more trees on the other side. A flurry of bright green laser bolts flashed by them on all sides, but the shots went wide. They were too far away and with too much vegetation between them for a clean shot. He ran along the trees on the other side of the road with Widow keeping pace right beside him. She snapped off periodic shots to return fire on their attackers.

"I hope you have a better exit strategy than this!" she said. "They're catching up!"

"I do," he confirmed.

A minute later they reached the yard where he and Ava had hidden the hoverbikes.

But there was no sign of her. And no time to wait.

Clayton reached the first bike and stabbed the ignition switch. It hovered up to waist height, and he pulled open the storage compartment at the back to make a space for Rosie. "Take the other one!" he cried as he tucked his pistol into his belt and began throwing survival gear out of the bike. Widow jumped on the back of the other vehicle and powered it up.

Clayton finished emptying the storage compartment and bent down to lift Rosie into it. "Stay," he warned her, and she sat down with a snort of protest. Clayton swung a leg over the side of the bike and pulled his feet up.

"Ready?" he asked.

Widow nodded. "I'll lead."

Clayton was about to argue when he heard the telltale *whirr* of a bike's engine approaching. The Chimeras weren't just following them on foot. "Go!" he cried.

Widow gunned the throttle and pulled up hard, vanishing in an instant. Clayton followed suit, but with slightly more restraint—conscious that he could send Rosie flying off the bike if he accelerated too fast.

He raced after Widow, throttling up slowly and weaving a snaking line around the tops of the tallest trees. A dazzling green laser snapped through the air beside him, giving him all the more reason not to fly in a straight line. "Shit," Clayton muttered. He ducked low behind the control bars and goosed the throttle up higher. Weaving more furiously now, he glanced at the bike's sensors and saw two purple blips racing ahead of a scattered dozen others who were now falling behind. Two hoverbikes were on their tail—and it was easy for them to shoot, but he would have to twist around in his seat and take his eyes off the road to accomplish the same thing.

Another laser beam flashed out, and this time it burned a sizzling hole through the side of the bike.

"Shit," Clayton muttered again. Widow was flying at least half a klick ahead of him, a tiny glinting speck at the furthest limits of visibility. So far, they were only shooting at him. He pushed the throttle up as high as it would go, jetting out after her. Another pair of lasers flashed by to either side of him. Wind whipped into Clayton's eyes despite the windshield he was hunched behind, and his eyes blurred with tears. He glanced back again to make sure Rosie was still there. She was hunched low in her seat, her tongue out and jowls flapping in the wind. At least she was enjoying this.

Another flash of emerald light tore out of

the darkness. Clayton flinched away from it, swerving dangerously toward a tree. He regained control a moment later and then spared a hand from the control bars to reach for his pistol. He snapped off two shots, aiming as best he could despite being half-blinded, and unable to see clearly in the dark. The pistol clicked dry. The clip was empty. Another curse tore from his lips and he threw the useless weapon over the side of the bike. Seeing Widow take a sharp right turn, he banked after her to the gleaming river of broken asphalt that was the I45. He realized she was following it North, and a flicker of curiosity broke through the more imminent concerns about their survival. Had Sutton and Lori found a ship in Dallas?

Maybe that's where everyone else was. Hope reared up inside of him as he wove a slaloming path along the highway. Glancing at his sensor display, he saw the two purple blips of enemy hoverbikes falling behind. And no more lasers snapped out after them. The Chimeras were breaking off their pursuit.

Clayton's brow furrowed with confusion. He kept jinking and maneuvering to throw off their aim, but soon they fell off his sensor display entirely as they drifted out of range. Clayton pulled alongside Widow. She jerked a thumb over her shoulder and gave him a one-handed shrug.

He shook his head.

They'd obviously been called off, but why? They'd had him and Widow at a clear disadvantage. Given a few more minutes of pursuit, they could have easily picked them off. So why hadn't they stayed the course?

And what had happened to Ava?

Clayton grimaced as he remembered her. She'd told him that she wouldn't wait around for him if he didn't make it back to the bikes in time. But *she* was the one who hadn't made it. He contemplated the road ahead and wondered if he and Widow should turn back and try to rescue Ava. But that would be impossible now. The entire camp was on high alert.

Clayton felt a heavy weight settle around his shoulders, pressing him down. He was leaving yet another Chimeran ally behind, a captive of enemy forces. But unlike Keera, at least Ava was among her own people. And she'd had her weapons set to stun, so maybe Tyris wouldn't treat her too harshly. After all, she hadn't killed anyone.

Clayton tried to ease his conscience with those thoughts. He vowed to come back for both Ava and Keera just as soon as he caught up with the rest of Phoenix.

CHAPTER 35

Keera sat in the pilot's seat of the shuttle with the leader of the Reapers holding a gun to her head. He smiled nastily at her. "You've done good, chalkhead."

Clearly visible, just below and ahead of them were two hoverbikes racing down the moon-silvered highway. The other two who'd been chasing them had fallen behind and broken off pursuit. All four were oblivious to the cloaked shuttle flying over their heads. Keera had expected the Reapers to want to leave Earth after she helped them take off and fly away from San Antonio. She'd been planning to open the airlock and blow them all out into space as soon as they left the atmosphere. Unfortunately, Zachary had other ideas. He wasn't willing to risk the unknown by searching for a habitable world beyond Earth, or the possibility of running into a Kyron fleet in orbit. Instead, he ordered her to fly due East to Phoenix base. He planned to use the cloaking shuttle to ambush and raid it, stealing their supplies and adding them to his own.

But when they arrived to see a large group of Chimeras now occupying Phoenix Base, he'd quickly decided against his original plan. Even with the advantage of surprise, there was no guarantee that they'd survive a confrontation with an organized military unit. And with the shuttle's cloaking shield engaged, they couldn't activate its energy shields, so they were vulnerable even to small arms fire.

Zachary had just ordered Keera to fly away and head for New Houston when they saw the twin fireballs of explosions erupting from the Chimeras' camp. They'd watched silently from above as some type of struggle played out on the ground, and then chased after the trouble-makers as they flew away on a pair of hover-bikes. Even before they'd checked the shuttle's sensors and identified those two bike pilots as *humans,* it had been clear to both Keera and Zachary that at least one of them was Clayton. Making that even more likely, a third life sign was sitting behind one of the pilots—an animal. Keera knew from its size that it had to be Rosie.

"Where do you think they're goin'?" Zachary mused. "They're headed due North. Ya think they got another camp up there?"

Keera didn't bother to guess.

Zachary went on, "My bet is they have a camp around here somewhere."

Footsteps clanked steadily down the aisle to the cockpit, and a new voice joined his, sultry and female: "Zack, the boys are gettin' restless. We've been cooped up for too damn long. When is this plane going to land?"

Zachary waved her away. "Soon, darlin. Soon. First we gotta see where the road takes us, and I'm wagering it's someplace cozy."

"And you trust her not to fly us into a mountain?"

"This is Texas, sweetheart! There are no mountains. Besides, she's got a vested interest now. One of those two down there is her human concubine. She's hoping that after we capture him that we'll give her a chance for a conjugal visit. Ain't that right, chalkhead?"

Keera refused to give him the pleasure of a reaction.

Zachary chuckled darkly and shook his head. "Never mess with a bitch in heat."

"That's sexist and demeaning," McKayla chided, but she said it with a smile.

"No it's not," Zachary replied. "She's not a woman. She's a chalkhead."

Keera resisted the urge to push the flight yoke down and plow the shuttle into the ground. She'd be sparing the world of these ignorant savages. The only thing that stopped her was knowing how close they were to their goal. She had a ship. Now all she needed to do was find the others and get rid of the dead weight on board. These Reapers made even the most brutal and twisted Chimeras seem like angels by comparison. So far Zachary hadn't allowed any of them to make good on their threats to harm her, but she knew that would only last as long as her cooperation and usefulness did. Once Zachary figured out how to fly the shuttle on his own, or if the ship took catastrophic damage, she'd be right back to where she'd been on that rooftop in San Antonio: fleeing from a band of perverted psychopaths.

* * *

"Goodnight, honey," Samara said into the audio pickup at the base of a thick window.

Dora planted both palms on the other side of the glass, her face stricken. She looked like she might already be having a change of heart about submitting herself to an isolation ward, but it was too late for second thoughts now.

"I'll see you in the morning, okay?" Samara said.

Nova stepped up beside her and spoke into the mic. "I'll come, too, Sis. Look on the bright side, no Dregs can get you in there!"

Dora nodded slowly but said nothing.

Samara resisted the urge to make a break for the airlock control panel. But Logan and Dr. Dartmouth were standing right beside them, and they'd take a dim view of her attempting to compromise the Enclave's environment.

Samara placed a palm to the glass, matching her hand to one of Dora's. An air gap of several inches remained between the two sides of the window, making even the illusion of physical contact impossible.

"I love you," Samara said.

Dora nodded again. "Me too." With that she dropped her hands from the glass and retreated to the hospital bed in the center of the room. Dora crawled into the bed and tucked herself under the covers, watching them from there. Samara waved to her and blew a kiss, but Dora made no attempt to respond.

"We can arrange for you to visit her first thing tomorrow," Dr. Dartmouth reassured.

"Until then, you should both get some rest," Logan added. "If you're ready, I'll take you up to see the others." Everyone other than Dora had been cleared by the body scanner, so they'd been taken straight to their quarters.

Samara nodded and turned away from the window, her eyes stinging with tears. She wiped them away quietly and she and Nova followed Logan down the corridor to the elevators. Dr. Dartmouth didn't follow them. Thinking that strange, Samara glanced back and saw her walking deeper into the facility with someone else—another woman, tall and elegant with razor short black hair. She was wearing some type of uniform rather than a doctor's coat like Dr. Dartmouth. Just then, both women turned a corner and passed out of sight.

"What about food?" Nova asked as they stopped at the elevators.

"The mess hall is closed," Logan explained. "But I called and had our staff send food up to your quarters. You'll probably find it in the refrigerator by now."

"Dinner in bed," Nova said. "I could get used to that."

Logan flashed her a tight smile as one of the elevators chimed and the doors parted to let them in. He spoke to the control panel, "Level five."

"Going up, level five," the elevator replied in a pleasant female voice.

The doors slammed shut and the elevator rocketed up for a few seconds before abruptly slowing. The doors parted and Logan stepped out, leading the way. They followed him into a wide, luxurious corridor with warm lines of recessed lighting running along the tops of the walls, leaving the ceiling in darkness and shadow, as if it might be much higher than it seemed.

The walls were white with gleaming flecks of gold and silver, a patterned metallic inlay in the shape of trees and grass that seemed to have depth like a hologram.

As they walked down the corridor, the walls seemed to come alive and move, as if branches were waving and metallic leaves were fluttering in an unseen breeze. The spongy blue floor felt like carpet, but it appeared to shimmer and roll like water, with wave-like patterns flowing along its length. A quiet whisper of accompanying sounds, like waves swishing along a sandy beach soothed Samara's weary mind. Mirror-plated silver and gold doors lined both sides of the corridor, again, with holographic properties. They looked gold when viewed from an angle, but silver when facing them directly. As Samara turned to look at them, floating holographic room numbers appeared.

"Amazing," she said.

"It is, isn't it?" Logan asked.

"Spectral," Nova added.

They hadn't seen this kind of luxury on their way to the isolation wards, but the corridor leading from the landing pad outside had been almost equally as impressive: a glass walkway crossing high above a lush green garden growing in a cavernous, wedge-shaped space that spanned at least five levels along the outer walls of the pyramid. Logan had told them that the greenhouses were there to grow food as well as to foster a sense of peace and emotional well-being through connectedness to nature.

Apartments ran along the inner walls with balconies and windows overlooking those vast gardens. The entire facility was like some type of luxury hotel straight out of the future.

"I think it's making me dizzy," Nova said as another wave of holographic water swished past their feet.

"You'll get used to it," Logan said. "During the day, the floor turns green and it looks like grass. "The water setting is supposed to soothe people and get their brains ready for sleep. Just like the soft lighting." He gestured to the dim golden glow of recessed lights that lined the top of the walls.

"Amazing," Samara said again. As she looked up, she noticed that the dark gulf of shadows between the walls was actually glittering with stars that slowly winked on and off. Apparently the Kyra didn't like looking at static backdrops, but she was beginning to agree with Nova: it was making her head swim to see movement everywhere she looked.

Logan stopped in front of a particular door and some of that motion ceased as they halted beside him. The number *547* glowed to life in front of the double doors just as Logan waved his hand to open them. A stunningly appointed living area and kitchen appeared. Sergeant Sutton was sitting on a clean white couch with his arms draped across the back, looking out at the view. A lush sprawl of greenery lay beyond the balcony and the glass outer wall of the Enclave. Sutton twisted around to see who had opened the door.

"You're back. Is Dora all right?" he asked.

"She's fine," Logan answered as he led the way inside. Sutton rose from the couch to greet them. He wasn't wearing his old, faded army fatigues anymore, but a clean, fuzzy white robe and matching slippers. His face was clean-shaven and no longer smudged with grease and dirt, revealing a shiny burn scar on one side of his face.

"Helluva place you've set us up with," Sutton said, turning in a circle to indicate their surroundings. "Seems like a regular Shangri-La. What's the catch?"

"No catch," Logan replied as they stopped in front of each other.

Samara and Nova walked straight by them to the balcony. Harold and Pyro were out there, admiring the view from even closer up. Like Sutton they were wearing fuzzy white robes and slippers, and their hair looked wet from a recent shower.

The doors slid open as Samara approached. She and Nova stepped out into a warm, fragrant breeze of fresh, growing things. A waterfall thundered beside them, flowing between their balcony and the next one over. It cast sparkling, undulating sheets of spray over the jungle below before falling into a dark, gleaming black pool on the ground floor.

Samara stopped beside Harold and slowly shook her head, gawking at the view. She peered over the glass railing, five floors down to the lush, orderly jungle. It was different from the farms—fuller and greener with flowers growing everywhere. Samara spotted several types of plants and trees that had no business growing in Texas. A massive glass wall with triangular window frames formed the outer wall of the pyramidal structure, protecting it all from the dry Texas air. Beyond the glass wall, illuminated streets and narrow paths cut between orderly plots of wheat and corn and the stately lines of trees that divided them.

"I can't look away..." Harold said. "It's too damn beautiful."

Samara looked down again to admire the jungle. Winding footpaths were illuminated with decorative lighting, and floating white spheres illuminated everything else as they slowly drifted above the treetops like Chinese lanterns.

"No wonder this place didn't make good soldiers," Pyro added. "I can't imagine it churning out anything but tree-hugging pacifists."

Samara nodded along with that assessment. Her thoughts drifted back to Dora, and she wished her daughter could have been here to see and experience all of this. Maybe soon she would get that chance, but Samara still didn't fully trust these people. Not with Dora, anyway.

"You think all of their rooms have a view like this?" Nova asked wonderingly.

"I think they just might," Harold replied.

Samara felt somehow tricked by the beauty of their surroundings, as if it was all part of a plot to lull them into a false sense of security while the residents of the Enclave subtly preyed on them. Maybe that wasn't true, not for all of them, but with Dora's condition and her obvious value to them, it could easily be true for her. Samara forced herself to turn away and march back inside, saying as she left, "I'm going to take a shower."

Nova followed her inside.

Samara's footsteps slowed as she noticed Sergeant Sutton and Doc pressed to either side of the double doors to their suite. Both of them were cursing and sweating in their fuzzy robes as they tried to pry the doors open. Richard and Lori were there, too, in matching white robes, standing a few feet away and looking worried.

"What's going on?" Samara asked, hurrying over to join them by the doors. Harold and Pyro came running in behind them.

"Damn it!" Sutton cried. He gave up trying to force the doors, and Doc gave them a kick. Sutton winced and Samara noticed that several of his fingernails were bleeding, having broken in the seam between the doors.

"Well?" Samara prompted.

Sutton met her gaze with a grim look. "They locked us in."

"They did *what?*"

"Question is," Sutton went on, "did they do it because they don't trust *us,* or because we can't trust *them?*"

CHAPTER 36

Clayton pulled his bike to a stop beside Widow's. The thunder of wind roaring by his ears left a ringing silence in its wake. He glanced around, checking for signs of pursuit or Dregs. A quick look at the time on his ARCs showed that it was nearly midnight.

"There's no one here," Widow muttered, while staring hard at her sensor display.

"Where did they go?" Clayton asked, guessing that she must mean the rest of Phoenix. "Is everyone okay?"

"Last I saw them they were all fine," Widow replied. "They probably went to the Enclave already. But it's strange that Sutton didn't leave someone behind to take us there."

"The Enclave?" Clayton asked.

Widow looked up from her bike. "It's some kind of safe haven the sergeant found around New Dallas."

"My wife and kids are alive?"

Widow nodded. "Yeah. Why, you thought..." Understanding dawned in her eyes.

"Don't worry about it. They're fine."

Relief washed over Clayton like a tidal wave. His shoulders sagged as a wall of tension burst inside of him. He let out a long breath. A wet nose began sniffing around his elbow, nudging him. He reached around to pat Rosie on the head. "Hey, girl." She began panting noisily. "Bet you're thirsty, huh?" He grabbed the canteen off his belt, unscrewed the cap, and cupped one hand to pour water for her. Rosie lapped it up in an instant and went on licking his hand until it was dry. He pulled away and poured some more.

"We'll have to wait here for the night," Widow said. "If Sutton and the others made it to the Enclave, he'll send someone back to check on the rally point as soon as he can."

Clayton took a break from pouring water for Rosie and jerked a thumb over his shoulder to indicate the road behind them. They'd stopped on a highway bridge across a dried-up riverbed. "We could still be followed," he said. "For all we know those Chimeras have longer ranged sensors than we do and they've been following us all along, just out of range."

"Maybe. Or maybe they don't need to follow us... that would explain why they broke off the chase."

"What are you talking about?" Clayton asked.

"They did a mind scan on me, so they know

exactly where this rendezvous is. But that's not all: I heard them talking about the Enclave after they interrogated me. They switched to Kryo when they realized I was listening, but I got the feeling that they recognized the name, like they already know about the place."

"Then they could be headed to the Enclave as we speak," Clayton scowled. "Do you have any idea where it is?"

"No. Sutton didn't even know. Scouts were supposed to meet them here and lead the way."

"Great." Clayton let out a sigh and nodded to a dense wall of trees on the other side of the bridge. "Let's get to cover." He glanced back to make sure Rosie was still seated in the cargo area, then pulled his legs up and twisted the throttle to jet across the bridge to the other side. He guided the bike down a grassy slope to the trees below and slowed to a crawl as he flew over a service road running beside the highway. Flying between the trees until the bike was hidden from casual detection, he powered down and jumped off the back. Widow parked her bike in the underbrush a few feet away from his and did the same.

"And now we wait," she said, sitting down with her back to the nearest tree.

Clayton moved to help Rosie out of the back of his bike, but she jumped out on her own—the cut end of her chain rattling and skipping through the grass as she ran around sniffing furiously to reconnoiter her new territory. She squatted down a few feet away and spent long seconds emptying her bladder.

Clayton looked away and nodded to Widow. She had the rifle he'd given her up to her shoulder and her right eye pressed to the scope to scan the service road and the highway beyond. "What else did Sutton tell you about the Enclave?"

"Nothing," Widow replied without looking up from the scope.

"He had to have said something."

"Yeah..." Widow trailed off and eased back from the scope, seeming to cast her mind back to remember. "He said they have walls. And enough food to feed an army."

"Good. That's something. Did he say how they found it?"

"No, but maybe they saw it from the air when they went to New Dallas"

"My thoughts exactly," Clayton said. "This Enclave might not be that hard to find. We could look for it ourselves. Sutton said it has walls and tons of food, so it can't be a small operation."

"Guess not," Widow said. "So why didn't those Chimeras go straight there instead of coming to Phoenix Base?"

"Maybe you're wrong and they don't know where it is," Clayton suggested.

"Let's hope so," Widow replied. "So that's

our plan? Get back in the air and see if we can find it on our own?"

Clayton nodded. "Beats waiting here for a guide to show up."

"And what if Sutton comes back for us while we're gone?"

"Then why isn't he already here? There might be a reason they haven't sent people back for us."

"Yeah, like maybe it's too good to be true and they just tossed their lot in with a bunch of cannibals."

Clayton winced at that suggestion. "All the more reason for us to find them on our own. Let's go."

Widow nodded and pushed off the ground to her feet. Before either of them could take more than two steps toward their bikes, they heard Rosie start barking incessantly.

"Shit. You better shut the mutt up before she draws every Dreg for a hundred miles!"

Clayton cursed under his breath and ran toward Rosie. He knew that bark. She'd found something. Back when he and Nova had been living on their own in the Wilds, Rosie would go with them on hunting trips. After he shot a stag or a deer she'd run ahead and start barking like that to let them know where it was.

Clayton crashed through the trees and bushes to a small, grassy clearing. Lying there in the middle of it were two dark mounds.

Rosie was barking at both of them. She looked at him and barked again. Clayton frowned as he approached. One was definitely an animal. A wild boar of all things. The other was a human male. It looked like he'd been gored to death by the animal's tusks. But then what had killed the boar? Clayton dropped to his haunches and patted Rosie on the head, stroking her back to calm her while he examined the bodies.

"What have we here," Widow said, stopping a few feet from the human body. "Careful," she said as Clayton reached for the body. "It could be infected."

He hesitated, then found an unbloodied spot on the man's clothes to grab him by. He turned the body over with a grunt. And saw the gaping hole where his heart should have been. The smell was horrible—charred flesh and fabric. He took a quick step back, holding his sleeve to his nose. "The boar didn't do that," he said.

"No..." Widow agreed. "Looks like a plasma weapon. There was a struggle here." She glanced around quickly, then looked at the animal.

Clayton's gaze followed hers. "Laser burns," he said. "Humans killed both of them."

"Or Chimeras."

"Or that," Clayton conceded. "But no, you said this was the rendezvous with people from the Enclave. This guy isn't from our group.

What are the odds that he'd be here randomly? Maybe he was a scout from that place."

"Or part of a larger group," Widow said.

Clayton cast about, checking the state of the ground. It was too hard to see tracks or trampled grass in the dark, so he couldn't be sure that this man hadn't been part of a larger group. "Maybe," he said.

"Okay, so what are we saying? The Enclave planned some type of ambush, it went bad, and our people killed one of them. But then what? They got the upperhand and took our people?"

"Could be. I guess there's only one way to find out," Clayton said. "We need to find the Enclave." Clayton bent down to pick up the end of Rosie's chain and gave her a tug to pull her away from the dead bodies. "Come, Rosie." She was reluctant to go, and he had to drag her for a few steps. She probably wondered why he was leaving all the meat on that boar to go to waste. His stomach grumbled, reminding him how long it had been since he'd last eaten, but there was no time for it now.

Hurrying back to their bikes, Clayton hoisted Rosie off the ground and dropped her in the cargo compartment once more. Widow jumped on her vehicle and powered it on with a rising *whirr* of the grav engines. Clayton did the same, and it hovered up underneath him. He twisted the throttle in reverse and backed out of the trees. Moments later he and Widow were pulling up and zipping over the tops of those trees. A canopy of leaves silvered with moonlight blurred beneath them as they flew alongside the highway, heading North for New Dallas.

* * *

Commander Tyris loomed over the captive Chimera, recently awoken from multiple stun bolts that had neutralized her just a few hours prior. She lay on her back in the trampled dirt around a roaring bonfire. The power cells in the woman's armor were depleted, her helmet off and sitting to one side. She was propped up on her elbows to face him, uninjured besides a split lip. For now.

"Corporal Ava Haraki," he said slowly. "I remember you."

"Likewise, asshole," Ava said.

Mutterings of shock rippled through the circle of soldiers surrounding her. One of them stepped out of line and delivered a sharp kick to the side of her head. "Watch your tongue, Dakka!" the man cried.

Ava cried out in pain, and the back of her head slammed into the dirt.

"At ease," Tyris snapped, and his man subsided. He nodded to Ava as she recovered and sat up. Her scalp was split and bleeding where the boot had connected. She blinked slowly at him, looking dazed by the blow. "As I recall, you deliberately transferred to another unit to escape my command."

"Because you're a degenerate piece of shit," Ava spat a thick black clot of blood in the dust.

Another wave of muttering went from man to man as Tyris's soldiers expressed their collective shock and grim anticipation at this traitor's defiance. Tyris smiled coldly at Ava. "*I* am the degenerate?" he asked, deciding to pluck at that thread. "What ever do you mean?"

"You raped three women. Two humans. One Chimera. And those are just the ones I know about. Tip of the iceberg."

Tyris took a quick step back, and pretended to be shocked by the accusation. "If that were true, then why was I not sent to die in the arenas? Kyron law is clear. Humans they might overlook, but a Chimera..." He slowly shook his head. "I would be executed for preying on one of our own in such a vile manner."

"You weren't sent to the arena because you're too smart to get caught," Ava said.

"I'm afraid those are just rumors, Corporal."

"Not rumors," Ava replied. "I knew the Chimera, and she told me about the others. Right before she shot herself in the head."

"Ah, yes. I recall. A deranged woman. There is another side to that story. She was caught giving credits to her human relatives. I reported her behavior, and she lashed out with her accusations after her parents were rounded up by the Guard."

"No, you *threatened* to report her parents so you could take advantage of her. Then when you got bored, you reported them anyway."

With that, a few of Tyris's female soldiers turned to look at him. Even Lieutenant Akora, his second in command, turned to look at him, her eyes sharp with suspicion.

This situation was getting away from him. He shouldn't have encouraged Ava to speak. Fortunately, women were the minority in V'tan Company, and their voices and fears would be silenced easily enough.

Tyris heaved out a belated laugh as if the very thought of him abusing his power was hilarious. He trailed off into a hissing grin. "You are quite the storyteller, Ava. Unfortunately, you have no proof of my offenses, but I have plenty for yours. You are found guilty of treason, the penalty for which is death. I wonder: why on Earth—" He paused to reflect on the irony of that idiom. "Would you attack us, your *own* people?"

"*You* are not my people," she replied. Ava looked away from him, her gaze sweeping around the group, and lingering on the females who's ears she'd begun to corrupt. "I didn't kill any of you! My weapon was set to stun."

"So what happened to them?" Tyris jerked his chin to the two dead Chimeras lying about eight feet to Ava's left. "I suppose they're just sleeping?"

Grim laughter answered.

"I didn't kill them. I told Clayton I would only help him if he didn't kill any of you. Apparently he didn't listen."

"Because he's our enemy!" Tyris blurted in a thunderous voice. "What did you think would happen? He's a Dakka, Ava. And now, so are you." He shook his head in dismay and then nodded to the soldiers standing closest to her. "Throw her in the fire."

Ava's eyes flew wide with horror. "*What?*"

His men hesitated, each looking to one another for confirmation of the order.

"You heard me!"

Akora leaned over and whispered to him. "Commander, under Kyron law, the penalty for treason is death by firing squad... not immolation."

"Look around, Lieutenant!" he thundered. "Do you see any Kyra?"

Akora looked confused. "No, sir."

"Exactly! We make our own laws now."

"You mean *you* do?" Akora ventured.

Tyris's eyes cinched down to angry slits. "Are you challenging my authority, Liuetenant?"

Akora hesitated. She was still favoring the side on which she'd been shot. Her injuries would heal quickly now that they'd been properly treated, but she was in no shape to duel him.

"No, sir," she said quietly.

"Good, because the next time anyone so much as hesitates when I give a command, they'd better be holding a Sikath." Tyris regarded his men balefully. None of them seemed willing to put a formal challenge behind their dissent. They all knew better. No one could defeat him in a duel.

"Good. As I was saying, burn the witch."

This time two of his men stepped forward, each of them grabbed one of Ava's arms, and she began to struggle and scream, kicking and clawing at the dirt. She lashed out and struck one of them on the cheek. He hissed in pain as dark blood bubbled from three long gashes in his flesh. The pain gave him strength, and he dragged her to the fire and threw her in.

Tyris stood watching as the flames engulfed her. Ava screamed and thrashed and flew out of the fire, fleeing from her fate. The circle parted for her and she dropped and rolled, putting out the flames. The corners of Tyris's mouth dipped in disappointment.

His hand flashed down to the Stinger pistol on his thigh and drew it. He leveled the weapon on Ava just as she was pushing off the ground, her face and hands blackened with soot and her armor smoking.

Tyris pulled the trigger and a bright emerald laser tore through the side of her head. Ava dropped with a muffled thump, and lay still, her armor sizzling in the dirt.

"The witch is dead," he declared, then turned and began to stalk away. "Akora, Rathos —walk with me," he said.

Lieutenant Akora and Corporal Rathos both caught up to him as he strode back to the log home that served as his temporary command center. Akora was limping and leaning to one side from the lingering pain of her injuries. "Sir?" she asked.

He glanced her way, but he was still irked that she had dared to question his orders. To express his displeasure, he addressed Corporal Rathos instead. "Report, Corporal. How did your pursuit of the escapees go?"

"We chased them out as ordered, sir. We made it look like they didn't get away too easily. Then we broke off the attack and flew North to conduct recon of the Enclave. It looks like they managed to avoid infection with the new virus. Everything seems to be running smoothly. They had all the lights on, the walls are intact, and we spotted armed guards on the walls."

"Really," Tyris said. He gave a thin, predatory smile. "That is very *interesting*. If true, the Enclave would make a perfect base of operations for us. Sadly we don't have the numbers to run it ourselves, so we'll need to subdue the human populace. But I suppose kings are nothing without their subjects."

"Yes, sir," Rathos agreed.

"The question is, how do we take the Enclave without compromising the integrity of the settlement? We can't break the walls."

"Our commandos could get in without being seen," Rathos suggested. "The Enclave won't have access to the tech they need to see through cloaking shields."

"True. Unless they stole it," Tyris pointed out. "We can't assume that they haven't. Dallas is right next door, and it's currently overrun. By now they could have stolen tech from the Garrison, or from dead soldiers in the street."

"Good point, sir," Rathos said.

"We could test the waters by sending one or two operatives. Better yet... we could have them sneak in and open the gates for us. Then the rest of V'tan Company will be able to walk right in."

"That's an excellent plan, sir."

Tyris paused on the rickety front steps of his command center to regard Rathos with a look somewhere between loathing and appreciation of the man's sycophantic fawning. This was why Akora was his second in command. Despite what Ava may have thought, he didn't like submissive subordinates or lovers. It was much more satisfying to find a strong, dominant personality and then break it and bend it to his will. *Strength admires strength,* he thought. It was just a pity that once broken, such individuals were only fit for disposal. Like the Chimera that Ava claimed he had extorted for his own personal satisfaction. When she had stopped objecting to his advances, she had become far too boring to bother with. He'd had no choice but to turn her parents in for accepting illegal financial aid from their Chimeran daughter.

"I'm glad you like the plan," Tyris said slowly. "Because you will be the one sneaking in. Go suit up, Corporal... and take Lieutenant Akora with you," he said, glancing at his number two.

"Akora, sir?" Rathos asked, glancing at her. "She's wounded."

Akora was still suspiciously silent. Probably because she understood just how thin the ice was that she was standing on. "Barely wounded," Tyris clarified. "Regenex is more than up to the task. By the time you arrive at the Enclave, she'll be back to fighting shape. Besides, she has something to prove after she let those Dakka children get the better of her. She'll get the gates open, even if she has to die to do it. Isn't that right, Lieutenant?" he asked, finally addressing Akora directly.

"Yes, sir," she managed.

"Good." He looked back to Rathos. "We'll need time to get into position. Wait outside the walls for us to make comms contact with you. Once we're close, I'll give you the word to sneak in."

"Yes, sir..." Corporal Rathos's brow had furrowed all the way up to his cranial stalks.

"Is something the matter, Corporal?"

"Just one thing, sir: how do you intend to get there? It would take a week to march that far on foot."

"The garbage hauler we captured will carry some of us, and the armored transports we brought from the city will carry the rest." Before leaving the *Sovath* to come here, they'd managed to sneak into the city under the cover of daylight, after all the Dregs had gone to bed, and they'd stolen two ground vehicles—automated *Rydes,* older model troop transports that had been re-purposed for civilian public transport. Those vehicles hadn't been enough to carry everyone, but with the addition of the garbage hauler they'd captured from Phoenix, no one would need to walk.

"You won't make good speed on the highway, sir," Rathos pointed out. "It's in bad shape."

"I'm aware of that, Corporal. I estimate that we'll arrive by early morning. But don't think that's an excuse to delay. I want you both in position as soon as possible. Now go."

"Yes, sir." Corporal Rathos saluted, then turned and left. Lieutenant Akora went after him without another word or so much as a parting salute of her own.

Tyris watched them go with a scowl. If Akora weren't so attractive, he wouldn't have let her get away with such insubordination. But the time would come to punish her for it. He smiled in anticipation of that moment, but he knew he'd have to be careful. First he'd need to find something that Akora cared about more than her own life. Ava was right, he was far too smart to get caught, and he wasn't about to break that streak now.

Turning away, he walked inside the moldy-smelling house that served as his headquarters. The guards at the front door nodded to him, and he said, "At ease," as he walked through.

Tyris contemplated the task ahead of V'tan Company. The Enclave would be well-defended, but the humans defending it had no real combat experience, whereas his men were all veterans from the war with the Chrona.

V'tan Company might be stuck down here with the Dregs and the Dakkas, but that didn't mean that they had to live like those animals. Soon, they would be living in utter luxury. For Tyris, that would be like a long awaited home-coming. He'd been trained and educated in the Enclave. For all he knew, his parents were still living there. Assuming they survived the assault, he might even have the chance to see them again. If that happened, would he simply rip out their throats, or would he make them suffer first? *Decisions, decisions...*

CHAPTER 37

Samara stood in front of the window in the sub-levels of the Enclave, staring into the isolation ward where she'd left Dora. Her daughter was sleeping peacefully.

"Doesn't she look a little too pale to you?" Samara asked, turning to Dr. Dartmouth for an answer.

The doctor looked to her with worry lines creasing her cheeks. Her blue eyes were wincing. "I'm sorry to be the one to have to tell you this, but Dora has been worsening steadily through the night. The infection has spread, and there's nothing we can do to stop it."

A sharp spike of dread shot through her and Samara stepped back suddenly. "No. You're lying. She was fine!"

A shriek sounded from Dora's room and Samara spun around to see her sitting up in bed, her skin waxy and translucent. Her scalp was showing in places, and dark black lines of blood were trickling from her eyes and ears. Bloodshot eyes, no longer green like her father's, but fast turning red like a Dreg's. "No!" Samara cried again. She planted both palms against the window, gaping in horror at what her daughter was becoming. "You did something to her! She was fine when I left!"

Dora shrieked again. Her eyes rolling like marbles in her head.

Samara felt a sharp prick in her neck, and she whirled around to see Dr. Dartmouth holding en empty syringe. "I'm truly sorry about this."

"What did you do to me?"

"At least now you can join your daughter. Take her to room one oh seven."

Strong hands seized both of her arms and she felt herself being bodily lifted and turned. Samara screamed in outrage. "I'll kill you!"

But Dr. Dartmouth just laughed. "You won't even remember me."

Another scream tore from Samara's lips, louder and more feral than the last.

And then she woke up with a start and a sharp gasp. She sat up quickly with her heart pounding in her chest and her head swimming with a hazy swirl of fear and confusion. "Lights!" she cried.

The lights swelled to a cozy glow. Nova stirred on the other side of the bed and woke up. She stared at Samara. "What's wrong?"

Reality sank in, and Samara sucked in a shaky breath. "Nothing. Just a nightmare."

Nova nodded slowly and pushed up onto her elbows. "I had one, too. Chimeras were roasting Rosie on a spit."

Samara smiled sympathetically. "I'm sure she's fine."

"How long have we been asleep?" she asked, glancing to the windows on the far side of their room. Darkness still cloaked the world beyond the glass walls of the Enclave. The apartment they'd been assigned had turned out to have four spacious bedrooms, each with its own bathroom and view to the gardens below. Samara swung her legs over the side of the bed and felt around with her feet for the fuzzy slippers she'd put on after showering and changing out of her filthy blue scrub dress.

Samara walked over to the windows. It was impossible to tell how much time had passed without access to a clock. Maybe it had been an hour. Maybe four. How did people in the Enclave tell time? Did they all wear ARCs like Clayton? Probably, she decided, although she hadn't noticed the telltale glow of that technology over Logan's eyes.

"Why do you think they locked us in?" Nova asked.

There'd been plenty of speculation about that while she and Nova had gorged themselves on the food in the fridge—egg salad sandwiches and roasted turkey with gravy and apple pie. They'd eaten it all cold, not even bothering to use the flash heater, which was the Kyron version of a microwave. The Enclave was replete with such technologies, unlike other occupied cities that typically sported replicated versions of old human tech.

"I don't know," Samara admitted. "But it might not be for a sinister reason. And like Sutton said, it could be because they don't fully trust *us* yet."

"Maybe," Nova said.

"Would you trust us? We came from the Wastes, and we were responsible for the Chrona's attack."

"Well, *you* weren't a part of that plot."

"No, but they don't know that," Samara said, shaking her head.

"So you don't think we should worry."

"I didn't say that. I think we should keep our eyes open, but I can't imagine them having any kind of agenda for taking us in."

"You mean other than Dora and the fact that she could lead to a cure."

"But they didn't know about that before they brought us here."

Nova grunted and sighed. "I guess you're right. But what about..." Her voice dropped to a whisper and she went on. "What about that man you killed? What if it was one of them? What if they *know?*"

Ice shot through Samara's veins. She hadn't thought about that. But lulling them into a false sense of security and then locking them all in their room didn't make any sense. They would have simply arrested her on sight and left the others free to go about their business.

"They don't know," Samara said. "And even if they did, what are the odds that it's one of them? He was on foot and unarmed. The Enclave has hoverbikes and guns." Samara shook her head and heaved a weary sigh as she walked back to the bed. "But still. Let's keep that to ourselves, okay? Don't mention it again. Just in case." Samara glanced at the ceiling and pointed up. "Besides, another reason to lock us in here might be to secretly observe us. That would be a good way to learn more about *our* intentions, don't you think?"

Nova went suddenly very still. "I didn't think about that. Do you think they heard us just now?"

"If so, I'm going to have a lot of explaining to do. But it *was* an accident." She said that while staring at the ceiling, as if to address anyone who might be listening.

While she was looking at the simulated stars in the ceiling, the lights around the top of the walls abruptly went from a soft gold to a dark, pulsing red. A siren began roaring through the room, muted and distant, but familiar, like an old air raid siren.

"What's going on?" Nova asked. "What is that?"

Even as she asked, hidden speakers crackled to life and a strident voice declared: "Action stations, action stations. All security officers and reserves report to the walls! We are under attack! This is not a drill. I repeat, this is not a drill!"

Samara ran back to the windows and stared at the sloping glass wall of the pyramid, trying to glimpse the fortifications of the Enclave beyond. Everything outside the pyramid was dark and hazy, filtered through two different layers of glass and washed out by the lights and reflections in between. It was impossible to see what was going on, but even the gardens below were bathed in a pulsing crimson light.

Nova arrived at the windows beside her, breathing hard. "Do you think it's the Kyra? Maybe their fleet finally arrived."

Samara searched the sky for signs of incoming Kyron fighters and transports, but all she saw were a handful of stars bright enough to make it through the light pollution coming from the Enclave. "Maybe, but I don't see anything," she said.

"That doesn't mean they're not there," Nova pointed out.

The door to their room burst open, and both of them turned to see Sergeant Sutton standing there. He was wearing his camo fatigues again, along with his utility belt, though his sidearm was notably absent.

"We need to go."

"I thought we were locked in?" Samara asked, striding across the room to reach him.

"They let us out. We've been called upon to help defend the Enclave. Logan is waiting at the door."

"So now they trust us to carry guns?" Nova asked.

"Guess so," Sutton said.

"Defend against what?" Samara asked.

"Dregs," Sutton replied.

Before he could say more, Logan pushed through the door behind Sutton. He was wearing dark clothes, painted black body armor that looked like it had been stolen from a Chimera, and a bandoleer of plasma grenades. He also carried a laser rifle and two sidearms.

"There's a horde of at least ten thousand Dregs headed this way from Dallas," he said. "They triggered our early warning system. We need to slow them down. There's a choke point between our two cities. It's blocked with old vehicles, so we're going to make a stand there and see how many of them we can kill before they get this far."

"Why are they coming here?" Nova cried.

"Maybe they saw the lights," Logan replied.

"Does it matter?" Samara asked. "They can't get through the walls, can they?"

"They can't get *through* them, but the bastards can still climb. We've had climbers sneak over before. They usually don't get far, but that's because they never come at us in organized groups like this one."

"And what happens if they get through?" Nova asked.

"Then our gunners on the walls will just have to do their best. Now come on. We need to hurry. There's a chance we can turn them back before they ever get here."

Sutton nodded to Samara and Nova as Logan stalked out of the room. "Get dressed," he said, and then followed Logan out.

Samara hesitated, wondering if she should mention that she barely knew how to handle a gun, but the thought of just sitting here, waiting for Dregs to break in was much worse than being a part of the effort to stop them. Nova was already picking her dirty clothes off the ground and shrugging out of her robe to put them back on.

"Wait," Samara said. She strode past the girl to the bedroom closet and pulled it open to reveal a line of gray and white jumpsuits. She passed one to Nova and then took another for herself.

"Thanks," Nova said. "That's much better."

Samara smiled tightly as she dropped her robe on the floor and began pulling her legs through the jumpsuit. Her mind jumped ahead to the threat marching on them from Dallas. Thousands of Dregs advancing in an organized horde. Was the new generation more intelligent than the old one? And what had set them in motion? They should have been foraging around peacefully inside the walls of New Dallas, not sallying out like an army to come here. It was almost like someone had *told* them that there was a whole city full of warm bodies next to theirs.

Samara shook her head and pushed that thought aside as she zipped up her jumpsuit and followed Nova out of the bedroom. That was ridiculous. Dregs were dumb brutes. They couldn't be reasoned with.

* * *

"Why'd she stop?!" McKayla demanded.

"Because I'm done taking orders from you idiots," Keera said. She could see the shining jewel of the Enclave on the horizon and the raggedy masses of Dregs below. The horde slowed, then stopped, climbing on each other's shoulders and leaping into the air to reach the transport hovering above their heads. Others looked around dumbly, as if to ask each other for directions. The Reapers hanging out the open airlock at the back of the shuttle were still waving their flares and guns around, shouting obscenities to the horde below. But with the shuttle stopped and hovering over the Dregs' heads, goading them was pointless—even dangerous. A piece of debris *thunked* off the hull. Then another *thunk* sounded and one of the men in the back yelled, "Hey! What's the hold up!"

"You fly where I say, or I put a hole in your head," Zachary warned as he leveled his plasma pistol at Keera's head.

Keera turned to look at him and bared her teeth in a hiss. "You kill me, and we'll crash."

"You're not touchin' the controls right now. We won't crash. And I'm pretty sure after watchin' these past hours that I can fly it all on my own."

"But can you land?" Keera challenged. She let the grin fall from her face. "I'd hate for you to turn yourself into a puddle on the pavement."

"Listen to her! She's bein' cheeky, Zack. I told you we should have let the boys have her. She wouldn't be giving you lip right now if we'd broken her in first."

"Maybe you're right, sweetheart," Zack said slowly. "But I like to think we can be more civilized. Last chance, chalkhead. Fly or die."

"Did you ever think that maybe destroying the Enclave isn't the best use of dwindling resources?"

"There's only five of us, thanks to you," Zachary said with a cold look in his eyes. "You really think we'd stand a chance of getting in there without a distraction?"

"Sensors indicate at least ten thousand Dregs down there," Keera said. "If you lead them to the Enclave, they'll kill everyone." She hoped Zachary had some sense of reason left to appeal to. "What is that human saying? You don't kill the golden goose. They're worth more to you alive than dead. It's a self-sufficient community. Maybe the last of its kind. We're talking about the survival of your species. You kill them, and it's over. The human race will go extinct."

Zachary smiled slowly, revealing dirty yellow teeth. "Humanity will, but I won't. I'm gonna live forever as king of the whole fucking world." His eyes sparkled with manic glee as he said that. "Now, as I said before. Fly or die."

Keera felt her blood run cold. She thought again about plowing the shuttle into the ground. Zachary would shoot her and grab the controls, but would he be fast enough to stop her?

There was only one way to find out.

"I'll fly," Keera ground out. She turned back to the forward viewscreen, and then pushed the control yoke all the way forward. The shuttle dived sharply toward the shrieking masses of Dregs, and the Reapers in the back cried out in alarm as they came tumbling toward the cockpit.

"Zack!" McKayla screamed.

He pulled the trigger and a wash of blinding light and pain strobed through Keera's head, incinerating her consciousness in the blink of an eye.

CHAPTER 38

As they flew North, Clayton began to see light swelling on the horizon. He couldn't communicate with Widow, but she must have seen it too. It was a hazy white bloom against the clouds, big enough and bright enough that it had to be generated by something huge. Then, out of nowhere, the glow of those lights abruptly vanished.

Clayton's mind spun in circles over that phenomenon. What could generate such a massive amount of light and then suddenly disappear? It hadn't been lightning, or an explosion. Those were fleeting events that wouldn't have lasted more than an instant. It had to be some type of city or encampment. And it had to be a big one.

Clayton flew alongside Widow and pointed in the direction that he'd seen the lights. She nodded and gunned the throttle to fly in that direction.

They continued on for about ten minutes, with the night air cold and whipping violently around them. Clayton pressed himself low against the seat, nearly lying flat against the hoverbike to avoid being battered by the air. He wished he'd stolen a helmet from one of the Chimeras in the camp back at Phoenix base, but there hadn't been any time or opportunity.

The crumbling, overgrown ruins of New Dallas and Fort Worth undulated beneath them like the waves on an ocean. Ruined buildings rose and fell; the shadowy specters of trees jutted up here and there, reaching with gnarled hands for their bikes. This was the real Phoenix: Mother Nature rising from humanity's ashes.

Something appeared against the shadowy sprawl of debris and vegetation below: dim but gleaming dark red, like a giant ruby at the furthest limits of their visibility. It was shaped like a pyramid and soaring well above the tops of even the tallest trees. The structure was luminous, and shining with lights from within. That had to be the source of the glow they'd seen a few minutes ago.

They slowed down but flew on steadily until they could pick out details of the structure. Walls had been built around it, just like any of the occupied cities. But it didn't look like any occupation zone Clayon had ever seen. Had it somehow escaped the Chrona's virus?

Widow slowed to a crawl and dropped closer to the ground as they drew near. Clayton matched her speed and altitude. He understood why she was hesitant about approaching the installation. For all they knew, it could be a Chimeran military base. There could be snipers on the walls waiting to pick them off if they flew too close.

Widow stopped and hovered at a safe distance, shadowed and sheltered by the remains of old skyscrapers on either side. Clayton pulled alongside her to hover some thirty meters above the ground, studying the shining jewel ahead of them.

"You think that's the Enclave?" Widow asked.

"I do," Clayton replied.

"It could be a trap."

"Yes."

"It's massive. That pyramid could be, what... a quarter of a mile at the base?"

Clayton nodded along with that assessment, though it was hard to tell from this far away, without some frame of reference. Widow pulled her rifle up and peered through the scope to the walls. "There's people up there," she said.

"Human?" Clayton asked.

"Yeah. I think so."

"Are you sure?"

Widow pulled back from the scope and regarded him steadily. "As sure as I can be at this distance. We'd have to get closer to be a hundred percent certain."

Clayton frowned. "I'm guessing they're armed?"

"Yes."

Clayton stared at the distant city, still glowing red rather than white. In fact, the pyramid was the only thing that was lit, and it was pulsing slowly. "Looks like the emergency lighting on a ship," he said. "That structure was shining with clean white light a few minutes ago. Now it's practically gone dark."

"You think there's some kind of trouble over there?" Widow asked.

"Could be." He glanced up at the sky, scanning the stars.

"What are you looking for?"

None of those stars appeared to be moving. Clayton brought his gaze down and shook his head. "I was looking for signs of the Kyron fleet that was supposed to be coming. If they have one in orbit, we should be able to see it with the naked eye."

"If it's in a low orbit, you mean."

"Right."

"You're thinking maybe the Kyra arrived and they're sending troops down to take that city." Widow pointed to the pyramid.

"I was... but now I'm thinking it could be something else."

"Like what? They have walls and armed sentries. They can't be worried about Dregs."

A sudden woof drew his attention to Rosie in the cargo compartment behind him. Clayton glanced at her. Her floppy ears were pricked up, and she was staring intently at the horizon, somewhere east of the Enclave.

Another woof.

"Would you shut that mutt up? She's going to give us away."

Clayton reached around to stroke her neck. "Hey girl, shhh. Take it easy."

She whimpered and shuffled forward in her seat, as if she wanted to get out of the bike. "She probably needs a pitstop," he said.

Rosie looked away from the horizon and began panting impatiently. Then something caught her attention again and she sat up straight, her ears erect. She growled softly.

"She's probably hearing those Dregs down there," Widow said, pointing to the nearest one—a pale stumbling speck picking its way along the street below.

"Maybe, yeah," Clayton agreed. He looked away from Rosie to glance at his bike's sensors. He spotted a few scattered blips below, staggered and moving slowly. All of them were blue—a color that identified them as Dregs on Kyron scanners. They were too far from the Enclave's walls to see what color the sensors would use for the sentries, but they couldn't afford to get any closer. Whether the Enclave was ultimately friendly or not, they were probably under orders to shoot first and check their fire later.

"So what's the plan?" Widow asked.

"I'm thinking..."

"Well, we can't just fly up to those walls unannounced. They might freak out and shoot us down."

"Agreed. Besides, we don't know that the Enclave didn't lure our people in and make them all their prisoners. It could be run by Chimeras, or even a hostile group of humans." Clayton's thoughts jumped to Keera, either captured or killed by those Reapers in San Antonio, and he winced, hoping that she was still alive—or if not, that at least she hadn't suffered.

"So how do we find out if they're friendly?" Widow asked.

Clayton was still staring at the sensors, his eyes drifting out of focus as he sank deeper into his thoughts. He was drawing a blank. Sneaking in would be impossible without cloaking armor. Ava had the only suit, and she'd either been captured or killed back at Phoenix Base. He grimaced at the memory of being forced to leave her behind. It was becoming a pattern with him: abandoning his Chimeran allies and never looking back.

Clayton pushed that thought away. He would go back for Keera. And Ava too. He just couldn't do it alone. He needed Phoenix's help.

"Hey, Clayton, are you listening to me?"

"Yes, I'm thin..." He trailed off as a solitary purple blip appeared, drifting across the sensor display from the right-hand side, coming from the east and the direction of New Dallas. Clayton blinked to focus his eyes. The blip was bigger and brighter than an individual Chimera. He tapped it with his finger, and detailed imagery appeared hovering above the display in a three-dimensional hologram: a ship with sharply-angled sides and wing-like projections. Roughly wedge-shaped and aerodynamic. That blip wasn't a Chimera. It was a Kyron shuttle, identified as a *La'rik-class transport*. Clayton gaped at the screen. This was what they'd been searching for from the start, and here it was cruising casually into view.

"I don't believe it..." Widow muttered, noticing the same thing on her sensors.

Then Clayton saw something else: a solid blue smear inching across the screen behind the transport. The smear spread and forked, sprouting tentacles like a living thing. It was flowing like a liquid into an unseen mold. Clayton frowned, wondering if it was an actual liquid leaking out inside of the display and flowing into nooks and crannies behind the screen. But then his eyes picked out individual blips along the edges of the shaded region—stragglers. It was a horde of Dregs, packed so tightly that their signatures all blurred together. The mold they were flowing through was the ruins of the cities below: old streets and alleyways.

Widow sucked in a sharp breath. "Holy shit."

"I think we know what that emergency lighting is about."

"There must be thousands of them," Widow said.

"Tens of thousands," Clayton corrected.

He glanced up from the display and turned his ear in the direction of signatures he'd seen, straining to listen against periodic gusts of wind. That was when he heard it: a distant rumbling, like a herd of stampeding cattle.

"That transport is leading the way," Widow said. "Look." She pointed, and Clayton followed her gesture to see bright white lights inching across the horizon, almost at eye level with them.

Widow brought her rifle up to check with the scope. "There's people hanging out the back. They're waving flares around!"

"People?" Clayton asked. "You mean Chimeras?"

Widow hesitated, silently tracking the transport's progress. She pulled back from the scope to look him in the eye. "No, I mean people. I don't see any cranial stalks on those fuckers. They're definitely human."

The picture belatedly snapped into focus. "Shit," Clayton said.

"What?"

"Those are the Reapers."

"Reapers? Flying a Kyron transport?"

"No. Keera's flying it. They must have threatened to kill her if she didn't help them."

"So she's alive," Widow said. "Figures. She would find a way to sacrifice what's left of humanity just to save herself."

Clayton shot Widow a glare that she probably couldn't make out in the dark. "She's not like that."

"Oh yeah? Well then I present Exhibit A for your consideration: the last surviving human settlement on the planet, and she's leading a fucking army of Dregs to destroy it."

"The Reapers are. Not her."

"She doesn't have to. She could sacrifice herself and those Reapers would be shit out of luck without her."

"Maybe. But right now none of that matters. What matters is what are we going to do about it."

Widow sighed. "Fine. We could try to hijack the shuttle and lead the Dregs away. They're going pretty slow, and it looks like the rear doors are open. Maybe they won't see us coming."

"That's actually not a bad idea," Clayton agreed. "Even if they do see us coming, I doubt they'll know how to operate the guns. And if Keera is the one flying, she might find a way to help us."

Widow snorted. "Yeah. Sure. So long as it doesn't mean risking her own neck."

Clayton glared at her. He wanted to ask what her problem was, but she'd already spelled it out multiple times.

"I need to land somewhere and drop Rosie off," Clayton said, already scanning the ruins for a rooftop that might be safe. He spotted one, down and to the right, a three floor building that looked mostly intact, with a flat roof and no apparent access to it besides the crumbled remains of a stairwell entrance. "There." He pointed. "Let's go." Not waiting for Widow to confirm his order, he flew down to the roof and parked his bike there. Hopping off, he hoisted Rosie up and out. She gave him a sad, knowing look, and he bent down to scratch her behind one ear. "It's just for a little while. I'll be back. It's for your own good."

Widow dived down beside them and came to a roaring stop, her bike's air brakes firing noisily. "We'd better hurry, Clay."

"Yeah." He nodded to Rosie and threw a leg over the back of his bike. He glanced around, checking to make sure there were no threats to her safety up here. The roof had a hole in it, but he couldn't hear or see any Dregs in the immediate area, and the door to the stairwell he'd seen was blocked by an old air car that had crashed into it. "See you soon," he said, nodding to Rosie. Looking to Widow, he said, "I don't have a gun. Can you check the back of your bike? There might be something in there."

Widow gaped at him. "What happened to your sidearm?"

"I emptied it while firing on the Chimeras that chased us from Phoenix Base. I threw it over the side to keep my hands free."

Widow muttered something under her breath and jumped off her bike to check the cargo compartment. She spent a moment rummaging through the contents before withdrawing a short-barreled laser rifle. She checked the charge pack and then pulled two matching ones from the storage compartment before walking over with the weapon. "Here," she said. "You're lucky I had something."

Clayton looped the shoulder strap over his neck and balanced the weapon in his lap. Flying with one hand on the control bars and another on that rifle was going to be a challenge.

"Ready?" he asked.

"Ready enough," Widow replied, as she stalked back to her bike.

"I've got point," Clayton said as he pocketed the spare charge packs Widow had given him. He grabbed the bike's control bars. "On me," he said, and then he gunned the throttle and pulled up hard, speeding toward the distant transport.

CHAPTER 39

Samara ran behind Logan and the rest of Phoenix. Nova kept pace beside her, flashing down a plain gray and white corridor with smooth black floors. It was far less decoratively appointed than the residential areas of the Enclave. The corridor bustled with armed and armored residents. A pair of soldiers walked by them pushing a hovering crate packed to the brim with spare charge packs.

They reached an open door at the end of the corridor and Logan stepped through. As he did so, the guards standing there straightened. One of them nodded and said, "General."

Logan nodded back, but didn't verbally acknowledge the man.

Samara didn't miss the significance of that exchange. "You're a General?" she asked.

He glanced at her as he led the way past racks and cabinets full of weapons and ammo. Several dozen men and women were busy arming themselves inside. They saw Logan coming and stood to varying degrees of attention.

"At ease! No time to stand on ceremony!"

Muttered *yes, sirs* echoed back, and Logan reached a wall of high-powered laser rifles —weapons that Samara recognized from Chimeran soldiers who'd carried them in Houston. These were military-grade, not civilian-issue like the ones Clayton had used with the SWMD.

Phoenix fanned out along the length of the wall.

"Grab a weapon and as many charge packs as you can carry," Logan said.

"Sure thing, *General*," Sutton said through a wry smile that told Samara he didn't think Logan had properly earned that rank. Sutton hailed from the old Union army, and he was a veteran of both the invasion and the resistance, so maybe he had a right to feel that way.

Logan glanced at Sutton as he grabbed a heavy rifle off the wall and loaded it with a fresh charge pack. Sutton took a matching rifle for himself, and Logan handed his weapon back to Harold, who was standing behind him. Logan was already armed to the gills, so he didn't need it. Richard, Lori, and Pyro stepped out from behind the general and went to grab their own weapons.

"Look, Sergeant," Logan began through gritted teeth, "You and I might have taken different paths to reach our respective ranks, but you can be sure that I've had plenty of combat experience. I've logged over three hundred hours in battle sims here in the Enclave. Not to mention all the years I've spent commanding this army and fending off Dregs from the walls."

Sutton nodded along with that. "And yet the Kyra passed you over when they were looking for officers that they could use in *their* army. I wonder why that is...?"

Logan's dark eyes collapsed into angry slits, and the muscles bunched at the corners of his jaw as he clenched his teeth. "Someone had to defend this place, and I will not have you questioning my authority within hours of your arrival! Don't make me wonder if taking in your people was the right call. Remember, we're all on the same side here. At least, that's what *you* told me."

Sutton shrugged and turned his rifle on its side, making a show of checking the safety. He looked up from the weapon, the old burn scar on his face tugging one corner of his mouth down while the other ticked up in a smile. "If we're all on the same side, then why did you lock us in our suite?"

"Because you're new here! You're on probation. We don't know if we can trust you yet. What if you came here to instigate a coup? You're all exiles. That means every one of you is a criminal."

"Political criminal," Sutton clarified.

Samara noticed that the other people in the room were glancing their way now, stopping to stare and listen to the confrontation.

"I only have your word for that," Logan said. "And the Chimeras didn't just exile political dissidents to the Wastes. They exiled murderers, thieves, and rapists. Would you honestly tell me if one of your people had been exiled for *those* crimes? Just more shit water under the bridge, right?" Logan heaved his broad shoulders in a shrug. "People can change. I bet that's what you told yourself when they joined the resistance."

Sutton held the general's gaze for a beat, saying nothing, but his lopsided smile widened slightly, as if he were enjoying a private joke.

Samara felt a cold tendril of doubt trickle through her like an ice cube sliding down her spine, and for the first time she thought to wonder about the people that she'd escaped Houston with. Could she trust all of them? *Any* of them?

"That's what I thought," Logan said, Sutton's silence having given him his answer. "You're damned lucky we let you in here at all, but it can change like that." Logan snapped his fingers for emphasis. "You can get exiled from here, too."

Sutton's eyes flared at that threat, and his smile faded. Doc laid a hand on his shoulder as if to calm him down.

Looking at Logan, Doc said, "You don't need to worry about us, General. We'll prove ourselves tonight. You won't regret letting us in."

"I certainly hope you're right about that," Logan replied.

Doc jerked his head sideways and caught Sutton's eye, pointing to some other equipment he'd found. An excuse to break up the fight. Sutton allowed Doc to lead him off, and then Logan tore his gaze away, too. He noticed his own men gawking, and his face flushed angrily. "Get your hands out of your pants and march your asses to the gates!" Several of his soldiers acknowledged the order, snapping into motion to grab the last of their gear before filing out of the armory. Logan turned away, shaking his head and muttering to himself.

The members of Phoenix quietly finished arming themselves. Logan gave Samara a rifle like the one he'd passed to Harold earlier. "You know how to handle this?" he asked.

She hesitated before reaching tentatively for the weapon. "Yes," she said in a quiet voice.

"Was that a question?" Logan demanded.

Samara shook her head and drew herself up. "No, sir."

"Good..." he trailed off, his eyes narrowing on Nova as if just noticing her for the first time. "What about you? What are you, twelve?"

"Fourteen, sir. And I'm a crack shot," Nova explained. "I lived in the Wastes my whole life."

"Well if that's not a résumé, then I don't know what is. Here." He grabbed another rifle for her, and then began passing stacks of spare charge packs to her and Samara. "Clip these to your belts," he said.

Nova and Samara each took a stack and did as they were told. Logan looked away from them to address the rest of Phoenix. Everyone else was already done and waiting for orders.

"Ready when you are," Sutton said in an even voice.

"Then it's time to go hunting! Fall in!"

"Hooah!" Sutton said, and Doc and Pyro echoed his battle cry. Samara frowned at that as she rushed after them, suddenly feeling out of place. What was she doing playing soldier?

"I guess they reached an understanding," Nova said as she ran beside Samara.

"I hope so," Samara replied, glancing over at the girl. But in the heat of battle, she had to wonder whose orders Phoenix would actually listen to: Sergeant Sutton's or General Logan's?

Her bet was on the sergeant.

CHAPTER 40

Keera awoke chained up in the back of the transport. Her head was thick and pounding with a stabbing headache. Her entire body felt heavy and numb, as though she were on a high-gravity world. Her ears were blocked and ringing. Distantly, she heard Reapers yelling, cursing at the Dregs below.

She glanced in that direction, and winced as the movement triggered painful spasms from the muscles in her back and arms. Her wrists were bound to an electrical conduit above her head.

Keera spotted two Reapers hanging out the rear airlock, jeering at the Dregs below and periodically firing their laser rifles into the horde. They couldn't do much against ten thousand monsters, but those shots weren't designed to thin the herd—quite the opposite. It was the equivalent of a cattle prod, enraging and goading the horde to chase the shuttle.

Her plan hadn't worked, Keera realized belatedly. She'd tried to slam the transport into the ground to stop the Reapers from leading these Dregs to the Enclave, but somehow Zachary had managed to stun her and regain control of the transport before it could crash.

"Hello beautiful," a deep voice said.

Keera looked away to see the portly Reaper with long stringy hair. His pudgy face stretched into a grin, revealing rotting brown teeth, several of which were missing. Keera glared at him but said nothing. The man was holding a rifle and wearing a sidearm on his hip. She quietly tested her bonds. Chains rattled and pulled taut, just a few inches from the conduit that she was chained to. If she had more slack in her chains she might have been able to goad that man into range and make a grab for one of his weapons, but the Reapers had obviously thought about that when they'd tied her up. She could barely move, but at least her legs were free.

"You missed our date on the roof. Lucky for you, I take rainchecks." The man released his rifle and reached for the clasp of his utility belt.

A mixture of horror and disgust rolled through Keera's gut. She scuttled away from him, pressing herself to the bulkhead behind her. She glanced to the opening of the cockpit, just a few feet away. The door was open, with Zachary and McKayla sitting in the pilot's and copilot's seats respectively.

The Reaper in front of her ducked out of his rifle's shoulder strap and placed it carefully on the floor beside his utility belt. He was unarmed now. He regarded her with another smile.

"Are we going to do this the easy way or the hard way?"

Keera's heart was hammering in her chest. Her eyes darted to the cockpit, wondering if Zachary and his mate knew what this man was planning to do to her. But this had been McKayla's idea. For all she knew, he was acting on their orders.

Keera pushed her emotions and fears aside and forced herself to meet her would-be assailant's dark, beady-eyed gaze. "The easy way," she said.

The man's smile faded, as if he'd been hoping for a fight. He nodded and started toward her. Keera bided her time, waiting for him to get close enough. He dropped to his knees and paused to consider her unbound feet.

"Just get it over with," Keera said.

He smiled again and nodded, reaching eagerly for her with two dirty hands. His head reached the perfect position, and Keera lashed out with her right foot. She caught him in the side of the head, dazing him. He cried out and withdrew sharply, and then she hammered his nose with the sole of her other boot.

Cartilage gave way with a satisfying

crunch, and he screamed. He clutched his nose in both hands, blood gushing between his fingers. "You bitch!" he raged.

Booted feet resounded on the metal floors. "What the hell is going on back here?" McKayla asked as she appeared in the entrance to the cockpit. "Shit," she cursed when she saw the state of the other Reaper.

Keera smiled coldly at her.

"Can't you do anything right?" McKayla demanded. She stormed over to an equipment locker on the opposite side from Keera, making sure to stay out of reach of her feet. The door of the locker was bent, the locking mechanism broken. She pulled it open and withdrew a familiar object: a meter-long sword in its sheath. A Sikath. She drew the weapon, revealing the gleaming black nano-edged blade.

McKayla flicked the power on, and a shield shimmered to life around the fragile sword. It blurred and hummed as the blade began to vibrate back and forth, several thousand times per second. McKayla stalked over to Keera, being careful again to mind her feet. She stood next to Keera's head and then leveled the deadly blade mere inches from her throat.

Keera eyed the weapon.

McKayala nodded to the man with the broken nose. "You still want her?"

The man went suddenly very still, his hands clutching his shattered nose. His dark eyes were full of pain, but something dark and ugly filled them now: desire. Keera shivered, wincing as the movement brought her dangerously close to the blade McKayla was holding to her throat. A Sikath would slice clean through the side of the transport, let alone Keera's neck.

"Then have her," McKayla said. "I'll make sure she doesn't struggle."

The man slowly dropped his hands from his nose, revealing a crooked, flattened tomato. His every breath was a watery wheeze, but somehow he was able to ignore the pain. Keera watched his hands drop to his belt, then looked away, up at the human woman who was not only condoning his depravity, but encouraging it.

"You're a woman," Keera said slowly. "Don't do this."

McKayla smiled thinly at her. "I'm a woman, but you sure as hell ain't. You're a chalkhead."

Keera felt the blood draining from her face as she realized what she was dealing with. This was racism in its purest, vilest form. McKayala had utterly dehumanized her just because she was a Chimera. She didn't matter. She had no rights.

"What did we do to you?" Keera asked in a cracking voice.

"Shut up," McKayla said.

Keera heard a belt buckle hit the floor, and she squeezed her eyes shut. Footsteps. Then she felt hands on her thighs, and her entire body went cold.

"Hey, leave something for us, Matt!"

A grunt and a wheeze were the balding man's only reply as he fumbled with the clasps of Keera's jumpsuit.

There was no point in allowing this to go any further. She was better off struggling and letting McKayla cut her throat. Keera steeled herself, preparing to lash out with another kick. She cracked her eyes open, judged the distance from her boots to the Reaper's head. Maybe she'd be able to kill him before McKayla slit her throat. He gave her a bloody smile.

And that was when she heard it: the rising *whirr* of hoverbike engines, approaching fast—followed by the screeching reports of laser fire.

"What the hell!" someone cried from the rear airlock.

Keera turned to look just as two laser bolts struck the tall, skinny man on the left. He stumbled and then fell out the airlock.

"Seth!" the first one cried. And then a laser bolt struck him in the chest as well, spinning him around. He landed face-first on the deck and his head bounced off with a reverberating clang. The blade vanished from Keera's throat as McKayla drew her sidearm.

"What's going on back there?" Zachary

cried from the cockpit.

And then a hoverbike sailed right into the back of the transport and wedged itself between the bulkheads. The man on the back fired before McKayla could, and a shining blue stun bolt hit her in the stomach, doubling her over with an airless gasp. A crackling sizzle of blue fire arced over her body from head to toe, filling the transport with an eery blue glow. She crumpled to the deck beside Keera with her clothes sparking and her limbs still twitching.

It all played out in just a few seconds. The man with the broken nose had frozen in front of Keera, gawking at the scene. She took her chance and grabbed his head between her thighs. He cried out in a muffled voice as she squeezed as hard as she could and twisted, rolling over in the process. Something popped in the man's neck, and he went limp. She kicked him away from her, slamming her boots into his head and back repeatedly. He ended up three feet away and lying on top of his own head with his neck twisted 180 degrees.

Clayton jumped off the back of the hoverbike, glanced her way, and then continued on before stopping to aim his rifle through the door of the cockpit.

"If you shoot me, we'll crash," Zachary said, his voice sounding clearly through the opening. "Drop your weapon."

"If I do that, you'll shoot me."

"Maybe. But what choice do you—"

Clayton pulled the trigger. Another electric blue stun bolt blinded and dazzled Keera's eyes, and then Clayton ran for the cockpit. A moment later, Keera felt the shuttle slowing to a stop, hovering in place. Then Clayton emerged from the cockpit, striding over to her. He spotted the Sikath sticking out of the floor beside McKayla. The dead-man's switch had turned it off just as she'd dropped it, but the blade was still sharp enough to bury itself several inches into the deck.

Clayton drew the weapon and flicked it on with a click and a steady *hum.* He stepped carefully over to Keera. She watched him with glazed and staring eyes. He hesitated, and a frown crossed his face as he noticed the Reaper she'd killed—his pants around his ankles. He seemed to realize what he'd prevented, and his face paled.

"Are you—"

"I'm fine," she snapped, much louder than she'd intended. Keera had drawn her knees up to her chest in a fetal position. She relaxed that posture now and rattled the chains around her wrists. "Mind cutting me free?"

He nodded slowly, but said nothing.

She held her wrists apart and he carefully slipped the blade between them. The chains broke and fell to the deck with a noisy rattle. A second hoverbike appeared behind the transport, hovering in place beside them, and a woman carefully climbed off the back to come inside. It was Widow. She took in the scene at a glance. "You really beat the hell out of him," she said, her gaze lingering on the dead Reaper.

Keera nodded as she stood up and fastened the clasps on her jumpsuit.

Widow cracked a fading smile. "Good."

A silent understanding passed between them, and Keera looked away. She'd heard rumors about Widow's past, and suddenly Keera understood why she was such a cold, angry woman. She didn't say anything—she couldn't have if she had wanted to; the inside of her mouth was so dry it felt like chalk. She scowled at her unintentional allusion to the racial slur that characterized her people. Stepping over McKayla, Keera deliberately ground the woman's hand beneath her boot as she went. She reached the cockpit and found Zachary on the floor between the pilot's and co-pilots seats.

"We'd better tie them up," Keera heard Clayton say. "Check the supply lockers for restraints we can use."

"With pleasure," Widow replied.

Keera walked over Zachary, stepping on him to get to the pilot's seat. She took a moment to survey the situation below with her eyes and the transport's sensors—

And a cold weight settled in her gut as she took in the sheer immensity of the horde. It looked a lot bigger than it had the last time she'd seen it. Now sensors were reading fifty-five thousand two hundred and six Dregs. And this time, after the transport had stopped moving, they weren't all gawking at it and wondering where to go.

In the foreground, barely a hundred meters from the shuttle, was the spire of an old stone building. Beyond that, a line of old vehicles blocked the entrance of a bridge across the river that protected the Enclave on three sides. The heavy metal gates of the Enclave lay right on the other side of that bridge.

And the Dregs were rushing onward, wrapping around the stone building in the foreground like a flood. They were spurred on not by the pulsing, ruddy glow of the Enclave's emergency lighting or by the Reapers goading them from above, but by the scent of fresh, human meat standing on the walls, and living in close quarters in the glass pyramid. The Enclave was home to five thousand people. They were outnumbered ten to one. If the horde made it across that bridge, the Enclave wouldn't stand a chance.

"Don't go anywhere yet," Clayton said as he stepped into the cockpit behind her. Keera turned to look as he went on blithely: "Widow's still securing the captives in the back. She needs a chance to get on her bike before we fly anywh..." Clayton trailed off suddenly as laser fire started up from atop the wall of vehicles on the other side of the stone building. Deadly emerald beams of light stitched back and forth across the frontrunners of the horde, illuminating thousands more in a sickly green light. Now Clayton's less sensitive human eyes could see what she was staring at. His gaze dipped to the sensor display and widened upon seeing the solid mass of blue seeping across the screen. Fifty-five thousand Dregs flowing toward the Enclave like a tidal wave.

"We have to do something," Clayton whispered.

Keera nodded slowly and powered up the transport's guns. She primed the targeting system to track the Dregs' unique bio-signatures and strictly avoid humans.

The ship's twin laser cannons began thumping steadily with high-pitched reports. Thick emerald beams slammed into the ground, lighting fires and incinerating three to five Dregs with each shot. It wouldn't do nearly enough, but at least the transport's guns were heavier than the small arms fire coming from the Enclave.

CHAPTER 41

Samara stood on a paved street behind the heavy metal gates of the Enclave, waiting for them to open. There had to be at least fifty armed soldiers there besides the surviving members of Phoenix. All of the ones from the Enclave wore bits and pieces of Chimeran armor, while she and the rest of Phoenix were unarmored. Samara cast her mind back to the armory, wondering if they'd somehow missed finding suits of armor there, or if there simply hadn't been enough to go around.

"Are you ready for this?" Nova asked, speaking loudly to be heard above the distant reports of laser fire and the rising tumult of fifty soldiers bumping shoulders behind the city gates.

Samara glanced at the girl and nodded. "Yes." She flexed sweaty hands on her laser rifle and checked the fire-mode selector for the hundredth time. The safety was still on. No chance she could accidentally shoot one of the men in front of her.

A loud *thunk* sounded as heavy locking mechanisms in the gates slid aside. They began rumbling open, and a dark gap of stars and sky appeared.

General Logan Hall's voice thundered to their ears, amplified through the external speakers in a Chimeran helmet he now wore: "Death to the Dregs!" he cried.

The soldiers standing behind him took up that battle cry with a deafening roar, pumping the air with their fists and rifles. And then the general cried, "Forward!" And he led the way through the widening gap. It took a moment for the lead end of the group to get out of the way.

"Stay close," Sergeant Sutton said as he glanced back at Samara from where he stood with Harold, Pyro, and Doc. Lori and Richard stood behind Samara and Nova. All told, there were only eight of them. They'd lost Preacher while fleeing from Phoenix Base. And Widow, Clayton, and Keera were still missing in action. "We need to watch each other's backs out there," Sutton added.

"Copy that," Pyro said.

Samara nodded.

The men in front of them surged forward with an unintelligible roar, and Sutton turned to follow them with a battle cry of his own: "Hooah!"

"Hooah!" the others cried as they ran after

him—even Nova. Samara ran silently behind them. As soon as she cleared the gates, she saw the bridge and the river on the other side. The city was surrounded by a U-shaped bend in the river. Dregs hated water, so that would have been enough to stop them were it not for the old, four-lane bridge that crossed to the Enclave. The bridge had collapsed on one side, leaving just two lanes clear. As Samara ran along the cracked and buckled concrete, she wondered why the Enclave didn't just blow out the bridge and cut the city off from the Dregs.

Then she saw the reason: a thick pile of debris had washed up against the bridge, making a second path across the river. It wouldn't be that simple to cut the city off from the Wastes. Even if the Enclave could collapse the two lanes that were still standing, the Dregs would still rush across the dam of debris below. It would take a hell of an explosion to eradicate both the bridge and the dam, and something told her they didn't have access to the kind of ordnance they'd need.

There had to be a reason General Hall was leading a charge across the river rather than planting explosives. Their only hope was to slow the Dregs down before they reached the city walls, or better yet, to make them think twice about pressing on, and find a way to rout the herd.

Up ahead, the ruins of an old two story stone building appeared. The clock tower at its center had crumbled and was leaning to one side, while fully half of the stone building had been wiped out. The other half of it and the steps to the columned entrance stood mostly intact, peeking over the top of a low wall of rusting vehicles that had been drawn across the entrance to the bridge. A dozen armed sentries stood there, firing down into the horde on the other side. Samara couldn't see the Dregs from here, but she could hear them: their hisses, growls, and shrieks all blurring together in a deafening roar that was thousands of voices strong.

Samara felt her entire body start to shake as fear and adrenaline flooded her system. Maybe she should have stayed behind. How would she be helping Dora if she got herself infected or killed?

Before she could have any more second thoughts, she fetched up against the wall of vehicles at the end of the bridge. The Dregs stampeding on the other side were so close now that the ground was shaking with their collective approach. The soldiers from the Enclave ran up makeshift wooden ramps and climbed ladders to reach the top of their barricade.

Samara ran with Nova up the nearest ramp behind Sergeant Sutton and the others. She crested the top of the wall to see soldiers fanning out along its length and adding their fire to that of the odd dozen men already standing there. They pressed in until they were standing shoulder to shoulder without a single gap. Flickering bursts of emerald light backlit the soldiers as they fired into the horde. Dregs screamed as they died, but the rumbling thunder of their approach never ceased. Samara ran after Sutton to the thinnest end of the Enclave's ranks, and they filled in gaps on the far right of the barrier.

"Holy shit!" Pyro swore.

"Holy hell," Harold added.

Samara found an empty space along the barricade and saw what they were remarking on.

"Weapons free!" Sutton cried. And all of them let loose with flickering torrents of laser fire.

All except for Samara and Richard. They'd both frozen, staring blankly into the screaming horde of Dregs. The flickering emerald light of laser fire illuminated them. Fires sprouted here and there as lasers missed and hit trees or grass, adding to the ambient light. A shadowy herd of pale-faced monsters appeared rushing toward them, shoulder to shoulder in an endless throng. Samara saw their gleaming red eyes, stringy patches of hair, and dirty, bloody clothes, and she realized that these were second generation Dregs, all still in the process of turning, but already driven insane by the virus. These had to be the former citizens of New Dallas. But how had they come together in such an organized way?

The pale, bobbing sea of faces stretched as far as Samara's eyes could see and then still further, wrapping around the street on both sides of the courthouse to untold numbers beyond.

"Help us!" Nova cried. She was firing steadily with her rifle on full auto, spraying the shrieking masses below. A wave of Dregs advanced on their section of the wall. Their ranks were falling and thinning by the dozens as lasers found them, but ever more advanced from behind, clambering over the fallen and using the growing piles of corpses like springboards to leap closer and closer to the top of the barricade.

Samara pulled her rifle up and turned it on its side, her hands shaking violently as she found the selector switch and flicked it to *kill.*

Pulling the stock up to her shoulder, Samara screamed and held the trigger down, raking deadly fire over the nearest Dregs. Her eyes teared with the blinding assault of lasers. Her nose ached and stung with the sharp scent of ozone. Her ears rang with the deafening roars and screams of Dregs and friendly soldiers alike. Dregs climbing up the barricade reached several men and pulled them over the wall, screaming as they fell. Their bodies vanished in the horde, their screams turned to gurgles as they were eaten alive.

Nova cursed as a gust of super-heated steam jetted out of the cooling vents in the sides of her rifle. Her weapon had just over-heated.

A pair of Dregs began climbing up directly below. Samara shot the first one in the chest, and it fell with a *thud,* while the second pulled itself up to within just a foot of Nova's face. It spared a hand from the side of the old school bus they were standing on and swiped at her with its claws. Nova stepped back quickly, narrowly missing the attack. Lori darted in and jammed her rifle against the side of the Dreg's head and pulled the trigger. A molten orange hole appeared in its pale white head. The creature went limp and fell to the ground.

"Thanks," Nova said, just as the indicator light on her rifle glowed green.

Lori nodded, and both women went back to firing.

Samara directed her attention to the horde and raked the nearest line of Dregs with a stuttering stream of lasers. Another line pushed through, climbing a wall of corpses rising ten meters away from the barricade.

Just then, a blinding explosion erupted there as a plasma grenade touched down. It exploded with a deafening *boom,* and flaming pieces of Dregs went flying in all directions. A heavy chunk of one slammed Samara in the shoulder and spun her around. She found herself staring at it, still flaming on the ground on the other side of the bus where she stood: a pale, dirty foot, quickly turning black as it burned itself to a crisp. Her stomach lurched queasily, and she spun back around to face the horde. That grenade hadn't even slowed them down. The snarling, shrieking masses were growing thicker not thinner. Two more grenades burst open the rising walls of the dead, sending out another gruesome rain of flaming carnage that pitter-pattered down around them. But it only bought them a momentary reprieve.

Samara's rifle clicked and stopped spitting fire. Steam gushed from the vents in the sides, and she dropped the rifle as it scalded her hands. The weapon swung free from the shoulder strap as Samara rubbed the backs of her hands as if to put out a fire. The steam gushed on, searing her stomach through her jumpsuit. She grabbed the rifle again, gritting her teeth against the pain and searching for some way to cool the weapon down.

"You have to flush the coolant!" Nova said. "Here!" she reached over and pressed a button just above the trigger guard on the opposite side from the fire-selector switch.

The steam hissed suddenly louder and

thicker before vanishing altogether. A green light flicked on at the back of the rifle.

"Thanks!" Samara said, and took aim once more. Dregs were climbing up right below her. Ten of them in a row, with a hundred more fighting to be next. She and Nova and the soldiers around them sprayed the monsters with lasers, dropping them all. The next ones clambered forward, stepping on the backs of the dead. They felled those too, and the pile grew one layer higher, rising like a ramp to reach them. Soon it would be high enough that the Dregs wouldn't even have to climb the barricade.

Their position was about to be overrun.

"We're gonna have to fall back!" Sutton screamed. "General Hall!" he cried, his head turning to search for the other man.

But his voice was lost to the raging thunder of laser fire and the shrieking horde. "Let's go!" he said, striding along behind them and waving urgently to the members of Phoenix. He pointed back to the gates on the other side of the bridge. "It's time to run for it!"

The Enclave's soldiers were still firing steadily, but General Hall was nowhere to be seen. Samara hoped he hadn't been one of the ones the Dregs had yanked down from the barricade.

And then a new sound came: a steady *thumping* of much heavier weapons, followed by the high-pitched whine of grav engines, rising swiftly as they approached. Samara glanced up toward the sound and saw a *ship* come flying over the crumbling clock tower of the courthouse.

It was a small transport flying low with floodlights shining down and laser cannons roaring. Thick emerald laser beams slammed into the street below, incinerating dozens of Dregs with every shot. The ship stopped right above them and raked its guns up and down the length of the mounded wall of corpses in front of the barricade. High-powered lasers ignited the dead and drew a wall of flames along the length of the battle lines. Samara felt waves of heat radiating from the fire, and smelled the horrid stench of burning flesh. Her stomach clenched and heaved once more. She took a quick step back and held her sleeve to her nose as the inferno grew uncomfortably hot on her face.

Finally, the horde had slowed in its approach. A scattering of Dregs dared to run through the flames, only to catch ablaze and fall shrieking to the ground on the other side.

The soldiers on the wall cheered and shouted out warnings about the ship that had just saved their lives. None of them seemed happy to have been saved by Chimeras.

But Samara knew better. She stared up at the ship with a mixture of awe and euphoric relief, watching as it flew over the wall and hovered down for a landing on the other side. A hoverbike screamed after it and landed beside the ship, and a woman with long dark hair jumped off the back of the bike. Samara knew who it had to be even before she saw the other two people come striding out of the back of the transport. She turned and sprinted down the wooden ramp from the barricade, flying across the glittering asphalt to reach them.

She recognized Clayton by his shaggy beard and shoulder-length hair just a few seconds before she slammed into him and buried her face in his neck.

CHAPTER 42

"Sam," Clayton breathed beside her ear. "You're okay."

"*I'm* okay?" she withdrew sharply to look him in the eye, her gaze hard and angry. "I thought you were dead!"

"Likewise," he said.

Nova crashed into him next and it became a group hug. She was laughing and crying at the same time, but then she stepped back with a suddenly stricken look. "Where's Rosie?"

"She's fine. I left her on a rooftop not far from here. We'll pick her up when this is over."

Nova nodded slowly, her eyes shadowed with worry as she glanced back to the line of old vehicles that separated them from the tens of thousands of Dregs on the other side.

"Captain Cross! You son of a bitch! You actually did it!" Sutton cried. Hurried footfalls thundered to Clayton's ears, and he saw the rest of Phoenix running down from the makeshift walls. "You found a ship! I wouldn't believe it if I hadn't just watched you save our collective asses with it!"

"More dumb luck than anything," Clayton said as Lori came running out to greet her daughter, Keera. "Reapers had it," he explained, watching as Lori and Keera embraced one another. He looked back to Sutton. "They must have followed Widow and me here, and we took it from them."

"Well dumb luck or not, it looks like you've found your new command. Congratulations, Captain. Irony is, we might not have to leave anymore."

Clayton shook his head. "Depends how this battle goes."

Doc stepped out from behind Sutton and crossed over to Widow. She watched him approaching with a frown, her arms crossed over her chest. He stopped awkwardly in front of her. "You're hurt."

Widow touched her cheek, running her fingertips along thick crusts of dried blood, as if only now remembering that Chimeras had flayed her cheek open while she'd been their prisoner. Doc shrugged out of his pack and began digging through it for supplies.

Clayton heard more footsteps rushing in and followed the sound to a group of soldiers running over from the barricade. Their weapons were out and they didn't look happy.

They stopped ten feet away, not aiming their rifles, but not lowering them either. The leader reached up and twisted off a gleaming black helmet, revealing dark hair tied back in a ponytail and equally dark eyes with crow's feet pinching around them. "Who is this?" he demanded, jerking his chin to Clayton and looking to Sutton for an answer.

"Captain Cross," Sutton said. "From the Forerunners."

The man's eyes widened in recognition, but he didn't reply.

"And you are?" Clayton asked.

"General Hall, leader of the Enclave's Army. But actually, Captain, I wasn't asking about you. I was asking about *her*—" He pointed over Clayton's shoulder to Keera.

Clayton stepped sideways to let the general address her more directly. Seeing the scowls and hateful looks directed her way from the general's men, Clayton pointed out, "She's the one who just saved all of your lives." He deliberately withheld her name and former rank, thinking it might not be a good idea to reveal that she'd been the admiral of the occupying fleet ten years ago. Who knew what kind of grudges these men might be holding.

"Fair enough," General Hall said. "But that wall of fire you kicked up is not going to last long. You have any other Hail Mary's left?"

Keera stepped forward. "You have to retreat."

"I'll be the judge of that... *ma'am.*"

Keera's eyes narrowed by a fraction of a degree. "There's fifty-five thousand Dregs out there, and you're not going to turn them all away just because you've killed a thousand. They can *smell* you. All of you. And like you said, as soon as the flames die down, they'll come rushing through, and you'll be overrun in a minute."

Silence answered Keera's warning, broken only by the periodic screeching of lasers firing down from the barricades on stragglers who made it through the flames. General Hall's men traded anxious glances, some of them muttering under their breath about the numbers they faced.

"Fifty-five thousand," the general said slowly. "That's practically the entire population of New Dallas. I wonder, how did they all find us at the same time? And how do *you* know how many there are?"

"Because she led them here!" a woman screamed from the direction of the transport before Keera could reply. The Reapers were awake.

"Who was that? Who's in there?" General Hall demanded.

"Reapers," Clayton said. "Human waste. They're the ones who led the Dregs here. We managed to commandeer their transport, but it was already too late."

"I see. And how did these Reapers find us in

the first place?" General Hall demanded. "Only chalkheads like her know of the Enclave's existence."

"I didn't tell them," Keera said, ignoring the General's insult. "They went to Phoenix Base and found it already taken by Chimeras. The transport was cloaked, so they followed Clayton and Widow north until they saw the Enclave for themselves. They realized that the only way they could raid your city was to have Dregs overwhelm your defenses first, so they went to New Dallas to gather the horde."

General Hall began nodding. "And all this time you were what—their accomplice? I'm guessing you piloted the shuttle."

"I was a prisoner," Keera clarified. "And I tried to crash it before they got here, but they stunned me and took the controls themselves."

"What a convenient story," General Hall said.

"We don't have time to stand around here arguing," Sergeant Sutton said.

"No, we don't," General Hall agreed. He looked to Keera. "You said we should retreat. Then what?"

"Then we blow the bridge," Keera said.

"We don't have the ordnance for that."

"You don't, but *I* do. The laser cannons on the transport can do it, but it'll take time."

"How *much* time?" the general asked.

"Five, maybe ten minutes to cut a hole."

"By then we'll have ten thousand Dregs at the walls." General Hall slowly shook his head. "We'll lose too many people, and the integrity of the city will be compromised."

"We can hold them here," Sutton said.

"But taking out the bridge will cut off our retreat," General Hall replied.

"The transport can pull us out afterward. At least fifteen at a time," Clayton suggested. "And we have two bikes. That's another four."

"I have fifty-six men here," Hall replied. "Counting all of you, that's at least three trips. By the time we get to the last one there won't be anyone left to evacuate."

"Sacrifice your city or your troops," Sutton said. "It's your choice."

"What about *your* troops? Who gets to evac first?" General Hall demanded.

"We can draw names at random," Samara suggested—and then winced as she appeared to realize that her name might not get drawn.

"There's no time for that!" General Hall cried.

"How about this: it's *our* ship," Keera growled. "Phoenix gets out first, or I pull them out now and you're all on your own."

"Oh, so it's like that, is it?" General Hall looked to Sutton for an answer.

"You said it yourself," Sutton said. "We're on probation. We're new to the Enclave. It wouldn't be fair to ask us to give our lives in its defense when we don't even know if we'll be allowed to stay."

General Hall snorted. "That might be a good way to get off probation, don't you think?"

"Not if we're dead."

Clayton struggled to fill in the blanks and figure out what he was missing.

"How about this," Sutton went on, "you give my people an unconditional pardon to stay in the Enclave, and then we'll fight to defend it with our dying breaths. Are you authorized to offer that?"

General Hall smiled. "Done."

"Good," Sutton said. "Keera—" He looked to her. "Better get that bird in the air and start chipping away at that bridge."

Keera hesitated before acknowledging the order with a nod. She ran back to the transport and disappeared inside. Muffled voices sounded from within, followed by a sharp cry from the woman who'd spoken earlier.

"Everyone to the wall!" General Hall ordered as he put his helmet on and turned to lead his troops back to the front line.

"On me, Phoenix!" Sutton replied as he ran after them. Doc was done patching Widow's cheek, and now they sprinted after Sutton with Lori, Harold, Pyro, and Richard. Clayton rolled his shoulders, feeling the dull stabs of pain from the shrapnel still lodged in his back.

Samara's hand found Clayton's and she gave it a squeeze as Keera disappeared inside the transport. "Dora was bitten," she said. "By a second generation Dreg."

Clayton's eyes snapped to hers, his heart suddenly hammering in his chest. "She was *what*? Is she..."

Samara shook her head. "She's immune. She's in isolation. The Enclave thinks they can use her to develop a cure."

Clayton's brow creased deeply and he nodded along with that. If it was true, maybe there was still hope for humanity on Earth.

"They're coming through!" someone cried from the wall, and then the sporadic sounds of laser fire became a steady barrage.

"We can talk about this later!" Nova shouted to be heard above the sudden din. "We have to go help them! Come on!"

Clayton stared at his daughter and saw a startling depth in her gaze, equal parts horror and grim determination shone beneath the flickering emerald light of laser fire. The face that framed her gaze was that of an adult—a veteran soldier. No longer just a teenage girl. Clayton nodded to Nova with a grim smile and grabbed his rifle in both hands. "Lead the way."

CHAPTER 43

Lieutenant Akora sat on her hoverbike beside Corporal Rathos, watching the unending horde of Dregs below. They flooded every street and alleyway for a square kilometer in front of the bridge to the Enclave.

"They're going to overrun the Enclave," Rathos said, speaking quietly over their comms.

"Maybe," Akora agreed.

"If V'tan Company were here..." He trailed off.

"Then we'd die with them," Akora said.

"We have heavier weapons than they do," Rathos said.

"It wouldn't matter. There's too many of them."

"Then... what do we do? Go back and tell the Commander to retreat to our previous position? By morning the city will be over-run."

Akora considered their orders. She was in no hurry to report back to Commander Tyris with bad news. Partly, because she couldn't stand to see his face. He was a pig, and a monster. If she hadn't been recovering from her injuries at the time, she might have challenged him on the spot after he'd thrown Ava into the fire. And that wasn't the only offense worth challenging him over. Something told her that woman's accusations weren't just rumors.

"Lieutenant?" Rathos prompted.

"No, we wait," Akora decided, answering both her own thoughts about challenging the commander and Rathos's inquiry at the same time. "Our orders are to wait and standby for the commander's arrival. There's still a chance that the Enclave will survive."

Even as she said that, something new happened. A ship blasted off the ground right behind the Enclave's forward lines. Akora recognized it as a La'rik-class cloaking transport. Commandos used them to sneak behind enemy lines. Somehow the Enclave had found a ship *and* figured out how to pilot it.

"Are you seeing that, LT?" Rathos asked.

"I am," she replied, just as the ship began raining hellfire down on the bridge between the Enclave and the Dregs. Sheets of laser fire continued flashing out from the Enclave's forward lines. They were buying time for the transport to cut the city off from the horde. Unfortunately, the soldiers on the ground weren't going to live through it. A calculated sacrifice to save the city.

"Maybe the Dakkas aren't so dumb after all," Rathos said.

Akora glanced at him. "They're just as smart as us, Corporal. Remember, we *are* them, and they are us. The difference is, we're genetically enhanced for war and interstellar travel, while they are stuck with what nature gave them."

"Still makes them inferior."

"Perhaps. But don't underestimate them, Corporal. It could mean your death."

"Yes, ma'am," Rathos said quietly.

Akora dragged her eyes back to the battle. If those soldiers only knew that they were saving the city for V'tan Company, they might not have been so willing to sacrifice themselves in its defense.

* * *

Nova stood between her father and Samara, firing steadily into the guttering wall of flames, dropping wave after endless wave of Dregs. The steady flashing of lasers blinded her. Steam periodically gushed from her weapon, scalding her hands as it overheated. She felt the skin blistering and stinging, but pushed through the pain, refusing to let it slow her down.

Blinded by the flashing light of lasers, she could barely see to aim, but it almost didn't matter where she fired, she was bound to hit a Dreg. With her vision impaired, Nova's ringing ears became the focus of her senses: weapons hissed with steam as they overheated, and empty charge packs clattered to the rusty metal roofs of the vehicles in the barricade; laser rifles screeched with constant reports, and heavy laser cannons thumped steadily in the distance as Keera took out the bridge; the shrieking snarls of the Dregs and the triumphant whoops of human soldiers mingled with the screams of the wounded and the dying. It all played over and over on a loop without end.

Nova's weapon clicked dry, and she hurried to eject the empty charge pack. It fell soundlessly on her foot.

"Nova, look out!" Clayton cried as a Dreg's filthy hand reached for her, materializing wraith-like from the strobing green light still flashing as after images before her eyes. She felt it seize her jumpsuit and drag her toward the low wall of metal and wooden panels in front of her. She stumbled forward, staggering under the weight of the creature and staring into the dirty face of a female Dreg that still looked halfway human with bloodshot blue eyes and half a head of stringy black hair. The creature shrieked and snapped at her with dirty, bloody teeth, showing a black tongue. Nova pitched forward as the Dreg abandoned its hold on the bus and grabbed her with its other hand to pull her neck down for a bite.

Clayton shot it in the face, but Nova was carried over with it. She felt herself falling, saw the knot of Dregs below look up and shriek with delight as they anticipated the kill.

And then someone pulled her back. It was Samara. "Are you okay?"

Nova nodded mutely.

And then a blood-curdling shriek erupted from their end of the barricade.

"Shit!" Lori cried. "Look out!"

A pair of Dregs had jumped over to the far end of the barricade from a nearby pile of corpses that had reached to the same height as the fortifications. They'd landed between Richard and Harold and now both of them were locked in a hand-to-hand struggle for their lives.

Nova reloaded her rifle and took aim, but she couldn't get a clear shot. Harold managed to draw a knife from his belt, and he sliced his Dreg's throat open. Blood gushed over him, and he scuttled away, no doubt worried about the possibility of infection. Pyro ran in to help Richard just as his Dreg turned its jaws on his arm and clamped down. He screamed, and Pyro shot the creature at point-blank in the side of the head.

And then three more Dregs jumped over. Sutton and Pyro shot two of them. Clayton shot the third, and Nova missed.

"Fall back!" Sutton cried as four more

came flying over. They landed in a crouch and bounded toward them. Phoenix cut them down as they retreated from the threat, and half a dozen more took their place.

General Hall came running in, drew a grenade from the bandoleer across his chest, and tossed it toward the pile of corpses on the other side of the barricade.

One of the Dregs standing on the wall snatched it out of the air and stared at the device. Its nostrils flared and twitched as it sniffed at the metal cylinder.

"Everybody down!" General Hall cried.

"Jump!" Sutton added, and he took a running leap off the barricade, followed closely by Pyro.

Nova was knocked down and flattened, a heavy weight pressing her down. She recognized the sour smell of her father's sweat just before the world flashed white. A deafening *boom* lifted the ground beneath them and sent them flying through the air.

Nova's stomach lurched into her throat as she fell, and she experienced a breathless flash of déjà vu from countless nightmares that she'd had as a kid—nightmares in which she discovered that she could fly only to suddenly lose that ability and plummet like a rock. And then came the worst part, the part where she always woke up—the bone-cracking *thud* of the impact. But that impact did the opposite of waking her: it knocked her out cold.

CHAPTER 44

Clayton landed hard, but his fall was broken by another soldier. He picked himself off the ground, his head thick and ears ringing, elbows aching and his back stinging with a fresh wave of shrapnel.

Strong hands found him, and he was pulled to his feet, eye to eye with Sutton's terrified gaze, one side of his bald head was gleaming with blood from a gash. *Run!* he said, but Clayton didn't hear it. He read Sutton's lips.

The sergeant turned and ran back into the fight, his rifle spitting fire as he went.

Clayton was about to join him, when he remembered who else had been with him on the wall. He spun around to look for Samara and Nova. A second later, he found them both lying face-down on the asphalt ten feet away. Neither of them was moving.

Clayton heard a snarl and spun around to shoot a Dreg in the stomach just before it could reach him.

It was a young teenage boy, balding, with

streaks of blood leaking from bloodshot eyes. A child, driven insane by the virus, now clutching a fiery hole in his gut as he died. Clayton stared in shock as the boy pitched over and fell on his face, dead before he hit the ground.

In the background, his eyes registered armored soldiers leaping off the barricades and firing backward at the horde flooding a flaming gap on the other side. General Hall held his ground along with Sutton and several others, raking the Dregs with solid sheets of laser fire. The general tossed another grenade into the heart of the shrieking horde, and Clayton looked away just before the explosion could blind him. A hot wind blasted by, peppering him with fiery bits and pieces that pelted his jumpsuit and seared his exposed skin.

"Fall back!" the general cried into the lull that followed that explosion. His voice boomed across the battlefield, amplified by the speakers in his helmet.

Looking back the other way, Clayton saw just three members of Phoenix go flashing by: Lori, Widow, and Doc. Keera's transport shone brightly in the distance, dropping down to a ragged gap in the bridge, the floodlights shining bright.

She couldn't evacuate them all.

Clayton snapped out of it and ran toward his family, his eyes stinging with tears. He couldn't tell whether they were from the pain of his injuries or the fear of losing Sam and Nova. He fell on the ground between them and shook them both simultaneously. "Get up!" he screamed with spittle flying from his lips. "Get up!"

Only one of them stirred. Nova rolled over with a groan, and he saw that her leg was broken. A bloody tibia jutted from her shin. She'd never be able to run like that.

"Dad?" she mumbled.

He glanced at Samara. She still wasn't moving. He realized with a blinding flash of terror that he couldn't save them both, and he didn't even know if Samara was alive.

Coming to a snap decision that he knew was going to haunt him for the rest of his life, he reached down and scooped Nova up. She cried out as the movement disturbed her broken leg.

"You'll be okay," he said, as much to himself as to her. And then he ran and didn't look back. His eyes blurred with tears, and this time he knew that it wasn't from physical pain. He heard the steady hammering of booted feet chasing him and of lasers screeching as soldiers retreated. Then came their screams and the Dregs' snarls, followed by silence and the thunder of bare feet slapping concrete, drawing ever nearer.

Just seconds before he reached Keera's ship, he could hear them panting and snorting as they breathed down his neck. Nova seemed to come to her senses and she cried out in a trembling voice, "Dad!"

Dead ahead, the roof of the transport had formed a bridge across a ragged gap that Keera had cut with the ship's lasers. Lori, Widow, and Doc jumped to reach it, and then Lori skidded to a stop and turned to beckon to him from the other side.

Clayton saw the asphalt run out just a few steps ahead of him and the transport hovering four feet away from that. He hit the edge and pushed off with every ounce of strength he had. The crumbling bridge gave way under his foot and his guts climbed into his throat as they began to fall.

Nova screamed, and Clayton caught a glimpse of the shining river below—at least forty feet down. His head swam dizzily.

Lori lunged, reaching for them with both hands—

And missed.

"Clayton!" she screamed after them.

"Hold your breath!" Clayton shouted to Nova.

Nova stopped screaming and sucked in a deep breath. Clayton pointed his toes and shifted his grip on his daughter.

And then the water enveloped them in its frigid embrace, and the shrieking horde faded to a muffled, cottony silence. The current grabbed them as their momentum carried them all the way into utter darkness, only to hit the pebbly riverbed with a bone-cracking jolt. He lost his grip on Nova, and the current rolled Clayton along the bottom a dozen times before he managed to orient himself and push off with a kick. He fumbled blindly for Nova, reaching through walls of liquid darkness to find her, but he couldn't locate her anywhere.

He kicked and clawed his way to the surface, heading for the faded silver glow of the stars and moon. His head broke the surface, and he heard a raucous roar of splashing. Thinking it might be Nova struggling to swim with her broken leg, he twisted around to look —

And saw a stream of Dregs sailing down from the bridge like lemmings, shrieking in abject terror as they fell. They hit the water with loud slaps, doing body flops and knocking themselves out cold. Even the ones that came thrashing back to life couldn't seem to remember how to swim, and they quickly dropped below the rippled surface of the water.

Realizing he couldn't see her anywhere, Clayton cupped one hand to his mouth and shouted, "Nova!"

But his only reply was the steady thunder of Dregs slapping water.

CHAPTER 45

"**N**ova!" Clayton shouted again as the transport dropped vertically to the riverbank in front of him. He cast about desperately, searching for her bobbing head, her blond hair sleek and wet.

He sucked in a breath and dived down, searching the depths of the river and swimming around aimlessly in the dark. His lungs burned for air, and he was forced to surface again. Taking in another breath, he repeated the process. And then twice more.

The third time he came up for air, a thrashing knot of Dregs came floating by, using each other's bodies as rafts.

Clayton kicked the nearest one in the face and quickly swam out of their reach. He headed for the shore of the river, swimming with the current. The transport was landed some twenty feet higher up. Lori, Widow, and Doc came running out to get him.

"Nova," he gasped while crawling up the pebbly beach on his hands and knees. His whole body shook with exhaustion. "She's still in the water!" he said as Lori pulled him to his feet. "Tell Keera to use the transport's sensors to—"

"We already have," Lori said. She jerked her head sideways to indicate Doc and Widow. They'd run past Clayton, farther down the beach. Doc was on his knees beside a dark shape lying on the shore, and Widow was standing over them, looking scared.

"Nova!" Clayton ran to reach her side.

Doc was busy doing chest compressions when he fell on his knees beside her.

Clayton's heart seized in his chest, watching impotently as Doc worked. Lori laid a hand on his shoulder. He couldn't lose both her and Samara.

"We have to go!" Widow said, stepping back and aiming her rifle at the river.

Doc looked up quickly, and Clayton twisted around to see a living raft of Dregs wash up on the shore beside them. It came alive with arms and legs kicking and clawing to free themselves. They began splashing in the shadows. Clayton reached for his rifle, but he'd lost it in the river. Lori jumped up and took aim with hers, just as Widow opened fire.

"Pick her up and let's go!" Lori shouted.

Clayton extended trembling arms for Nova. He didn't even know if she was alive.

And then her whole body bucked and

heaved as she coughed and water bubbled from her lips. Relief crashed through Clayton, sweeping over and through him more powerfully than any emotion he'd ever felt in his life. He scooped Nova up; she coughed and spasmed in his arms as he ran.

He reached the open airlock of the shuttle within seconds. The two Reapers were there chained up inside, and Clayton's hoverbike was still wedged between the bulkheads. When the Reapers saw him come in carrying his daughter, Zachary sneered and McKayla spat on him as he walked by to the cockpit. He didn't even glance at them. Several sets of booted feet followed him in, and then he heard Widow shout, "Get us in the air!"

Keera pulled up hard, and Clayton's knees almost buckled under him. He saw Nova studying him with a knitted brow, then watched as she looked around and struggled to peer over his shoulders. He set her down in the co-pilot's seat, and she clung to it while peering into the back of the transport with a horrified look on her face.

"What is it?" he asked, feeling numb from the cold water, and emotionally numb from everything else.

"Where is everyone?" Nova asked in a shrinking voice.

"Dead," Widow grated out as she entered the cockpit.

"Samara, too?" Nova asked in a cracking voice.

Clayton nodded, and the last of his strength left him in a rush. He hit the deck hard and sat there, dazed and staring at his hands and feet.

"Wait," Keera said. "What's that? I'm reading two human life signs in the water."

"Are you sure?" Widow asked.

"Positive."

Clayton jumped to his feet and saw it for himself: two yellow blips, drifting along the current beside each other amidst a dozen scattered clumps of blue ones that were rafts of Dregs.

"Who is it?" Nova asked, leaning toward the viewscreen as Keera took them down to the river. The transport's cannons opened fire, flashing out and cutting down the Dregs who'd washed up on the shore.

Clayton spotted a pair of bobbing heads, swimming steadily for the riverbank. He couldn't see well enough to identify them, but Keera could. He looked to her for her answer, but her eyes were fixed on the water as she landed the transport.

***

Ten minutes earlier...

Samara came to, her ears ringing and head hammering from the blast and the subsequent impact. She pushed up on her elbows, unable to believe she was alive. Dozens of soldiers were running toward her, firing sporadically and screaming in terror as a solid wave of Dregs came at them like a flood, overtaking them and sucking them under one after another.

Samara blinked bleary eyes and tried to struggle to her feet. A sharp, blinding bolt of pain erupted in her ankle, and she collapsed. She cried out and bit her tongue. Her ankle was either broken or twisted. Either way, she wasn't going to make it.

But she had to try. She pushed off the ground again and this time she made it, standing one-legged like a flamingo before the onrushing horde. She tried to put weight on her foot, and it gave out instantly once more. Four soldiers broke ranks and ran out ahead of the rest, managing to escape a grisly death. One of them was armored from head to toe in gleaming black armor. General Hall. Another was equally familiar: bald with dark skin and the shiny patch of a burn scar on his cheek. Sergeant Sutton. Their eyes locked, and his widened. He angled toward her, running straight at her like a linebacker. He slammed into her and pushed her down.

"What are you doing?" she cried.

"Shut up and play dead!" he said, holding her down and shielding her with his body.

And then Dregs fell on him, ripping and

clawing at his back, and his face contorted in agony. No teeth or claws found her, but she could feel warm blood soaking through her clothes. Samara sobbed and silently cursed the Dregs and the Chrona who'd made them. It only lasted for a few seconds before she felt hands grabbing her and pulling her out. That was followed by a shrieking report of laser fire, and then the gut-sucking *boom* of another grenade exploding. She came face to helmet with General Hall, her ears ringing anew. The Dregs appeared similarly dazed, clawing at their eyes and stumbling around blindly. General Hall dropped his rifle, leaving it to hang from its strap, and then he scooped her off the ground and ran.

Samara saw Dregs running to all sides of them, jaws snapping, and eyes wild. One of them sliced open her arm with its claws. She cried out in pain, but General Hall didn't even react. He just kept running. They reached the ragged end of the bridge and sailed out over thin air, falling more than a dozen feet short of the other side.

"Get ready to swim!" General Hall cried.

Samara pulled in a shaky breath.

And then they hit the water with a world-shattering *slap!*

CHAPTER 46

The shuttle touched down briefly, right in front of Samara and General Hall as they kicked and struggled together through the water to reach the open airlock at the back of the transport. The general had one of her arms draped over his shoulders.

Clayton stood in the open airlock, clutching a handrail and reaching for Samara with his other hand. "Sam!" he cried, unable to contain the swirling storm of joy, relief, and guilt that washed over him.

Samara was sobbing as she came limping inside. General Hall helped her in and then Clayton took over, stumbling with her the rest of the way through the airlock. The transport took off and Clayton and Samara fell down together. He grabbed her face and kissed her hard, as much to be sure that she was real as to welcome her back from the dead.

"How did you..." he trailed off, shaking his head as they came apart.

"I didn't. Sutton saved me. He threw himself on top of me and the Dregs went for him instead. He died a hero."

"He's no hero!" General Hall scoffed as he pulled off his helmet.

Widow and Lori gathered around, their eyes cold and glaring.

"He was bitten! He was going to die anyway."

"Fuck you!" Widow screamed.

Clayton felt an exhausted echo of that same anger flash through him, warming his frozen body.

"Are you fucking kidding me? He's dead!" Widow cried as she took a step toward the general and shook a fist in his face. "Take it back," she said through gritted teeth.

Logan Hall smiled thinly at her. "You think you're the only one who lost people tonight? Crawl out of your ass and take a look around!" Logan thundered. "At least you still have people! Mine are all gone, to a man."

Widow took a step back with the force of the general's outburst. She stalked away, heading for the cockpit.

"We did it," Samara whispered. "I can't believe we made it."

General Hall glanced at her. "You didn't." He nodded to her arm, and Clayton noticed the parallel furrows of a Dreg's claws. Not deep and gushing with blood, but washed white by the water.

"No way you're not infected," General Hall said. "That Dreg broke your skin."

"She's immune," someone else called out from the cockpit. It was Nova. Clayton looked down that way and saw Doc busy wrapping her broken leg in a bandage, using the sheath of the Sikath for a splint.

"Immune, huh?" General Hall grunted.

"She's right," Clayton said. "Dora's been bitten, and she's not infected. The whole reason she's immune is because her mother is."

"Well, I sure as hell hope you're right about that," General Hall said, looking away. His eyes fell on the two Reapers and he grew suddenly very still.

Zachary gave him a nasty grin. "How's it feel to be saved by a chalkhead?" The general said nothing, and he went on blithely, "Pretty soon she'll be ruling you all like a queen! The new overseer! It's back to captivity for the human race!" He laughed and shook his head.

"Zack..." McKayla said in a low, warning voice.

But it was too late. A dark flash of anger stole across General Hall's face. He stalked toward the two Reapers and punched Zachary straight in the mouth with an armored fist.

Zack's teeth clacked together noisily and he sagged against his chains.

"Turn this shuttle around!" General Hall said as he pulled the Reaper up and drew a sidearm from his waist to aim it at the chains.

"What? Why?" Keera asked.

"You heard me! Fly us over the horde! We have a load of garbage to dump out the airlock."

Clayton felt the transport turn.

General Hall shot Zachary's restraints, and he screamed as the bolt of plasma burned his hands.

"Zack!" McKayla sobbed.

General Hall dragged him through the transport, delivering blows to his head the whole way to subdue him. And then he threw the man out the back. Clayton grimaced as Zack fell screaming to the shrieking horde below.

Samara buried her face in his chest and covered her ears. Then the general came marching back, headed straight for McKayla. She strained against her chains, pressing herself against the bulkhead and shrinking away from his approach. Her jaw was slack and eyes wide with terror.

"No!" she screamed as he reached for her chains and took aim. She kicked him, her boots bouncing off his armor. And then he fired, and she screamed in pain just as Zachary had.

"No! No! No!" she cried, batting and clawing at his hands and face as he dragged her to the airlock, too. He slammed the butt of his pistol into the top of her head and she quieted somewhat. But then she shrieked like a Dreg as she fell. Her screams faded quickly into silence as she reached the eager embrace of the horde.

"All right! Take us to the Enclave!" General Hall shouted. But he stayed right where he was, hanging out the open airlock to watch the Reapers die.

Clayton let out a shuddering breath, shocked to the point of numbness at the callous fury of the General's retribution—but then he remembered what they'd been about to do to Keera, and the fact that every single death tonight was their fault—Sutton, Harold, Pyro, Richard... and over fifty other soldiers whose names he didn't even know.

Remembering all of that, suddenly Clayton wanted to watch the Dregs tear the Reapers apart, too.

CHAPTER 47

The fading screams of the Reapers only reminded Keera of all the other people they'd killed—among others, her father, Richard Morgan.

Keera couldn't believe he was dead. She'd never had a great relationship with him, but somehow that didn't make it any easier. Richard Morgan, former Ambassador of the Union, resistance operative, coward... Father... gone forever. Keera blinked in shock. Nova watched her from the co-pilot's seat while Doc finished bandaging her leg.

"Are you okay?" the girl asked, her eyes searching.

Keera's cranial stalks twitched. She dipped her chin in a shallow nod, but said nothing. Dead ahead, the dull, pulsing ruby glow of the Enclave brightened to a shining white diamond once more, the state of emergency now past.

Her thoughts blanked, then drifted in a new direction. What would life be like there?

Would she be the only Chimera? And where was the Kyra's fleet? They were supposed to have arrived half a day ago, and yet the transport's sensors showed nothing in orbit. Either the fleet was standing off at extreme range, or it had never arrived.

Footsteps rang on the metal deck. Keera heard a man clear his throat. "How's the leg?" Clayton asked.

"Fine," Nova replied. "Doc gave me a painkiller."

"She'll need surgery to set the bone," Doc said. "I did the best I could."

Clayton gave a weary sigh. "You did great."

Keera aimed for the nearest landing pad. It was illuminated brightly with concentric rings of floodlights. The transport's landing lights added to the glow as they drew near. Dust billowed out underneath them as she set down, the ship's grav engines repelling stray matter just as surely as the Earth attracted it.

The ship touched down with a jolt and a *thunk* of metal struts hitting the concrete landing pad. Keera killed the engines, and a heavy silence fell but for the tick-tick-ticking of metal parts cooling.

More footsteps tracked steadily to the cockpit. "Let's go," General Hall said in a gravelly voice.

Keera unbuckled and stood up. Doc left the cockpit, and Keera waited for Clayton to help his daughter up and out. She hopped along on one leg, using him for support. General Hall lingered, his eyes cold as he stared at her, his gaze measuring.

Keera hissed at him and bared sharply-pointed teeth. "What?"

He smirked and shook his head before following Clayton through the ship. Keera scowled at his back, watching his ponytail swing back and forth as she trailed after the man. She knew his type—humans with an axe to grind, bigoted men who couldn't see that Chimeras were people, too. *Not just men,* she corrected herself. There were plenty of female bigots out there—McKayla, for example. An involuntary shiver rocked Keera's body and she pushed the memories away with a violent shove. Someone had cleared out the corpse of the man who'd tried to force himself on her, but that didn't make it any easier to forget.

Keera's footsteps were leaden, her body heavy with defeat. They'd won the battle, and yet somehow it felt like they'd lost the war. They'd lost too many people. As she reached the airlock, she spotted Widow bending down to help Samara off the floor. They went limping out ahead of Clayton and Nova.

General Hall glanced back at her, then away, as if he was just checking to make sure she wasn't about to stab him in the back.

Keera thought about saying something to

either allay his fears or goad the man, but she didn't have the energy.

They walked down a landing ramp at the back of the transport. A stiff breeze blew in, bringing with it the still smoldering stench of burning Dregs, and the unwashed scent of the living ones, their dirty bodies still pressed together and fanning out along the river in a throng tens of thousands deep.

Sentries fired periodically from the walls, picking off the survivors that had jumped from the bridge and managed to reach the opposite shore.

General Hall took the lead as they crossed the landing pad, striding steadily forward. He crossed a long walkway flanked by railings to a curving glass wall. A door slid open, and a group of four armored soldiers bustled out, along with someone else in a clean white hazmat suit. Keera was surprised they still had enough soldiers to spare that they could muster an armed response to newcomers.

"Stand down!" General Hall called out as he approached, and the soldiers appeared to relax somewhat. The person in the hazmat waited patiently for them to arrive.

Keera's sensitive eyes pierced both the darkness and the transparent faceplate of the suit to see a woman with light blue eyes, blonde hair tucked back from her face, and aquiline features. Her nose, chin, and cheek bones were sharp, giving her a predatory look that rivaled the Kyra. Keera felt her eyes narrowing and wished for the umpteenth time that she could read *human* thoughts as easily as she could read Kyron and Chimeran ones.

"You're... alive," the woman said slowly, her eyes lingering on Keera for a moment before flicking to the general. He stopped in front of her and waited. "Were you compromised?" the woman asked, her eyes flicking up and down, studying him for signs of bites or scratches. His shiny black armor was dull with infected blood, but otherwise pristine.

The general shook his head. "Not as far as I know. Let's get on with the tests."

The woman scanned his forehead with a thermometer. It beeped a moment later.

"No fever," she said, "But I guess it's too soon for that, anyway." She reached around behind her to a hovering storage crate and keyed something into the control panel on the side.

The top of the crate opened up and a stream of hovering black spheres raced out. They assembled themselves into three floating rings in front of the open door to the Enclave. Keera recognized the technology. A portable Kyron body scanner. Chimeras used them to test people who might have been exposed to the virus. The scans were meant to determine if they were infected, and also later on in the process of turning, to determine whether they would ultimately become Dregs or Chimeras.

General Hall walked toward the scanner and the hovering spheres parted to let him in. He stood still in the center of the rings as fans of blue light washed over him from head to toe. The scanner projected a holographic report in the air, and the woman in the hazmat suit studied it.

"You're clean," she said after a moment.

General Hall stepped out and went to join the guards at the entrance of the facility. The hazmat worker looked to Keera next, unable to contain herself any longer. "She's a Chimera."

"She saved your lives," Clayton pointed out.

The woman's eyes flicked to him, then to General Hall. She pointed to Keera as if to accuse her of something. "Director Hall won't allow a Chimera to join us. Not without a vote from the council."

Director Hall? Keera wondered. It sounded like the leader of the Enclave was related to the general.

"So let them vote," General Hall said.

"They won't be able to convene until tomorrow. Where are you going to put her until then?"

"In the detention level, where else?"

"What?" Lori demanded. "You're joking. She saved you!"

Keera felt a bitter smile lifting one side of her mouth. This didn't come as a surprise to her.

"The council will be apprised of her actions; you have my word of that," General Hall said as he turned to regard the others.

"Can we testify on her behalf?" Clayton asked. "We can all vouch for her."

Even Widow nodded along with that.

"You'll all have your chance to speak before the council tomorrow," General Hall confirmed.

"You mean today," Nova said. "It's after midnight."

The general waved dismissively at her. "That's what I meant. Now, who's next?"

Doc stepped forward and into the ring of hovering spheres. His scan came back clean. Then Clayton and Nova limped over and both of them stood together inside of the scanner. They both passed their scans as well.

Keera went next. The woman in the hazmat eyed her warily as the fans of blue light washed over her.

"No active infection."

"You were expecting otherwise?" Keera asked.

"You're not immune anymore," the woman said through a nasty smile.

She made a good point. Keera stepped out of the scanner to let Widow and Samara shuffle into it. Samara's arm was bleeding now, with three parallel gashes peeking out from under her sleeve.

Fans of blue light washed over her and Widow. The scan finished and the doctor studied the results.

"You're clean as well," she said.

Samara looked surprised. "Are you sure?"

"Yes, why?"

"Because Dora was bitten, and she didn't pass the scan." Samara rolled up her sleeve to reveal the three bloody gashes in her arm. The doctor studied them briefly and then shook her head. "An older Dreg did that. You're fully immune to the first strain of the virus. Your body must have eliminated the infection already."

"How can you tell it was an older Dreg?" Clayton asked.

"Look at her jumpsuit. It's torn. New Dregs are still turning. They won't have claws yet, and human nails aren't sharp enough to get through that fabric."

Samara nodded along with that explanation. "Doctor Dartmouth..." Samara began.

"Yes?"

"How is my daughter?"

"Sleeping peacefully. She's fine. The infection hasn't spread, if that's what you're wondering."

Samara sagged against Widow, seeming to

deflate as the air left her lungs.

The doctor cracked a more genuine smile at that, then looked away, her gaze sweeping over the rest of them. "You're all cleared to come inside. Congratulations. You saved a lot of lives tonight. It's time for you to get some rest. I'm sure you're exhausted. Please follow me."

The doctor touched the control panel on the body scanner's storage crate and the hovering spheres streamed back inside with a sound like marbles clacking together.

Dr. Dartmouth stepped past the crate and led the way through the door to a glass walkway on the other side. The crate hovered along behind her, set to auto-follow. The four guards and General Hall waited for the others to approach. "Leave your weapons at the door," the general said.

"Are you fucking kidding me?" Widow asked.

"No," he replied.

Widow glared at him. "Are you at least going to help?"

General Hall held Samara up while Widow placed her rifle and sidearm on the ground. They traded places at Samara's side again, and the rest of the group disarmed themselves, adding to a growing pile of weapons at General Hall's feet. Keera came last. She wasn't carrying any weapons, so she walked straight on behind

Clayton and Nova.

"Bind her hands," General Hall ordered.

The guards at the door stepped in front of Keera and one of them produced a length of stun cord from his belt. Keera put her hands together and watched while the man cinched the stun cords around her wrists.

He stepped aside, and then Keera walked through to a long glass walkway that crossed high above the gardens below. Strips of light running along the top and bottom of the tunnel pulsed red and blue, humming steadily as they disinfected everyone's clothes and skin with harmless UV and infrared radiation. The lights continued to pulse, warming Keera's face and skin like actual sunlight as they walked down the length of the corridor to the gleaming banks of elevators on the other side. While they waited there, General Hall's hand flew up to his ear to answer a call on his comms.

"What is it?" Clayton asked.

The general looked to him with sudden suspicion and drew his sidearm. He didn't aim it, but everyone tensed up immediately.

He jerked his chin to Samara. "Ensec has just put out a warrant for her arrest."

Samara paled, but Clayton's cheeks flushed dark red beneath his scraggly beard. "For what!" he thundered.

"Murder," General Hall replied. "You're

going to have to come with me," he said to Samara.

The doctor in the hazmat suit took a quick step back, looking shocked. "Murder? Who did she kill?"

"One of ours," General Hall said, his eyes never leaving Samara's face.

To Keera's surprise, she didn't even try to argue. "You'll have to help me. I can't walk on my own." She glanced at Widow as she said that. The other woman looked angry, as if she wanted to argue about the charges.

"Sam, what's going on?" Clayton asked. He slowly lowered Nova to the floor. The girl looked worried, but not shocked—as if she knew something about this.

"How did you find out?" Nova asked the general.

And Clayton gaped at his daughter, his suspicions confirmed.

"You were under surveillance in your quarters. Ensec just reviewed the logs. They caught you two speaking about a man Samara killed near the rendezvous. That was our forward scout, Norman Murphy. He was supposed to be the one to meet you."

Samara swallowed visibly and winced.

"It was an accident!" Nova cried. "He surprised us!"

"That's for a tribunal to decide." General Hall pointed to Keera. "Would you help Samara, please? You're both going down to the detention level." One of the elevators opened, and General Hall nodded sideways to it. Two of his soldiers waited with hands on their side-arms while the other two went in to hold the doors. Widow, Lori, and Doc watched these developments with dark, hooded eyes.

Lori caught Keera's gaze and smiled reassuringly. "We'll get you out tomorrow."

"Don't be too sure," Keera replied as she went to Samara's side and took Widow's place. Keera wrapped the other woman's arm around her shoulders to help her keep weight off her injured ankle.

"We're going to fight this," Clayton said through gritted teeth.

Samara gave him a shaky smile as she hobbled along beside Keera. They stepped into the elevator and General Hall and his other two men came in behind them, keeping a wary distance.

"Sub-level four," the general said to the control panel.

"Going down. Sub-level four," a pleasant voice announced. The u-shaped glass wall gave a clear view of the gardens below as the elevator raced down. A few people watched from their balconies along the inner wall of apartments.

Keera felt Samara's entire body start to shake, but she couldn't tell whether that was from fear, remorse, or simply spent adrenaline.

"What happens if I'm convicted?" Samara asked quietly.

"That depends on the seriousness of your conviction."

"If it's ruled an accident?" Samara pressed.

"Then it's manslaughter. You'll get to stay in the Enclave, but you'll have to spend a number of years in prison."

"You actually waste resources on prisons?" Keera asked.

General Hall smirked. "What would you rather we do, exile all of the petty criminals to the Wastes? I suppose that is the Chimeran way...." A few snickers erupted from the guards.

"That's not what I meant. I meant, isn't there a more productive way to deal with deviants?"

"Such as?"

"Community service. House arrest."

The elevator dropped below the decoratively lit gardens and plunged into darkness. Rings of light from the sub-levels flashed through the glass elevator, periodically casting General Hall's features into sharp relief. The elevator slowed, then chimed and said, "You have arrived on sub-level four, the Detention Center."

"She'll get community service, no question about that, but we don't keep convicted criminals in luxurious accommodations," General Hall said as he stepped out. "That would be counter-productive to their punishment," he added as he waited for them to leave the elevator.

Keera blew out an angry breath and followed him out.

"It's okay," Samara whispered.

"And what if it's not ruled an accident?" Keera countered, wondering just how much justice they could expect to receive from a tribunal that might easily be biased in favor of the Enclave's own residents.

"Then she'll be exiled," General Hall declared in a level, matter-of-fact voice, as if exile were anything other than a death sentence.

CHAPTER 48

Another elevator opened, and a woman with short dark hair and warm brown eyes stepped out in a sleek black jumpsuit. She smiled warmly at them. "Welcome! My name is Cava Turing. Please, join me," she said, waving to them from inside the elevator. "I'll take you down to your quarters."

Clayton stepped through with Nova hopping along beside him. Widow, Doc, and Lori came in behind them.

"Level five," the woman said.

"Going down, level five," the elevator replied.

The doctor in the hazmat suit waved once to them before the doors slid shut and stole her from view.

Clayton stared out the curving glass walls of the elevator, watching as lush greenery swept up to greet them. But the elevator stopped almost as soon as it had started, and their guide stepped out, saying, "This way please."

"Wait, what about her leg?" Clayton asked, pointing to Nova. "It's broken. She needs surgery."

"Can it wait until morning?" Cava asked.

Doc nodded. "Yes. It was a clean break."

"Good." The woman turned and started down the corridor on the other side. The others followed, and Clayton struggled after them with Nova.

The strange, luxurious appointments of the Enclave were all but utterly lost on Clayton. He walked down the corridor in a daze, trailing behind the others.

"It's going to be okay," Nova said quietly.

But Clayton didn't even attempt to respond to that. He wasn't sure that she was right. They'd fought and died to save the Enclave, and now its people were treating them like the enemy. At least, they were with Samara and Keera.

"What happened out there?" Clayton whispered back, unable to keep the accusation from his voice. He didn't like all the secrets being kept from him. First Dora's bite and now this.

"This guy came running out of the woods," Nova said. "He surprised us, and Sam shot him by accident."

Clayton drew in a deep breath that tasted stale despite the pleasant floral fragrances in the air. They stopped at a particular gleaming silver door. The number 547 glowed to life in front of it, and then the door parted down the middle, sliding open to reveal a beautiful apartment.

"If you need anything," their guide said from outside the doors. "Just ask for hospitality services, and one of my staff will answer you."

The doors slid shut.

"No thanks," Widow muttered.

Clayton looked away, his eyes drifting out of focus. He felt like he could drop where he stood and sleep for days, but a dozen other needs were busy nagging for his attention. Hunger. Pain. Thirst. And a sharp urge from his bladder. He helped Nova over to the living room couch and eased her down into it.

"You look like hell," Doc said, coming alongside him and shaking his head.

"You don't look so hot yourself," Clayton pointed out, nodding to indicate the dozens of scrapes and cuts on Doc's face—shrapnel wounds from the explosion that had taken out the barricades.

Doc frowned and shook his head as he looked away. "Everyone get changed and take a shower," he said, raising his voice. "I'll check and dress your wounds as soon as you're done."

Clayton glanced about, trying to decide where the nearest bathroom was.

"This way," Widow said. She grabbed his

arm and pulled him along toward one of several decorative gold and silver doors that led away from the main living area.

Clayton allowed her to lead him. She left him alone inside. He spotted a large bed with the sheets rumpled. Fuzzy white robes and slippers were strewn across the floor. Widow came back with Nova and left her at the foot of the bed. She shut the door behind them, and Clayton spotted the open door to an en-suite bathroom. He walked over there on wooden legs, and the lights came on automatically for him. He stared at his face in the mirror, and blinked in shock at the person staring back at him.

His face was covered in blood from small cuts and scrapes, just like Doc's. His cheeks were still smeared with black grease from the attack on the Ascension Center in New Houston. That had been exactly one day ago, and yet somehow it felt like a lifetime. Adding to his disheveled appearance, his scraggly beard was matted and tangled with blood. His long hair likewise. His haunted green eyes were wide and bloodshot and deeply shadowed.

Clayton quietly shut the door and began to strip out of his jumpsuit. He found it stuck to his back with dried blood from shrapnel injuries old and new. As he pulled it away, some of them broke open, stinging with fresh waves of pain. He hurried over to the shower and turned it on, setting the temperature from a touch control panel in the wall until it was steaming hot.

He stepped in and let the water wash away the filth and blood. He watched it pooling at his feet in a bright red swirl. Water dripped steadily from his overgrown hair and beard until the water at his feet ran clear. He found a bar of soap and passed it all over his body as gently as he could, finding new cuts, bruises, and scrapes as he did so. He stood there for a timeless moment, feeling numb despite the waves of blinding pain washing over him.

When he was done, he found a towel on a rack and dried himself as best he could, staining it red with his blood. Then he wrapped it around his waist and walked out. Doc was waiting for him, looking no less exhausted than he felt.

"Ready?"

"What about the others?" Clayton asked.

"You're the last one."

Clayton glanced at his daughter. Nova had curled up on top of the sheets in her dirty clothes, already fast asleep. She wasn't hurt besides her broken leg, so Clayton decided to let her rest.

"All right," he said, whispering now. "Let's get it over with."

CHAPTER 49

Commander Tyris stood in the shadow of a crumbling skyscraper, watching as the sun inched across the jagged, shattered remains of mirror-plated green glass that had served as the building's outer walls. Barely a block away were the concrete walls of the Enclave, and beyond that, soared the gleaming glass pyramid of the facility itself. The human sentries standing watch atop the walls had steadily thinned all through the early hours of the morning. Now they were down to scarcely a few dozen men to watch a perimeter of several kilometers. The others gone to bed after a long night of guarding against the horde of Dregs on the other side of the city. Those filthy beasts had fled with the sunrise, unable to find a way around the river, while V'tan Company had crossed it at another bridge higher up and then crept into position around the back of the Enclave.

"Commander, we're in position," a familiar voice crackled through Tyris's helmet comms.

"Excellent work, Lieutenant Akora," he said. "Open the gates. It's time to remind these Dakkas who really owns this city."

"Yes, sir," Akora replied.

Technically, it belonged to the Kyra who'd built it with their mobile factories and their legions of alien Chimeras, but they'd abandoned Earth to its fate, so the Enclave belonged to Tyris and his people now. He smiled eagerly at the thought of this long-awaited homecoming. Would his parents be surprised to see him?

Maybe he wouldn't kill them, after all. It might be more fun to watch them beg and squirm, just as he had once begged them to understand his choice to become a Chimera. They'd disowned him after that. Now they'd wish he'd never been born.

* * *

Clayton woke up, going from a deep, dreamless slumber to wide awake in an instant. His heart fluttered wildly in his chest, like a bird trying to escape its cage, and his hollow stomach ached.

He sat up with a groan and listened to the silence, wondering what had woken him. Sunlight was streaming in through the window, dazzling his eyes. The window in the bedroom had been polarized last night, but he'd been aware of it lightening gradually with the sunrise: an ever-brightening glow stabbing through his eyelids each time he woke up and changed positions to keep pressure off his injuries.

Beside him Nova slept soundlessly, never stirring. He glanced over at her, suddenly afraid, and waited to see the subtle rise and fall of her chest. There. It rose, then fell, then rose again—her nostrils flaring as she inhaled.

Relief overcame him. His bladder spasmed and burned with an urgent demand. He groaned once more and almost fell out of bed on his way to the bathroom. The soft, spongy floors were warm, not cold, to the touch. His stomach growled, reminding him of the next order of business. Food. Last night, after Doc had finished picking debris out of his back and spraying the wounds with Regenex, he'd been too tired to eat a proper meal. In lieu of that he had stuffed himself on a crusty loaf of bread that he'd found in the kitchen before shuffling off to bed.

As Clayton emptied his bladder in the bathroom, a sound caught his ear from the neighboring room: a muffled shout, then a rush of heavy footfalls, and the muted crack of a weapon going off. *Thud.* A body hit the floor. Clayton froze mid-stream. Zipping up, he planted his ear against the bathroom wall. More booted feet shuffling. Muffled voices arguing: deep, gravelly voices. Too distinctive to mistake. Chimeras. An icy chill overcame him, and his skin prickled with goosebumps. Booted feet retreated from the room next door. Clayton pulled away from the wall and looked urgently to Nova. With her broken leg, she wouldn't even be able to run.

A blaring alarm started up. The lights darkened to a bloody red and pulsed steadily. "General quarters! General quarters! We are under —"

The voice cut off with the cracking report of another weapon firing, and this time the sound came over hidden speakers in the ceiling.

A moment later, a new voice came on: deep, and gravelly, and distinctly male. A Chimeran voice. Clayton was shocked to find that he recognized it. "There's no need to panic. I'm one of you! Quite literally. Some of you might still remember the quiet, unassuming boy, Caleb, who later became Commander Tyris— Mom, Dad, I'm home!" He broke off into hissing peals of laughter and then the transmission died in static.

Finally, Nova woke up. "What's going on..." she asked sleepily, her brow furrowing as she belatedly processed Tyris's broadcast. "Who was that?"

Clayton hesitated. If the Chimeras were already going door to door in the residences here on level five, and they had control of the operations center where the general quarters would have sounded from, then it meant that they must have already secured all of the other more critical areas of the Enclave: the armory, the outer walls... the security system. The fight was over before it had even begun. The only chance they had was to make a run for the transport that Keera had landed outside.

Clayton tore out of the bathroom. "Get up!" he whispered sharply to Nova.

"I can't, my leg..."

Rather than argue with her, he scooped her off the mattress and started for the door.

It burst open before he could reach it, and two fully-armored Chimeras stepped through. Their rifles tracked up. He heard the muted reports of more rifles firing on the other side of the suite a split second before the ones in front of him flashed with electric blue fire. Clayton's muscles all gave way in the same instant, and he fell to the ground with fiery blue arcs of electricity leaping from his clothes and snaking over both him and Nova. He saw her eyes rolling up in her head just before plunging into darkness himself.

CHAPTER 50

Keera lay awake in her bed in the cell beside Samara's.

"Do you think they'll let me see my daughter?" Samara asked.

"I don't know," Keera said.

The doors to both their cells were open, blocked with deadly razor beams rather than physical bars. That made it easy to talk to each other. It also made it easy to kill themselves, if that suddenly became the lesser of evils. All they had to do was run through the door, and they'd be sliced into half a dozen smoking slabs of meat.

Samara sniffled audibly, and Keera realized that she was crying. She cringed. Emotional displays made her uncomfortable. At least she couldn't see the woman's tears.

"They won't exile you," Keera said in an attempt to cheer her up.

"How do you know that?"

"Because it's easy enough for them to learn if you're telling the truth about the accident.

They'll have Kyron brain scanners here. So, assuming you're telling the truth..."

"I am," Samara said.

"Then don't worry about it."

"I'll still go to prison."

"Probably, but it could be worse. And something tells me the Enclave's prisons will be a five star resort compared with the way we've been living out in the Wastes. At least you'll get regular meals and you won't have to worry about Dregs tearing you apart in your sleep."

"I guess that's true." Keera heard Samara let out a shaky breath, and her voice grew steadier and less fraught with emotion. "What about you?" Samara asked.

"Me?"

"I get the feeling they don't like Chimeras here."

"No more or less than anywhere else," Keera said. "Now that they don't have a fleet hovering above them ready to vaporize the Enclave if they step out of line, they're feeling more free to express their pent-up hatred and resentment. They don't seem to realize that we were slaves just the same as them."

"But you were the boot pressing down on their necks," Samara said.

Keera snorted. "I suppose so."

Before she could contemplate her fate any further, the lights in Keera's cell plunged to a ruddy color and pulsed steadily. Then came the announcement across the PA system: "General quarters, general quarters, we're under—"

A stun bolt silenced the announcement, and Keera sat up in a hurry. She listened to Commander Tyris come on to continue the announcement, and then she cursed under her breath and jumped off her cot. "This is bad," she said.

"How did they get in?" Samara cried. "We have walls and sentries!"

Keera began pacing the floor inside her cell. "They must have waited for the turnover of the watch. Most of the soldiers would have gone to bed after staying up all night to deal with Dregs. The walls would have been virtually undefended. They timed it perfectly. This is bad, Samara. Really bad. Commander Tyris is a psychopath."

"You know him?"

"I know *of* him. Rumors from captains in my fleet who had to deal with him. His company kept getting transferred around because no one could stand him. He tried to put in a transfer to my ship, but I blocked it."

"What kind of rumors?" Samara asked.

"Various abuses of power, some sexual, others violent. He picked on humans and Chimeras alike. An equal opportunity asshole."

"Why wasn't he punished? I didn't think the Kyron Guard put up with that kind of thing."

"They don't. But he was too smart to get caught, and now he probably never will. But if he ends up in charge around here..."

"I get it. What can we do?"

"Us?" Keera blew out a frustrated breath. "Nothing. All we can do is hope the Enclave fights them off." But even as she said that, Keera realized that Tyris had to be close to gaining full control of the city. He might be a psychopath, but he was a smart psychopath. He wouldn't have come on the comms to gloat unless he already had the Enclave right where he wanted it.

Keera stood in front of the glowing razorbeam door to her cell, wishing Tyris would cut the power so that she could get out. But he wouldn't do that. He needed the power on to gain full control of the facility, and to use the doors to lock people in their rooms.

A door swished open somewhere in the distance, and she heard several sets of footsteps approaching steadily.

"Who's that?" Samara whispered.

"Shhh," Keera replied. "Hide."

"Too late!" a familiar voice crowed. It was Commander Tyris himself. He came to a stop in front of her cell, smiling broadly. His thickly muscled arms, broad shoulders, and barrel chest matched perfectly with the image she had of him in her head: a brute. But he was also a handsome brute, and somehow that made him even more vile.

"You really should know better than to whisper around a Chimera," Tyris went on. "Our hearing is a hundred times better than a mere Dakka's." He glanced sideways to one of his soldiers. "Open the cells, Corporal. Get them out."

"How did you find me?" Keera asked, wondering if she should throw herself through the razorbeams before they could disable them. To go by the smug grin on his face, Tyris surely recognized her, and that meant this wasn't going to end well.

"I was browsing through the Enclave's personnel records to isolate key individuals— councilors, soldiers, the director... when I happened to see your name logged in the detention level. Imagine my surprise to find the infamous traitor, former Admiral Keera Reed locked up like a dog in a Dakka jail." Tyris's mouth twisted with wry amusement as the razorbeams snapped off. He pointed to her and said. "Drag her out to the courtyard with the others! If she struggles, stun her."

Two soldiers stepped forward and grabbed Keera on either side. She decided not to struggle. It wouldn't do her any good anyway. "I'll go peacefully," she said.

"Pity," Tyris said. "I was really hoping you'd struggle..."

Keera smiled sweetly at him as she walked out between the two soldiers. "Can't have everything."

"Oh, but I can." Tyris stepped in front of her and lightly ran the claw of his index finger up the curve of her throat to her chin, tipping her eyes up to his. She heard his thoughts without wanting to, and her whole body went stiff. A blinding rage built up inside of her, as she realized the rumors about him were all true. This man was pure evil and proud of it.

He stared into her eyes for a heart-stopping second, his putrid fantasies assaulting her in advance of any physical contact.

"Sir?" one of the soldiers holding Keera prompted. She recognized a female voice.

Tyris glanced at her and scowled, as if only just realizing that he had witnesses. He stepped aside. "Take her to the courtyard, Lieutenant Akora." Another two soldiers carried Samara out, and she met Keera's gaze with naked terror.

Lieutenant Akora's hatred of the man in charge rolled over her, the other woman's violent thoughts flashing through Keera's mind. She knew what Tyris was, and she was itching for the chance to kill him and steal his command.

A feeble hope soared in Keera's chest, and she focused on the woman's thoughts, trying to determine how serious she was about her intention to challenge Tyris.

But her hopes were dashed a moment later as Lieutenant Akora's bloody thoughts took on verbal form: *If only he weren't so deadly with a Sikath...*

Akora's plans went in a new direction, thinking that if she could gather proof of Tyris's wrongdoings to show to the rest of her company, she could have him removed from command without dying as a martyr in a pointless duel.

She decided on that course of action.

But Keera had a feeling that moment of revelation would come far too late to save her, Samara, or anyone else that Tyris had singled out and sent to the courtyard. She knew the strategy well. It was standard Kyron military doctrine, and she'd followed it many times herself when conquering native populations: find the leaders and execute them publicly, then replace them with Chimeras.

CHAPTER 51

A pair of extra-wide, tall glass doors in the base of the pyramid parted. The Chimeran soldiers dragged Samara through to a group of humans and more Chimeran soldiers standing in the courtyard behind the city gates. She still couldn't put much weight on her injured ankle, so she didn't attempt to struggle.

Birds sang cheerily from the tops of tall trees growing to either side of the paved road to the gates. The morning sun beamed down, just now peeking above the walls and the gate-house. Chimeras stood up there, aiming rifles down from above, their cranial stalks silhouetted by the rising sun and distinguishing them clearly from humans.

"Clayton!" Samara cried, recognizing him and the rest of Phoenix standing there. Now she did struggle to break free, but she received a sharp elbow in her ribs that knocked the wind out of her in a *whoosh.*

"Don't resist," Keera warned her.

Samara glanced at the other woman, while

gasping soundlessly for air. Had Keera really given up that easily? She'd been a battle-hardened admiral with a reputation for cunning and brilliant tactics.

But what could she do?

They were marched over to the others and then released. Samara collapsed with a sharp cry as her twisted ankle gave way, and the Chimeras holding her withdrew, laughing and muttering to each other about how pathetic Dakkas were. Clayton ran over to her and cradled her in his lap. "Are you okay?" he whispered.

She nodded. Nova appeared behind him with a trembling smile.

"They didn't kill anyone?" Samara asked.

"Not yet," Clayton whispered.

General Hall and a woman that Samara recognized only vaguely were standing in front of a huddled group of ten other men and women, all of whom looked as if they were about to be physically sick. Widow, Doc, and Lori came over to Samara, their eyes darting to the armed Chimeras that stood to all sides of them.

"Hell of a nice day to die," Widow said, nodding up at the clear blue sky. As if to punctuate that thought, a pair of Blue Jays darted through the air, chirping as they went.

Keera stood to one side, watching as Commander Tyris went straight up to General Hall and said. "Hello, Father."

Samara reeled in shock with that revelation. And then the Chimera's head turned a few degrees to the right to find the vaguely familiar woman standing beside the General, and he added, "Hello, Mother. Or should I say, Director and General Hall. I suppose those titles are more appropriate after you disowned me..."

* * *

Keera couldn't believe it. She'd sensed the revelation in Tyris's thoughts long before he actually reached his parents.

"Are you ready to die?" Commander Tyris asked his mother. "I promise I'll make it quick."

"You always were a hateful child," Director Hall said. She had razor short black hair, dark green eyes, and was tall and elegant with a long neck. She looked regal even in her fuzzy white robe and slippers, and she had a smooth, stunning face that was so blank and emotionless it could have been chiseled out of stone.

"And you always were a cold bitch," Tyris replied. "But, that's all water under the bridge now, *Director*."

"What is this? Revenge?" General Hall demanded. "If it's revenge you want, go ahead, kill us! But let everyone else go. These people have done nothing to you."

Commander Tyris took a quick step back, and a hand flew up to his chest in an oddly effeminate gesture for such a large, brawny man. He even made General Hall look small by comparison. "I'm insulted. You really think that I'm that petty?"

"Yes," his mother spat.

"You never understood me. I came here for my men, not for *you.* Why scrimp and scrape together a life in the Wastes when we could be living in comfort and safety here?" Tyris smiled and spread his hands to indicate their surroundings. "When I learned that the Enclave had miraculously avoided infection, there really was no other choice. It was inevitable that we should come here and claim our rightful place as the Enclave's new rulers."

"Our people will never submit to Chimeran rule," Director Hall said.

"They won't have a choice," Tyris said. "And after all of you are cut down in front of their eyes, they won't dare to oppose us." He turned to indicate the glass wall of the pyramid, and Keera followed that gesture to see hundreds and hundreds of balconies beyond the glass wall all packed with people. They were locked in their rooms and drawn by morbid curiosity to watch the spectacle in the courtyard below.

Keera was running out of patience with Tyris's posturing. There was only one chance to end this. She started striding toward him. The soldiers flanking him raised their rifles.

"Stop!" one of them cried, and she did.

"What do you think you're going to do?" Tyris asked through a booming laugh. "You think you can just waltz over here and kill me with fifty crack troops watching?"

"Only if you tell them not to interfere," Keera replied. She bared her teeth at him in a predatory smile. "I challenge you, Commander Tyris Hall, for the command of V'tan Company."

The courtyard grew suddenly very quiet, and Tyris's smile faded dramatically. "You can't challenge me," he said. "You're no longer a member of the Guard, and you're a traitor to your people. Kyron Law doesn't apply to you."

"Nor to you," Keera replied. "Look around!" she swept her gaze through the courtyard to take in all of his men. "The Kyra are gone. They abandoned you. Their fleet should have been here long ago. But there's a reason they never arrived. They've written Earth off completely."

"Then what do challenges matter?" Tyris demanded. "Who cares."

It was the wrong thing to say. Mutterings of discontent rumbled through the ranks of his soldiers. He turned to regard them. "Shut up! You know I'm right! The Kyra forced their culture on us. They made us fight and kill each other in order to rise through the ranks and assert our dominance. But we're better than that now! We don't need to fight each other!"

"Then why did you throw Ava into the fire?" someone shouted.

"Who said that!" Tyris's face flushed black, and dark fish scale patterns of veins appeared beneath his skin. Keera smiled. Her plan was working.

"It sounds like you're afraid to fight me," Keera said. "It's okay to admit you're a coward, Tyris. Be true to who you are. There's nothing worse than living a lie."

Tyris spun around to face her, his nostrils flaring and cranial stalks twitching furiously. "Bring out the Sikaths!" he thundered.

Two soldiers broke ranks and scurried over.

"This will not save your people," he cried, leveling a finger at her as he shrugged out of the strap of his rifle and unclipped the utility belt with his sidearm and holster. He handed them to one of the two soldiers holding ceremonial swords. "Even if you win, you will *not* assume command of V'tan Company. You are a traitor. They would never follow you."

Keera nodded along with that. "I don't aspire to command anyone anymore. I'll be satisfied just to watch you bleed."

Tyris smiled coldly at her and drew his blade from the sheath. "Good luck."

Another soldier ran over and handed her the second blade. She whipped it through an abbreviated arc to throw off the sheath, and then flicked it on. The gleaming black sword snapped to life, blurring and humming with tiny hypersonic movements, and shimmering with the pale light of the shield that kept the nano-edged blade from breaking.

Tyris strode steadily toward her. Keera waited, focusing on his thoughts to read his actions before he took them. He stopped in front of her, right at the edge of her reach and held the blade crosswise in front of his chest, in a two-handed grip. Keera forced herself to be calm, holding her own sword in one hand and not even bothering to raise it in a blocking stance.

She deliberately left her left side open, knowing that Tyris would think his reflexes were fast enough to take advantage of the opportunity. She sensed his decision to strike even before his arms began to move.

And she darted left, ducking out of reach just as his blade sailed through the space where she'd been standing. He recovered quickly, leaving very little time for a counter-attack, but Keera managed to slide her blade past his just as it came back around to block. The tip of it pierced his left shoulder before he batted it away. Tyris recoiled from her, screaming in equal parts rage and pain. His left shoulder had been sliced open as he'd knocked her blade aside, his bicep tendon cut cleanly and gushing black blood. His left arm dropped limp to his side and he switched to a one-handed grip on his Sikath. Keera began circling him just out of reach, searching for another opening. His thoughts were blowing up like fireworks, too loud and scattered for her to read clearly.

"Congratulations," Tyris growled. "Now I'm going to make you suffer." He smiled nastily, his eyes tracking her as his blood bubbled and dripped to the courtyard in noisy *splats*. But within seconds it slowed and stopped entirely as his body stopped the bleeding. If he were a human, he might have bled out in just a few more minutes, but Chimeras were much harder to kill.

Tyris's thoughts slowed and focused once more, and Keera stopped circling as she sensed his intention to rush her. He planned to use his superior strength to knock her sword aside, and then run her through and end the fight before it could drag on.

And that might have worked—were it not for the fact that she knew what he was thinking.

Tyris pushed off the ground, launching himself into a sprint. Keera waited until the last possible second. And then, rather than block his sword, she darted to one side and dropped to the ground, throwing out one leg to catch his feet. His sword swept up clumsily to slice her open as he fell, but his strength wasn't behind the blade anymore, and she was the one who batted it aside.

Tyris fell on his face with a grunt and began immediately springing back up. But Keera had already taken full advantage of the opening. She threw her sword like a javelin. It impaled him clean through his back and buried itself in the ground. The dead-man's switch had turned it off, but Tyris had been fully impaled. He slumped to the ground, shrieking and hissing like a Dreg as he reached blindly to pull the blade out of his back.

Keera lunged toward him to finish the job, but at least a dozen of Tyris's men raised their rifles. "Halt!" one of them cried, and Keera had no choice but to stop where she was.

But then a woman raised her voice and stepped forward: "Stand down!" Keera recognized from her voice that it was Lieutenant Akora. The one who secretly wanted to kill Tyris and take his place.

The men aiming at Keera hesitated.

Tyris went on thrashing and screaming, the sword pinning him down. He grabbed the blade with his good hand and sliced it open. The hilt was out of reach. He couldn't free himself.

Akora went on. "If you shoot her, then our laws and our ways mean nothing! Think of all of the people who died or were maimed so that we could rise up and take their place! Shoot her, and you're spitting in your own eyes. Tyris was a willing challenger. No one forced him to accept. Now he must submit if he wishes to live. Commander Tyris! Do you submit?"

His screams and struggles went on for several seconds more. He tried to pull the sword out again, and one of his fingers fell off with a meaty *thup.* "I submit!" he shrieked through the pain.

"As the next highest-ranking member of V'tan Company, I accept your submission. Commander Tyris Hall, you are disgraced and hereby stripped of all rank and privilege."

Lieutenant Akora came striding over to him and yanked the Sikath out of his back. He rolled over with a hissing groan, his eyes clenched shut and his right hand clutching a bubbling fountain of blood in his lower abdomen. "Get on with the executions," he mumbled.

Akora glared briefly at him, then looked away and strode purposely toward the leaders of the Enclave with the Sikath. Keera watched as she stopped in front of them and leveled the bloody blade at Director Hall.

"Your people are no better than mine," Lieutenant Akora said.

"I never said—"

"Quiet!" Akora thundered. She looked away, her gaze passing over the Chimeras. "We, are no better than them!"

A rumble of discontent passed through the

group.

"We share the same genetic roots. We were all human once, the same as they are! We are one people, not two, and it's time we started acting like it. The Kyra abandoned us down here. If we're going to survive, it won't be because we won a pointless war against each other. This city might very well be the last surviving settlement on the entire planet. Have you stopped to think what happens if it fails? If it falls to the Dregs? Or if we burn it to the ground while fighting amongst ourselves?"

To Keera's surprise, the councilors were all nodding their heads. Even General Hall and Director Hall, and the surviving members of Phoenix seemed to be in agreement.

"Chimeras can't breed," Akora went on. "We cannot survive as a species without humanity's help, and they won't survive without trained soldiers to defend them."

More murmurs of agreement. Now most of the Chimeras were nodding. Someone cried out, "They're Dakkas! They can't be trusted."

"And we're chalkheads!" Akora shouted back. "And they would say the same about us. It's time we put petty bigotry to rest and challenge *ourselves* to be better. That is the only way we're going to survive going forward. Chimera or Human, we will go extinct on this planet if we don't stand together."

Keera couldn't believe the turn things had

taken. She had expected Akora to take command and be a better leader than Tyris, but she'd never expected her to be *this* good.

"She's right!" Director Hall shouted. "We don't have to fight each other! You haven't killed anyone here today, have you?"

A few Chimeras shook their heads.

"Your weapons were set to stun," Director Hall went on. "And why is that?"

"So we could execute you publicly!" Tyris managed to grit out.

"No," Director Hall replied. "That's not why. You could have spared us and still gone on a killing spree to pacify the civilians inside. Instead, you locked them in their rooms and sought out the leaders. You did that because even Tyris knows that we need each other. He wasn't going to kill everyone. He needs us to run this city. To grow its food and wash its clothes, and clean its corridors."

"But not to govern," Akora said.

That stopped Director Hall's speech, and her expressionless face grew lined with worry.

Even Keera was worried. Had she misread this? Was Akora planning to execute them all anyway?

"There will need to be changes going forward," Akora said. "We will need a voice in your government, and guarantees of equal rights."

"Done," Director Hall said, and the councilors standing behind her nodded along with that. "What else?"

"We need a pardon. From this day forward, none of us will have our pasts count against us. No matter what crimes you may later uncover, perceived or real."

Director Hall glanced at her son before she replied, and Keera understood why. If she pardoned all of them, she would be pardoning him, too.

"Granted."

"What about Samara?" Clayton shouted. "And Keera!"

Director Hall looked to him, then back to Akora. "The pardon will apply to everyone, and it goes both ways! Your people cannot hold anything against ours, either."

"Agreed," Akora said.

"You fools!" Tyris cried. "You'll be killing each other inside a week!"

Everyone looked at him, and Akora said, "There is one person that I would like to exclude from this deal."

"What do you want to do with him?" Director Hall asked.

"Exile him to the Wastes."

Despite his injuries, Tyris managed to push himself up on one elbow to regard his judge and jury.

"I've done nothing to deserve Exile!"

"Nothing that we can prove, you mean,"

Akora said. "Until Ava. You executed her in the cruelest way imaginable. Lucky for you, I am not as sick as you are. At least in Exile you will have a chance to survive."

Tyris's eyes darted frantically around the ring of soldiers, searching for support.

But he found none.

"Get him on his feet!" Akora cried.

And two soldiers ran forward to do just that.

"Dakkas! You're all Dakkas! The Kyra would execute every single one of you!" he screamed as they grabbed his arms and yanked him up. He spat at them, and hissed.

"Maybe they would," Akora admitted as Tyris came alongside her. "But the Kyra aren't here, and that means we're finally free." She turned to regard the human councilors and Director Hall. "All of us!"

A cheer broke the tension in the air, and the Chimeras relaxed their guard and broke ranks. A mixed group of humans and Chimeras followed Tyris to the gates and saw him out.

Tyris was thrown through the doors, and left bleeding and broken in the dust. He picked himself off the ground and stared incredulously at them, clutching his side. "You'll all burn for this! I swear it!"

And then the gates slammed shut, punctuating that statement and sealing him off.

"Who'd have guessed we could have peace

just by getting rid of one bad egg," Clayton said through a sigh.

"Me," Akora said.

"And me," Keera added with a nod of recognition to the other woman.

"Good riddance," Lori muttered.

Director Hall cleared her throat. "I believe its time to let my people out of their rooms and inform them of the new social paradigm. Lieutenant, I would like you to choose two of your soldiers by popular vote, a man and a woman, to sit on our council. They will represent your interests here."

"We will have their names for you by the end of the day," Akora said.

"And General," Director Hall said, turning to him. "I could be mistaken, but it looks to me as though you have found ready replacements for the soldiers that we lost last night."

General Hall nodded back, but his eyes never left Akora and her soldiers. "So it would seem, Director," he replied. "So it would seem."

CHAPTER 52

One week later...

Clayton sat on the balcony of his newly-assigned quarters, sipping a convincing cup of coffee beside his wife and his daughter, Nova. The waterfall they'd been next to before was situated on the other side of the balcony, one level up, and four suites over. Rather than sharing this suite with the rest of Phoenix, they had it all to themselves. Apparently families didn't have to share, but singles did. Clayton supposed they had to find a way to encourage procreation somehow.

"Not bad," Samara said, cradling her cup between her hands.

"Tastes like sour dirt," Nova said.

Clayton arched an eyebrow at her and smiled. "That's what coffee tastes like."

"In that case, I don't like it," she said.

"More for me." Clayton shrugged and took another sip. His eyelids slid shut and a contented sigh passed between his lips. After ten years away from civilization, he'd almost forgotten what coffee tasted like.

A sullen woof drew their attention to Rosie. She sat beside Nova and placed a paw on her thigh, begging. She hadn't gone for her walk in the gardens yet.

"You wouldn't like it," Nova quipped, deliberately misinterpreting the dog's request.

Woof!

"I don't think that's what's she's after," Clayton said.

Nova cracked a wry smile. "I was being obtuse."

"Obtuse?" he asked. "Where the heck did you learn a word like that?"

"The library. Mrs. Barton is teaching me to read."

"Really," Clayton said, nodding appreciatively. All the things he'd never taught Nova while they'd been out in the Wilds together. It made his heart ache just to think about it.

Nova nodded. "She says I won't last a minute in school if I don't learn how to read first."

"Sounds like a good place to start."

Samara reached up and wiped her cheek. Clayton noticed that it was wet.

He was about to ask what was wrong, but stopped himself. He could guess. "We're going to see Dora in a minute."

She shook her head and drained her cup.

"Let's go now," she said, and jumped up from the bench where they both sat. I can't wait any longer. Dr. Dartmouth said she had news to share."

"She also said to come down at nine. It's only eight-thirty," Clayton pointed out.

Samara just looked at him. He winced at the intensity of her stare and nodded, draining his cup, too. "I guess it'll take at least ten minutes to get down there."

"I want to go, too," Nova said.

Rosie barked and spun around, misreading their intentions. "You can see her later," Clayton decided. "Go take Rosie for a walk before she starts making puddles everywhere."

"Or piles," Samara added.

"Ewww," Nova said.

They stepped toward the apartment, and sliding glass doors parted automatically to let them in. Rosie bounded through eagerly, and Samara was right on her heels. The doctors at the Enclave had fixed what had turned out to be a fractured ankle with bone-knitters and nanite injections, and now, a week later, she didn't even walk with a limp. Nova's broken leg had been fixed just as readily.

Clayton smiled as he followed them inside. He couldn't blame Samara for being in such a hurry. He was also anxious to see Dora, but fear tempered his enthusiasm. What if the doctor's news wasn't good?

* * *

"The infection is completely stable," Dr. Dartmouth said. "We have to cover the wound, because the bite weeps and bleeds periodically, and those fluids are mildly infectious."

Director Hall nodded along with that assessment, but her expression was as stoic and blank as ever.

"So we cover it!" Samara blurted out. "What's the problem? We'll be careful. I promise. We could even put her arm in some kind of a cast... or... or..."

"Yes, we're working on a solution," Dr. Dartmouth said.

"So that's the news? That the infection still hasn't spread?" Clayton asked, while peering through the window to Dora's bed. She was sitting up and watching them with dull, lifeless eyes, but making no move to leave her bed. The confinement and isolation was wearing on her. She looked depressed.

"Yes," Dr. Dartmouth replied. "But now we're confident that the infection won't spread. She won't succumb to it. The wound may never fully heal, but she's in no danger from the virus."

"Okay, that is good news," Clayton said through a sigh.

Samara was grinning from ear to ear and wiping fresh tears from the corners of her eyes. "Does she know? Can we go in and see her?"

"No, and yes you can. We thought you should be the ones to break the news to her."

Samara grabbed Clayton's hand and pulled him toward the hazmat lockers. "Thank you!" she said as she ran by Dr. Dartmouth and Director Hall. "Thank you!"

Clayton tried to match her enthusiasm as she pulled on one of the suits. They both got dressed in a hurry, and then filed into the quarantine airlock, waiting endless seconds for the UV and IR lamps to stop flashing. The lights snapped off, and the airlock opened. Samara ran to the side of Dora's bed. Clayton arrived beside her half a second later.

Samara was already holding both of Dora's hands in her bulky gloves. "The doctor says you're fine! You won't get sick. You're going to get out of here!"

Dora's eyes lit up. "When?"

"Soon!" Samara said, her eyes bright with tears behind the faceplate of her suit.

Clayton put on a smile, but said nothing. That wasn't what the doctor had said. In fact, he was painfully aware that she'd neatly avoided specifying any kind of time frame for an end to Dora's isolation.

Dora started crying, but now she was smiling and laughing, the dark cloud over her momentarily broken.

"I can leave now?" Dora pressed.

"I'm going to work something out," Samara

said, glancing back at the window to where Dr. Dartmouth and Director Hall were having an animated discussion. Samara looked away, but Clayton's gaze lingered, wondering what they were talking about. Their voices were silenced by the thick panes of glass and the six-inch air gap between them. "We have to make sure it's safe for you to be around other people," Samara went on.

Clayton looked back to their daughter in time to see her face fall. "But you said I'm fine."

"You are!" Samara agreed. "But your bite is contagious, so we still have to be careful."

Clayton considered that excuse. At this point it should have been a simple matter to bandage her arm and let her out, but that wasn't what Dora's doctors were doing, and he had a bad feeling there was something they weren't telling him. Clayton looked back to the window. The doctor and the director were still arguing. He wished he could read lips. They appeared to notice him watching. Director Hall pulled the doctor aside, and they both passed out of sight.

"I don't understand," Dora sobbed.

"We'll get you out soon. If not today, then tomorrow. Okay?"

"You promise?"

"I promise."

"Dad?" Dora asked.

He looked back to her, saw the feeble hope

shining in her eyes, and he didn't have the heart to crush it. He nodded. "We'll get you out, Dora."

"Okay."

"Just hang in there, okay, sweetheart?" Samara said, rubbing Dora's back with her thick rubbery white glove.

Dora nodded and sniffled.

Clayton smiled grimly at that and placed a hand on top of her shoulder to give it a reassuring squeeze. That bad feeling that he was missing something was screaming for his attention again. And suddenly he realized what it was: neither Dr. Dartmouth nor Director Hall had mentioned their hope that Dora's immunity would lead to a cure. And with that, a single word ricocheted around inside his brain like a bullet: *why?*

The Enclave might have found a brittle peace with Chimeras and humans now passing each other in the halls without trading racial slurs or trying to rip each other's throats out, but there was a much more personal battle looming on the horizon, and he had a bad feeling that Dora was going to be right at the center of it.

GET THE FINAL BOOK FREE

Read the stunning conclusion in...

Second Encounter
(Coming September 2020)

Pre-order it now from Amazon

(https://geni.us/aw4jts)

OR

Get a FREE Kindle copy of the book. All you have to do is post an honest review on Amazon: https://geni.us/fereview

And then send it to me here: https://files.jaspertscott.com/encounter2free.htm

Thank you in advance for your feedback!
I read all of my reviews and use
them to improve my work.

Note: as an Amazon Associate I earn a small commission from qualifying purchases.

KEEP IN TOUCH

SUBSCRIBE to my Mailing List and get two FREE Books! (http://files.jaspertscott.com/mailinglist.html)

Follow me on Bookbub:
https://www.bookbub.com/authors/jasper-t-scott

Follow me on Amazon:
https://www.amazon.com/Jasper-T-Scott/e/B00B7A2CT4

Look me up on Facebook:
https://www.facebook.com/jaspertscott/

Check out my Website:
www.JasperTscott.com
Follow me on Twitter:
@JasperTscott
Or send me an e-mail:
JasperTscott@gmail.com

MORE BOOKS BY JASPER T. SCOTT

Keep up with new releases and get two free books by signing up for his newsletter at
www.jaspertscott.com

Note: as an Amazon Associate I earn a small commission from qualifying purchases.

Final Days
Final Days | Colony | Escape

Ascension Wars
First Encounter | Occupied Earth | Fractured Earth | Second Encounter

Scott Standalones (No Sequels, No Cliffhangers)
Under Darkness | Into the Unknown | In Time for Revenge

Rogue Star
Rogue Star: Frozen Earth | Rogue Star: New Worlds

Broken Worlds
The Awakening | The Revenants | Civil War

New Frontiers Series (Standalone Prequels to Dark Space)

Excelsior | Mindscape | Exodus

Dark Space Series

Dark Space | The Invisible War | Origin | Revenge | Avilon | Armageddon

Dark Space Universe

Dark Space Universe | The Enemy Within | The Last Stand

ABOUT THE
AUTHOR

Jasper Scott is a USA Today bestselling author of more than 20 sci-fi novels. With over a million books sold, Jasper's work has been translated into various languages and published around the world. Join the author's mailing list to get two FREE books: https://files.jaspertscott.com/mailinglist.html

Jasper writes fast-paced books with unexpected twists and flawed characters. He was born and raised in Canada by South African parents, with a British heritage on his mother's side and German on his father's. He now lives in an exotic locale with his wife, their two kids, and two Chihuahuas.

Printed in Great Britain
by Amazon